Talking to Wendigo

Talking to Wendigo
copyright © John C. Goodman 2008

Published by Ravenstone
an imprint of Turnstone Press
Artspace Building
018-100 Arthur Street
Winnipeg, MB
R3B 1H3 Canada
www.TurnstonePress.com

All rights reserved. No part of this book may be reproduced or transmitted in any form or by any means—graphic, electronic or mechanical—without the prior written permission of the publisher. Any request to photocopy any part of this book shall be directed in writing to Access Copyright (formerly Cancopy the Canadian Copyright Licensing Agency), Toronto.

Turnstone Press gratefully acknowledges the assistance of the Canada Council for the Arts, the Manitoba Arts Council and the Government of Canada through the Book Publishing Industry Development Program and the Government of Manitoba through the Department of Culture, Heritage and Tourism, Arts Branch, for our publishing activities.

Cover design: Doowah Design
Interior design: Sharon Caseburg
Printed and bound in Canada by
Hignell for Turnstone Press.

Library and Archives Canada Cataloguing in Publication

Goodman, John Charles, 1951–
    Talking to Wendigo / John C. Goodman.

ISBN 978-0-88801-304-0

    I. Title.
PS8613.O64T34 2008   C813'.6   C2008-900893-6

TALKING TO WENDIGO

John C. Goodman

RaveN STONE

*For Heather
who made the journey
with me*

Talking to Wendigo

PROLOGUE

The wolf ran swiftly through the shadowy forest. William ran behind. He had the impression that he was a deer, but why would a deer be chasing a wolf? The wolf disappeared into a narrow cleft between two outcroppings of dark rock. William followed it through the passageway onto a plain of loose, jagged stones at the foot of a cliff. A half-moon hung overhead like a drop of pus from an infected sky.

William found himself in a cave kneeling nose-to-nose with the wolf, staring into its malevolent green eyes. The wolf bared its teeth and snarled. William backed away. The wolf straddled something on the ground. It was the body of a man. There was blood everywhere. William glanced down at his hands and feet; they were covered with blood.

When he looked back, the body on the floor was sitting upright, staring at him with round, dead eyes. The face was disfigured as if eaten away by a wasting disease. A cadaverous arm rose, pointing a bloody finger at William. The leprous lips parted and whispered, "Tag. You're it."

Pure primal fear rushed through William as he tried to run, stumbling on the animal bones that covered the rough ground. He fell into darkness, fell into a bottomless depth. William screamed. He could feel something beside him, like a flickering blue flame, holding him as he tumbled, pulling him back out of the darkness.

"Smooth move," the flame said.

CHAPTER ONE
SUNDAY

Dazzling pinpoints of morning light splashed off the wind-rippled lake. William stopped dead. Squinting against the brightness, he strained to make out a blurry figure on a rock by the water's edge. William rubbed his eyes. Without his glasses he couldn't see distances and those glasses were resting patiently on top of a pile of books beside his bed. He frowned indecisively.

Autumn mornings come slowly to the northern Ontario woods. A pale luminosity in the east gradually brightens; the dawn breeze brushes the night clouds over the horizon, leaving a sky of translucent blue glass.

William had been awakened early that morning by a sense of urgency in his bladder, one of the joys of being fifty-six. Pushing out of the warm cocoon of the covers, he pulled on the khaki trousers and green flannel shirt he had worn the day before and hurried outside, fastening his belt over his paunch as he went. He stumbled, still stiff from sleep, toward the outhouse; his puffing breaths making light, quickly dissolving clouds in the autumn air. The smack of the spring-hinged door slamming shut echoed sharply off the last pieces of night left under the evergreen trees at the edge of the clearing around the cabin.

When, with enormous relief, William left the outhouse, he stretched, yawned, and let the crisp scent of pine clear his sinuses. The sunlight felt good on his face after days of overcast skies and heavy rain. He was weary from a restless night. Woken by a nightmare shortly before midnight, he had not been able to get back to sleep until almost dawn. He couldn't remember details of the dream, something about a wolf and a cave and a dead body—and falling, he remembered falling. He shuddered.

William smoothed back his brown hair, aware that it was beginning to show the first traces of grey. He had been at the cabin only a few days and was not yet used to waking to silence, to the little dramas of mist on the surface of the lake. It was very different from the familiar hum of the city he had left behind. He frowned at the jumble of rock and bush around him, his mind fussing with needling details: why hadn't his phone been connected yet? Where had he put the name of the man who could deliver firewood? When would the bank transfer his accounts? Should he sign a contract with the propane company now or pay by delivery? He shook his head impatiently at the barrage of pressing trivia. I should make a list, he thought. As he started back toward the cabin, William was brought up short by the sight of the figure by the lake. Backlit by the sparkling water, the shape seemed to flicker like a flame. What if it's a bear? William worried. After a moment's hesitation, he set off cautiously down the path to the lake.

As he approached, the form resolved itself into the figure of a man, a stranger standing perfectly still by the water's edge, blending into the rugged landscape, almost part of the rock.

The dawn breezes were dying, the lake settling into a glassy smoothness. William didn't quite know what to do when confronted with a trespasser on his property. Should he go back to the cabin and wait until the man went away? Was there some kind of backwoods etiquette to be observed? Would a polite, Can I help you? be appropriate? Or a terse, What are you doing here?

The man continued to stare out over the water as William came up behind him. William decided on a noncommittal approach. "Uh, hello," he mumbled. There was no response. He cleared his throat. "Hello," he repeated, more forcefully.

The stranger turned; his eyes were dark brown, almost black. He was slightly shorter than William, with a wiry build, wearing old blue jeans and a faded, red-checked shirt buttoned to the neck. He appeared to be a little weather-beaten, around forty, but a handsome-looking Native man. "I hear you need some help around the place," he said softly.

"Um, well, yes." William hadn't expected anyone to apply for the job so soon, or in such an unusual manner. It was only yesterday that he had mentioned to Doug Trimble at the General Store in the nearby town of Jubilee that he was looking for help. William was at a loss; he should have made a list of questions to ask in an interview.

Before William could say more, the man stepped around him, walking up the path toward the cabin. "Wait a minute!" William called, turning to follow too quickly, losing his balance. He made a few stumbling steps sideways to regain his footing. The man glanced back. "Smooth move," he said before setting off again, taking the uphill path in easy strides. William blinked. Something about those words disturbed William, but he didn't quite know why. With an irritated shake of his head, he called again and hurried after the man.

By the time William reached the door, the stranger was already inside, examining the cardboard box of food on the floor in front of the kitchen cupboards where William had dropped it the day before. "What do you think you're doing?" William asked, disconcerted, out of breath.

"Making breakfast," the man replied, searching in the box.

"Uh, look," William began, "I don't really need anyone to make me breakfast. What I need is someone to help me fix up this cabin for the winter; check the roof, seal up drafts, that sort of thing. I want, uh, a sort of odd-jobs kind of person, not a cook."

As William talked the man opened the small refrigerator and took out eggs and bacon. He pulled a frying pan from the cupboard and set it on the stove to heat.

"Um," William started again, "I think you should leave."

The man looked up, his expression calm, eyes steady. "Most people don't realize the power of words," he said with certainty. "People chat and talk; they stop hearing what they are saying. You say I should leave, but that isn't what you want. You want someone to help you. I am here to help. If you put out words like that, they will come true and then there will be no one to help you." He returned to the frying pan. "There are spirits all around us. They listen and hear what we say. The spirits fulfil our words. You are in the bush now. You are not in the city anymore. Be careful what you say."

Not knowing what to say, William decided not to say

a word. Retrieving his glasses from the bedroom and sitting at the table, William watched the man prepare breakfast with a graceful, purposeful economy of motion. It reminded him of the way he had seen geese land on the lake, backing and folding their wings at the precise moment they touched down smoothly on the water.

William had the vague impression that he knew the man from somewhere, but couldn't place him. This was his first visit to the cabin in the two years since his wife Barbara had died, and he guessed he might have run into the man on a summer vacation in the past.

William soon had a plate of bacon and eggs on the table before him with toast, jam, and a cup of sweet, black coffee. The man brought over a plate for himself and sat down. "I hear you're up here to work on a book."

Raising his eyebrows, William thought, News sure gets around in a small town. "Yes," he answered simply, pointedly refraining from further elaboration.

They finished their breakfast in silence. William chewed on unspoken words, concentrating on his plate, trying to decide how to deal with the situation, not coming up with anything. In spite of himself, he enjoyed the meal. When they were finished, William looked up, his own hesitant glance meeting the man's unwavering eyes. "Why do you want to work for me?"

The man shrugged. "The spirits called you; they brought us together. I need you, you need me." He pushed his chair back, stood up and walked to the door. He stopped with his hand on the knob. "I cooked. You wash up," he said, then stepped outside.

William exhaled loudly and rolled his eyes to the ceiling. "What have I got myself into now?" he mumbled under his breath. But he cleared the dishes off the table and put a pot of washing-up water to heat on the propane stove. I'll bet he needs me, he thought wryly, he probably plans to rob me at the first opportunity.

The cabin didn't have running water, just a handpump at the sink. William regarded it apprehensively. His mind began to wander over all the things that could go wrong; there were an awful lot of them. His plan had been to live in the cabin over the winter, some self-imposed seclusion to work on his book, his serious, scholarly contribution to literary criticism—the depressing fate awaiting retired English literature professors such as himself. Now it was starting to look as if it wasn't such a good idea. The ease with which the man had pushed his way inside troubled him. So far the man hadn't acted violently, but what if he *did* intend to rob the place? William grew concerned about his isolation. In the summer, with other cottagers around, it was different, but all the neighbours were gone by September. He was alone. What if dangerous characters were lurking in the woods, mad trappers or psychotic hunters?

William took a deep breath. It was too late to turn back. He had given up his house in Toronto and sold most of his possessions. His metaphorical bridges had been burned; he had nothing to go back to. When you have no reason to be anywhere in particular, one place is as good as another.

The sound of a car outside interrupted his gloomy thoughts. William leaned over the sink for a better view out the window. A white Ford Explorer with an Ontario Provincial Police logo on the door and a red and blue light rack on the roof pulled up beside the cabin. A uniformed police officer began talking to the man who had just hired himself as William's helper. Oh my God, William thought, panicking, he is a criminal!

The pan boiled over on the stove. William shut off the propane and poured the steaming water into the sink, barely avoiding scalding his hand as he tried to keep an eye on what was happening outside. After talking for several minutes, the man and the policeman nodded to each other; the policeman returned to his vehicle and drove away.

The front door opened and the Native man entered. "Dishes done yet?"

William gave him a deadly look. As the man turned away, William caught a glimpse of a smile. Feelings clattered inside him like dropped silverware. He felt irritated that he wasn't assertive enough to tell this interloper to go away and angry about the police coming to his house. Folding his arms across his chest, William glared. "Are you in trouble with the police?"

"Not that I know of," the man replied.

"Well, what did he want?"

"A cabin was broken into up north of here on Eagle Lake. He wanted to know if I knew anything about it."

"Do you have a history of breaking into cabins?"

The man shrugged. "No, it's just that sometimes I hear things about what's going on around here. The cops figured I might know who's been out in the bush and could have busted into that place."

William looked away. "I don't want you here if you're in trouble with the police." He stopped at the sound of tires crunching on gravel. Through the window, he could see that the police car had returned. *They've come to arrest him!* William thought.

The man opened the door and the police officer stepped inside. "Hey, Jack, I forgot to ask, have you seen George Ferris around lately?"

"George? No, not for a while. Why?"

"He's gone missing. It's kind of strange. He called his daughter and asked her and her husband to come up here, all the way from California. They arrived last Wednesday and George wasn't around. When he still hadn't shown up yesterday, the daughter reported him missing."

"I didn't even know he had a daughter."

The officer nodded in agreement. "Yeah, no one else did either. I've been asking around, but nobody seems to have known George very well. Doesn't look like anyone hired him as a guide." He paused for a moment. "It's funny though, when they got to the cabin his truck was parked there, so either he walked somewhere or someone else drove him."

"Maybe he went out in the bush," Jack suggested. "Could be he went hunting."

The officer shook his head. "As far as I know he only had an old Winchester deer rifle and a Remington 12 gauge shotgun, and they were both in the rack at his cabin. He filled some gas cans in town on Tuesday, and that's the last anyone saw of him." Turning to William, he smiled. "You must be Mr. Longstaffe. I'm Sergeant Ray Selkirk from the O.P.P. detachment down in Fayette. I hear you're up here to write a book?"

"Uh, yes," William mumbled.

"And Jack here's going to help you through the winter, eh? Good; you couldn't be with a better man than Jack. Nothing like having a medicine man around to help you survive in this country." Selkirk nodded to Jack. "Let me know if you hear anything." The sound of the door closing wasn't any louder than normal, but to William it sounded like the thump of all his collapsing assumptions. He busied himself with the dishes to cover his confusion. William had suspected that Jack was a criminal, yet here was a police officer saying he couldn't be with a better man.

"See you later," said Jack, opening the door.

William called after him. "Your name's Jack?"

"Yeah, Jack Crowfoot." He waited, holding the door open.

"You're a medicine man?"

Jack dropped his eyes. "Well, I don't know what you mean by a medicine man. I go into the spirit world and ask for guidance from my spirit helpers. If that's a medicine man, then yes, I guess I am one. If you mean someone who casts spells and works magic, then no, I guess I'm not." A silence fell between them. "See you later," Jack repeated and slipped out the door.

William finished the dishes.

"I wouldn't go out there if I were you."

William stopped at the sound of Jack's voice. He looked down at his hand—it was on the front door knob. The last thing he remembered was going to bed early with a book. The next thing he knew, he was standing by the front door in his pyjamas.

"I wouldn't go out there if I were you," Jack repeated. "Wendigo is out there."

Jack was sitting on a blanket on the floor. The doors to the airtight woodstove were open, the glow of the coals throwing a demon-red cast over his face, his shadow looming large on the wall behind, dancing in the flickering light. In his hand, Jack held a round, flat drum. William had a vague impression that he had heard drumming and that the compelling rhythm of the drum had drawn him from his bed. It had been soft and rapid, echoing as if from a long way off, and yet at the same time there was an immediacy to it, as if it were right there in the room beside him.

"What?" William hadn't seen Jack since the morning and vaguely wondered when he had come back.

"You go out there, Wendigo will take you for sure," Jack said.

William stood still, unable to make any sense of the situation. "What time is it?"

"It's late." Jack walked over and took his arm. "C'mon, sit down. I'll make some tea." He led William over to the table and guided him to a chair. Picking up the blanket from the floor, he wrapped it around William's shoulders. "There, don't want you to catch cold." He went to the kitchen to put the kettle on the stove.

"What's Wendigo?" William asked, recovering a little from his disorientation.

"Wendigo is a very bad spirit," Jack explained. "The worst. He finds people alone in the woods at night and makes them go crazy and then he eats them. You have to be careful around Wendigo. Nearly caught you tonight."

"Caught me? What do you mean?"

"Wendigo was calling you, like he did last night."

"Last night?" A tingle ran along William's spine, stirring up something about his dream.

"I saw you there," Jack whispered.

"Saw me? Saw me where?" William was fully alert. Fears fluttered through him like bats in a house.

Jack brought over two cups of tea and set them on the table. He pursed his lips. "You don't remember, do you?"

"Remember what?"

Jack shook his head as if dismissing an unimportant detail. "I hear your wife is dead."

The sudden change of topic took William off guard. "Uh, yes."

"Were you happy together?"

William had to think before answering. "It's complicated."

Jack laughed. "It usually is! Married long?"

"Oh, we married when I was still a graduate student. Then I landed a teaching position at York University. We bought a house in Toronto and lived there right up until she died."

"Yeah," Jack said, "I heard you were a literature professor. Retired, eh? And now you're up here meeting Wendigo, just like me."

William sipped his tea. It tasted like straw.

"I'm going out into the bush tomorrow," Jack announced. "I need you to go with me."

William blinked. "Oh, I don't think so," he protested.

Jack leaned forward. His eyes held an intensity that both scared and fascinated William. "The spirits called you," Jack said in a low voice. "It's important to do what they ask, otherwise they will abandon you, and who knows what will happen then?" He sat back and drank his tea. "I'm going to look for George Ferris tomorrow. The spirits have asked you to help. It's up to you if you want to follow their call or not."

William hesitated. "Why do they want me? I'm new here, I don't know anyone, or anything."

Jack shrugged. "Nobody knows why spirits do what they do. They have their own reasons. We don't even know why people do the things they do, let alone spirits." He gave a slight smile.

William wanted to say no, but found he couldn't. He faltered. He felt impelled to go, as if something was pulling him, a force he couldn't resist. "Well—"

"Good. Go to bed now," Jack said gently, like a father to a sleepy child. "You'll need your sleep if you're going into the bush tomorrow." He helped William up and steered him to his room, the blanket trailing along the floor behind. William tumbled into bed, scattered thoughts keeping him from sleep. They gathered like winter clouds before bursting in a blizzard of self-pity. The questions about his relationship with Barbara had stirred his sorrow. It wasn't a new sadness for William, but an old ache he had been pushing away, or more accurately, running away from. It was the reason he had moved up north, trying to put distances between himself and the pain.

He and Barbara had bought the cabin almost on the spur of the moment, years ago, on a family vacation—one of the rare ones when everyone managed to get along. It was as close to happiness as his family had ever come. They saw an advertisement for the property in the window of Cornerstone Realty in Thunder Bay, drove up to see it, and put down a deposit the next day. It was to be their Shangri-La, a place where their happiness would be preserved timelessly, where they could come back and recover it anytime they wanted.

It hadn't worked out like that. The cabin became another battleground, a three-way tug-of-war between Barbara, himself, and the children. The stout log walls held years of resentment and recriminations. It was another failure for William in an endless series of attempts to create a family out of stifled feelings and unspoken anger. He had intended to sell the place after Barbara died, but found he couldn't live in their house in Toronto anymore. The memories had crowded in on him, like heavy curtains drawn across winter windows, blocking out the light, blocking out the air so he couldn't breathe, choking him.

William lay in the dark bedroom, mired in a gnawing loneliness. He had tried to avoid his emotions with unpacking, organizing the cabin, planning his book and positive thoughts about starting a new life. But the truth was that by leaving Toronto he had removed himself even more from his children and his friends, plunging into a deeper isolation than before. Maybe that's what he had really wanted all along, what he was afraid to admit to himself. Sleep finally engulfed him like an ocean swallowing a drowning man.

CHAPTER TWO
MONDAY

It was still dark when Jack shook him awake. William rolled sleepily out of bed and struggled into a pair of beige, safari-style pants and a flannel shirt from The Rainforest Outdoors Store in Toronto—the kind of clothes people in the city imagined people wore in the woods. In the kitchen area, a bowl of cereal waited for him beside a cup of steaming coffee. After a quick dash to the outhouse, William sat down to eat his breakfast.

Jack busied himself preparing two backpacks. "Let's go," Jack said when William finished eating. "Wear your hiking boots."

"Where are we going?" William asked.

"To find George Ferris." Jack picked up the packs and slipped out the door.

William pulled on his boots, grabbed his jacket and hurried outside. The air held the chill of heavy dew. Jack was already sitting in William's truck. Before moving north, William, in anticipation of severe winters, had bought a 1988 four-wheel-drive, flat black Bronco II from an off-road enthusiast former student. It was so dented, scraped, and banged up that it looked like it had fallen off a mountain—more than once.

It was almost full daylight. William stared out over the lake as it quietly reflected the pink and grey dawn. The pines around the cabin were still in deep shadow, looking like cardboard cut-outs of tree shapes pasted on the sky. The troubled feelings of the night before had not been laid to rest by sleep. The sharp points of the trees were a bed of nails for his mood.

William rubbed his face. He didn't know what was the matter with him, he wasn't usually so emotional. Taking a deep breath, he climbed into the Bronco. The vehicle was covered in condensation, large droplets running in rivulets down the windshield. "Where are we going?" William asked as he started the engine. His voice sounded like sandpaper on rusty steel. He ran the wipers to clear the windshield. Jack pointed down the drive.

William released the clutch and drove along the gravel road. Too fast. The washboard road was rough as memory and jarred so badly when he hit the ruts that he had to slow down.

"Sometimes," Jack said, "when you first encounter the spirits, it breaks a lot of stuff loose and you feel a little out of control."

William didn't want to talk about spirits; he had enough on his mind. He followed the potholed road to the highway and stopped. A battered blue pickup truck came barrelling down from the north at high speed. The driver braked hard, made a screeching turn, fishtailed onto the gravel road opposite, and was lost in a cloud of dust.

"Whew!" William exclaimed. "He was in a hurry."

"Hmm," murmured Jack. "That was George Ferris's truck."

"George Ferris? The man we're going to look for? I guess he's back now if that was his truck."

"Hmm," Jack murmured again. "Let's go see."

William crossed over the highway and followed the blue truck along the road to Reese Lake. The road was in worse condition than the one they had left. The potholes were impossible to avoid. Proceeding in low gear, they passed a few cabins, shuttered and closed up for the winter. Through the trees on their left flashed glimpses of a small lake. "Keep going to the end," Jack pointed ahead.

The road ended at a run-down cabin. A wisp of smoke rose from the metal chimney. The moss-covered roof sagged; the ends of the joists were rotting under the eaves. The weathered trim around the windows bore patches of flaking white paint; a broken windowpane was covered with a piece of cardboard. Half the front porch was missing; the remains of a railing clung uncertainly to one side. Beside it, a tattered tarp partly covered a snowmobile and some kind of trailer with ski-runners instead of wheels. The area around the cabin was a junkyard filled with rusted pieces of metal; stacks of old tires; a filing cabinet with a bent drawer; a bale of wire overgrown with weeds. Behind the cabin, pushed up against the outhouse, sat a wheelless red pickup, its rusty hood open over a cannibalized motor. William felt depressed just looking at it.

William and Jack parked and went up to the porch. The beat-up blue truck they had seen on the highway was parked out front. In the bed was a haphazard pile of camping equipment. William put his hand on the hood. It was still warm.

The front door creaked open and a woman in her early twenties stepped out. "Can I help you?" she called. Even with her puffy morning eyes and curly blond hair awkwardly pinned back she was a beautiful woman, her face as softly rounded as an angel from a Renaissance painting. She wore a blue denim shirt and tight jeans; a wide leather belt accentuated her slim waist.

William became acutely aware that he had neither shaved nor washed up that morning. In fact, he hadn't shaved or washed the day before either. He rubbed the stubble on his chin, embarrassed, trying to remember if he had put on a clean shirt.

"Hello," Jack called. "We're looking for George. Have you seen him?"

"No, I haven't. Are you friends of his?"

"Yeah. My name's Jack. This is William," he responded. "We heard he'd gone missing. Thought we'd come over and see what we could do. Have you heard from him at all?"

"No. We arrived last Wednesday, but he wasn't here. He called and asked us to come up, said it was important."

"And you waited until yesterday to report him missing?"

She rubbed her hands nervously. "I wanted to before, but Lance, my husband, said to wait, that he might turn up. We just didn't know if he was coming back or not."

"You're his daughter, right?" asked Jack.

"Yes, I am," she replied with a bright smile. "Caroline. Caroline Rockwell." She straightened up and stretched out a confident hand in a rehearsed gesture, like someone presenting an award. Jack shook it briefly.

"Did he say what was so important?" continued Jack.

"No, he didn't say anything," said Caroline, a little knot of creases forming between her belladonna eyes. "I didn't actually talk to him, he spoke to Lance." She smiled again; this time it seemed a little more forced, like a practised expression to promote her husband's name. "Lance Rockwell, the actor. You've probably heard of him. We're from California." She brushed at her wayward curls.

Jack nodded toward the blue pickup. "George's truck is here. Was it here when you arrived?"

"Yes," Caroline confirmed. "The keys were in it."

"George had an all-terrain vehicle, but it's not here now," Jack noted. "Think he went off on that?"

"I have no idea," said Caroline.

"Boat's gone, too," observed Jack, pointing down to a jetty at the edge of the lake. "Could be he went off in that."

"I don't know," Caroline said, "but he couldn't have gone off in both of them, could he?"

Jack smiled. "Nope. Was that you driving that truck a while ago? We saw someone turn off the highway, driving kind of wild."

"It was Lance." A tinge of sadness crossed Caroline's face. "He went off to do some thinking, you know, figuring out his life and stuff."

"Came back in an awful hurry for somebody who was off thinking," Jack remarked.

Caroline smiled wryly. "Lance and his enthusiasms. Once he has an idea he gets all fired up and can't stop till it's done."

The door creaked again and a man stepped onto the porch. He was tall and rangy with lined, rugged features under thick, dark brown hair. He wore cowboy boots, a beige denim shirt, and black jeans with a bucking bronco buckle on the belt. Taking a sip from a coffee cup, he sized up Jack and William over the rim. His eyes were a startling blue. A cigarette smouldered between the fingers holding the cup, smoke drifting in front of his face, adding mystery to the piercing eyes.

"What's going on?" It was more a demand than a question. The languidly relaxed pose he assumed beside Caroline couldn't disguise the tension in his body.

"Oh, this is my husband, Lance Rockwell." Caroline gestured toward him with both hands as if presenting a new model of toaster. Again the practised smile as she said his name. "Lance, these gentlemen are asking about Daddy."

Lance scowled belligerently. "Who wants to know?"

"George is a buddy of mine," said Jack, his attention riveted on Lance. "Thought we might try to find him."

Lance's blue eyes opened a fraction wider as he raised his eyebrows. "Not much point, is there? He could be anywhere. Where would you start?"

"Maybe I have an idea about that," said Jack. Lance's eyes narrowed slightly. Jack pointed to the Bronco. "Mind if we leave our truck here?"

Lance shrugged with forced indifference. "Go ahead. How long will you be gone?"

"Just the day," said Jack. "We'll be back before dark."

"Think you can find him in that time?" Lance stared into the distance over the lake. "It's a pretty big country. We don't even know if he's around here."

"Well," said Jack, "out here in the bush, if somebody is lost and nobody looks for them, they don't get found." He kept his eyes on Lance. "Saw you out on the highway there. Early morning is a funny time to be coming home. Where were you?"

"None of your goddamn business!" Lance practically spat the words.

Jack turned his back and went to the Bronco, opened the rear door and took out the two backpacks. He passed one to William and shouldered the other himself. "We'll go this way," he said, heading toward the lake.

William waved to the couple on the porch and hurried after Jack. Following the lakeshore, they set out at a good stride, but very soon Jack had to slow down for William to keep up. Once William was at a comfortable pace, he began to enjoy the walk. The shoreline was made up of wide stretches of flat rock, a pretty pinkish granite. Sombre pines interspersed with golden-leafed poplar and aspen ringed the small lake. The beauty of the country had a positive effect on William, gradually lifting the gloom that coloured his thoughts. The calm surface of the lake reflected the green and gold, mixing it with the blue and white of the sky. To William, it was like hiking through a Tom Thomson painting.

At the end of the lake, Jack stopped. "We can rest for a minute," he said, "then we'll leave the lake and head off through the trees. It will be rough going."

They sat quietly, looking out over the water, soaking up the warm sunlight. William opened his jacket. "Is George a good friend of yours?"

Jack stood up and stretched. "I wouldn't say we're exactly friends. We both work as guides for Andy Polsky's outfit, taking groups out into remote areas for wilderness hikes." A ripple dimpled the centre of the lake as a fish rose to feed. "Andy cut some trails around a lake up north of here, Bearpaw Lake up by Tremont Ridge. He flies groups in and out." Jack paused; his eyes wandering wistfully over the water. "Some nice hikes up there. Country few people have ever seen, except for loggers and prospectors."

After a short break, they pushed on through the bush, William following as best he could. Jack's comment that it would be hard going was an understatement. Even with Jack breaking trail, William found himself fighting through a thick tangle of branches. The undergrowth was dense by the lake, thinning out as they moved further inland. The landscape became rockier. The bare lower branches of the pine trees, too shaded to support any needles, clawed at William like black dead hands. Sometimes they had to make their way over or around huge boulders and outcroppings. Except for the occasional squeaking chipmunk, there was no sign of wildlife.

William struggled along, awed at the ease with which Jack travelled through even the thickest bush. He moved like a boxer on skates; bobbing, weaving, and gliding all at the same time. William tried to copy his movement and immediately fell down, landing on a soft bed of brown pine needles. Jack glanced back over his shoulder. "Smooth move," he said. "Won't get far lying down there." William heaved himself to his feet and battled on.

Occasionally Jack would stop and squat down to study the ground, or examine a fallen log. After a while it became evident even to William that, although there was no distinct trail, they were not the first ones to pass that way.

William fingered a broken branch. "Someone's been through here before, haven't they?"

"More than once," Jack replied, thoughtfully. They had paused to rest on the edge of a small ravine. "Looks to me, though, that the last trip was made going north, like us. Whoever went through here didn't come back this way. And it was before the rain we had last week, too. What do you think?"

William shrugged.

"Tracking isn't your area of expertise, is it? It's a little different than the halls of academia!" Jack laughed. "The funny thing is, though, there aren't any blazes. If someone is cutting a trail through the bush and wants to use the same trail again, they make an axe cut, or blaze, on the trees to mark the route. Whoever it was knew the bush well enough to find their way without any blazes. I would say our mysterious woodsman didn't want this trail to be noticed. He wanted his tracks to just disappear again; he was trying his best not to leave any trace."

"You think it was George Ferris?"

"Well, we'll see. We are heading to the place my spirit helpers showed me." Jack started north again.

"What!" William exclaimed. He grabbed Jack's sleeve to stop him. "What do you mean, the place your spirit helpers showed you?" The mention of spirits made him nervous.

The corners of Jack's eyes creased with amusement at William's anxiety. "I visited the spirit world last night. One of my spirit helpers showed me a place in the bush. That's where we're headed now."

"What place? Will George be there?"

Jack merely smiled. "Come on, it's not far."

The ravine led to a cliff of dark rock, the top slightly higher than the surrounding trees. Jack turned to the right and made his way along the base toward a part of the cliff that had broken off and stood by itself like a massive column. William had a vague feeling of having been there before. "What is this place?" he asked Jack.

"This—" Jack gestured toward the cliff, "—is Hellbent Stump, and that," he pointed to the separate column, "is called the Chunk." Jack moved into the gap between the two, a space about as wide as a hallway. William followed him into the shaded cleft. The moody darkness of the sun-starved passage pressed on William. He stumbled on the jagged rocks littering the path. After about ten or fifteen paces they emerged into the light on the other side.

A scree of fallen boulders and rubble formed a clear space around the bottom of the cliff, a barren moonscape in the midst of the evergreen woods. At the very foot of the cliff, enough soil had gathered to support a thick screen of bushes, most of their leaves already turned a dull autumn brown. William gazed up at the rocky wall. After the closeness of the cleft it was a relief to stand under open sky. He leaned his head back and looked into the blue infinity above him, noticing that a light cloud cover was beginning to move in. He stretched his arms out wide and yawned.

Looking back at the passage they had come through, William's mind tumbled down it like a hole through time. He was sure he had been there before, but he couldn't remember clearly. It was all jumbled, like remembering a dream. He had the sensation of running through darkness, and there was a wolf, a big, dark wolf running ahead of him. Then the gap became another hallway, passing Barbara after a fight, averted glances raking the walls, tight lips gripping silence, shoulders brushing stiffly, anger in the air acrid as a chemical fire.

William jumped as if he had stepped into icy water, shocked at the suddenness and completeness of his vision—it had felt as if he was actually in the hallway with Barbara. He looked for Jack; he was nowhere to be seen. "*Jack!*" William yelled as hard as he could, over and over. Jack stepped out of the bushes at the bottom of the cliff, a flashlight in his hand.

"Okay, William," he said. "I heard you. You keep making noise like that and you'll scare everything away. There won't be any wildlife around here for the next fifty years."

"But—" William protested.

"I know, I know," said Jack, "you did the right thing. Come on." The lightness had gone out of his manner, tension strained his features. He turned back toward the cliff face, disappearing into the bushes. William followed, pushing through the branches, ducking his head to keep them from scratching his face, using his arms to clear a way. Dead leaves showered around him and dropped down his neck. Behind the bushes there was a narrow opening in the rock wall. Crouching down, Jack flicked on his flashlight and squeezed into the gap.

William followed on hands and knees. Darkness closed around them. Crawling along, he was led by Jack's light through a narrow tunnel. It was so low at one point he had to wriggle along on his belly. He began to worry that there might be bats around, or, even worse, snakes. Jack switched off his flashlight and William could see a faint glow of natural light ahead of them. The light at the end of the proverbial tunnel, he thought. The passageway widened and they were able to walk hunched over, then stand up completely. They entered a rock cave about the size of a small living room. The ceiling narrowed above their heads into a vertical shaft open to the sky, admitting a shadowy, indirect light. William had an overwhelming sense of déjà vu.

The floor of the cave was covered with a deep layer of forest debris. A nauseating smell filled the air, like a backed-up toilet. In front of them, on top of the detritus and tangled branches, lay a man. His eyes were wide open and staring; unblinking. William stared back, frozen with surprise; everything around him began to spin. He had a fleeting vision of a wolf. He gasped sharply and the world steadied. Fear bubbled along his nerves, then subsided, leaving him in a tenuous calm.

Jack bent over the man.

"Is he all right?" William asked lamely. He already knew the answer to that question.

Jack shook his head. "That's George Ferris," he said. "He's dead."

William started to tremble. His impulse was to run, to put as much distance as possible between himself and death.

Jack touched his arm. "Calm down. He won't hurt you. We'll leave in a minute."

William breathed deeply, a hand over his mouth against the smell. Jack, signalling William to stay where he was, began to circle the body, studying the ground. He shone his flashlight on the walls and examined the cave in detail. At last he said, "Okay, we can go now."

William was calmer, but still a little shaky. He gazed at the body with a mixture of fascination and revulsion. "Shouldn't we do something?" William asked, alarmed at just leaving the man there. "Cover him up or something?"

"Not much point," said Jack.

The dead eyes stung William like accusations. "Shouldn't we close his eyes at least?"

Jack knelt and forced the eyelids closed.

William stammered, "What, um, what happened? How did he die?"

Jack pointed to the opening above. "Looks like he fell through that hole first, but that wasn't what killed him. Here, look. See how his leg's broken? That's a really bad fracture." The leg was twisted back on itself, the pants stained dark with blood. "The fall broke his leg, but this is what killed him." Jack shone his light on George's head. The whole right side was crushed, the scalp torn back in a gruesome mess of skin, hair, bone, and dried blood. William held back vomit.

"A blow like that would kill you instantly," said Jack.

"You can see that his leg bled quite a bit after he fell. Dead people don't bleed, so he was alive after he broke his leg. Then there's the rock." Jack shone his flashlight on a football-sized rock nearby. "See the blood on it? That's what killed him."

William felt a shiver race up his spine. "You mean someone hit him with that rock?"

"Yep," said Jack. "Unless that rock jumped up and hit him itself, George Ferris was murdered."

William had the sudden certainty that the body was about to sit up and point at him. Terror froze him to the spot.

"It's okay," comforted Jack. "There's nothing more to be done here. We're leaving now. Stay close behind me." Jack turned William around to face the wall, then ducked into the opening.

William stood in the half-light, tense with confusion and surprise. Jack had vanished. In the jumble of rocks and shadows William couldn't see the entrance to the passageway. Panic built in his throat. He was trapped with a dead body behind him. William trembled uncontrollably. He cried out, "Jack!" A beam of light shone out from one of the dark cracks in the wall and Jack stepped into view.

"Calm down," Jack soothed. "Here, take hold of my jacket and follow me."

William clutched the jacket in a desperate grip. Jack entered the gap in the wall, pulling William behind him. The tunnel narrowed, forcing them to stoop, then crawl. William lost his hold on Jack. The confined space had not bothered him on the way in, but now the tunnel seemed impossibly small. He struggled through, getting jammed, unable to move. His breathing grew shallow and rapid. He kicked his legs and strained with his shoulders.

As William's panic reached its peak, a strange feeling of calm overcame him. The inflexible rock became soft and comforting, almost inviting. William relaxed and let himself drift away. Slowly he became aware of a voice. "William! Grab your pecker and follow me." It was Jack. The barked command shocked William out of his stupor. He crept after Jack through the narrowest part of the tunnel and at last stepped out into the daylight.

Pushing through the bushes, Jack led William out onto the open scree. "Sit down here for a minute," said Jack, helping him onto a rock.

"I couldn't get out," William mumbled, feeling a little dazed.

"Yeah," said Jack, "the spirit in that cave, he really liked you, wanted you to stay and keep him company."

"What?"

"Some spirits like to hang out in caves; you have to be careful when you go into a cave. If they like you, they try to keep you there, make you confused so you can't find your way out. Lots of people get lost in caves. Those spirits feel lonely sometimes and want some company."

"What do you mean, the spirit liked me?" William's mind was muddled. He felt a strong urge to return to the comfortable darkness of the cave.

"Spirits are like people when it comes to that. Did you ever meet someone you took an instant like or dislike to?"

"Yes," William answered, still trying to clear his head.

"Well, spirits are the same. Some people they like, some they don't. Nobody knows why, it's the way things are."

"How did you know there was a spirit in the cave?" William's analytical mind was clawing its way back.

"Tried to make you stay, didn't he?" Jack smiled.

William shook his head at the absurdity of the idea.

Jack laughed at the look on his face. "You just met a spirit and you don't believe it; you don't believe your own experience."

"We just found a dead man," rebutted William. "I believe that!" As he said it, a wave of the nausea he had felt at the sight of the bloody head washed over him.

Jack looked at him inquisitively. "Do you remember now?"

"Remember what?" William swallowed hard.

"Remember when you were here before?"

Little prickles of fear ran up William's arms as Jack spoke. "I haven't been here before…" His voice trailed off as he recalled the feelings of déjà vu, the wolf, the body sitting up and pointing.

Jack appeared disappointed. "I thought maybe seeing George would make you remember, but I guess you're not ready yet."

"Ready? Ready for what?"

Jack continued as if William had not spoken. "Out here in the bush, there's no instruction manual, no rational explanation of how or why things work the way they do, all we have to rely on is our experience. You have to trust your experience; out here, your life depends on it."

They sat in silence for a while. William's mind was in turmoil. He wondered, Have I been here before? Did I really meet a spirit? Or was I simply confused by an unfamiliar environment? This was, after all, a long way from his old life. He'd like to see how Jack would cope surrounded by students, term papers, examinations and university politics!

Jack regarded him closely. "You'll probably find yourself feeling very moody, like your emotions are running away with you. You may have visions, memories so strong they seem real. It's what happens when you first encounter the spirit world. The reality you knew starts breaking down, all your defences are stripped away, your emotions come to the surface. If you have the strength to withstand it, it will pass."

"But—" William was flustered.

"The spirits have called you. How you answer that call will determine your path." Jack stood up. "Wait here," he said and walked out of sight into the space between the Stump and the Chunk. After a few minutes he reappeared and returned to where William was seated. He picked up his pack. "Come on, we'd better keep going if we want to be back before nightfall. Don't want to be out here in the dark."

"What were you doing?" William asked.

Jack thought for a moment before responding. "There are some sacred places in these rocks," he said. "I was checking on them. This place has many secrets."

"What kind of secrets?" William felt there had already been enough secrets.

"Maybe one day I'll show you," Jack replied. "My people have been coming here for a long time to visit the spirits. You're lucky. The spirit of that cave, he liked you. If you make a friend of that spirit, you will have a powerful helper."

William blinked in surprise. "How do I do that?"

"I don't know," Jack deadpanned. "He's your friend."

William shouldered his pack. "You know," Jack said, with a twinkle in his eye, "maybe it wasn't you that spirit was after, maybe he just liked your shirt." William looked down at his shirt, a bright red-and-yellow check. "With a shirt like that," continued Jack, "we don't have to worry about getting lost. It's so loud, when you take your jacket off they hear it all the way down in Jubilee!" They both laughed. Jack looked into William's eyes. "See, that spirit is helping you feel better. A few minutes ago you were trembling with fear beside a dead man, now you're laughing."

William, mortified that he might be acting disrespectfully to the dead, began to stammer a defence. Jack held up a hand to stop him, cocking his head to listen. His whole face changed. Jack's expression contracted in a focused intensity that filled William with alarm. Following the direction of his gaze, William saw a movement in the trees a short distance away. A crouched figure crept onto the scree, a small man with unkempt hair sticking out from under a brown-striped toque. He wore too-big jeans and a torn black-and-red-checked jacket over a dirty wool sweater. In his hands he held a rifle.

Jack and William didn't move. The man stopped, eyes flicking rapidly from one to the other. He held the gun at his hip, pointing straight at them, unwavering.

"Hey, Maurice," called Jack, "how's it going?" The man didn't reply. He remained perfectly still, except for his darting eyes. "Nice day for a hike out here," Jack went on conversationally. "We're headed up to the top of the Stump, going to have some lunch up there. Should be a great view today. Probably see clear down to the lake." The man held his rifle steady; he didn't move or say a word. "You seen George lately?" asked Jack.

The man's eyes narrowed with suspicion. "George here?"

Jack shrugged. "Wondered if you'd seen 'im. You and George are pretty good buddies, aren't you?"

"What do you know about George?" The rifle rose slowly from his waist to his shoulder. "That's my gold!" he shouted, suddenly agitated. "That's my gold!"

"Sure it is," Jack assured him gently, "sure it is. We

don't have any gold. We aren't even looking for gold. Any gold around here, it's yours."

"That's my gold!" the man shouted again. "You keep away!"

"Yeah, we're going," reassured Jack. "Finished our hike, now we're going home."

"That's my gold!" the man screamed.

"*Run!*" shouted Jack.

The sound of the rifle going off was deafening.

William ran for the trees. The gun blasted again as he dashed for cover. William crashed into the bush, fighting his way through the undergrowth. Branches clawed at his face and grabbed his clothing. Twigs and sticks writhed like snakes around his ankles, tangling in his bootlaces. Rocks leaped in front of his feet. Sweat streamed down his face, his vision distorting as his glasses slipped down his nose. He struggled on through a blurred nightmare, waving his arms before him to keep the raking branches away from his face. The rifle cracked behind him, but the reports were becoming more distant.

William couldn't run any more. He had to stop. Even fear and adrenaline couldn't push him any further. He leaned against a tree, gasping for breath, bending over to ease the stitch in his side. Jack came up beside him, listening over the sound of William's laboured breathing. The shooting had stopped.

"That spirit really likes you," said Jack at last.

William wanted to say, Why are you talking about spirits when there is a madman with a gun out there somewhere? But he was puffing too hard to speak.

"You think even Crazy Crazy could miss at that close range?" Jack asked. "And he's a good shot, I know. That spirit, he likes you. He made those bullets go wild. Saved our lives, I guess."

As soon as he could breathe again, William asked, "Who was that? You know him?"

Jack nodded. "Maurice Crécy. He's a little unusual. People started calling him Crazy Crécy, which soon became Crazy Crazy. He was a friend of George's."

"You really think he would have killed us?" William asked, still breathing hard.

"Sure looked like it to me," said Jack. "People don't usually point guns at you and pull the trigger unless they mean to kill you. That Crazy Crazy, he's unpredictable, you never know what he's going to do next."

"We should call the police. He should be charged with attempted murder."

Jack frowned. "It wouldn't do any good. How could we prove it? And anyway, what would they do with him? Put him in an institution? No, the spirits have other plans for Crazy Crazy."

"He's dangerous! He could shoot someone else."

Jack gave William a penetrating look. "I know you don't understand this yet, but this is the bush, we do things differently out here."

William gave a disgruntled sigh. "What if he follows us?"

Jack shook his head. "No. He's obsessed with his gold, that's more important to him than following us."

"Do you think he'll find George's body?"

"Maybe he will."

"Could he have killed George?"

"Maybe he did. I wouldn't have thought Crazy Crazy was homicidal until today. I guess if he would take a shot at us, he could have hit George on the head with a rock. You never know what a man's going to do once gold fever takes hold of him—old Crécy was double crazy to begin with; now I think he's gone triple crazy.

Gold's not supposed to be toxic, but it sure seems to poison some people."

William gave him a skeptical look. "Gold fever? I thought that was something they made up for boys' adventure stories."

"Nope, it's real enough." Jack shook his head sadly.

"And he was George's friend?"

"Well, they both drank quite a bit," said Jack. "They used to hole up at George's cabin drinking, sometimes for days at a time. I don't know if they were really friends or if it was just the bonds of alcohol."

As soon as he felt he could move on again, William said, "Let's go," anxious to put more distance between himself and the gunman. William had, unknowingly in his blind scramble, run parallel to the cliff. They walked along beside it, the height diminishing gradually until the edge was low enough to step over. Jack made a hairpin turn and began to climb the gentle slope toward the top of the bluff. Even though it was uphill, the going was easier over the smooth rock. William stooped to study the delicate, multicoloured rosette patterns of the lichen. So intent was he on his examination that he jumped when Jack put a hand on his arm. "Watch your step." In front of them, two slabs of rock split apart, creating a small fissure. It was nearly covered by dead branches and piles of brown pine needles. Jack picked up a stick and cleared the debris away, revealing a dark hole. "This is a small one," said Jack. "Some of them are big enough for a man to fall through. Even a small one like this, you fall into it, you could break a leg. Always walk on bare rock when you can; don't put your weight on anything else, even if it looks solid. Watch your step."

William straightened up. "That trail we were following, do you think Crazy Crazy made it?"

Jack shrugged. "Could be."

They started off again. William fell in behind Jack, matching his steps as closely as possible.

When they reached the highest point of the cliff they stopped to take in the view. The deep green of the northern pine forest, occasionally dotted with small stands of poplar and birch in their fall colours, stretched before them to the horizon. The trees undulated with the erratic landscape like a dark ocean. It appeared completely unspoiled, as if no one had ever set foot there. The sky was solid grey to the west, but there were only a few scattered clouds overhead. A slight breeze ruffled William's hair. He thought of the first European explorers and wondered how they had found their way through such seemingly impenetrable and unchartable forest. The answer, William knew, was that they were motivated by greed, dreams of riches from new trade routes and furs. He looked over the land, logged off, stripped of minerals, lakes poisoned, wildlife dead. What people will do for money, he thought cynically.

"See that," said Jack pointing to a small glimmer to the south, a slash of silver in the carpet of green, "that's Reese Lake where we came from."

William squinted into the distance. "Where's Jubilee?"

Jack pointed. "Can't see the town, but you can make out the water tower, there."

William searched and strained, unable to distinguish Jubilee's water tower from the trees.

"Let's have lunch," Jack suggested. From the backpacks he produced a thermos of coffee and a couple of sandwiches. They sat on the sun-warmed rock and ate. An enterprising whisky jack landed on the ground close to William and, cocking its grey-crested head, fixed an eye on his sandwich.

William chewed appreciatively. "This is good." He peeled back the bread. Ham, cheese, lettuce, mayonnaise, mustard. "Did you make these?"

Jack nodded.

William looked out over the broad vista before them. "Sure is beautiful out here."

"Yeah," said Jack. "This view is courtesy of the glaciers."

"The glaciers?"

"This is an outlier of Ghostwalker Ridge over there behind us."

William could clearly see a low ridge to the northeast. "An outlier?"

"Like a piece broken off. During the last ice age, about 11,000 years ago, all of this," he made an expansive gesture, "was under a glacier. The ice was so heavy it compressed the ground and even today this whole vicinity is lower than the surrounding landscape. It's called the Wiwishnee Depression. Believe it or not, the land is still rebounding after 11,000 years and every year rises a little higher. Some of the land rebounded faster than other parts; that's why it's so uneven in this area. Ghostwalker Ridge rebounded quickly, popped up as soon as the ice retreated. This piece broke off somehow and ended up here like a little island. The rest of the land is slowly catching up."

"Is this the only outlier?"

"No, there are a few others along the length of the ridge. Locally they're called stumps. Like I said, this one is Hellbent Stump."

"Is there a lot of mining around here?" Hearing Crazy Crazy rant about gold had piqued William's interest. Although he had vacationed at his cabin for years, he didn't know a lot about the geology of the area.

"Not around here. There was the Jubilee Copper

Mine; not much else after that played out. There's a palladium mine over there by Lac Des Isles. There was a silver mine down by Thunder Bay and there are amethyst mines along the north shore of Lake Superior. There's even been talk of diamonds in this area, although nobody's ever found anything."

"What about gold?"

"Well, there are gold mines northwest of here over at Red Lake near the Manitoba border, but the really big gold strike was the Holsum mine north of Sault Ste. Marie. What's interesting is that the same Beardmore-Geraldton greenstone belt runs right through here. It runs all the way from Red Lake over to Holsum. Disappears underground for a while, but a shift of it breaks out here."

"Greenstone?" The term was new to William.

"Yeah, it's a type of granite. It's often veined with quartz-carbonate and that's where gold is usually found, in the quartz veins. Ghostwalker Ridge, that's the greenstone belt. This is greenstone we're sitting on."

William was intrigued. He noticed the rock was much darker than the pink granite they had seen at Reese Lake. "I thought it was just rock."

"Everything has a story," said Jack, "everything has a history, a life, and a soul. Every tree, every leaf, every animal, every insect. We're all part of the story."

William felt the rock, wondering how many millions of years old it was, what changes it had seen. "There's never been any gold discovered here?"

"Well," Jack leaned closer, speaking into William's ear, "there's the legend of The Last Waltz Mine."

"What's that?"

"I'll tell you about it some time." Jack winked as he rose to leave. William tossed the last bite of his sandwich to the whisky jack. The audacious bird accepted the gift, gave a little bow, and, with a flurry of grey feathers, darted into a nearby tree to enjoy its prize.

They hadn't gone far when Jack stopped and pointed to a large hole. "What do you make of that?"

William shrugged.

"Look some more," Jack encouraged.

The ground on one side of the hole still had a covering of dead branches and pine needles, but the opposite side had been cleared, the brush in a pile with some loose stones. Patches of lichen were scraped away around the edge. William made a wild guess. "Has something been dragged over the rock?"

"Very good," said Jack. "We'll make a woodsman out of you in no time."

William walked to the lip of the hole and looked down. He gasped as he saw the body of George Ferris lying on the floor of the cave below. He jumped back. "Is this the opening we could see from the cave?"

Jack nodded.

"This is where he fell from?"

Jack nodded again. "Wait here." He slipped off his backpack and, crouching down, began to pace slowly around the gap in the rock. Jack never took his eyes off the ground as he repeatedly circled the hole, gradually working his way to the east.

William moved a good distance away and sat down heavily. He was beat. He wasn't used to hiking for hours at a time, especially through dense bush—and they still had to walk all the way back.

Eventually, Jack returned to where William waited. "Nothing more to see here. Let's go."

William reluctantly lumbered to his feet, glad to be moving away from the scene of the tragedy. He gave the opening to the cave a wide berth as they passed, as if he could feel death creeping out of it like a black mist spreading over the rocks, a darkness that would engulf him and draw him down into oblivion if he ventured too close.

They made their way to the edge of the cliff and looked down, but could see no sign of Crazy Crazy. The clouds were becoming sullen and threatening, making the sky look like a bad toothache.

William wanted to go home, but didn't want to walk into another encounter with Crazy Crazy. "I think it's going to rain. What should we do?"

Jack looked at the sky, then dropped his eyes to the ground; his body tensed. Kneeling, he examined the rock closely. "Someone's been here recently."

"How recently?" asked William.

Jack brushed a hand over the rock. "Today."

"How can you tell?"

Jack pointed. "Look, here. And here." William stared blankly at the ground. He couldn't see anything. "Of course," continued Jack, "the gum wrapper was a dead giveaway."

William searched around for gum wrappers, but there were none to be seen. "What—?" he began, then noticed the look of amusement on Jack's face. "That was a joke, right? There is no gum wrapper, is there? Very funny."

Jack laughed. "Come on, let's see if we can find out where he went." He set off through the trees.

"Wait!" called William, full of alarm. "Do you think we should? What if it was Crazy Crazy?"

Jack considered. "I don't think so. Crazy Crazy would have left more sign with those caulk boots of his."

"But, what if this other person has a gun too?"

Jack pursed his lips. "Do you know what Indians do when they get attacked by a bear?"

William shook his head.

"Well, you never go bear hunting alone, always go with a friend, then, if a bear attacks, you trip your friend and run like hell!" Jack looked at William straight-faced. "Same thing will work here."

William didn't get it. He stared at Jack with his mouth open. "You're not taking this seriously," he said.

"Yes I am," Jack reassured him. "Come on, we'll be careful."

William followed him into the bush.

The forest was darker under the cloud-troubled sky. The opaque green of the pines seemed to absorb all the light, leaving Jack and William adrift in an eerie twilight. The high treetops whispered occasionally in the wind, but no stir of air reached the ground through the thick skirts of boughs. All was quiet and still. William glanced nervously around as they walked. They headed north, away from the edge of the cliff, in the opposite direction from George's cabin. Although the terrain was rough enough to make for hard going, there was more of a definite trail to follow than on the trek out from Reese Lake. William's knees were beginning to ache; he had to stop and rest them every ten minutes or so.

"Where are we going?" William asked, lowering himself cautiously to the ground, as if setting a delicate crystal vase on a precarious table.

"We're heading toward Trout Lake, the next lake north of here."

"How far? My knees won't last much longer."

"We're almost there."

William massaged his knees. "I'm glad we didn't try to go back the way we came. This is a better trail."

Jack agreed. "It's an old logging road, abandoned before this area was even settled. The forest has pretty much taken it over now."

"You were going to tell me about a mine around here, a gold mine?"

"Yeah," said Jack. "The Last Waltz Mine. The story goes that after the First World War there was a prospector out of Winnipeg called Skinny Joe Lazare. Skinny Joe was supposed to have found gold, but never laid a formal claim, he kept the location a secret. He called his strike The Blue Danube Mine because 'The Blue Danube' waltz was his favourite piece of music. He always said that when he struck it rich he was going to dress up in the finest suit money could buy, go to the Plaza Ballroom in Winnipeg, find himself a beautiful woman and dance to 'The Blue Danube' waltz.

"Every spring Skinny Joe would come out to Thunder Bay from Winnipeg and go off into the bush, and every year he took a woman with him. But in the fall he always came back alone—with a sack of gold. Always said the woman had died of some illness or other. Talk was that Skinny Joe made sure those women never came back so they couldn't reveal the location of his strike. People began to call it The Last Waltz Mine.

"One year Skinny Joe hitched up with a local woman named Katey Devine. The other women he had brought out with him from Winnipeg, but Katey was local and knew the story. Her family begged her not to go and her brother actually pulled a gun on Skinny Joe. But Katey had her mind set and off she went mining.

"The next fall everyone waited for Skinny Joe's return. Katey's brother had spent the summer cleaning his gun and practising his marksmanship, planning to kill Skinny Joe if Katey didn't come out of the bush alive. Some old soldiers back from the war said that the tract behind the house he used for target practice looked as blown up as parts of France after a severe shelling.

"Finally, someone did return from the Blue Danube Mine, and, much to everyone's surprise, it wasn't Skinny Joe, it was Katey Devine. She was alone—except for a sack of gold. She told everyone that Skinny Joe had died from a fall, although people suspected that it was more likely from a push.

"Katey and her family left the area and were never heard from again. She never returned to the mine, but legend has it that she sold Skinny Joe's map. Every so often someone will turn up here with a map looking for The Blue Danube Mine, or The Devine Mine, or The Last Waltz Mine, or whatever name it had in the version of the story they heard."

"But no one's ever found anything?" asked William.

"Not yet," replied Jack. "Come on, we'd better keep moving."

William looked for an excuse to rest longer. "Who do you think was up there on the cliff?"

"That I don't know. But I doubt it was a casual passer-by," answered Jack. "Let's go."

"What do we do if we catch up with him?" William asked apprehensively, staggering to his feet. In his condition, he wouldn't be able to run for safety.

"Well," said Jack, "I intend to make myself invisible. Don't know about you." He began to move off down the trail.

"Jack, wait!" William's apprehension spun toward panic. "What do you mean, make yourself invisible?"

Jack paused. "Did you see me when you were running away from Crazy Crazy?"

William could only recall jangled fragments of his run. "No."

"That's because I became invisible," Jack said. William's face sagged in doubt. Jack gave him an appraising look. "I'll show you." They stood face to face about an arm's length apart. "Now," instructed Jack, "turn around, count to five, then turn back again."

William did as instructed. When he turned around, Jack was gone. William studied the scene before him, but couldn't see where Jack was hiding. "Okay," he called, "I give up. Where are you?"

Suddenly, there was Jack, taking a step toward him. It was as if he had materialized out of thin air. "How did you do that?" William asked, amazed.

"It takes practice, but you can do it too. It's not hard. That spirit will help you." He prodded William's paunch. "And you'll need some help to make that invisible!" he added, laughing. "Our eyes react to movement, so the first thing is to be completely still. Next, and this may sound strange to you, you have to pretend to be something else, and pretend so completely that you will look like what you are pretending to be to anyone who sees you." He saw the skeptical look in William's eyes. "It's like acting. We are the only beings that can do it because only humans have the capacity to lie."

William looked even more doubtful; Jack laughed. "You don't have to believe it, you just have to know it works. You couldn't see me, could you?" William shook his head no. "That's because," Jack clarified, "I had turned my awareness away from you and toward the tree beside me. The only way I can explain it is that I blended my awareness with the tree, so that what you thought you saw was a tree. I was standing right next to it, but you couldn't see me. Make sense?" Again, William shook his head no.

Jack laughed, enjoying himself. "You try it." He put a hand on William's shoulder and gently pushed him toward a small pine tree, moving him deep among the branches. "Grab hold of it," Jack prompted. William put one hand on the trunk and grasped a branch with another. "Now," said Jack, "close your eyes and imagine you are part of the tree. Focus all your consciousness on the tree. I'm going to turn around and then see how you do."

William closed his eyes and concentrated. He focused on the roughness of the bark and the stickiness of sap beneath his hands; felt the prick of needles against his cheek; smelt the sharp smell of resin. Imagining himself as a branch, motionless in the quiet air, he tried to let himself blend with the tree, become part of it.

"That's pretty good," he heard Jack say. William opened his eyes to see Jack standing a short distance away, regarding him intently. "You're a natural. With a little practice you could become a master of invisibility. Come on out of there."

William moved out from among the branches.

"There have been some really great medicine men," Jack continued, "who could disappear in the middle of open spaces even when people were watching them, whole crowds of people. They could move around too, appearing in different places. It can be a very useful trick."

"You honestly couldn't see me?" William asked wonderingly.

Jack chuckled. "Let's just say you did good. In fact, you did great for a first try. I would say that if you were wearing black on a moonless night and a blind person who wasn't looking for you walked by, they would probably never have known you were there." He patted William's shoulder. "Come on, we'd better keep moving."

William trudged on. It felt as if someone were lighting matches behind his kneecaps. Jack, as he had on the trail to Hellbent Stump, stopped occasionally to study the ground. William was hardly paying attention to where he was going, stumbling more and more, lapsing into a fog of exhaustion and pain. He could hear Barbara berating him, You shouldn't have gone out in the woods without knowing how you were going to get back. Her voice ricocheted off images from the past, scenes of Christmases and birthdays, memories of tiny student apartments, restaurants, and theatres. The old loneliness pursued him again, like a snake after a wounded mouse.

Since Barbara had died, he had faced the emptiness of a life alone. What made it hard was that William had harboured such hope that their antagonistic relationship could heal and grow strong again. Their marriage was good at the start—they were happy when they were young; in love, looking forward to a life that held prospects for the future. Then the children came and everything changed. Somehow the kids were always between them. William felt as if he could never be a good enough father to them, or a good enough provider. And he blamed all his feelings of inadequacy on Barbara, as if she were the salt that poisoned the ground of his soul.

The children, Peter and Stephanie, had grown up and moved out on their own, leaving the two of them in that old brick house with its tiny garden and gabled roof that leaked every winter when ice crept under the flashing. At first, in their forced togetherness, he felt that the closeness between them was beginning to return. It developed slowly, like a rose and a briar ruthlessly cut back, sprouting anew, putting out fresh shoots from the still living roots. Then death stepped in and changed everything. Now he had no wife and two distant children whom he had never learned to love. Or perhaps, never allowed himself to love.

William had been struck by Jack's comment that people could turn invisible because of their capacity to lie. Was that how he had kept his emotions invisible through all those years, by lying? Had his whole life been a lie? Was that why he felt like a ghost in his own past?

Jack stopped so abruptly that William almost bumped into his back. Jack pointed. William peered up the trail, but could see only trees and shadows. He adjusted his glasses, looking again. Then he saw it. Standing a short way ahead, plain as could be, was a deer—a doe looking directly at him, ears alert, eyes soft and brown.

The moment stretched into a peaceful silence. William fancied she had something to say to him. He dismissed the notion as nonsense, and as he did so, the doe moved silently off into the bush, her pale brown coat dissolving into the tangled shadows beneath the trees.

William was awestruck; he had never been that close to a wild animal before. He looked at Jack, but couldn't find any words.

Jack raised his eyebrows and nodded appreciatively. "That spirit brought the deer here for you. This is powerful medicine. Deer will be one of your spirit helpers."

William searched the forest hoping for another glimpse. "Spirit helpers?"

"Yes, when you go into the spirit world, Deer will be there to guide you, give you advice, lead you to healing, that sort of thing."

"I'm going into the spirit world?"

Jack laughed. "You've already been there, my friend." He flowed into the bush as easily as the deer. William teetered on his troublesome knees.

After a few steps Jack stopped again. "Be careful here." In front of him was a roughly circular chasm, big enough to drop a bus into. William peered over the edge, his gaze disappearing into the darkness.

"What's that?"

"It's called the Gulp. Legend has it that it's bottomless. Fall in there and you're gone forever."

William snorted. "The Stump, the Chunk, the Gulp? Who named these places, Walt Disney?"

Jack laughed. "See that?" He pointed to a course of tumbled rocks. "After a heavy rain or in the spring after snowmelt, water runs down there into the Gulp and the Gulp never fills up. The water disappears down there. Some people say there's a network of underground caves and rivers stretching all the way from Lake Nipigon to Lake Superior. There are lots of lakes around here that have streams running into them, but no outlet, so where does the water go? The theory is that the underground rivers maintain the water levels in the lakes. This is one of the entrances to that subterranean network."

William backed away from the edge. "'Abandon all hope ye who enter here.'"

Jack's brow creased as he tried to remember. "I've heard that before."

"Dante's *Inferno*—it's the inscription over the Gates of Hell."

Jack nodded. "Very appropriate. Let's keep moving."

The short fall day was turning into a long fall night when Jack finally stopped. William lifted his tired head. He could see a pale glimmer through the trees. Another few minutes brought them to a dirt road beside a lake, the surface covered with a soft mist. It captured the last of the daylight and held it dancing over the water, glowing like the eyes of someone in love, undaunted by the pressing darkness all around.

Across the road, a wharf protruded into the lake. Beside it, an open parking area was half taken up with overturned boats, their painters of grey rope stretching out from their bows like limp tongues of exhausted dogs. A single boat floated in the water beside the wharf, a vague shape in the mist.

"Where are we?" William asked Jack.

"The boat landing on Trout Lake. People take their boats out of the water and stack them up like that for the winter."

"How are we going to get home?"

Jack pointed to a light off to their right. They went toward it, William shuffling in a stiff-legged walk, trying to conserve his knees. The light came from the window of a cabin at the end of the road. It was full dark by the time they reached it. Jack climbed the three steps to the porch and knocked on the door. William waited below, leaning on the side of a dark green Jaguar, his knees too painful to negotiate the stairs.

An outside light came on and a face peered through a window before the door was opened by a tanned, athletic-looking man in a black track suit, his grey hair in a military buzz cut. Although the grey betrayed his age, he was obviously someone who kept himself in shape.

"Good evening," said Jack politely. "Sorry to trouble you; my friend and I are a little far from home. We wondered if you could help us out by giving us a ride back."

"A ride where?" The man's tone was stern.

"To our camp on Rainbow Lake. My friend William and I," Jack pointed to William beside the Jaguar, "went for a hike, but his knees started acting up, so we took a shortcut back and ended up here."

William straightened up and moved toward the light,

allowing the man a better look at him. He put on what he hoped was an expression of innocent suffering.

"Sure would appreciate it if you could help us out with a ride." Jack smiled ingenuously.

"I know Rainbow Lake, that's where the resort is." The man's eyes flicked between William and Jack. "You're camping there?"

Jack laughed. "No, William has a cabin there, he lives there. It's a local expression; we call everything outside of town a camp."

The man nodded decisively. "I'll get my keys." He made even the simplest statements sound like executive decisions. Returning a moment later wearing a down vest, he unlocked the car. Jack took the back seat, letting William sit up front where there was more room to stretch out his legs. William settled into the soft leather seat as the Jaguar's big motor leaped to life. The car smelled of luxury. As he started down the drive, the man inquired, "Where did you hike from? You said you took a shortcut."

"Hellbent Stump," Jack replied.

"Hellbent Stump, picturesque name," the man remarked. "By the way, my name's Harry, Harry Perkins; I'm from Toronto."

"I'm Jack, this is William."

Harry Perkins nodded affably as he navigated the ruts and potholes by the light of his high beams. As they passed the boat landing, William saw that the light had gone from the mist, night closing over the lake like a black fist.

Jack asked, "Did you see anyone else around this evening, anyone coming out of the bush like we did?"

"No," Harry responded. "Been quiet around here. Quiet as the grave, as they say. I was just out for a jog and didn't see anyone the whole time. Why?"

"Thought there may have been someone else out in the bush today, that's all. Do you know a man named George Ferris?"

Perkins's head jerked up sharply. "Who?"

"George Ferris. He lives over there on Reese Lake. Been missing for a few days. Wondered if you knew him."

"No, never had the pleasure," Perkins responded. By the dim light from the dashboard William saw Perkins's knuckles tighten on the steering wheel. "Was he a friend of yours?"

"Sort of," replied Jack. "You said you came up here from Toronto?"

"Yes, taking a little time away from the hurly-burly of the business world." Perkins gave a forced chuckle. "I have my own brokerage firm down in Toronto, dealing mainly in mining stocks. I can handle the major trades over the Internet, and my staff can cope with the smaller trades, so I decided to get away for a little while. I keep in touch by e-mail and phone." His lips parted in a toothy grin. "Hell, except for not having to worry about me overhearing when they complain about what a bastard I am, they don't even know I'm gone!"

"Seems like a long way to drive to a camp. Don't most people from Toronto have cabins around Muskoka or Haliburton?"

"This is God's country around here," Perkins said. "I'd move up here permanently if I could swing it. I first came through here as a teenager when I hitchhiked out west. Most beautiful country I've ever seen, and I've travelled, let me tell you. Always said if I could live anywhere in the world, it would be here. When the chance came up to buy that cabin last year, I jumped at it. I haven't been able to spend as much time up here as

I would like. Can you believe this is my first visit this year? Summer's over and I'm just arriving."

They reached the highway and Perkins turned south. They drove in silence for a few minutes before he asked, "What prompted you to take a hike up to that, um, Hellbent place today? Did it have anything to do with your missing friend?"

"Turn left here." Jack directed him onto the Reese Lake road. "We want to go right to the end, to the last cabin."

Perkins stopped the car. "I thought you said you lived on Rainbow Lake, where the resort is. Rainbow Lake is the other way."

"We left our truck over by Reese Lake," explained Jack. "That's where we started the hike from. We need to get the truck and go home."

"Ah." Perkins didn't sound quite so confident, but he made the turn and drove down the rutted road to Reese Lake. "Why were you out at that Hellbent place today?" Perkins braked sharply as the underside of the Jaguar scraped gravel in a large pothole. Perkins swore. Conversation stopped as he concentrated on driving.

"There's the camp," Jack pointed between the headrests, "you can see the lights. And there's our truck."

"So, why—" Perkins began again. His question was cut short, the car bottoming out again as it bucked another pothole.

Perkins pulled up behind William's Bronco. Jack and William both voiced their thanks as they climbed out of the deep leather seats.

"Glad I could help," called Perkins with a friendly wave.

Jack walked up to the front door of the cabin and knocked; William hobbling behind. Lance opened the door. "Your wife here?" asked Jack. Lance gave him a sour look and called into the house. Caroline came to the door.

"Did you find anything?" she asked, pushing in front of Lance.

"Yeah," Jack took a breath, "we found something. Found George."

"Where is he?" Her voice was tight with fear. "Is he all right?"

"Found him out there in the bush, about halfway to Trout Lake," said Jack, pointing into the distance. "Place called Hellbent Stump." Jack sighed. "He's dead."

"Dead?" Caroline's brows knitted as she cocked her head slightly to one side as if to hear better.

Jack nodded.

Caroline stared at him for a moment, uncomprehending. Then, slowly, her mouth opened, her eyes sank into pits of grief. "No!" she shrieked, burying her face in Lance's chest. She sobbed and pounded his shirt with a fist. "No, no, no!"

Lance stared over William's shoulder at the Jaguar in the drive, then fixed his bright blue eyes on Jack. "What kind of way is that to tell someone their father is dead?" he demanded, anger like acid on the tip of his tongue.

"There is no easy way," countered Jack, returning his gaze.

"You guys get out of here!" Lance yelled. "Go on! Get the hell out of here!" His eyes flicked back to the Jaguar.

"No! Wait!" Caroline's voice shook with the spasms of her sobs. "I want to know what happened. Tell me what happened!"

"We don't know" said Jack in a soft voice. "His leg was broken. Looks like he had a fall."

"Was he in pain? Did he suffer?" Caroline clutched at the front of Jack's shirt. "Tell me!" she screamed.

Lance held her from behind. "Hey, honey, come on, calm down."

She shook herself free. "I don't want to calm down! I want to know what happened!" A huge wave of sobbing overwhelmed her, her body jolted as if to electric shocks as she sank down on the porch. She lay curled there, shaking, tears falling onto the rotting boards.

Lance bent over her. He looked up at Jack. "Beat it," he ordered in a cold voice, hovering protectively over Caroline.

Jack and William turned to leave. Harry Perkins was parked behind the Bronco, his head straining forward over the steering wheel, trying to see what was happening on the porch. William wondered why Perkins was still there; then saw that there was no room for him to turn around until William's Bronco was moved. No one would try to reverse down that road in the dark.

"I'll drive," said Jack. William handed him the keys without protest.

Jack started the Bronco and moved forward, clearing the drive. Harry Perkins turned his car around and Jack, mimicking the manoeuvre, turned the Bronco and followed Perkins at a crawl toward the highway. William put his head back and closed his eyes. The scene with Caroline had ignited his memories of Barbara's death. His mind replayed the nightmare. His daughter Stephanie screaming at him, How could you let this happen! Don't you care? Even now the words were like razors across his throat. As if it was his fault, as if he could control death. At the time he had just stood there, numb with shock. Now tears welled up in his eyes. He felt them seep between closed eyelids, run down his cheeks, soak the stubble on his chin. He took a deep breath; it caught in his throat, half sigh, half sob. William wiped his face with the backs of his hands, hoping the darkness would cover his tears.

They reached the highway and Perkins turned off north. Jack crossed the highway onto the Rainbow Lake road. He pulled into the shadows, switched off the headlights and killed the engine. "We'll wait here a while," he said. William dozed off, to be awakened by the sound of an engine. He looked out the rear window in time to see the sweep of headlights as George Ferris's old blue pickup truck turned onto the highway and went racing off toward the north.

CHAPTER THREE
TUESDAY

William woke the following morning on his bed, fully dressed with a blanket pulled over him. He had no recollection of returning to the cabin. Even after a night's sleep he still felt exhausted; the events of the day before, both physical and emotional, had left him completely drained.

When William limped out of the bedroom, Jack was already up, sitting by the window drinking a cup of coffee. "There's coffee there," Jack said. On hearing Jack's voice, something stirred in William, something half-remembered from the night. He couldn't be sure, but he had a hazy recollection of drumming. Maybe it was a dream.

"Thought we'd go into town for breakfast this morning," Jack called as William headed outside.

"Okay," he agreed groggily. He was so stiff from

the previous day's unaccustomed exercise that he could barely walk to the outhouse. His knees ached, but at least they were no longer flaming. The day was overcast, the clouds an uneven pattern of dark islands in a pale grey sea. A wet wind blew from the lake. Although the rain had held off the day before, the threat hadn't gone away.

Back in the cabin, William poured himself a cup of coffee and drank it while he washed up, shaved, and put on clean clothes. He looked despairingly at the bed. The bedding needed changing after he had slept all night in clothes that had been dragged through the woods, but he didn't have the energy. He pictured himself as one of those stereotypical bachelors living with piles of dirty dishes and unwashed clothes. In the two years since Barbara's death, he had managed to keep himself reasonably decent, but that was in Toronto with other people around. Perhaps out here in the bush the thin veneer of civilization would peel away, allowing a life of contented squalor. By the time he was ready to leave, some of his stiffness had worn off. Jack hadn't moved from the window.

"Let's go see if Billy's around," said Jack when they were in the Bronco.

"Who?"

"Billy Dawes; he runs the floatplane service over there by the resort."

The Rainbow Resort was on the other side of the lake from William's cabin. William carefully manoeuvred around the potholes until he came to a fork in the road, one fork leading north to the Rainbow Resort, Rainbow Airlines and Andy's Adrenaline Wilderness Tours; the other east to the highway. They followed the north fork to the float plane dock.

"I was wondering," William said, "if that Harry

Perkins we met last night was the one who was out at Hellbent Stump?"

"Maybe," Jack nodded. "He said he'd been out jogging, but he could have been up at the Stump. He sure seemed interested in what we were doing out there."

"I also wondered," William continued, "if he hadn't given us a ride, how were we supposed to make it home?"

"Yeah," Jack frowned in mock seriousness, "I wondered about that too."

A yellow, single-engine plane was moored to the dock, the engine cowlings stacked on the wharf, the engine itself covered with a tarp. "Billy flies hiking groups into the backwoods for Andy's Wilderness Tours," Jack explained.

A small, prefab building beside the dock had RAINBOW AIRLINES painted across the side in large, multicoloured letters. Jack's knock on the door was answered by a big bear of a man in an undershirt and boxer shorts. His tousled dark hair tapered down into a scruffy beard.

"Hey, Jack," he drawled, blinking sleep out of his eyes.

"Hey, Billy," said Jack. "This is William."

"Hey, William." Billy opened the door wider and stood back. "Come on in. I was just making coffee. Want some?"

They walked into the office. In the centre of the room was an old grey metal desk with a computer and a gooseneck lamp. Behind it, a printer and fax machine shared a stand with a shortwave radio and a large silver microphone. William shuffled over to an old sofa and eased himself down. Beside it, a coffee maker joined the clutter on a table patterned with dark splashes of dried coffee and white grains of spilled sugar.

Billy pressed a button on the coffee maker and with

a mumbled, "I'll be right back," disappeared through a door at the back. He reappeared a few minutes later wearing pants and pulling on a checked shirt. "What's up?" he asked, buttoning the shirt.

"Haven't seen George Ferris around anywhere, have you?" Jack asked, straddling a straight-backed chair. William looked up in surprise. George Ferris is dead, he thought, but then realized Billy wouldn't know that—or, if he did know, how did he find out?

"George? Nope, haven't seen George in a while. Can't remember the last time I saw George." Billy looked up into the corner of the room as he sifted through his memories. "It was a while ago anyways." He went over to the gurgling coffee maker and poured three cups. Without asking if anyone wanted sugar, he spooned some into each cup and stirred.

"Heard there was a camp broken into up on Eagle Lake," Jack said, accepting a cup from Billy. "You know anything about that? You know of anybody out in the bush who could have done that?"

"Nope. Heard one of those camps on Eagle Lake belongs to Brad Pitt. Closest I've been to Eagle Lake was when I went to pick up those two geologists on Saturday. They were up by Stillwater Lake, over Ghostwalker Ridge north of Eagle Lake. Can't see how it could have been them. I was supposed to take 'em down to Thunder Bay, but my carburetor started acting up, so I had to take it apart and clean it out."

Jack nodded. "I heard those geologists were back. Any idea what they were doing up there?"

"Told me they were looking for amethysts," said Billy. "Although I don't know why they'd take gold pans with them if they were looking for amethysts. The same two guys were up here last year, too. Weren't you supposed to go with them as a guide?"

"We talked about it," confirmed Jack, "but they went with George Ferris instead."

"That's right!" Billy exclaimed. "I forgot, George was their guide last year. They didn't go up with anyone this year though."

"Why's that?" asked Jack, sipping his coffee.

"Don't know, didn't ask," Billy said emphatically. "Not my business. I just fly 'em where they want to go." He flattened his hand and raised it like a plane taking off.

"You said they had gold pans with them?" Jack asked.

"Yeah. They had a lot of gear. Took more stuff up with them than they brought back, that's for sure. Said they lost some equipment in the bush. Came back early too. Supposed to be up there another week, but they called on the radio for me to pick 'em up. Said they finished sooner than they expected."

"Why was that?" asked Jack.

"Don't know, don't care." Billy shook his head. "I don't ask questions. If you start asking questions you start getting answers and that usually leads to trouble, so I mind my own business." He finished his coffee and poured himself another cup.

"Nobody else out there, eh?"

"Not that I know of," said Billy. "Kind of slow this time of year. Took some wilderness hikers up to Bearpaw Lake for Andy Polsky, they're doing the Tremont Ridge loop, but that's it." He thought for a moment. "Say, you should talk to Andy, he's been cruising the bush around here, that whole area around Hellbent Stump. He might know something. I saw him the other day. Says he's marking out some new trails, local loops so people staying at the resort can take day hikes."

"Well, we better go. Thanks, Billy." Jack drained his

coffee cup. William reluctantly dragged himself up from the depths of the sofa.

"Hey, any time, Jack. I'd better remount that carburetor. Have to pick up those hikers tomorrow at Bearpaw Lake. For some reason they get real snarky when you leave them out in the bush a few extra days." He made a wry face and shook his head. Jack laughed as they stepped outside. "If I hear anything I'll let you know," Billy added. "Nice ta meetcha, William."

William waved good-bye as he climbed into the Bronco and gave Jack a puzzled look. "You didn't tell him George was dead."

"Nope."

"Why not?"

Jack shrugged. "He'll find out when it's time for him to find out. The spirits will see to that."

William sighed his irritation. Talking about spirits still made him feel uncomfortable. "Who were the geologists you were talking about?"

"They came up here last year doing a mineral survey, worked that area up by Stillwater Lake. Word was they didn't find anything worth developing; it was kind of a surprise when they came back this year."

"Billy said they were looking for amethysts."

"Hmm," Jack murmured.

"Where to now?"

"Town," said Jack. "You know the Kozy Korner Kafé?"

"Yes, we used to eat there once in a while when we were up here on vacation."

"Do you know Maggie, the woman who owns it?"

William tried to remember. "No. I might recognize her if I saw her, but I can't say I know her."

Jack leaned back on the headrest and lost himself in thought.

Rainbow Lake, where William's cabin stood, was the first lake north of the town of Jubilee, a ten-minute drive down a frost-heaved highway so patched that hardly any of the original asphalt remained. The road was lined on both sides with gnarled scrub pine behind ditches filled with wasteland weeds, their dried seedpods already empty, seeds scattered on hopeful winds.

There wasn't much to the town of Jubilee. Originally a boomtown built around a copper mine in the 1930s, it was a thriving community with a hotel, a newspaper and three taverns until the mine played out in the late fifties. After that, its economic survival depended on seasonal business: summer cottagers, hikers, fishermen, hunters, winter snowmobilers, and patrons of the Rainbow Resort. The original Jack o' Clubs Hotel managed to survive, due mainly to having the only remaining bar in town. Most of the full-time residents eked out a living as guides or ran businesses supported by the seasonal trade. Anyone needing a doctor or a dentist—or the police—had to go down to Fayette, a forty-minute drive to the south.

William drove along the main street and stopped at the Kozy Korner Kafé, a white stucco building, indistinguishable from a thousand other small-town restaurants. William hadn't been there in over two years and the place still looked exactly the same. The plate glass window announced ALL DAY BREAKFAST in splashy red letters. The inside was clean, but old and worn. A counter ran the length of the room on one side; tables with mismatched chairs crowded close to the window on the other. On the floor, patches of dark underlay showed where the linoleum was scuffed through.

Jack and William sat at the counter. William's stool wobbled dangerously as he put his weight on it. The original beige of the countertop had been buffed white by repeated cleanings. Behind the counter a green Beech milkshake machine stood alongside a glass-fronted pie case, a stainless steel Braun coffee maker and tiers of glass shelves heavy with ice cream sundae dishes.

The waitress came over as William studied the menu. She was a small, softly rounded woman, a few years past fifty, her rich auburn hair swept up and gathered in a loose chignon framing a peaches-and-cream complexion, reminding William of a tinted Victorian photograph. A fawn sweater over a green calf-length skirt complemented her colouring. She gave a big smile. "Hi, Jack, how are you?"

"Hello, Maggie. I'm pretty good," said Jack.

Maggie looked at William. "Hello. We haven't seen you around here for quite a while. You are—?"

"William." He put out a hand. He only vaguely remembered the woman, although she seemed to recognize him. "William Longstaffe."

"Maggie Fraser." They shook hands briefly. "How long has it been?" Her large, velvet brown eyes reminded William of the deer he had seen in the forest the day before.

"Two years," said William.

"That long!" Maggie sounded surprised. "Doesn't seem that long. Of course, I can never tell. I don't have any sense of time whatsoever! You could have said two years or ten years and I wouldn't know the difference. You've aged well."

Jack laughed. "Is that a compliment?"

Maggie put her hand over her mouth. "Oh, did I say the wrong thing? I meant—"

"Thank you," said William gallantly, "compliment accepted." He studied her face. Networks of fine lines patterned the corners of her eyes, as if she had walked through a spider's web and the strands had etched themselves into her skin.

Jack stepped in to cover her embarrassment. "I'm staying with William at his camp over by Rainbow Lake. We'll have a couple of breakfast specials, okay, Maggie?" said Jack. "And Maggie," he continued in a serious tone, "I need you to call the police for me."

"Oh, Jack," said Maggie, concern in her voice, "is something wrong?"

"It's about George Ferris. He's gone missing," said Jack.

"Yes, I know," said Maggie "The police came through here the other day. They went to see Doug Trimble over at the General Store, and once you tell Doug something the whole town knows."

"We found George," Jack stated flatly.

"Oh, thank goodness. Is he all right?"

"No," said Jack, "he's not all right. He's dead."

"Oh, how sad! That's terrible! Poor George! Where did you find him?"

"Found him yesterday out there by Hellbent Stump," replied Jack

"How awful. The poor dear! What happened?"

Jack's lips tightened. "Better let the cops look into it."

"I'll call them right now." Maggie moved to the far end of the counter where an old black rotary-dial telephone sat beside an antique cash register. She made the call, repeating the sparse details Jack had given her. "They'll be here soon," she said, hanging up the phone. "By the way, did you hear that Brad Pitt's cabin was broken into?"

"Yeah, heard a rumour it belonged to Brad Pitt."

She sighed. "So many terrible things happening, deaths, robberies—" She completed the sentence with another sigh.

"Met a man named Harry Perkins last night, has a

camp over there on Trout Lake. You know him?" Jack asked as Maggie poured coffee.

"Not very well, he's been in here a couple of times. He bought that camp late last summer; it used to belong to the Monroes, remember them? Mr. Perkins is up here from Toronto. I don't know how long he's here for though." Maggie went to prepare the food.

They ate in silence, William's weariness disinclining him to conversation. Occasionally other customers came into the café, sometimes nodding a greeting to Jack.

"We'd better go," Jack called to Maggie when they had cleaned their plates. "When the cops arrive, tell them we're over at William's place, okay?" He turned to William. "You got any money?"

William slipped a good tip under the edge of his plate and went to pay for their breakfasts at the ancient cash register.

When Jack stepped outside, he stopped for a moment to observe a car on the far side of the road. It was a huge old white Lincoln Town Car that the years had not been kind to. It was dented and rusted as if it had been put through a car-crusher and then straightened out again. The tires were bald and there was only one headlight, the other a gaping black hole. The front and back seats were packed with young Native men. One of them leaned on the front fender, belligerently returning Jack's stare. His long black hair was tied back with leather thongs tipped with coloured beads. Over a black sweatshirt he wore a checked bush jacket with the sleeves torn off. His air of defiant toughness put a chill up William's spine.

"I want to talk to these guys," said Jack and set off across the road.

"Wait," William clutched at his sleeve to hold him back. "What for?"

"I want to ask them something," Jack replied, giving William a slight smile. "Don't worry, you'll be all right. But if any of them says anything to you, tell the absolute truth. These guys have no time for anything else." Jack crossed the road, William tagging along behind.

Jack stood directly in front of the man leaning against the car and, looking him in the eye, spoke in his native tongue. The man gave a curt reply, returning Jack's stare, unblinking. Jack spoke again and appeared to be explaining something. When he finished, the man nodded. He did not look at William or acknowledge him in any way. Jack turned, walking back to the Bronco.

William stayed close beside him. "What was all that about?"

"Maybe nothing," said Jack. "I asked them to do something for me."

"You know those guys? They look like gang members."

Jack laughed. "They are Ogichidaw, warriors," explained Jack as William started the engine. "They follow the warrior's path. They are ready to kill or to die at any moment. That's why they don't have time in their lives for anything but the absolute truth. They will only kill or die for truth. That's what makes the warrior's path so hard. It forces you to get rid of all the bullshit in your life. No one wants to die for bullshit."

"And they'll do favours for you?"

"Sure," Jack smiled, "I'm *mishweegen*, a spirit talker. I talk to Wendigo. They respect that." After a moment he added, "I'm one of their teachers."

William couldn't hide his surprise and Jack laughed at the look on his face. "I'm what you would call a shaman," Jack continued, "although shaman isn't a word in our language, it was introduced by anthropologists. The medicine person in our culture is a healer, but not in a drug-dispensing, disease-fighting kind of way; more in a way that promotes physical, emotional, and spiritual well-being. *Medicine* has spiritual connotations and healing is primarily a spiritual thing. Even the herbs we use are medicinal, not because of their chemical properties, but because of their spirit and how it interacts with the spirit of the person who takes them."

William considered Jack carefully. As he spoke, there had been a change in his language. Before he had always talked in a clipped, backwoods dialect. But as he explained about medicine to William his syntax had improved and his vocabulary expanded to include words like *connotations* and *interacts*. William began to suspect there was a lot more to Jack than met the eye. He sighed, not sure if he should pursue the discussion. He followed some advice his wife had given him to help him through faculty parties: when in doubt, change the subject. Barbara had been more socially adept than William. She would always be there to guide him whenever he found himself in an awkward situation, telling him what to say, how to behave, what to wear. It helped him cope with social pressures, yet at the same time made him feel inadequate and bungling, as if he couldn't be trusted to make decisions on his own. He needed her help and at the same time resented it.

William gave himself a shake to break the spell of his thoughts. He changed the subject. "Maggie seems like a nice person."

"Yeah, she is," Jack agreed. "Maggie's a real fixture in town. That restaurant's been in her family since the copper boom in the thirties." He paused before adding casually, "She's single, you know."

"Oh really." William tried to keep the interest out of his voice.

"Yeah," Jack continued, "was married once. Husband was killed in a hunting accident years ago. Maggie was devastated. Then she hooked up with a guy, a real charmer, convinced her to expand the restaurant. She took out a mortgage to renovate the place and the guy ran off with all the money, left her alone with this huge debt. It's been tough for her. Be nice if she met someone decent." He gave William a sideways glance.

William concentrated on making the turn onto the Rainbow Lake road.

William awoke to the sound of voices. In his exhausted state, he had passed out on his bed as soon as they returned from the café. It was the first time in his life he could remember taking a nap in the morning. Yawning, he stumbled groggily into the living room.

Jack stood up and smiled. "You look like you could use some coffee! Sit down, I'll pour you some."

At the table sat two uniformed police officers, one of them was Sergeant Ray Selkirk, who had come to the cabin before. "Hello, Mr. Longstaffe." Selkirk indicated the other officer. "This is Constable Shaw." They both looked ridiculously young. In contrast to Selkirk's finely chiselled features and short, sandy hair, Shaw's face seemed roughly moulded out of putty, a dark moustache frowning over his upper lip. "We'd like to ask you some questions about the reported discovery of a body yesterday."

"Sure," said William, "although I can't tell you much. I was just following Jack, really."

Jack returned to the table and put a mug down in front of William. Selkirk turned his attention back to

Jack. "You said you went out to look for George Ferris. How did you know where to look?"

"Oh," Jack leaned forward, dropping into a conspiratorial tone, "I went into the spirit world and asked my spirit helpers for guidance. First I asked Bear, but Bear was in a silly mood and wanted to play. Then I found Raven, but that Raven, he was too haughty to be concerned with a missing man. So I went to Wolf and Wolf took me on a journey into the bush and showed me a body."

Selkirk jotted it all down in a notebook. Shaw looked doubtful, his tone gruff. "You're saying a wolf showed you where George Ferris's body was?"

"Showed me where *a* body was," corrected Jack. "Didn't know it was George until we got there."

At the mention of the wolf, William's skin prickled with the same peculiar feeling of déjà vu he had experienced near the cave.

Shaw sighed. William drank his coffee as Selkirk questioned Jack. Jack answered every question openly and appeared eager to provide information; however, William noticed that he left out any mention of the meeting with Crazy Crazy, or the fact that George Ferris was murdered. He also noticed that Jack had dropped into his backwoods dialect.

Shaw glowered at William. "You actually saw George Ferris's body?" He sounded like he didn't believe there was a body. William affirmed that he had indeed seen a body, but couldn't say who it was as he had never met George Ferris.

"And did you see the wolf?" Shaw asked.

William hesitated, then denied seeing any wolves. Shaw's eyes tightened to suspicious slits.

Selkirk frowned. "I guess we'd better figure out how we're going to retrieve the body. Could you take us back there?"

Jack shrugged, "I could take you to Hellbent Stump, but that body, probably gone by now. Lots of animals out there fattening up for winter. Wolves, bears, martens, lots of things. Probably can't find that body again."

"Let's cut the crap!" said Shaw, standing up, angry. He pushed his face toward Selkirk. "These guys are jerking us around. They report a body, but can't take us to it. They were shown it by some ghost wolf. This is such a bunch of crap. Let's charge them with mischief or something; run them down to Fayette and stick them in a cell to stew for a while."

"Shut up, Shaw," snapped Selkirk, like an exasperated parent to an unruly child. He looked at Jack and rolled his eyes. "He's new here. Transferred up last week, didn't you, Shaw?" Shaw scowled in silence. "From Windsor!" Selkirk added with another roll of his eyes. "He'll learn," Selkirk prophesied, adding under his breath, "I hope."

Selkirk stood up, addressing Jack and William formally. "We may have to question you further and we may request your assistance in locating and recovering the remains. We'll inform the coroner and see what he says."

"That camp that was broken into," queried Jack, "how many people were there?"

"Only one, we think," Selkirk informed him. "The perpetrator heated up some canned food and slept overnight."

Jack frowned and nodded thoughtfully. "How'd they get to that camp?" he asked. "By boat or they walk, or what?"

Selkirk shrugged. "Don't know. There's no road to Eagle Lake, so they must have come by boat or by plane. Can't see anyone hiking through that bush."

"Heard a rumour that camp is owned by Brad Pitt," said Jack.

Selkirk laughed. "I heard that too! Also heard it's owned by Harrison Ford, Meg Ryan, and Tom Hanks! We checked the registry when the report came in; most of the cabins up there are owned by numbered holding companies, no names on the deeds. Apparently, the one that was broken into belongs to Tyler Westman, you know him? Another actor; he made a bunch of tough cop films, back in the seventies, maybe the eighties, I can't remember." He put away his notebook. "Although people do say Brad Pitt has a place up there."

The officers left and Jack made sandwiches for lunch. While they ate, William talked about what needed to be done to prepare the cabin for winter. He started to make a list and lay out a timetable.

His planning was interrupted by the sound of a vehicle pulling up, followed by a firm knock on the cabin door. William began to clear the table as Jack went to answer the door. On the threshold stood a Native woman. She was of solid build, the top of her head level with the bridge of Jack's nose. Her long, dark hair ran like a river over her shoulders, falling in a glossy stream nearly to her waist. A denim jacket topped a blue-checked shirt, pale blue jeans and worn white sneakers. On a leather thong around her neck hung a large silver pendant inset with an amethyst crystal. It was difficult to judge her age; William guessed mid-thirties. She had a black eye.

"Hey, Jack," she said.

"Hey, Denise," he responded.

She pushed past him into the cabin, stopped and pointed at William. "This him?"

"Yep," said Jack, "that's him."

"He's cute." She looked William up and down appraisingly, then glanced around the cabin. "Nice place."

Dropping her overstuffed bag by the door, she walked into the open-plan living area. "You just moved in here, right?" she asked William over her shoulder.

"Uh, yes," William stuttered.

At the rear of the living area, two doors led to the bedrooms. Denise looked into William's room with its unmade bed, scattered clothes, and haphazard piles of books. "This your room?" she asked. William nodded. "Okay, I'll stay in here," she tilted her head toward the vacant bedroom beside it. "I'll grab the rest of my stuff from the truck."

"Wait a minute, wait a minute," William held up his hands. "You can't stay here. This is my cabin and you can't stay here." Other words trembled in his throat, unable to find release.

"This is Denise," Jack's eyes were directly on William's. "She doesn't have anywhere else to go."

William stared back, but couldn't hold his gaze. He felt cornered. Misplaced anger bared its fangs and struck out. He pointed at Denise's black eye. "Did you do that to her?"

Denise hooted with laughter. "Hah! If Jack ever hit me I'd hit him back so hard he'd land in the middle of next week!"

"No," said Jack quietly, eyes unwavering.

William looked at the floor. After his initial doubts about Jack, William had started to trust him. Now Jack was stepping over the mark, forcing this woman on him without even asking. "Look," he said, "I'm sorry if you have problems, but you can't stay here. I'm not running a boarding house. You'll have to stay somewhere else." He leaned on the kitchen counter and glared out the window, jaw set.

The three of them stood in silence. Mote-filled sunbeams poured through the windows bringing an incongruously joyful note to the scene. Jack spoke quietly. "I told you before, you're not in the city now. You are in the bush. If you live up here you have to live the bush way. This is a lesson. Never turn someone in need from your door. The spirits pay attention. They remember. One day, you may go to someone's door when you are in need and the spirits will turn you away. You must welcome Denise. Then the spirits will be good to you. Denise will not take advantage of you. She will take only what she needs, and not more than you can give. That is the way in the bush."

William stared out the window, ignoring them.

"Besides," Jack added, a little more brightly, "that Denise, she's a witch. You throw her out and who knows what kind of awful spell she will put on you."

Denise laughed. "Aw, you shut up," she said to Jack, but there was affection in her voice. She frowned at the cardboard box containing William's meagre supplies. Her lips formed a doubtful line. "If we're going to have any dinner we'd better do some shopping. Come on. We'll go into town for groceries. I'll drive." She smiled at William. "Don't want to die of starvation your first week in the bush, do you?" William didn't answer. "C'mon," she called from the door, giving William another big smile. "It'll be fun!" She stepped outside, leaving the door open behind her.

The inflow of cool air through the open door seemed to change the atmosphere in the cabin, as if new possibilities had been allowed in. William's ire dissolved as easily as it came. Slow to anger, quick to forgive, his wife always said of him. But it wasn't forgiveness he felt. It was the same feeling of impotence that had followed a thousand marital arguments, a hollow feeling that somehow he had been manipulated, but didn't quite know how. He had hoped that was all over, that he had left those old patterns behind and started a new life. William looked at Jack with a face as sad and empty as a condemned house.

"You got any money?" asked Jack.

"Uh, yeah," William stammered, still a little overwhelmed.

"Then let's go." Jack walked outside. William slipped on his jacket and followed, locking the door. Denise sat behind the wheel of an old green pickup truck, already running. The wheel wells were ragged with rust, the passenger side fender was loose and rattled to the engine's vibration, the front bumper tilted at a crazy angle, licence plate dangling by a single screw. Jack slid into the passenger seat next to Denise. William squeezed in beside him and shut the door. It didn't latch. He opened it again and slammed it, hard. That did it.

Denise threw the truck into reverse and put a heavy foot on the gas, spinning the truck around in the drive, narrowly missing the fender of William's Bronco. Not that it would have mattered much if she had hit it, William thought. Any damage she might inflict would be lost in the existing dents and bruises. To William, it was a metaphor for his own feelings, the world continuing to batter his already buffeted emotions.

He fished around down the back and side of the seat. "Where's the seat belt?"

Denise and Jack exchanged a brief glance before she put her foot down and rocketed off down the gravel drive.

Barrelling down the potholed road at high speed made William's teeth chatter. Gripping the door handle tight with one hand and the dashboard with the other, he looked over at Jack and Denise. Denise held the wheel with both hands, leaning slightly forward, intent on the road ahead. The amethyst pendant danced over her breasts. Jack remained relaxed and rode the jolts and bounces like a hawk on a boisterous wind. When they reached the highway Denise jammed on the brakes, locking the wheels in a skidding stop. William was relieved when she screeched onto the somewhat smoother asphalt.

Barely slowing down as they entered town, Denise braked hard and made a sharp turn into the unpaved parking lot of the General Store. She flashed a smile at William. "Let's go!" She jumped out of the truck, giving the door a hard slam behind her.

The Jubilee General Store was an old frame building, the inside divided into two halves: one side was a small grocery store complete with fluorescent lights, freezer compartments and a vinyl-tiled floor; the other half consisted of a dimly lit assortment of tables and shelves laden with clothes, hardware, kitchen utensils, camping gear, boating accessories, and anything else that would come under the heading of General. The original wooden floorboards, dark with age and wear, creaked and groaned beneath cautious shoppers.

William and Jack followed Denise into the store. They walked smack into the middle of an argument. Denise grabbed a cart and began to cruise the aisles with the same abandon with which she drove her truck.

One of the people in the argument was Doug Trimble, the owner of the store. The other disputant was Crazy Crazy. He was shouting.

"That's my gold!" he screamed, standing on his toes to push his face up close to the taller man. "That's my gold!"

On the floor in front of the counter lay an ageing golden retriever. At the sound of the raised voices it lifted a listless head, gave a hoarse bark, and collapsed back onto the shiny vinyl.

"Look, Maurice." Trimble ran his hands through his thinning hair in an effort to remain calm and reasonable. "I'm not going to grubstake you just because you want to go off prospecting. You bring me a nugget or something and sure I'll stake you, but there's no gold around here, people have searched, it's—"

"That's my gold," shouted Crazy Crazy. "It's there! It's mine! My gold!"

He stormed out, seemingly unaware that William and Jack, whom he had taken a shot at the day before, were standing next to him. Through the window, they watched him stomp down the street, still shouting. The dog woofed.

Doug Trimble leaned on the counter and shook his head. Long, thin arms stuck out of the short sleeves of a madras shirt adorned with a clip-on bowtie. "Don't know what's got into Crazy Crazy these days. He's been sayin' there's gold around here for years, but lately he's been gettin' really wild about it." He looked quizzically at Jack. "You don't think he found anything, do you?"

"Don't know," said Jack. "You can never tell what's going on with Crazy Crazy."

Trimble raised an eyebrow. "Gold fever?"

Jack nodded. "Could be." He gave William a sideways glance. "William here doesn't believe in gold fever."

Trimble raised the other eyebrow. "Oh, it's real all right. Once it catches hold of a person it can destroy them. They can't think of anything except gold. Can turn an ordinary man into a killer. Seen it happen. People go mad with gold fever. Lose all control." He looked down and shook his head sadly. "Say," he held up a finger, remembering something, "I heard about George Ferris. That's too bad."

"Yeah. When did you see him last?"

"Don't remember exactly, not for a week or so anyway; that's not unusual with George. The police were in here the other day askin' about him, it was Ray Selkirk from the Fayette O.P.P.; I told him you were out there by Rainbow Lake."

"Yeah, he came by and talked to me," said Jack. "He asked about a camp that was busted into, you know anything about that?"

"Nope," said Trimble, "I'll let you know if I hear anythin'. Rumour has it Brad Pitt owns a place up there on Eagle Lake."

Jack nodded. "Yeah, I heard that too. Sure are some nice places up there. You know a guy named Harry Perkins?"

"Not very well," said Trimble. "He was in here just the other day. Bought that camp on Trout Lake about a year ago. Hasn't been around much. Comes up from Toronto."

"Come on," Jack said to William, "let's stop Denise before she buys the whole store." Stepping over the dog, they found Denise humming as she pushed a shopping cart along a narrow aisle. Even though the shelves weren't well stocked at that time of year, Denise had managed to find enough to fill the cart. "We only needed stuff for dinner," said Jack. "Remember?"

"Well, when dinner is over, what are we gonna eat then?" Denise craned her neck to read the labels on the top shelf. "I don't know about you, but I like to eat regular."

"Um," William began, unresolved anxieties darting through him like startled hamsters escaping from a cage, "we haven't come to any arrangement about your staying—"

"Oh, don't you worry," Denise cut in, "it'll be fun.

I'll feed you good. Gonna be some long evenings though, with you not having TV out there."

"I was planning to write in the evenings," William manoeuvred for position, "and I need quiet, I need to be alone to write."

"Oh, that's no problem," said Denise cheerfully. "Jack here, he's a medicine man, *mishweegen*, a spirit talker. He talks to Wendigo. He can make your place invisible and he can call Wendigo to keep everybody away. Don't you worry, nobody will bother you while Jack's around!" She smiled. "Now what about crackers? You like these ones with little seeds in them? Or do they get caught in your teeth? You still got your own teeth?"

"Those are fine," William said resignedly.

"Come on!" Denise grabbed William by the arm. "Let's go find some ice cream!" She dragged him over to the freezer compartment, opened the lid and considered the various flavours. "You got kids?" she asked as she picked up a container of Maple Delight.

"Um, yes," said William. "Two. A son and a daughter."

"How come they're not here with you?" She put the Maple Delight back and chose a Double Fudge Ripple.

"Oh, they're grown up, they have their own lives, they don't have much time for me."

"Grandchildren?" Denise exchanged the Double Fudge Ripple for Raspberry Surprise.

"Yes, my daughter has two boys of her own. Colin and Stephen."

"I've got a couple of kids too," Denise volunteered. "Toby and Jessie. Toby's twelve; Jessie's gonna be eight next month. They're staying with their grandmother right now."

"Uh, Jack, is he the, uh, the father?" William stumbled over what seemed to him a very personal question.

Denise's eyes widened as she put a hand over a mouth open in shock. "Jack! Oh no! You didn't think—oh no! Jack!—I'm his sister!" She hunched her shoulders and giggled.

William blushed furiously. "I thought—when you came to the cabin—" he blurted to cover his embarrassment.

Denise laughed, putting a hand on William's arm. "Don't worry about it. Easy mistake to make. I'd be a lucky woman if I could find another man like Jack!" She picked up a Belgian Cream Vanilla and compared it to the Raspberry Surprise. She sighed, put the Raspberry Surprise back and closed the freezer lid. "This'll do. Let's go." With William in tow, she retrieved her cart and headed for the counter.

"Jeez Denise!" Doug Trimble exclaimed when he noticed her black eye. "What happened to you? Somebody smack you, or what?" William felt foolish for not having shown any concern of his own for Denise's eye. He shoved his hands into his pockets and frowned.

"Yeah," said Denise. "That Danny, he got a little bit too drunk and started swingin' so I took off out of there, but not before he caught me one up side o' the head." She gingerly fingered the bluish blush under her eye.

Trimble squinted at her. "You gonna leave 'im?"

"Yeah," said Denise sadly. "We're done."

"You should put some ice on it, keep the swelling down."

"Nice chattin' with you," said Denise, "but this ice cream is starting to look a little warm."

Trimble took the hint and rang up the groceries.

"You got any money?" Jack asked. William sighed and reached for his wallet.

They piled back into the truck, William hanging on grimly as Denise raced over the broken highway. "If that ice cream is melted," she mused, "you think we can take it back? Or maybe we can pour it over pancakes for breakfast."

At the cabin, Denise made dinner. She emptied a couple of cans of beef stew into a casserole dish, poured instant biscuit batter on top for a crust and baked it in the oven. When it was ready she plunked it in the middle of the table for everyone to help themselves. William was surprised at how much he enjoyed it.

As they ate, Denise asked William, "What's your book about?"

"Um, well, it's about early-twentieth-century poetry. It's a study of the period around the First World War. I'm trying to examine the war's effect on English poetry by exploring changes in voice, imagery, and subject matter before and after."

"Was there an effect?" she asked.

"Oh, well, uh, there was a gradual transition. A new tone of despair entered English poetry, and this is in evidence actually in the years leading up to the war. After the war, under the influence of a movement called Modernism, there were more poems expressing feelings of alienation, of the loss of meaning in a fragmented world."

"Hmm," said Denise, "why write about something sad?"

"What?" William's fork hovered over his plate as he looked across the table at Denise.

"Well," she said, "if you have a choice, why not write about something happy? Why write about despair?"

"It's not that I'm writing about despair, I'm writing about the characteristics of a certain period in the history of English literature."

"Weren't there any happy periods in English literature?" Denise asked.

William had to think about that. "Not many," he said finally.

"If it was me, I'd write about something happy." Denise carried her plate to the sink.

The sound of gushing water as Denise worked the pump handle drowned anything William might have said in response.

Jack went to check the woodstove as William cleared the rest of the dishes from the table. He noticed Denise's black eye again. "I'm, uh, sorry about your husband," he offered awkwardly.

"What?" Her eyebrows raised in question.

William touched the side of his eye.

Denise laughed. "Oh, you mean Danny! No, Danny's not my husband. Danny's, I dunno, Danny's a big kid!" She laughed again.

"Your children—the father—" William prompted hesitantly.

"No! Danny's not the father. Their father's long gone. Last I heard he was living over there in Michigan. Haven't seen him in years."

William gave a sidelong glance to make sure Jack was still busy with the fire, then said in a low voice, "Jack called you a witch."

Denise chuckled softly. "He only says that to tease me," she whispered. "But I was serious about Jack. He talks to Wendigo. Only a really powerful medicine man can talk to Wendigo. You be careful; you fall into Wendigo's clutches and you're a goner." She held out a dishcloth. "Here. I'll wash, you dry."

After the dishes were done, Jack and Denise went out. "We're going to see the kids over at my mother's," Denise announced. William retired to his desk in the loft over the kitchen area, booted up his laptop computer, laid out his notes, and prepared to start work on his book. He didn't feel much like working, but he suspected they had gone out to leave him some space to write and so felt obliged to take advantage of the situation.

It was quiet in the cabin, no sound except for the occasional snap of a log from the woodstove. William found himself unable to concentrate. Escaping into work was something he had always been good at, a way of showing Barbara he could do something useful. In the silence of the northern night with the smell of burning birch soft on the air, however, the riddles of literature didn't seem very important. After a futile struggle to gather his thoughts, William gave up, put on his jacket and went out for a walk.

The lights from the resort shone across the lake, sputtering the water with flashes of yellow. A three-quarter moon flickered through fast-moving clouds overhead, whisked by stratospheric winds. William had moved north in an attempt to take control of his life, but it seemed to be slipping from his grasp. Jack, Denise, George's body—he felt overwhelmed. The old loneliness began to fester in his gut. He stood staring into the darkness brooding over what his life had come to. A ripple of wind troubled the tops of the trees, making them moan. Is that Wendigo? he wondered. His spine tingled like a young child being told a ghost story. Hurrying back to the safety of the cabin, he went to the loft to put his notes away.

A few moments later, Jack and Denise returned. They came in quietly, glancing up toward the light in the loft. William stared back at them solemnly. As he looked from the face of one to the other, their eyes reached out to him. It was almost a physical sensation, like fingertips brushing his cheek. William felt a budding sense of relief. Perhaps he wasn't alone after all.

CHAPTER FOUR
WEDNESDAY

Denise had already gone out when William woke up the next morning. He and Jack again went for breakfast at the Kozy Korner Kafé. On the drive into town, William fussed about money. He hadn't budgeted for eating out so often, in fact he hadn't budgeted very carefully at all. Finances were another facet of life beyond his control.

Only two other people were in the café, two men sitting at a corner table looking sullen. Their expensive haircuts and good-quality clothes gave them away as visitors.

Jack and William sat at the counter; William studied the menu. He looked up and almost fell off his stool. Behind the counter stood Denise. She wore a white bib apron over a green-checked shirt and jeans. Another silver pendant inset with an amethyst crystal graced her neck.

"Denise!" William stared at her, dumbfounded. "What are you doing here?"

"Hello to you too," she said. "I work here, what do you think?" Her eye was changing to a mottled brown-yellow as the bruise faded.

"Hey, Denise," said Jack. "We'll be back in a minute; I want to talk to these guys. Make us some breakfast, okay?" He slipped off his stool and walked over to the corner table. William followed. "Mind if we sit down?" Jack asked. One of the men raised his eyebrows and glanced around the restaurant to indicate that there were lots of other tables available. He finally shrugged, "Sure."

"You were up here last year," Jack stated, taking a chair. "You almost hired me as a guide, but took George Ferris instead."

The man's eyes narrowed as he searched his memory. "Oh yeah, I remember, you're—"

"Jack. And this is my friend William."

"Yeah, that's right, Jack. How you doin', Jack?"

"I'm doin' fine," Jack replied. He turned to William. "These two gentlemen are geologists, been doing some prospecting around here. This is—"

"Steve," the man filled in. "I'm Steve Mason, this is Frank Happer." They all nodded hello. Steve Mason appeared to be in his late forties, Happer about ten years younger.

"And," added Steve, "we haven't been prospecting; we merely conducted a geological survey of the area."

"Must be some pretty interesting geology up there on Ghostwalker Ridge to bring you back two years in a row."

"Yes, there is," agreed Steve. "Most of that ridge is meta-sedimentary rock, but there's an upthrusting of meta-volcanic around Stillwater Lake. It was under a lot of pressure during the last ice age and this is one of the few places where we can study the effects of that pressurization because of the rebound—you know about the rebound?" Jack nodded. "The rebound," Steve continued, "exposed rock that in other areas is still buried deep underground."

"What did you find?" Jack asked.

Steve smiled condescendingly. "It's kind of hard to explain to a layman."

"Find any gold?"

Steve's reaction to Jack's question was covered by the arrival of Denise with coffee. She put down full cups for William and Jack, refilling the cups of the geologists from a glass carafe. "You want anything else?" she asked. Steve and Frank shook their heads no. "Breakfast is coming," she announced to William and Jack as she left.

Steve managed to arrange his features into a perplexed look. "No. We didn't find any gold. We weren't prospecting for gold."

"Heard you had gold pans with you," said Jack.

"Oh," Steve smiled and relaxed. "Yes, we had pans. Listen," he looked over his shoulder to see if he could be overheard, then leaned across the table, his voice a stage whisper. "We didn't want this to get around," he exchanged a glance with his partner, "we were hoping to find some amethyst up there."

"Amethyst?" Jack appeared doubtful.

"Yes. Last year we found a fault in the subhorizontal unconformity between the Archaen and Proterozoic rocks. It seemed like a good place for amethyst. We came back this year to check it out."

"Why the gold pans?"

"There are often traces of carbuncle in streams adjacent to amethyst formations. You can pan for carbuncle the same as for gold."

Jack nodded. "Heard you came back early, that you lost some equipment up there."

Steve breathed out heavily, shaking his head. "Guess everybody knows your business in a small town. Yes, we came back early and yes, we lost some equipment. It was stupid really. We should have hired a guide like we did last year, but we thought we could find our way around well enough. Turns out we couldn't. We were out in the bush when the rain started, remember that rain? What a downpour! We left our gear and went back to camp. Next day, when the rain stopped, we couldn't find our way back to where we had left the gear. We were wet and miserable, everything was soaked through, and without the Geiger counter—"

William jumped. "Geiger counter?"

Steve smiled at William's alarm. "Yes, a Geiger counter—to check for radiation. Amethyst is a quartz crystal; its purple colour comes from radioactive minerals, like uranium."

"There's uranium around here?" William felt anxious that he might be exposed to deadly radiation.

"Yes," Steve confirmed. "Not enough to mine commercially, but there are a few hot spots. I'm surprised this whole town doesn't glow in the dark." He grinned. William couldn't tell if he was joking. "So we lost it all, pans, counter, everything. There was nothing to do except come back and dry out. If that old plane hadn't conked out, we'd be home in Toronto by now."

Frank Happer spoke for the first time. "Rainbow Airlines," he sneered, "should be called Brokedown Airlines. One plane and they call it an airline! And that plane isn't even safe to fly. Damn thing should be grounded." He lapsed back into his sullen silence.

"Breakfast's ready!" Denise yelled from the counter.

Jack ignored her. "Did you see George Ferris at all this year?"

Steve flicked a glance at Frank. "No, we haven't seen him, not since last year."

"Did you know he was missing?"

"Missing? No, we hadn't heard anything. When was this?" Steve looked concerned.

"The other day. Did you ever meet his daughter or son-in-law?"

"No. Didn't even know he had a daughter. We didn't know George very well. He preferred drinking to talking."

"Breakfast's getting cold!" Denise hollered.

Jack stood up. "Well, see you around, I guess," he said; then added casually, "By the way, did you find any amethyst?"

"No," Steve said sadly. "Surprising really; the geology seemed perfect."

"Going to try again next year?"

Steve shook his head. "No. We searched hard enough. There's nothing there."

"Breakfast is getting old and cold here!" Denise called from the counter.

Jack and William nodded good-bye and returned to their stools. The two geologists paid and left.

William asked Jack as they ate, "Is there really radiation around here?"

"Don't worry about it," said Jack. "It won't hurt you. The only way radiation could kill you around here is if a truck with a load of nuclear waste ran you over."

"But—" William's response was interrupted by the jingle of the bell over the front door. A man walked in, slamming the door behind him.

"Hey Denise!" he called.

Denise came out of the kitchen at the back, wiping her hands on a towel. "What do you want, Danny?"

William had assumed Denise's boyfriend would be Native; he was surprised to be confronted by a large Caucasian in a black leather motorcycle jacket. He had on worn work boots and ragged jeans.

"Hey, babe, I need some bread to get my truck fixed," said Danny, leading a little with his left shoulder as if ready to throw, or dodge, a punch.

"After what you did? You hit me and you want me to give you money? I don't think so." Denise dropped the cloth on the counter and folded her arms across her chest.

"C'mon, it's only a loan." Danny put a hand out, palm up, beseeching. "Couple o' guys need a ride to Thunder Bay. They're gonna pay me and I'll pay you back." A big, easygoing smile spread across his face. "But I need a new fuel pump in my truck, you know? Gimme some money and I'll take it down to Drake's Garage and everything will be cool."

"You've been drinking."

"I haven't been drinking!"

"Danny, I can smell it on you from here."

Danny straightened up, his enunciation improving markedly. "A couple of beers, that's all. I haven't been drinking. Give me some money out of the cash register, just a loan."

"That money's not mine, you know that!"

"Maggie'll never know. We'll put it back before she misses it! C'mon Denise, I've got a chance to make some bread here, don't blow it for me!" He took a step forward.

"Don't you come near me!" yelled Denise, grabbing the first thing at hand, which happened to be the grill scraper.

"Deneese!" Danny whined, continuing to walk toward her. "Come on, baby, help me out!"

"Back off, Danny." It was Jack who spoke.

Danny stopped dead. His jaw dropped, eyes opened wide. "Hey, Jack," he said. "Didn't see you there." He paused awkwardly. "How's it goin'?"

"I think you'd better leave," said Jack quietly.

"Hey, take it easy. Just trying to get some shit together here," Danny held both palms out, innocence in his eyes. "About Denise, you know, I didn't mean to pop her like that. I was making a point and she walked right into it." He jabbed the air with his fist. "Pop!" He cast down his eyes in mock remorse. He looked at Denise, the bruise a dark accusation. "How you doin' now, babe?" he asked. Soft, boyish features under curly black hair gave him an incongruously tender look.

"Danny," Denise shook her head in disgust. "You are so full of shit!"

"Aw, come on, Denise!" Danny protested, his voice rising.

"Leave her alone, Danny," said Jack, as quietly as before.

"Yeah, right," Danny spat, turning to the door in fury.

"Danny!" Jack called sharply. "Before you go, have you seen George Ferris around lately?"

"What?" Danny stopped with a hand on the doorknob, confused. "George? No, I ain't seen George. Wish I could find him though. Bastard owes me ten bucks. You know where he is?"

"When did you see him last?"

"Last week over at the hotel." Danny strained to remember. "He had this big fight with Andy Polsky, then he hit me up for a ten spot for a bottle and I haven't seen 'im since."

"When last week?"

Danny thought hard. "I dunno. Tuesday, maybe Monday—no, must've been Tuesday—"

"What was the fight about?"

Danny shrugged. "Dunno; something about some money or something. Andy said he'd blow George's ass off if he ever saw him around his place again, something about amethysts, but I didn't hear anything else. Had my own conversation goin' on, you know?"

"Anybody punch anybody?"

"Naw, they just argued. If anybody had started poppin' anybody I'd have been in on it."

"Okay, see you, Danny," Jack said and turned back to his plate.

"Hey," said Danny, letting go of the door handle, taking a step toward Jack, "you couldn't lend me some cash, could you? Enough to fix my truck? How about it?"

Jack shook his head without looking up.

"Shit!" Danny slammed out of the restaurant leaving the little bell jangling after him.

"Whew!" William breathed, "he sure is a piece of work."

Denise laughed, dropping the scraper on the counter. "Oh, he's not so bad when he's under control. Problem is, he's never under control!"

"You're not thinking of taking him back, are you?" asked Jack.

Denise rocked her head from side to side, considering. "No," she said, not very definitely. "Not until he quits drinking, anyway." She disappeared through the swinging doors to the kitchen before Jack could say more.

William tried a bite of his now stone-cold breakfast, put his fork down and pushed the plate away. "Danny said Andy Polsky threatened to shoot George."

"Yeah," said Jack. "Maybe we should go and talk to our friend Andy."

Denise emerged from the kitchen with a tray of clean coffee cups. "You want more coffee?" Both Jack and William nodded yes. She slapped a couple of cups on the counter. Denise served like she drove her truck. "Have to charge you extra for these," she said as she poured. "If it's the same cup, it's a refill. But these are clean cups so I have to charge you extra. You left your cups over there on that table," she indicated the geologists' table with a nod of her head.

With a sideways glance at William, she spoke to Jack in their native language. Jack guffawed and said something back. They both chuckled. William realized he didn't really know anything about the two of them, about their backgrounds or their heritage. "What tribe are you?" he asked, the way he would ask a new acquaintance where they worked.

Jack gave him a direct look. "I'm a Canadian," he said, "how about you?"

William's face flushed. He stared into his coffee.

"Oh Jack!" Denise admonished, "you can be such a jerk sometimes!" and returned to the kitchen.

The café door opened and Maggie came in. She gave a big smile. "Hello, Jack. How are you? And William?"

"Hello, Maggie. I'm pretty good," said Jack. William grunted. The ring of the bell brought Denise out from the back.

"Hello, dear," Maggie called warmly, "been busy this morning?"

"Not so's you'd notice," replied Denise. "Only these couple of loafers," she added, smiling mischievously at Jack and William. "Had some other customers, but these two scared 'em off."

Maggie laughed and, turning, caught William

watching her. He quickly flicked his eyes away and huddled over his coffee.

"Let's go see Andy Polsky," Jack said as they left the café. William drove back to Rainbow Lake and followed the fork in the road that led to Andy's Adrenaline Wilderness Tours beside Rainbow Airlines. In contrast to Billy Dawes's prefab, the Adrenaline office was a modern log building faced with large, plate glass windows. The front was v-shaped to maximize the view over the lake. It looked like a wood and glass luxury liner sailing out of the forest.

A sign over the front door announced TOUR CENTRE. Jack and William went inside. *Rustic* was the word that came immediately to William's mind. All the furniture was made from sapling wood with the bark still on. A black bearskin rug covered the polished pinewood floor. Deer and moose trophy heads hung on the walls. A stuffed hawk with outstretched wings soared on a wire strung from the rafters. On the back wall, a gun rack containing several rifles was secured by a chain-lock.

"Jack!" bellowed a large man with a barrel chest, a big blond beard and long blond hair tied back in a ponytail. He had on a fisherman's vest bristling with little pockets over a flannel shirt and blue jeans. His black belt was fastened with a silver buckle in the shape of a grizzly bear. He came forward with a broad smile and gave Jack's hand a hearty shake. "Haven't seen you around lately. Wondered what happened to you!"

"Andy, this is William. William, Andy Polsky." Jack made the introductions.

A large, rough-furred German shepherd stood pressed against Andy Polsky's thigh. It looked like it ate Dobermans for lunch. It lowered its head and growled.

"Spur!" barked Polsky. "Be quiet!" The dog slunk to the back of the room.

Andy smiled at William, shaking hands with an overly firm grip. "William is it? Mind if I call you Bill?"

"I prefer William."

Andy guffawed. "We're not so formal around here, are we, Jack? You know, Bill, Jack here, he's one of my top guides. You want to go somewhere in the bush, couldn't be with a better man than Jack! Where you from, Bill?"

"Toronto," answered William.

"Good! You looking to go hiking? We have some great wilderness trails we can put you on."

Jack interrupted the sales pitch. "Andy, we came by to see if you knew anything about George Ferris."

"George?" Andy gave his head a dismissive shake. "No. There's nothing to know about George. George is gone forever! No more trouble from George!" As he spoke his voice rose in anger, his face flushed.

"What went on between you and George? Heard you had an argument last week over at the hotel."

Andy Polsky roared and waved his arms around. "Ha! Argument! We didn't argue! I *told* him! I said, You'll never work for me again, you son-of-a-bitch! And that was the end of it. You know what that sneaky son-of-a-bitch was doing? He was charging my customers extra camp fees! Can you believe that? He'd take them out on a hike and at the end he'd tell them they had to pay these camp fees, then he'd pocket the money. Well, somebody complained because my packages are all-inclusive, says so right in the brochure. Said they'd never take one of my tours again. Turns out I'm losing customers because of George! After all the years I spent building up this business, starting with nothing, building it up by my own sweat until I had something going here." At the sound of his master's raised voice, the dog sprang forward, nails clicking on the wood floor. He stopped behind Polsky, teeth silently bared. "You know, my customers come from all over the world: Canada, the US, Asia, Europe. Just had a bunch of German tourists do the Tremont Ridge loop. You've been on that trail, Jack. That is some rough country. I cut that trail myself, all myself! I told George straight out that he'd never work for me again!" His waving arms stirred enough air currents to make the suspended hawk sail back and forth on a turbulent updraft.

Jack said, "Heard you said you were going to shoot his ass off."

Andy scowled, making an empty gesture with his hands. "Well, I might have said something like that. I was angry, I don't remember. I didn't mean anything by it if I did say it. I was angry, that's all."

"You know George is dead?" Jack asked quietly.

"Yes, I heard. Nothing to do with me though. Haven't seen him since that night at the hotel."

"Tell me about the amethysts," said Jack.

"Amethysts?" Andy gave Jack a suspicious glance from the corner of his eye.

"Yeah. Heard you and George argued about amethysts."

Andy looked away. "Don't know who you've been talking to. I don't know anything about any amethysts." He shook his head to confirm his denial. "Now that I think about it, it could have been something George said to Danny, you know Danny Burke? Of course you do, he's hooked up with your sister Denise, right? Well, Denise makes amethyst jewellery and George was asking Danny where she got the amethysts from. That's all I can think of."

"Hear you've been cruising the bush around Hellbent Stump."

"Jeez, Jack, really into my business, aren't you? What's it to you?" The dog moved up beside Polsky.

"A lot of people will be upset if you start cutting trails around there. That's sacred ground. Lots of burials in that area."

"I'll cut trails wherever I damn well please!" Andy's face darkened in a thunderous expression. "Already sent in a permit application to the government. There's a great view from the top of the Stump, it'll make a good day hike."

"Been out there recently?"

"What's it to you where I go and what I do?" Andy's violent arm waving sent the stuffed hawk spinning again. "I've got a business to run here and I do whatever is best for my business! You mind your own damn business and keep out of mine!"

"Okay, Andy, we'll be going. Come on, William." They left without good-byes. Outside, William looked back to see the dog, paws up on the window sill, barking violently after them.

In the Bronco, William said, "He's a volatile character."

"Yeah, old Andy is pretty excitable," Jack agreed.

"You said there are burials out at Hellbent Stump?"

"It was one of the places we used to bury our dead. That's where the name came from. For us it was the-place-where-the-deceased-travel-to-the-Lodge-of-the-Dead. That got translated into Hellbent. All heathens go to Hell."

William thought about Andy Polsky's tirade. "Do you think Andy had anything to do with George's death?"

"Hard to say," Jack frowned. "He was being evasive; whether that was because he had something to hide or if he was just being Andy, I don't know."

When they reached the highway, Jack said, "Let's go back over to Trout Lake. There's something I want to check out." A thin drizzle had started. The clouds appeared low enough to touch. William drove, wipers slapping away the spray.

"Stop here," said Jack when they came to the boat landing. They went down to the wharf; William turned his collar up against the little fingers of cold rain that tickled his neck. The overturned boats huddled disconsolately in their winter storage, hunched against the weather like huskies in a blizzard. William noticed that the painters he had seen before were missing. Probably taken off for the winter, he mused. Only one boat was still in the water, as on the night before, an ordinary aluminum runabout with an outboard motor.

"You see that boat?" Jack asked.

"Yes," replied William, as if he could miss it.

"That's George Ferris's boat," said Jack. William looked at it in surprise. Jack walked along the pier to the runabout and examined it in detail.

There were two spare gas cans in the boat. Jack lifted them out and shook them to see if there was anything in them. "Let's go," he said. He set off toward the Bronco with a gas can in each hand.

"Are we going home now?" William asked.

"Need to run some errands," Jack replied. "You got any hip waders?"

William shook his head no.

"Let's fill up with gas first. Then we'll go find the hip waders and other stuff."

"What other stuff?" William asked apprehensively.

"We're going to take a little trip," Jack said. "Need some camping gear. We're going to spend a night out in the bush."

"No, Jack, I'm not going anywhere." William was

exasperated. "We're supposed to be working on making my place ready for the winter. I'm not going on any camping trip and I'm not spending a night out in the bush." He looked up at the glowering clouds. "Especially not in this weather. My knees still ache from the last time; I'm in no condition to go hiking off to God-knows-where."

"Whatever you want." Jack said. "No hiking involved though. We can ride all the way. I'm going, sure could use your help." William remained stubbornly silent. "Going to be mighty lonely out there all by myself," Jack continued. "Not very safe either. Suppose I get hurt and need help? I could die out there."

"You get yourself into it, you get yourself out," William carped like a petulant adolescent.

"Good philosophy," said Jack. "George's killer is out there somewhere. Suppose he tries to rub you out? You'll be home by yourself. Don't forget Crazy Crazy is still roaming around with a gun. Tried to shoot us; what if he decides to finish the job when you're there all on your own? Could be those warriors will come by looking for me. I won't be there, but they'll find you. I sure wouldn't want to be alone with them at night. Or maybe Wendigo will come around and—"

"Are you trying to scare me?" William interjected.

"Nope," Jack smiled. "I don't have to do that. I'm merely telling you what might happen, you'll do the scaring all by yourself. Which is worse, being in the cabin all night alone or being out in the bush with me?"

William made a grumbling noise in his throat. "The choice would be easier if you were a whole lot prettier," he said, deadpan. Jack put his head back and laughed out loud.

After filling up the Bronco at Drake's Garage, along with the gas cans from George's boat, they drove around for a couple of hours as Jack visited people, borrowing various bits of camping equipment. Some were in town and some were cabins stuck out in places William would never find again on his own. Most of the houses in town were frame boxes about as big as a two-car garage, built by the mining company for their workers back in the thirties. They had a dilapidated air with their peeling paint, rotting wood and sagging roofs. The grey day washed them with another layer of neglect, leaving everything looking as hopeless as an overdrawn bank account.

Nearly all the houses were guarded by ferocious dogs that barked savagely as the Bronco pulled up; they quieted down when Jack walked toward them. Because of the dogs, William waited in the Bronco while Jack paid his visits.

By the time they made it back to town the drizzle had let up. They went to the General Store to buy food for the impending expedition. Doug Trimble was behind the counter, the old retriever sprawled on the floor in front of it. "You seen Crazy Crazy lately?" he asked as he rang through the groceries.

"Not today," replied Jack.

"Remember when he was going on about gold yesterday?"

Jack nodded.

"Well, he came into town today all worked up again about gold, and do you know what?" Trimble picked up a can of stew, examined the price, then set it down. He put his hands on the counter and leaned toward Jack. "He had some!"

"Gold?" asked Jack.

"Yep," continued Trimble, "big chunk of ore with

veins of solid gold in it. Wouldn't say where he got it; kept repeating it was *his* gold. Asked Billy Dawes to fly him down to Thunder Bay to file a claim and have the samples assayed, but Billy's plane is broke down again. Old Crécy always said there was gold around here somewhere and I guess he was right. Who would have thought it, eh?"

"Yeah, that's a big surprise." Jack didn't sound surprised at all. They gathered up the groceries, then loaded them into the Bronco with the camping equipment.

"Crazy Crazy found gold?" William felt a thrill run through him.

"Looks like it," Jack responded indifferently.

"That's incredible!"

Jack cut him off. "Thought we might get something to eat over by the Kozy Korner," he said. William wanted to go back to his cabin. "Maggie'll be there," Jack added.

"Okay." William tried to sound resigned instead of eager. The day had been so dark that the transition from daylight to night was hardly noticeable. The wet road glistened softly in the glow of the few streetlights dotting the main road. When they arrived at the restaurant, Maggie was clearing tables. Jack and William sat near the window. Looking outside, William noticed the warriors' car still parked across the street.

"I'll be right back," said Jack. William watched him leave the restaurant and cross to the Lincoln. Maggie came over with a big, welcoming smile. "Hello, William! Back so soon!" She put water glasses and menus on the table.

William smiled back. "Um, yes." He fumbled with his menu. "Did you hear about the gold?"

"Oh, yes!" Maggie's big brown eyes sparkled. "Crazy Crazy came to town with some ore samples! Everyone is excited! The whole town is buzzing with the news!"

William was about to tell her about his confrontation with Crazy Crazy at Hellbent Stump, but Maggie steered the conversation back to him.

"Denise says you're planning on moving up here permanently. It will be nice having a new face around over the winter."

"Well, I'm going to give it a try," William replied noncommittally.

"You're from Toronto, right? Don't get too many people from the south up here, mostly people from Thunder Bay or Sault Ste. Marie, The Soo as we call it. What made you buy a camp up here? It's a long way from Toronto."

"I came up here on a vacation with my family years ago and we loved it; we decided to buy a cabin and spend all our vacations here. Seemed worth the drive. Also," William tried a wink, but ended up blinking, "it's a lot cheaper to buy a cabin here than around Muskoka!"

"I'm sure that's true!" Maggie laughed. "Denise tells me you're a university professor."

William corrected her. "Was. I'm retired."

"Must have been an early retirement," she teased. "You don't look old enough to retire." William blushed. "You and Jack getting along well? You must have a lot to talk about, you both being professors."

"What?" William didn't know what she meant. He wondered if she was referring to Jack teaching the warriors.

"You and Jack both being university professors, you must have some interesting conversations out there in the evenings."

"What do you mean? Jack's a university professor?"

"Yes." Maggie looked perplexed. "He taught over there at Northern University in Sudbury. Didn't he tell you?"

"No, he never said a word about that."

Maggie laughed. "That Jack. If he isn't one of the strangest people I ever met. Imagine not telling you! He was a philosophy professor, I think. He was there quite a while and then all of a sudden came back here. You should ask him about it."

"Yeah," William agreed, sourly. "I will."

Maggie put a hand over her mouth. "Oh, I hope I haven't said too much. Perhaps I shouldn't have told you if Jack didn't mention it. After all that business with his wife—"

William's eyebrows jumped up. "His wife?"

"Yes, she—" Maggie stopped herself in mid sentence. "Oh, he didn't tell you about that either, did he?"

"Not a word."

"Oh dear, here I am gossiping away again." She looked around the restaurant to see if the other customers needed anything. "Do you mind if I sit down for a minute?"

"Not at all." William reached across the table to pull a chair back for her and knocked over a glass of water. He froze guiltily, like a child who had spilled chocolate milk on his mother's new white carpet.

"Oh, don't worry, dear," comforted Maggie. "Happens all the time. I'll clean it up." She bustled off to fetch a cloth.

William sighed. He felt inept. It had always been one of his shortcomings. He could hear Barbara's voice: When God gave out social graces you must have been standing on your head and got it all backwards. His self-pity rose like a tide pulled by a bitter moon. Put him in a social situation and he would be sure to commit some blunder. It had kept him estranged from other people, pushing them away, always seeking to be alone.

"Smooth move." Jack stood beside the table.

"What?" William was startled. He had become so lost inside himself he had forgotten where he was.

"Saw you through the window," said Jack. "Knocking the glass over. Smooth move."

William grumbled as Jack sat down.

Maggie brought a cloth to wipe the table. "There," she said brightly, "no harm done. What can I get for you?"

Jack ordered a hot beef sandwich and William said he would have the same.

"Won't be long." Maggie hurried away.

William gave Jack an annoyed look. "Where are we going tomorrow?"

"Won't know till we get there," Jack replied cryptically.

"A wolf going to show you the way?" William sounded as sarcastic as Constable Shaw.

Jack looked up, surprised at William's tone. "No," he said softly. "Last night I went into the spirit world and Raven took me on a journey. Tomorrow we'll see if we can find where Raven took me."

William maintained eye contact. "Maggie says you used to teach philosophy at Northern University," he said, his voice neutral.

Jack nodded without shifting his eyes. "Yes, that's right. I was a lecturer. I was there six years."

"So what's all this dumb Indian crap about spirit worlds and ravens and wolves? What's going on?" William's indignation flared in his words.

Jack sighed, dropping his gaze to the table. "I am *mishweegen*, a spirit talker. This is my life now. That other life is behind me, not part of me anymore."

"But, why didn't you tell me?" William felt duped, suckered into trusting someone, then finding out the relationship was based on lies and deception.

Jack looked into the distance. "All I can tell you is that circumstances drove me here. My own teacher says the spirits called me. Coming back here was the only choice I had left." He fell silent. His eyes drifted down to the floor.

"You still could have told me," William pouted. "You could have been straight with me."

Jack's head came up, his expression changing from sadness to anger. "Would it have made a difference?" His bitterness burned William like spits of hot water from an over-boiled pot. "Would you have treated me differently knowing I was a university lecturer instead of a dumb Indian? Would you respect me more, accept me as an equal, instead of condescending to drive me around and buy me meals?"

William's body pressed against the back of his chair. He tilted his head to the side, avoiding the full force of Jack's gaze.

Jack looked away, his mouth a hard line. He folded his arms across his chest. William remained silent, stunned by Jack's uncharacteristic outburst. Jack's words rang in his head. Was he condescending? Would he have treated Jack with more respect had he known more of his past?

Maggie came over with their meals. Seeing the expressions on their faces, she put the plates on the table with a polite waitress smile and went away without a word.

Jack's mouth softened. "I'm sorry," he said without looking up. "I spent my youth being angry, angry at white men for what they did to my people. I thought I was over it, but I guess it's still inside me." He turned back to face William.

William opened his mouth to apologize for his insensitivity, his prejudices; Jack held up a hand to stop him. "You don't have to say anything. But William, you have to trust that the path I am on is the right one for me." He paused, then added, "If you let me, I can help you find your path too. You have a real stubborn streak in you."

William didn't respond, wary of being drawn into a discussion he didn't want any part of.

"There's something in you that keeps you in your old ruts and won't let you out," Jack continued. "You have trust issues."

William kept his head down and ate, even though the food tasted like sand in his mouth.

"I thought you would have remembered by now." Jack looked pensively into the distance.

"Remembered what?" William asked with a sidelong glance.

"Remembered being in the cave, remember finding George's body."

"I was in the cave. We hiked to Hellbent Stump together. What do you mean?" William met Jack's eye.

"Before that. You were there before. I saw you."

William's eyes darted from side to side before fastening once more on his plate.

"The spirits called you on a journey. When Wolf took me to the cave and showed me George's body, you were already there. You ran, but you ran in the wrong direction, you ran into the darkness. I pulled you back. Remember?"

William kept his eyes down. Jack's words had sparked unsettling feelings. It wasn't clear what he remembered—it was all vague and muddled, disjointed dream images. A wolf, a cave. Whatever it was filled him with fear.

"That's why I came to find you," Jack continued. "You have a spirit journey to make and I am here to help you."

"You know—" William laid down his knife and fork "—I don't want to do this anymore. I've had enough. I want to return to my normal life; I want to fix up the cabin and work on my book, nice and simple."

Jack shrugged. "It's your choice. You don't have to accept the spirits' help. If you don't, you will be in that same rut forever."

"At least it's my rut," William stated sourly.

Jack laughed. "See? I said you had a stubborn streak. But you don't want to stay in the same old groove. You want out. The spirits know that, that's why they called you. They want to help you. You have to trust."

Conflicted emotions struggled within William. His teeth made a grinding sound, like changing gears with a bad clutch. If he was truthful with himself, he did want to change. Wasn't that why he had moved there, to break the old patterns, to find a new life? Maybe he didn't know how to change. He sighed. Whether it was the call of the spirits or not, he did not know, but he had to take the path that led to a new life. If it embraced the future, or simply escaped the past, didn't matter.

With that acknowledgement to himself, William's mood turned mellow. Maybe the spirits are helping me, he thought.

Jack watched William's expression change as he waded through his inner turmoil.

"Take it easy," said Jack. "Your feelings are all mixed up from your encounter with the spirits. You overreact to everything; it's normal. It's part of finding the right path."

William didn't feel reassured.

The warriors' car started up across the street. Without a muffler, the big engine sounded like a jumbo jet taking off. The single headlight on high beam swept the street as the car turned and roared off toward the north.

Maggie brought over the bill and slipped it delicately on the table between them. "Everything okay?" she asked hesitantly.

William looked up and experienced a momentary dizziness, as if he were falling into those big brown eyes. "Yes," he said. Then looked at Jack. "Everything's fine."

Jack nodded. "You got any money?" he asked. William laughed out loud.

As they entered the cabin, William wrinkled his nose at the sharp smell of solder. Denise sat at the table. In front of her were rolls of silver and copper wire, amethyst crystals, pliers, and a soldering iron. She wore a pair of large glasses, giving her an owlish look.

"Hi guys," she said, intent on her work, not looking up. "There's some dinner there if you want it."

"We ate in town," said Jack.

Denise put down her pliers. "Fine. Save me cooking tomorrow."

"We won't be here tomorrow," Jack informed her. "We're going out in the bush."

"Okay, I'll eat it." She picked up the pliers again. "Did you see Danny in town?"

Jack shook his head. "Not since this morning."

William remembered Andy Polsky saying that Denise made jewellery. He went over to inspect her work. He picked up an amethyst crystal caught in a net of silver and copper wire. "That's beautiful."

"Thanks," said Denise.

"Where do you get the amethysts?"

Jack and Denise exchanged a look. "I belong to a Native Arts co-op," Denise explained. "A lot of my supplies come from there."

"Oh." William glanced from Jack to Denise. They both avoided his eye. "I wondered because those two geologists we talked to said they were looking for amethysts on Ghostwalker Ridge." He yawned. "I'm going to bed. Good-night." He went to his room.

William jolted awake. The light was on; he had drifted off while reading, the book still open on his chest. He lay rigid, listening for the sound that had sliced through his sleep. It came again, a blood-curdling yell. The hairs on William's neck stood on end.

He jumped out of bed and ran into the living room. More cries came from outside.

Lights were on, but Jack was nowhere to be seen. William's mind raced, trying to decide what to do. Should he hide? Should he run? As he stood frozen in hesitation the yelling suddenly stopped. The silence that followed felt even more chilling.

Denise's door opened and she swished into the room swathed in a big blue bathrobe and fluffy blue slippers. "What's up?" she asked as if being awoken by terrifying screams in the middle of the night was perfectly normal.

William's eyes were wild with panic. His hands shook. "Did you hear that? That yelling?" His throat was so tight he could barely force the words out.

"Oh," said Denise airily, "it's Jack doing some of his medicine stuff. I'll make you a nice hot drink. It'll help you calm down."

"That was Jack?" William asked in wonder. He didn't think those sounds could come from a human throat.

"Probably him and those Ogichidaw, the warriors. They can be pretty loud sometimes." Denise went to the kitchen and put a pan on the stove. "No milk," she observed, scrutinizing the interior of the refrigerator. "Herb tea okay? Let's see what we've got."

"What were they doing out there? Will they come in here?"

"Better ask Jack about that. I guess they could come in. Think I should make more tea?"

"Denise," William cried in desperation, "I'm terrified!"

Denise narrowed her eyes and regarded him. "You have a dead spirit stuck in your chest. You should let me take it out."

William stared at her dumbly.

"Part of your spirit has died and it's stuck there in your chest. You have to get it out to let yourself heal and grow again." Denise continued calmly making tea. "That's why you're afraid. That part of the chest, around the heart, that's where courage comes from. With that dead spirit there, it's like you have a hole in your courage—makes you timid. When we take it out, your courage can grow back, make you strong."

William didn't know how to respond. His mind darted from thought to thought, unable to form coherent connections.

Denise gave him a big smile. "Don't worry. It won't hurt." She poured hot water into a cup. "Sit down; I'll bring your tea."

William couldn't stop trembling. He went to his room and wrapped himself in a bathrobe before sitting down at the table. The steam rising from the cup smelled like dry grass. William took a tentative sip. It tasted like dry grass.

"At first I thought it might be your dead wife's spirit stuck in you. Happens like that sometimes. A dead person's spirit will suck the life right out of you. But it's been there a long time, since before she died, so it can't be hers. Must be part of your own spirit. Something wounded you in the past and a little bit of you died."

William shrugged his shoulders. "I don't know what to make of all this, Denise." The trembling had stopped, although he still felt a little light-headed from the excitement.

"You don't have to make anything of it. Drink your tea, it'll help you calm down." William sipped obediently. "I belong to the *misgigitswan*, the healing lodge," Denise confided.

William shuddered. She is a witch like Jack said! he thought.

She cocked her head to one side and squinted at him again. "That spirit's jammed in there pretty good. We're going to have to loosen it up somehow." She nodded thoughtfully. "Can't get over your wife's death, can you?" William's head spun. "See," Denise explained, "that dead spirit is keeping you from coming to terms with your life. Problem is, you don't want to get rid of that dead spirit. You've had it so long it feels like part of you. You think you can't change and that's just the way it is." She leaned toward him and, looking into his eyes, said with intensity, "But that's not the way it is. You can change. You can heal and grow into a whole person again."

William sighed and leaned back in his chair. It was all too much for him.

Denise watched him. "Just like Jack. He came back here with more dead spirits than a porcupine has quills. Couldn't accept what happened to his wife."

"Is Jack's wife dead?" At last William found something to focus on.

"Dead? No, Sarah's still alive—at least her body's alive. It's her mind that's gone."

"You mean, she's in a coma?"

Denise shook her head sadly. "No, she's wacko, crazy, loony, out of her mind. She's in Lakeview Hospital down there by Thunder Bay. Been there nearly ten years."

"She's mentally ill?"

"Sarah's had almost every label in the psychiatric encyclopaedia; schizophrenic, paranoid delusional, compulsive-obsessive, bipolar disorder, manic-depressive, you name it, she's been called it. But they haven't been able to help her. After they'd been married about four years she started having episodes. She'd fly into a rage for no reason, or she'd start talking about imaginary people and places, sometimes in an imaginary language. Her mind drifted away into her own world until eventually there was no more of this world left and we lost her."

"And Jack?"

"Well, this all happened while he was teaching at the university. When things got too bad, Jack quit his job and brought her back here. He couldn't manage with her on his own; he had to put Sarah in the institution. Broke his heart. He felt like he'd failed her. Started drinking heavily, angry all the time. If you said hello to him he'd swear at you. Don't know what would have happened to him if Anton hadn't found him."

"Anton?"

"Yeah, Jack's teacher. Anton recognized his great heart. He shook all those dead spirits loose and pulled them out. Started him on his path, showed him how to become a spirit talker."

"How did he shake the dead spirits loose?" William asked.

Denise winked at him. "He met Wendigo. That did it."

The front door opened and Jack came in. "Hi," he said nonchalantly. "What's up?"

"Having a cup of tea," said Denise "Guess it's time to go to bed now."

"Wait a minute!" William protested. "I want to know what's going on. What was all that noise?"

"Some of those Ogichidaw out there," said Jack, hanging his jacket on a hook. "The warriors. Those were their death-cries. They scare you?"

"They scared the crap out of me!" exclaimed William. "What were they doing out there?"

"I asked them to keep an eye on your camp. Lots of strange things have been happening. Didn't want anything strange to happen here."

William wasn't reassured. "You're not telling me everything, are you?"

"That's because I don't know everything," Jack replied. William would have thought he was being flippant if his voice hadn't been deadly serious. "Go back to bed and get some sleep. We need an early start in the morning."

"What were the warriors doing out there?" William persisted.

"Being scary. They scared you, didn't they? That's good. It takes time to develop a real death-cry, one that puts the chill of death into whoever hears it."

"But they weren't only trying to scare me—"

"Nope. Scaring you was a bonus." Jack chuckled. "What did you make?" he asked Denise, indicating the cups on the table.

"*Maskikik*," Denise answered.

"Good," said Jack. "Medicine plant. It'll help you sleep and have good dreams."

"Who were they trying to scare?" William was determined to get an answer.

"Whoever was out there." Jack smiled.

"Jack!" William was completely exasperated. "Who was out there?"

Jack smiled again and patted William on the shoulder. "Don't worry about it. It's all over now. They won't be back. Those Ogichidaw did a good job. Drink your medicine."

William gave up. He drank the rest of the tea and went back to bed. In spite of his agitation he fell asleep instantly. All night he had vivid dreams.

CHAPTER FIVE
THURSDAY

When Jack woke William the next morning, Denise already had breakfast waiting. It was still dark. Two backpacks waited like anxious terriers by the door. William walked outside into a thick fog. It swirled around him, coating his face with fine moisture. He navigated to the outhouse, tripping and stumbling, guided by the stiff, sharp branches of the bushes bordering the path. Isolated by the darkness and fog, William felt a peculiar floating sensation. His mind wandered adrift in the black cloud. All his terrors crept out of the gloom, growing with each step he took. Loneliness gripped his chest, choking the breath out of him. Self-pity sank cold claws into his belly. By the time he reached the outhouse he was crying. He wiped the mixture of warm salt and cold mist from his face. Was this what it was like to have a dead spirit in your chest, he wondered?

He hadn't cried when Barbara died—he had been sad, but had not cried. As always, he had pushed everything away; avoided feeling anything so that he could carry on; so that he could take the giant step from one numb moment to the next. Now, here, in an outhouse in a fog-shrouded wilderness, a lifetime of buried hurts were beginning to struggle out of their graves like nightmare creatures, tearing him to pieces. William didn't want this, didn't want any of this to happen. He ran, flying down the path to the cabin. At the door, he leaned on the jamb, panting, scrubbing his face with his sleeve to erase the tears. He wanted to be himself again—himself—whoever that was.

Pushing open the door, he fell into the room. Jack and Denise both stared at him. His eyes were red-rimmed, hair awry, breathing heavy.

"What happened to you?" asked Denise. "You meet Wendigo out there?"

"Shh," Jack cautioned her, making a calming motion with his hand. "William, what happened?"

"Uh, nothing," said William. "I, uh, got lost in the fog, that's all."

"It's okay, William," Jack said. "Your emotions are a little out of control. Trust in the spirits, they will help you. Sometimes we need to reshape the past before we can shape the future."

William pushed his feelings down, retreating into his habitual cold denial. He asked matter-of-factly, "We're not going out in this, are we? You can't see a thing out there."

Jack smiled kindly. "It will clear," he said. "You'll see." William was still standing at the door, his hand on the knob. "C'mon," said Jack, "eat your breakfast, then we'll leave. Better pack a change of clothes."

Hardly another word was spoken before they left.

The fog made the going slow; the Bronco's headlights diffusing into a blank whiteness. Jack stuck his head out the side window. "A little to the left," he called when they veered too close to the ditch. William would have missed the Trout Lake road if Jack hadn't told him when to turn.

By the time they reached the boat landing, daylight was displacing the murky fog. George Ferris's runabout floated beside the dock, its painter slack, the aluminum hull grey as solidified mist. William bailed the accumulated rainwater while Jack carried the gear from the truck. When the boat was as dry as William could make it, Jack began to pass things for William to stow.

A soft crunch of gravel made them both look up. Harry Perkins stood beside the Bronco. "Hey there," he greeted. "Saw you pull up. What's going on?" He wore grey slacks, an open-necked blue pin-stripe shirt and a blue blazer with a Jaguar crest on the pocket.

Jack finished what he was doing and asked, "You know whose boat this is?"

Harry Perkins walked down to the dock, his hands in his pockets, and regarded the runabout. "No idea. Should I? I guess it belongs to someone from one of the other cabins on the lake. I don't know much about boats, don't own one myself."

"This boat belongs to George Ferris." Jack watched closely for a reaction. "Remember, the man who went missing?"

"Really?" Perkins looked concerned. "He didn't live around here, did he? What's his boat doing here?"

"That's what we're going to find out." Jack untied the painter, stepped into the runabout and primed the motor.

"Where are you off to?" Perkins asked.

"Don't know yet." Jack gripped the pull cord on the

motor, then paused, looking up at Perkins. "Did you know that George Ferris was dead?"

Perkins eyes opened wide with surprise. "No, I didn't. When did this happen?"

"William and I found his body the other day," said Jack.

"Well, that's unfortunate." Perkins fumbled for words of commiseration. "I didn't know the man, but, uh—"

"Now we find his boat here. Kind of strange." Jack pulled the cord to start the motor.

"Where are you going?" Perkins asked again.

Jack revved the engine. He cupped a hand behind his ear. "What?"

Perkins shouted. "Where are you going?"

Jack pointed to the motor, then to his ear, shrugged and shifted into gear. He cranked the motor over sharply to turn the bows out into the lake, opening the throttle as they moved into open water. William watched the figure of Harry Perkins disappear into the lingering mist.

The calm water rolled away from the bows in smooth grey braids. As they motored north the mist thinned to a light haze. William could see the dark ribbon of the shore sliding past. By the time they reached the north end of the lake, the mist had cleared completely. Jack slowed the boat, pointing it toward the shore. William couldn't see what had drawn Jack's attention; all he could see were rocks and trees. Jack steered the runabout through the weeds in the shallows and entered the mouth of a small creek. The opening was completely invisible from the water; William would have passed by without seeing it.

As they motored up the creek, the stony bottom was sharply visible through the clear water. William called excitedly to Jack when he saw a couple of fish, their tails lazily waving against the current. Jack nodded and smiled.

The creek began to narrow and become shallow. From ahead, the gurgle of running water could be heard over the putter of the outboard. Jack cut the motor and steered toward the bank where a small clearing made a perfect place to land. William stood up, balancing carefully, and stepped ashore. He found a post driven into the ground to tie the painter to. The landing place was not a convenient accident of nature. It had been made.

Jack rummaged around in the bottom of the runabout, throwing a bag ashore before climbing out himself. He opened the bag and removed a pair of hip waders.

"Here." He tossed them to William. "Put these on." He took another pair out of the bag and slid into the rubber legs. Fastening the suspender straps over his shoulders, he stepped into the creek. It came up to his knees. William adjusted his waders and followed Jack into the water.

They walked upstream, the current pushing against their legs. The babbling sound became louder as they neared a small rapids. The water, ankle-deep at that point, burbled over the gravel bottom. Jack waded out to centre stream and crouched down, examining the creek bed.

"What are you looking for?" William asked.

Jack straightened up. "Trying to see if a boat has been through here."

William peered into the water. "It's too shallow for a boat, isn't it?"

Jack made a noncommittal *mmm* sound.

"Can you see anything?" William asked, studying the bottom through the clear running water without a clue as to what he was supposed to be looking for.

"Been too long," said Jack. "Water tends to level

everything out. It's deeper here in the centre, but whether or not that's the normal water channel or if someone has dug it out to make it deeper, I can't tell. Can't see any scratches or scuffs on the rocks; small stones like these shift around too much."

"You think George Ferris came through here in his boat?"

"It's a possibility. Let's go." He retraced his steps downstream to the runabout. Wading to the stern, he lifted the motor out of the water and leaned over the gunwale to grab a length of rope. He tied the line to the bows and handed it to William, keeping the painter himself. "All set?" he asked with a grin.

"What are we doing?" William had no idea what he was planning.

"We're going to tow the boat upstream and over those rapids." He smiled again.

"Oh," William frowned doubtfully.

"It's either that or carry it."

"Let's tow," said William. They set off upstream. It was easier than William had expected. Where the water was deep enough for the boat to float the towing was effortless, and even hauling it over the gravel bottom of the rapids wasn't difficult with two of them pulling, but it was hard enough that William wouldn't want to do it by himself. He guessed that was why Jack wanted him along, as a tow horse, and not for his sparkling company.

When they reached deeper water the runabout floated free again and Jack waded toward the bank where there was another small landing place. "We'll have lunch here," he said, climbing out of the water. From a backpack he produced sandwiches, a flask of coffee, and a couple of bottles of water. William struggled out of his hip waders and they ate sitting side by side on a fallen log.

It was early for lunch, but William found he was starving. Around a mouthful of sandwich, he asked, "Where do we go from here?"

"Up to the next lake and see what we find."

"That's Eagle Lake, isn't it?" William wasn't entirely sure of his geography. "Where the cabin was broken into?"

"That's right."

"Who made these landings?" he asked.

"There aren't any roads to Eagle Lake. The people who have camps up there, more like mansions really, come in by plane. The only other way is up this creek from Trout Lake. They sometimes bring supplies in this way by boat."

"If Brad Pitt has a place up there, wouldn't people have seen him around town?"

Jack laughed. "The people in those camps don't come into town. They have assistants to do that for them. I can't see Brad Pitt poking around the General Store comparing prices on soup cans!"

William munched and mulled things over. "If a boat did come through here recently, it didn't have to be George, it could have been from one of the cabins, right?"

Jack nodded. "Yeah. But there's nobody up there this time of year. Anyone coming through here would need a good reason."

"If no one's up there, how did the police know a cabin was broken into?"

Jack laughed again. "Flew in. The people up there are rich. They can afford to pay for extra security. The police fly in with a boat between the pontoons, cruise around a bit to check the camps, then fly out again.

Won't find too many cops walking bush trails or hauling boats over rapids."

William watched the creek meander away through the trees. "What are we looking for?"

"Won't know till we get there." Jack was being evasive again.

"Jack, don't do this to me. Every time I ask a question you give a vague answer. Stop treating me like some dumb white guy. It's frustrating."

"I'm not being evasive; I'm telling you the truth. You're not used to hearing the truth. You're used to hearing what people think or what their opinions are, but that's all it is, supposition and conjecture. The spirit world cannot distinguish between fact and fantasy. If you go into the spirit world with ideas and opinions, you will get back ideas and opinions, but that's all it will be, fantasy and imagination. It may be exciting, but there's no substance to it, just colourful pictures. But if you enter the spirit world with truth, then you will learn great truths." Jack finished his sandwich. "So when I talk to you, I tell you the truth about what I know. I can't talk about guesses or suppositions. I can only tell the truth."

William held his tongue by wrapping it around the last bite of sandwich.

"The way of the spirit is the way of truth," Jack went on. "Once you start living the truth, your life will never be the same."

Sarcastic comebacks bit at the back of William's throat; he pushed them down into the frozen darkness where all inner voices were silenced.

Jack carefully gathered up the sandwich wrappers and put them in the bag before boarding the boat.

Bitterness niggled under William's tongue like sand in his shoes. The last thing he needed was to be dragged out into the middle of nowhere and lectured on how to live by a burned-out philosophy professor turned backwoods voodoo witch doctor. He had come up here to write his book and so far had hardly a word down on paper. His cabin still wasn't prepared for the fast approaching winter and here he was hauling a boat up a creek on some Platonic quest for Truth. He stood up wearily, threw the hip waders into the runabout and untied the painter. Jack, seemingly oblivious to William's peevish mood, lowered the motor into the water and started it up.

The creek grew deeper and wider as they followed its twists and turns until, abruptly, the broad expanse of Eagle Lake opened up before them. Jack revved the motor, racing north under full throttle. The wind picked up, raising a short chop. The sky overhead had faded to pearly grey; a threatening mass of dark cloud, like distant hills, loomed on the horizon. The exhilaration of speed lifted William's depression. He began to enjoy himself. He opened his mouth and felt the cold wind sing in his fillings.

Eagle Lake was larger than Trout Lake. Cottages dotted the shore, bright splashes of reflective glass amid the dark trees. Jack had been right, these were more like mansions than cabins. A few of them looked bigger than the resort on Rainbow Lake.

William was awed. "Who owns these places?"

Jack laughed. "Some pretty rich people, Hollywood people mostly. They use them as getaways. The lake is stocked with fish, they spray for mosquitoes—it's like a wilderness paradise."

The lake narrowed at the north end and this time William could see a slight opening in the trees signalling the mouth of a creek. Jack headed straight for it. The eelgrass was thick where the stream entered the lake. Jack cut the motor and lifted the prop from the water. He took an oar and used it to pole the boat through the weeds.

At least we won't be up this creek without a paddle, William thought wryly.

Soon the weeds gave way to a clear gravel bottom and Jack started the motor again. They hadn't gone far upstream before the water became shallow again. William looked for fish, but didn't see any. He did, however, spot the landing place right away. Pleased with himself, he turned to Jack and pointed. Jack nodded and nosed the runabout toward it, although William suspected he already knew it was there. William climbed ashore and tied off the painter. Jack killed the motor and stepped out beside him.

A high ridge to the north loomed over them. William pointed to it. "What's that?"

"Ghostwalker Ridge," said Jack.

"The same one we saw over by Hellbent Stump? It comes all the way up here?"

"Yes. It's a little higher here, but it slopes off sharply not far to the north. Around Iron Lake the greenstone drift disappears underground, back where the glaciers put it."

Jack put a hand on William's shoulder, motioning him to stay where he was. Jack surveyed the area. William did the same, noticing a rough trail following the stream north toward the ridge. The mud was rutted with the tracks of wide, ribbed tires. Off to the left were the remains of a small campfire; beside it, an edge of blue tarp peeked out from under a pile of brushwood, the needles on the cut pine branches still green. William didn't know how long it took for pine needles to turn brown, but as they were green, they probably hadn't been cut very long ago.

Jack knelt and examined the ground, then walked over to the rough trail and studied the tracks. He went to the pile of brushwood and called William over. "Help me clear this away."

After pulling the branches off the blue tarp, Jack grabbed a corner and folded it back. Beneath it was a Yamaha Kodiak 400 all-terrain vehicle painted in a camouflage pattern.

Jack stood looking at it thoughtfully.

"Is this what you expected to find?" William asked.

"It was a possibility." Jack continued to stare at the ATV in deep thought for several minutes. "Let's make camp," he said abruptly. "We'll stay here tonight and head home tomorrow."

They hauled the gear out of the boat and set up a small tent. It was one of those modern tents held up by metal hoops instead of the wooden poles William had used as a boy, the last time he had been camping. He didn't know how it went together and hindered the erection more than he helped. The wind had become stronger and did its part to tangle the nylon fabric. Finally the tent was up and William was able to pound in some anchoring pegs without hurting himself.

"You're turning into a real woodsman," said Jack, smiling.

"I can do without the sarcasm, thank you very much," William shot back. Jack laughed.

The wind brought the dark clouds tumbling over Ghostwalker Ridge. It began to spit with rain. While storing their gear in the tent, William came upon a round deerskin bag. He peeked inside to find the circular, flat drum he had seen Jack with in the cabin.

The rain increased. Jack entered the tent, primed a

lantern and lit it. "How about some nice hot tea?" he asked.

"How?" William asked. "You can't light a fire in this rain, can you?"

"We'll use an old Indian trick," said Jack. "Camping stove." From the pile of gear he produced a small, one-burner propane stove. He lit it while William dug out a pot and filled it with water.

"You borrowed all this stuff, didn't you?" William asked. "Don't you have any of your own camping gear?" It seemed strange that someone who knew his way around the woods as well as Jack wouldn't have his own equipment.

"I don't own anything except my clothes, a blanket, a knife and my drum. I have no possessions and carry no money."

William knew that renouncing material possessions was a part of many sacred traditions. "Is that part of the spirit path?"

"It's part of my path, not necessarily part of the spirit path. When I was at the university I was never satisfied with what I had. I guess I was trying to prove myself all the time; that a dumb Indian could make it in the white man's world. I always wanted the next upgrade for my computer and a newer car; I was caught up in wanting more. When I came back here I decided I wouldn't own anything. I wanted to relearn the real value of things."

"Is it working?"

Jack laughed. "I'm not sure yet. We'll have to wait and see. I think I'm still pretty greedy. One thing about being Indian is that there's an ingrained stereotype in North American culture that Indians are poor. Indians aren't considered to be contributing members of society. It's different for white people. If white people are poor it's because there's something wrong with them, they're lazy or stupid or shiftless, or something. They aren't pulling their weight. But if you're Indian and poor, it's because you're Indian."

The water began to boil. Jack took a small mustard tin out of a pack and sprinkled some of the contents into two mugs.

William eyed the tin dubiously. "That's not mustard, is it?"

Jack grinned. "No, it's tea, medicine tea, builds strength. I just keep it in this tin. Recycling. Good for the planet." He filled the mugs with hot water, handing one to William.

Jack reclined on his sleeping bag, balanced his cup on his chest, and stared at the tent roof. "That's part of the answer to your question about why I don't own anything," Jack went on, "the other part is Wendigo."

"Wendigo?"

"Yes. It takes all my concentration to keep Wendigo at bay. If I let my attention be distracted by possessions, Wendigo will consume me." He looked at William. "And I have to keep Wendigo away from you. He's been gnawing at you. With your mixed-up emotions you're an easy target. He nearly got you this morning. He was attracted by those death-cries last night. Wendigo's out there prowling around, stalking you."

William sipped his tea. It tasted like grass. He wanted to keep the conversation away from spirits. He changed the subject. "What is that ATV doing here?"

"That ATV belonged to George Ferris. Remember when we first went to his cabin I noticed it was missing?"

"Yes," said William. "How did you know to look for it here?"

The rain pattered on the tent roof. "To understand that, I have to tell you more about the spirit world.

Remember I said it was Wolf that took me to where George was and that Raven showed me the way here?"

Here we go again, thought William.

"That's how the spirit world works; we learn truths from our animal spirit helpers. It may sound like mystical nonsense at first, but you need to understand the reasoning of the spirit world. The spirit world has its own way of connecting things. Normally, we think in logical steps like: If this, then that. In the spirit world, an animal helper will take you on a journey and show you things. The spirit helpers solve the problem and show you the solution in images, in signs and symbols, sometimes in dreams. It's all very logical, but a different kind of knowing, more of an intuitive sense."

William remained silent.

"We had a known fact," Jack continued, "that George Ferris was missing. We also knew that a cabin had been broken into. I went into the spirit world and told those facts to my spirit helpers. Wolf took me to the cave where we found George's body. How did Wolf know where to go? Let's look at the whole picture." He sat up and searched around the tent. Reaching into a pack, he picked out a can of stew, peeled the label off, and smoothed it out on his knee. Then he climbed over William and unzipped the tent door. Reaching underneath the tent floor, he came up with a dry twig. Sharpening it with a pocket knife, he burned the end with a match and used the charred point to draw a makeshift map on the back of the label.

"This is where we are at the top of Eagle Lake, here's Trout Lake, and this is Reese Lake, where George's camp is. The cabin that was broken into, the landing where we found his boat, and George's camp are in pretty much a straight line, see?" He drew a rough dotted line to connect the xs. "Let's suppose George was the one who broke into the cabin. We know he was at the Trout Lake landing, because that's where we found his boat, and we know he never reached home. So where is the most likely place for him to be? In between Trout Lake and his own camp. And what lies between those two points? Hellbent Stump. Therefore, the most likely place for George to be is Hellbent Stump. Make sense?"

"Yes. It sounds pretty simple when you put it like that." William thought for a moment. "But we don't know that George was the one who broke into the cabin."

"That's right. I presented the facts to Wolf; Wolf put it together and took me to the cave. The spirit helpers know things in ways we can't. It was Wolf who told me to look for George's boat at Trout Lake; that was Wolf's intuition. If George's boat wasn't there, we would have been on a wild goose chase looking for him at the Stump."

"But," William struggled to order everything in his mind, "we didn't find the boat until after we found George, so how—"

"You're right. We had to test my vision by going to the cave. First we found the secret trail that confirmed we were on the right track. And later we found his boat; that gave us more facts. I went into the spirit world once more and Raven brought me here." Jack lay back on his sleeping bag and closed his eyes. "Spirit helpers work only with facts. If you give them lies or falsehoods, they may turn on you and send you on endless, meaningless journeys that will exhaust you and lead nowhere." He opened his eyes and looked dreamily into the distance. "Sometimes you don't have all the facts, so you have to go with what you've got. Sometimes things don't add up the right way and you end up on the wrong path. We must always test our visions in the real world, otherwise we end up living a fantasy—or maybe a nightmare." His face tightened; his eyelids twitched as if in pain. After a moment he spoke again, quietly, as if to himself. "That's the adventure of life. We keep taking wrong paths until we eventually find the one way that is right for us."

William listened to the sporadic rain drumming on the tent roof. The wind rustling the nylon made him feel like they were lying beneath fluttering moth wings. He sat up. "Shall we make dinner?" He took out another can of stew. "We have two kinds here," he said, reading from the can, "beef with potatoes and onions, and," turning over Jack's map, "turkey vegetable."

"That's okay," said Jack. "I'll tell you a secret about wilderness cooking: if you put them both in the same pot, they'll both taste the same."

William emptied the cans into the pot and put the stew on the stove to heat. "You still haven't explained about the ATV," he prompted.

"Oh, that was Raven's journey," said Jack. "Raven is a trickster. Raven likes a secret. Wolf is pretty straightforward, but Raven, you have to watch out for Raven."

William stirred the stew.

"Raven brought me up here," Jack went on, "and showed me that things were hidden. He didn't show me what, only that there were secrets here."

"What do you mean, Raven brought you here?" William asked. "You mean, you had a vision of this place?"

"I became a raven and we flew here together."

William would have thought Jack was joking, if his face and voice weren't so serious.

"Lots of things are possible in the spirit world, things sometimes beyond what we can imagine," Jack said gravely. William remained silent and let him continue.

"George left his boat at Trout Lake, then went south to Hellbent Stump where he died. That means he must have come from up north. You can't go any further north than this by boat, so this is the logical place to start looking for clues about what he was doing. At least, that's the way I interpreted Raven's journey."

"How did he bring the ATV up here? He couldn't have brought it in his boat, could he?"

"I've been wondering about that," said Jack. "Remember when we first went to his cabin, beside his snowmobile there was a big sled, sort of like a trailer without wheels? Well, that gave me the clue." Jack reached over and stirred the stew. "Let's consider all the possibilities. George couldn't have brought the ATV in by road, because there isn't any road. He couldn't have brought it in by boat because his boat isn't big enough, and even if he had managed to somehow raft it up, the raft would still be here, but there's no raft, so that's out. And he couldn't bring it in by plane, there's no way to land it on the water. That only leaves one way to bring an ATV up here."

William waited expectantly.

"Over ice," Jack concluded. "He could have put the ATV on a sled and pulled it behind his snowmobile."

"But," William objected, "that would have been last winter."

"Yeah," Jack nodded in agreement. "What was he planning?"

William tested the stew and poured half into a bowl. He passed the bowl to Jack and ate his own out of the pot. Jack was right, it all tasted the same. "If he brought the ATV up last winter, why did he wait until now to come back by boat?"

Jack shrugged. "I don't know. Maybe because there aren't as many bugs this time of year."

William shook his head. "I can't figure it out."

Jack scraped the last spoonful of the stew from his bowl. "There's only one thing I can think of that ties all this together."

William still had stew left in his pot and wondered how evenly he had divided the dinner. "What's that?"

"The geologists," said Jack with a decisive nod.

"The geologists?" William repeated, finishing his meal. He put his empty pot down, then sat up with a sudden revelation. "Amethysts!" he shouted. "The geologists were looking for amethysts! And George was at the hotel talking about amethysts before he disappeared. Do you think the amethysts are the connection?"

Jack laughed at William's excitement. "Let's see where we are." He picked up the map and re-charred the end of the twig to draw another x. "The geologists' camp was north of here, over the ridge at Stillwater Lake, where Billy picked them up in his plane. George was their guide last year, so he knew the location of their camp. George must have known they planned to return and been ready for them. He brought his ATV up here in the winter and cut that trail. There was something at their camp he wanted. I bet if we follow the trail it will take us right up near the geologists' camp."

"Are we hiking up there?" William asked timidly, secretly hoping they would be heading home the next day.

"*Mmm*," Jack made a noncommittal noise while he considered. "I don't think we need to. The geologists are back in town; I don't think there'll be any more to learn up there. If there was, I'm sure Raven would have taken me there."

William, relieved, settled back on his sleeping bag. "What does all this have to do with the geologists? They said they didn't find any amethysts, but what if they did?" Possibilities sparked in William's mind like fireflies on a summer evening. "George might have known they had found something and gone up there—yes!" William sat up again. "That's why he needed the ATV, he used it to steal the amethysts from the geologists' camp!" His eyes shone with excitement.

"Where are they now?" Jack's skeptical tone was like a bucket of water on the flames of William's enthusiasm.

"Huh?"

"There weren't any amethysts with George when we found him, so where are they?"

"I don't know." William thought for a moment. "Perhaps he hid them. Or whoever killed him took them! Yes! That's why he was killed, for the amethysts!" His mind raced through imaginative scenarios. "Do you think the geologists could have done it? Maybe they followed him and caught up with him at Hellbent Stump and they had a big fight and George fell into the cave and they murdered him and took the amethysts!"

Jack laughed softly. "Slow down. We're a long way from figuring out what happened yet."

"But it could have happened that way," William persisted.

"Yes, it could have," agreed Jack, "except for one thing."

"What?"

"The geologists didn't have a boat. How did they follow George over two lakes?"

William growled, disgruntled that his ideas could be dismissed so easily. "What do you think happened?"

"What I think doesn't matter," Jack replied. "All that matters is what did happen."

William lay in frustrated silence, listening to the hiss of the lantern. Rhythmic dripping from the trees tattooed the tent. William sat up, listening intently. From somewhere in the darkness came the unmistakable howl of a wolf. William couldn't tell how distant it was; it sounded closer than he liked.

"Did you hear that?" he asked Jack.

"Yeah," said Jack. The howl sounded again, other voices joining in the chorus. "The wolves will be hunting tonight."

"Will we be safe?" William's skin tingled.

"Oh yeah." Jack spoke calmly. "Those wolves won't bother us. They're hungry, but not starving. You can tell from their howls. You can hear the difference when they're starving; there's a note of desperation in their voices—then it's really scary. But they don't bother people unless they are totally famished. They generally stay as far away from people as they can."

"Why?" William wasn't quite reassured. "Because we can defend ourselves?"

"No," said Jack. "Because they don't like the way we smell. To a wolf, nothing smells worse than a human. It makes them keep their distance."

"I thought they only howled at the full moon."

"No, they howl before they hunt. Full moon is the best hunting time, so they howl most around the full moon."

"Why is that?"

"Because wolves hunt at night and it's easier to see what you're hunting in the moonlight. They hunt mainly by scent, but when they close in for the kill, they like to see what they're chasing. Most of the time wolves survive on small game: rabbits, chipmunks, mice, things like that. But at the full moon, that's when they go after the big game, like deer, because they may have to run the animal down for hours, and it's easier by the light of the moon." Jack thought for a moment. "We're the same. You know how people go a little crazy around the full moon?"

"I've heard that," William said.

"We used to be night hunters once," said Jack. "It's still deep in our psyches. Every full moon our survival instinct remembers and charges us up for the hunt, just like the wolves." Jack leaned over and dimmed the lantern. "Or maybe it's because, long ago, the full moon was when we were hunted by things with bigger teeth and sharper claws." Jack turned onto his side. "Better get some sleep. It's a long trip back tomorrow. Hope there's enough gas."

William lay awake, his thoughts scattered as raindrops. "I had some paper," he said into the darkness.

"What?" Jack asked.

"This morning when I packed my clothes, I packed a notebook and a pen. You could have used them to draw your map."

Exhaustion took over and William fell asleep. Sometime during the night he awoke to the throb of Jack's drum, but quickly drifted off again into a slumber troubled by dreams of wolves.

CHAPTER SIX
FRIDAY

The rain had cleared by morning. Jack was already gone when William woke up. William washed the dinner dishes in the stream; by the time he finished, his hands were numb from the cold water. Icy drips from the night rain dribbled from overhead branches and splattered on his neck. He looked around the dreary campsite with its damp tent under glum trees. Feeling stiff after a night of sleeping on the ground, William decided to work out the kinks by hiking down to Eagle Lake. He thought his knees could take it. Pulling on his hip waders, he headed downstream. The creek, almost still at the edges, ran fast in the middle, the water singing a rippling song as it twined and wove over itself. William watched, enthralled, as if the rushing water were a live thing, a liquid-skinned snake sliding through the trees.

William waded through waist-deep water, holding onto overhanging branches of willow and poplar for balance. Every handhold shook loose a flurry of fall leaves that settled on the running surface like golden messages from the dry land to the watery depths of worlds beyond the sun.

Where the rolling reflections of the stream opened into the calm expanse of the lake, William climbed onto a flat rock. The water at his feet was ribboned with green weeds tying the lake to the shore. William gazed out over a scene so breathtaking that the beauty was like a physical wind. It blew the dried leaves of his thoughts away, leaving him bare and open.

The sky was a jumble of colour. The ragged overcast broke clear along the horizon, letting the morning sun shine in beneath the clouds, lighting them up with pinks and purples; reds and mauves; yellows, greens, and blues. Impossible colours for a sky. The lake was covered with a low-lying mist that picked up the sky tones, reflecting them back in pale pastel patterns.

The hushed glory of the hazy stillness relaxed William's chaotic thoughts. Everything became unhurried and peaceful. In spite of all the summers William had spent at his cabin, this was the first time he had ever had a real sense of belonging with nature; with the rocks, the trees, the water; a feeling of oneness. He slipped into a reverie. It was as if his mind became part of the mist and he saw the world from a new perspective, a place of intricate dynamics, of heats and currents, airs and granites, moistures and infinities. He had no idea how long he stood there. Jack's voice, almost a whisper, brought him back to reality.

"Wilderness got you now, eh?" Jack's voice was subdued. "You'll never be able to live in a city again; you belong in the bush now. You're lucky. That spirit from the cave likes you. Took you gently; no struggles or trials. You're a woodsman now; no turning back."

William didn't understand what Jack meant about being taken gently, but, infused with the serenity of the scene before him, accepted it uncritically. An image formed in William's mind of the Gulp where they had seen the deer. He felt himself drawn into the opening, very rapidly, as if he were flying down, down into a darkness that opened into a forest. William found himself crouching in the shadows of a small clearing amid dark pine trees. Before him, almost close enough to touch, stood a buck, antlers like frozen lightning over its head. Their eyes were level. The deer's eyes seemed bottomless, a timelessness that William could reach into. They stared at each other for a moment before William felt himself pulled away, back to the edge of the lake.

"Tell me what you saw." Jack's voice came from behind, close to his ear.

"A deer." William swayed off balance. The world spun around him.

"Thought so." Jack took his arm and steadied him. "When I heard the wolves howling last night, I knew they were calling you; calling your Deer spirit. Deer is one of your spirit helpers." Although it was all very strange, William wasn't surprised by Jack's words. "That was your initiation into the spirit world."

William felt a little groggy, as if half-asleep, but became very animated and wanted to tell Jack every detail of what he had experienced. Jack listened patiently as he blurted out his account. When he finished, Jack said, "Are we going to have breakfast now?"

William was deflated. His vision had been so vivid he felt sure Jack would be excited by his account. Jack saw the disappointment in his face. "Don't worry," he said comfortingly. "You will learn. You have to keep the spirit world and this world separate. If you mix them up, you lose reality and go crazy. That's part of the *mishweegen* training, how to control the insanity. You're not in the spirit world now. It's time to make breakfast. So, let's make breakfast." He walked away.

William sat down and looked out over the lake. The sun had risen above the clouds taking all the colours with it, leaving the sky a flat grey. The mist had dispersed, the lake surface the same dull monochrome as the sky. The trees glowered.

William slipped back into the water and made the journey upstream. It was difficult wading against the current, but William took his time, the cold water soothing his knees. When he reached the campsite, Jack was stirring a steaming pot over a small fire. "Hey there, thought you were lost," he called, pouring porridge into a bowl.

William sat down on a rock to eat. "How did you get here so fast?"

Jack smiled, "I turned invisible. Made it back here in no time."

"When you're invisible you can walk through things?"

"Not exactly walk through them, just—it's hard to explain—it's something you have to experience. Finish eating and I'll show you."

When William put down his bowl, Jack dragged him over to a tree. "Grab a branch and hold on," he instructed. "That's good. Now imagine yourself becoming a tree, make it so real that you feel as if you are a tree, like you did before."

William concentrated on the scaly bark under his palm, trying to imagine it covering his whole body. His fingers became small branches, bristling with needles. He blended with the colours of the tree, the dark grey of the trunk, the lighter, almost orange tinge of the branches. Sensing the drops of rainwater clinging to the tips of the needles, he searched out the compacted energy in the buds where new cones waited to develop.

"That's very good," said Jack. "You're getting the hang of it. Now, let go of the tree and come here." He took William's arm and led him to a nearby rock.

Crouching beside it, William ran his hands over the textures of the surface. There were so many subtleties in what he would normally think of as an ordinary rock. He became the rock, hard and grey, cracked by frost.

"That's better!" exclaimed Jack. "You're doing great! Okay, stand up, shake it off, be yourself again. You see, that's how you become invisible, by blending into the things around you so that you can't be distinguished from them. And when you move, you move by becoming one thing after another. It may sound silly when said out loud; you have to experience it. Some of those old medicine men could move so fast that people believed they could be in two different places at the same time." William felt a little dazed. "You've been opened up to the spirit world," Jack continued. "All this will come more easily to you now; you'll find you won't need rational explanations for everything. The spirit world is a place of experience, not reason. The more you learn to trust your experience, the more will be possible for you." William stood with a dumb look on his face. "Okay," said Jack, laughing at William's expression, "lesson's over. Let's break camp and go home."

They struck the tent, packed up the gear, and headed downstream.

As they travelled southwards across Eagle Lake, a cold wind blew up and raised a chop. It was a rough ride. Partway down the lake Jack steered over to the western shore and slowed the motor.

"Something wrong?" William asked.

"No." Jack cruised along the shore. "Just wondered if we could see which cabin was busted into. It's only a day trip down to the boat landing on Trout Lake, so, if it was George who broke in, why did he do it?"

"Maybe it was rough, like this, and he wanted to wait until the wind died down," William suggested.

"You could be right," agreed Jack. "Or else he started too late in the day. We know he camped by the creek, we could tell from his fire. Let's say he made the trip from the boat landing at Trout Lake to the campsite at the north end of Eagle Lake in one day, camped overnight, and the next day drove the ATV over the ridge and raided the geologists' camp. He then drove back to the creek and left the same day in his boat. That would have him leaving in the boat late in the afternoon. Instead of trying to make it back in the dark, he decided to spend the night in a cabin."

William looked down at the wet tent in the bilge of the runabout. "If he had camping gear with him, why break into a cabin? Why not sleep in his tent?"

"It rained that day, remember? That's the day the geologists said they lost their equipment in the rain. Could be George decided it was easier to stay in a cabin than to pitch a tent in a downpour," Jack mused.

"Why did he leave if it was raining? Why not stay in the camp at the creek until the rain stopped?"

"I suspect," said Jack, "he wanted to get away from there pretty quick in case those geologists came looking for him. Did you check the tracks in the mud on the trail?"

"No."

"Well, I went partway up there this morning. Somebody came down that trail on foot. Two somebodys, as a matter of fact. They were probably looking for George."

"You mean the geologists?"

"Looks that way."

"Aren't you making a lot of suppositions? I thought you dealt only in truth?"

Jack laughed. "Before you can deal in truth, you have to figure out what the truth is!"

William gave a judgmental frown. "It seems to me that, in your spirit world, there is very little to distinguish between truth and guesswork—intuition, as you call it."

Jack was still smiling. "That's because you don't understand what truth is."

"I learned that in first-year philosophy class," countered William. "If something doesn't mean what you want it to, you change the definition!"

"Good strategy," laughed Jack. "I'll remember that." He slowed the motor even more and pointed the bows toward the shore. William saw a curl of smoke rising from the chimney of the nearest luxury cabin. It was one of the smaller places, but still palatial. From a wide deck in front, steps led down to a floating dock. "Somebody's home. Let's stop and say hello."

"Do you know who it is?"

"Not yet," said Jack. "Might be Brad Pitt," he laughed.

Tying off beside an orange Zodiac inflatable with twin 50 horsepower Mercury outboards on the back, they climbed the wooden steps to a door at the side of the house. Jack pointed to the lock. The wooden jamb was splintered.

Before they could knock, the door was opened by a stocky man with no neck. He wore a grey suit of shiny material over an open-necked purple shirt. Gold chains dangled a number of small ornaments and medallions into his chest hair. His right hand held a large sandwich. "What?" he said with his mouth full.

"Who is it?" called a voice from inside.

"Nobody," the man answered over his shoulder, taking another substantial bite.

"Well, show nobody in," said the voice. The man stood aside, motioning Jack and William inside with a jerk of his head. They went through a small vestibule and entered a sunken living room overlooking the lake. Off to the side, a dining area opened to a galley-style kitchen. Beyond that, a staircase led up to the second floor.

The stocky man went over and sat at the dining table, concentrating on his sandwich. In the living room a tall man lounged in a leather easy chair before a large-screen TV. He wore tailored jeans, cowboy boots, and a rodeo shirt. On the leather couch next to him reclined a woman. She was completely naked. A Cleopatra haircut framed eyes heavy with mascara and apricot eye shadow. Her pubic hair was shaved into an exclamation mark. She lay there languid as a diamond necklace. William was so shocked at the sight he couldn't do anything but stand with his eyes bulging and his mouth open.

"Would you look at that!" the tall man said to the TV. "How did he ever get a part like that? Casting director should be shot." Flicking his eyes at William and Jack, he spoke over his shoulder to the woman. "Fiona, go and put some clothes on, you're distracting our guests."

The woman rose obediently and walked away without a glance at William or Jack. William's eyes followed her through the dining area and up the stairs. Her buttocks moved like two pearl onions floating in a dry martini.

The tall man pointed a remote at the TV and clicked it off, turning to William and Jack. "To what do I owe the pleasure of this visit?"

"We were passing by," said Jack. "Saw someone was here, thought we'd stop in and say hello."

"Passing by?" the man noted doubtfully. "This isn't some kind of *Deliverance* crazy-inbred-locals-terrorize-hapless-city-folk, is it? Hey, Dink!" he called to the man at the table. "You terrorized by the crazy inbred locals?" Dink grunted. "Don't think you scare Dink," the man said, smiling. "Got a better story?"

William recognized the man, but at first couldn't place him. Then it came to him. Tyler Westman. He was an actor who had made a few westerns in the sixties, copies of Clint Eastwood's spaghetti westerns. Later he'd gone on to make a series of tough-cop movies, copies of Clint Eastwood's Dirty Harry films.

"Actually, we were trying to track somebody down," said Jack. "Do you know a man named George Ferris?"

"George Ferris." Tyler Westman rolled the name around in his mouth as if he were judging the taste of a single malt whisky. "Now, why would I know George Ferris?"

"Might have been him who broke in here."

"Really?" Westman opened his right eye wide and squinted with this left. "Just how did you know about the break-in?"

"Door jamb's all busted up," said Jack.

Westman snorted, one side of his mouth curling up into a smile. "So it is. Cops called my office to let me know about it. I decided I'd better come up here and have a look-see. Nothing stolen though."

"Wonder why he chose this place?" Jack looked around. "Out of all the cabins on the lake, why this one? Thought maybe he knew the place, been here before, something like that."

Fiona came back down the stairs. She was wearing tight black stretch pants and a leopard-skin print top.

Her nipples jutted through the fabric. She splashed herself on the sofa like a spilled drink. William stared.

"How did you get here?" Jack asked.

Westman gave a surprised laugh. "We flew in. A friend of mine keeps a private plane down at Thunder Bay. He gave us the use of the plane and that boat out there. What's it to you?"

Jack shrugged. "Just curious. You didn't fly in with the local service, Rainbow Airlines; I wondered how you made it up here."

"Well, I guess you boys better be on your way." As Westman spoke, Dink stood up from the table.

"Do you know Steve Mason or Frank Happer?" Jack asked. "They're a couple of geologists who were working over the ridge north of here." Westman squinted at him. Jack calmly stared back. "How about Lance Rockwell? Or Caroline Rockwell?"

"Rockwell." Westman looked up out of the corners of his eyes, as if trying to recall a distant memory. "What's this got to do with Lance Rockwell?"

"George Ferris was Lance Rockwell's father-in-law."

Westman pursed his lips. "Who did you say you were?"

"My name's Jack Crowfoot. This here's William Longstaffe."

Westman laughed "Longstaffe! There's a name to live up to, eh, Dink?" Dink grunted. Westman became serious. "Why do you think I know these people? What's it to you who I know and who I don't?"

"George Ferris was a friend of mine," Jack replied. "I'm trying to find out what happened to him."

Westman did his squint. It seemed to be one of his stock expressions. "What did happen to him?"

"He's dead."

"That's too bad." Neither surprise nor sympathy

showed in Westman's voice. "Always sad when someone dies. Especially when they die for nuthin'." He smiled, revealing a row of even teeth. "A line from one of my movies. Especially when they die for nuthin'," he drawled again, laughing to himself. "You know who I am?" he asked with a challenging look.

William spoke for the first time. "Tyler Westman."

Westman smiled again, pleased to be recognized. "Call me Ty." He had perfected the easy, deadly grace of the gunfighters he played. "Dink! Show Lo-o-ongstaffe and his friend out." He mockingly drew out William's name. "Better hustle them out of here before they start inbreeding right in front of us, eh, Fiona?" The woman didn't respond. She watched the blank TV screen.

Dink escorted Jack and William to the door. "Beat it," he said, pushing them outside.

"Is that a line from one of your movies?" William asked, sarcasm flicking out like a rawhide whip. Dink gave him a don't-mess-with-me look and slammed the door.

They went back to their boat. Jack revved the motor and headed south, throttle open full against the wind.

Jack steered into the creek that flowed from Eagle Lake to Trout Lake. They stopped at the landing place and, as before, put on their hip waders. Manoeuvring the runabout downstream was much easier than the trip up; they could let the current do the work, merely guiding the boat to the landing. Not only did the current help, but the rain from the night before had raised the water level so the runabout floated easily over the shallows.

"Isn't that interesting?" Jack commented. "That might be another reason why George decided to stay overnight in the cabin. He waited for the rain to bring the water level up and make it easier for the boat to ride over the rapids. His boat was probably pretty heavily laden; it would have been a tough job for one man to haul it through here."

"Heavily laden—you mean with the amethysts?" William asked.

Jack made a noncommittal *mmm* sound.

At the second landing they removed their hip waders and Jack prepared to leave again.

"Aren't we going to stop for lunch?" William asked.

Jack considered, then shrugged. "We can stop for a while, but we need to travel fast if we want to be back before dark." Fishing in a backpack, he produced a plastic sandwich bag full of brown lumps. Tossing it to William, he pulled out another bag for himself.

"What is it?" William asked, skeptically.

"The long thin ones are jerky. The short fat ones are pemmican. Trail food. Homemade." He grinned.

William tested the jerky with his teeth. It was too tough to bite a piece off so he settled for chewing on the end. The pemmican was softer, but still exceedingly chewy.

"Good, eh?" Jack grinned again. William didn't say anything. Perhaps their definitions of *good* were not precisely the same. "Don't worry," Jack laughed, "we'll go and have dinner tonight at Maggie's."

William chewed.

"So," said Jack, "you finally met a movie star. Too bad it wasn't Brad Pitt."

"He didn't really tell us anything, did he? He didn't say if he knew George, or the geologists, or Lance."

"I'm surprised you heard anything at all," Jack grinned, "the way you were staring at that woman."

William's face coloured. He started talking fast to cover his embarrassment. "Do you think Westman knows anything? Did George break into his cabin because he knew him? Do you think he knows Lance? They are both actors; if he knows Lance then he probably knew George."

Jack shook his head and chewed in silence. William had another question for him. "What did you mean this morning when you said the spirit took me gently?"

Jack lowered his eyes. "Some people have a difficult time finding their place in the world. Although you've had a cabin here for years, you never felt you belonged here, until now. People are funny. Sometimes, even when they find out where they belong, they put up a fight. I was like that. I didn't want to admit that my path led here. But here I am after all."

"It, um, it hasn't been that easy for me," William began, faltering over the unusual experience of talking about his feelings. He gave Jack a jumbled, rambling account of his encounter in the fog the previous morning, about his fears and his loneliness, about his tears. He told him what Denise had said about the dead spirit in his chest.

Jack listened quietly. "Spirits help us on our path. If we are on the wrong path, they raise obstacles in our way to steer us toward the right path. But if we're on the right path, they help us."

They sat in silence for a few minutes; only the murmur of the stream spoke to the listening trees.

"You said before that the spirits would be kind to me because I helped Denise—?" William let the question trail off, not quite sure what he was asking.

"Well, it didn't hurt." Jack considered his answer. "Spirits aren't like vending machines; you can't deposit good deeds and automatically get rewards." He looked wistful. "Sometimes you can do your best for someone and it all turns out wrong." He stared out across the water. "When you took Denise in, the spirits saw that you had a good heart. The spirits pay attention. You've had it easy; you have no idea how easy."

William hesitated. "Um, Denise told me about your wife."

Jack nodded, standing up quickly. "Let's go." Without looking at William he boarded the boat and started the motor.

William untied the painter and was about to step into the runabout when an idea hit him with such force that he missed his footing and fell, with a great splash, into the water.

"Whoa!" exclaimed Jack, quickly cutting the motor. "Smooth move!"

William stood thigh deep in cold water, the painter still in his hand, a look of wonder on his face. "The radio," he said.

"What?" Jack looked at him quizzically.

"The radio," repeated William. "You said the geologists couldn't have followed George because they didn't have a boat. But they had a radio! They called Billy to pick them up, remember? What if they radioed down to someone to intercept George the day he raided their camp? What if they called someone who followed George to Hellbent Stump and killed him?"

Jack raised his eyebrows and nodded. "That's a good thought."

"That means they had an accomplice—"

"Slow down!" Jack laughed. "Let me help you out of there and dry you off. It's easier to solve murders when you're not soaking wet!"

On the bank, William babbled about his idea as Jack found him a change of clothes. "What if—?" "Do you think—?" Ideas burst out of him faster than popcorn at a Saturday night movie.

Jack hemmed and hawed, noncommittal. William changed his pants and socks, but didn't have any dry shoes, so he put his hip waders back on.

On their way again, they followed the course of the stream to Trout Lake, where Jack opened the throttle full. The runabout bucked on the light chop, agitating the pemmican in William's stomach. The stiff wind made his eyes water. By the time they reached the wharf at the boat landing, William's bones were jangled from the rough ride. He stood up stiffly. He had to walk up and down the dock a few times to work out the aches before he could help Jack load the camping equipment into the Bronco.

William snapped on his headlights against the gathering dusk. He was starving and looking forward to a full meal at the Kozy Korner Kafé. Both he and Jack were astonished at what awaited them when they arrived in town.

The little town of Jubilee was bursting with people. The whole of the main street was lined with cars. They parked the Bronco on the south edge of town, near the school. The schoolyard itself had become a tent city.

William discovered that hip waders weren't the easiest things to walk in on dry land, forcing him to waddle penguin-like down the sidewalk. On the way to the café they counted cars from Minnesota, Manitoba, Wisconsin, Michigan, and as far away as North Dakota and Quebec. The restaurant was full and noisy with a small crowd waiting for tables. Maggie was running around serving while Denise cooked furiously behind the counter. Maggie hurried over when she saw Jack and William. Her hair was falling down and she hadn't bothered to gather up the stray red-gold strands. She looked tired; there was an air of frazzled distraction about her. It made William feel protective.

"What's going on?" he shouted over the din, surveying the throng of bustling elbows and working jaws as if the place had been overrun by horror-movie insects.

"News of Crazy Crazy's gold got out," Maggie explained. "People have been pouring in from all over. Would you two be dears and give us a hand? Denise and I are both worn out."

William shrugged. "Sure," he said, "what do you want us to do?"

"Jack, could you help Denise? And William, we're running out of dishes; if you could wash some dishes that would be a big help." Maggie led them through the swinging doors into a small kitchen. She gave them each white aprons, quickly showing William how to work the dishwasher.

The next few hours were among the busiest William had ever experienced as he hurried around clearing tables, stacking and unloading the dishwasher, carrying trays of clean dishes to Jack and Denise. He found it exhilarating. The hip waders brought out the comedians in the crowd who shouted comments as he galumphed around the tables. "Caught the fish for my dinner yet?" called one. "Up here in Jubilee, that's formal wear. They call that outfit a tuxedo!" yelled another. William beamed at everyone, clowning a little with the laughter, high on being the centre of attention.

In his mood of silly abandon, William formulated an inspired idea. Making sure everything was under control for a few minutes, he hustled awkwardly back to the Bronco, unlocked the rear door and retrieved the breakfast dishes from the morning. He had packed them still caked with porridge and his brilliant plan was to load them into the café dishwasher and save himself the trouble of scrubbing them at home.

Returning to the restaurant, he pushed open the door

to find his way blocked by a broad swath of grey suit material. The suit wearer turned around as William collided with his back. It was Dink. Beyond him, William could see Tyler Westman sitting on a stool at the counter, his back to Fiona. She balanced on the stool next to him in a tight, black leather mini-dress. Westman had on a brown leather jacket over his rodeo shirt and a tan cowboy hat. Maggie stood beside him, leaning in close to hear what he was saying.

She saw William by the door and waved him over. William edged around a threatening look from Dink and shuffled over to the counter. "This," Maggie said, starry eyed, "is Tyler Westman! We've never had a real movie star in here before!"

"I'll tell you what," Westman crooned to Maggie, "I'll send you an autographed picture to hang on your wall so everyone will know you're a special friend of Tyler Westman." He tapped the tip of her nose, she giggled girlishly in response.

William tightened up inside. "Better see to your customers," he said, indicating a group waiting to pay by the cash register.

"Oh, yes!" Maggie was flustered. "Where's my head at! Excuse me, Mr. Westman!"

As she turned to go, Westman took her hand and, looking directly into her eyes, brought it up to his lips and kissed it. "Call me Ty," he said through an ingratiating smile. Maggie blushed, gave a little tremble, and fluttered away.

William stabbed Westman with his best attempt at a hard look. Westman sneered back, nodding at the hip waders. "Well, Mr. Longwilly. Goin' fishin'? Or are you here to clean out the septic tank?"

"How did you get here?" William tried hard to make it sound like, Why don't you leave?

"Well now," Westman drawled. "Came in a boat. The Zodiac with those big motors is pretty fast. Even then it was after sundown when we reached the dock. Sure was a hell of a place to find in the dark. Dink nearly ruined his suit—and that put him in a bad mood. Won't be pretty for anyone who messes with him." There was a this-town-ain't-big-enough-for-the-two-of-us tone to his voice.

William turned at the touch of a hand on his shoulder. It was Maggie. "William dear, there are tables to clear." She smiled radiantly at Westman as she moved away. William scowled and returned to his work. The waders, which had been the source of so much fun, were now an irritation. He fought their limitations with every step, causing him to stumble and bash into customers. Alone in the back he took them off, chilling his feet on the cold tile floor, soaking his socks in spilled water.

The Kozy Korner usually closed at 8 o'clock, but that night it stayed open until 11, and even then Maggie had to turn people away before she could lock up. Only three customers remained: Tyler Westman, Fiona, and Dink.

Jack and Denise cleaned the grill while William finished the last of the dishes. When William came out of the back, Maggie was sitting at a table talking to Westman. Dink lounged near the door. "—the thing is," Westman was saying, "Fiona, Dink, and me don't have any way of getting around. No wheels, if you know what I mean?"

"Oh! You can borrow my car!" Maggie volunteered. "It's not much, but it runs."

"Why, that's real sweet of you." Westman exuded country-boy charm.

William stood over him. "If you don't have a car, how did you get from the boat landing to here?"

Westman pushed his hat back and smiled, putting on

a show for Maggie. "That was a bit of a puzzle. Up there on the lake, we have a real private little community; a place where people like me can avoid being bothered by fans and the pressures of being a star. We never come into town; we don't want anyone to know who's up there or when. We fly in, fly out, all nice and quiet like. We knew there was a boat dock near the town, but we didn't realize it was way out there in the boonies. Dink nearly crapped himself when he thought he might have to walk!" He laughed.

"So how did you get here?" William repeated.

"Met a man," said Westman, giving William an appraising squint from under the brim of his hat. "Fella has a cabin out there, was nice enough to give us a ride. Harry his name was. Parker, Pecker, Perkins, something like that." He leaned forward and tapped William on the nose the same way he had with Maggie. William didn't giggle. "You're bein' mighty inquisitive there, Mr. Longwilly. Best keep your nose out of places it don't belong." Westman leaned back and smiled.

Denise spoke up as she slipped into a denim jacket and picked up her purse. "I'm leaving now. I was supposed to go see my kids at my mother's tonight, but it's too late to even tuck them in."

"Oh, yes, of course," said Maggie. "Denise, would you be a dear and give me a ride?"

"I'll go with Denise," said Jack. "William, why don't you give Maggie a ride home?"

Maggie retrieved her purse from under the counter and removed a key from her key ring, handing it to Westman. "Here you are. It's the blue Plymouth parked out front there. I think there's gas in it, enough to get you around anyway."

"Why thank you, ma'am." Westman tipped his hat and winked. "I won't forget this." Maggie swooned.

"Let's go, Dink! Fiona! Our chariot awaits!" With a large wave matched by a broad smile as if he were leaving a thousand screaming fans, Tyler Westman breezed out of the Kozy Korner Kafé.

William carried his hip waders, making the journey to his Bronco along the cracked concrete sidewalk in his stocking feet. He also carried the breakfast dishes—in his annoyance with Tyler Westman he had forgotten to wash them after all. As they walked, Maggie chatted about the gold rush and some of the characters she had met in the restaurant, the places they were from, how people from Ontario seemed to be the worst tippers.

"Is this your car?" Maggie asked when they reached the battered black Bronco. There was a touch of surprise in her voice. "It doesn't look like your kind of car. I would have imagined something more sedate."

As he drove Maggie home, William explained how he had acquired the Bronco. Driving in socks was a new experience for William, but he didn't have far to go—nowhere in Jubilee was very far from anywhere else. Maggie's place was on the west side of town; a little frame house, white clapboard, blue trim, a couple of narrow dormers in the roof. The street was dimly lit by the kind of streetlights William hadn't seen since he was a kid: a metal pie plate with a bare incandescent bulb beneath it.

William parked in the gravel drive and sat with the engine idling. Maggie swung her door open and hesitated. "Would you like to come in?"

"Uh, well..." William floundered.

"It's going to take me a while to wind down from the day. I thought maybe we could talk a bit. I could offer you a glass of wine. I know I need one!"

"Ah, um—" William's mind teemed with things to say, but his brain seemed to have become disconnected from his mouth.

Maggie opened the passenger door. "Are you hungry? Did you eat tonight? I could make you something."

William's mouth opened and closed like a stranded fish.

"Okay then," she said, "I guess I'll see you—"

"No, wait," William finally choked out, "um, I'd like to come in."

Maggie tilted her head and smiled warmly. "That's wonderful!" She fumbled in her purse for her keys. The front door opened into a narrow hallway of dingy floral wallpaper. Maggie caught sight of herself in the hall mirror. "Goodness! I do look a fright. I'm surprised I didn't scare half those customers away looking like this." Brushing futilely at the wispy strands of amber hair floating around her face like plasma storms around the sun, she led the way to the kitchen at the end of the hall. The walls were covered with old-fashioned striped wallpaper. The cupboards were dull beige, the paint worn through to the wood around the handles. "You'll have to forgive this place. It needs a lot of fixing up, but I never seem to find the time or the money. The roof needed doing a few years ago and that cleaned me out. And I don't have the incentive living here by myself; I'm used to things the way they are. Do you find that living alone, after a while you stop noticing the flaws?"

"Um, well, um—"

"This was my grandparents' place and then Rick and I lived here, that's my husband. Since he died, it's just been me. Well," her lips pressed together in a dissatisfied line, "there was someone else for a while afterwards, but it didn't work out." As she talked she examined the contents of her refrigerator. "How does an omelette sound? A cheese omelette?"

"Sounds great," was William's contribution to the conversation.

"This should take the chill off; I should have done this first." Maggie stuffed kindling into the firebox of a big old cast iron range and lit it.

"You cook on a woodstove?" William asked. He thought they had gone out with horse-drawn carts.

"Yes, it was my grandmother's; it was all she would cook on. She taught me and I kept on using it. It's not hard once you know how, just takes practice. Like everything else in life, I guess!" She laughed. William allowed himself a polite chuckle. Maggie put on an apron, greased a cast-iron skillet and placed it on the stove, then whisked up half a dozen eggs in a bowl. "Oh! I forgot! The wine's in the fridge; glasses are in the cupboard."

William hunted down a half bottle of Chardonnay and a couple of glasses. He poured wine as Maggie deftly made a fluffy omelette. "My grandparents came over from Iceland. Can you believe it? That's where my colouring comes from. My grandfather always said I had Icelander eyes." She turned her gentle brown eyes on William and smiled. William's breath caught in his throat. He fumbled at replacing the cork in the bottle and knocked it over, catching it before more than a splash spilled.

"Are you uncomfortable here with me?" Maggie asked, holding her spatula like a bouquet of roses.

"Uh, no, no," protested William not very convincingly.

"It's okay," Maggie said, working the omelette with the spatula, "I know what it's like. After Rick died I felt uncomfortable around other men. Guilty, like I was cheating on him or something. They say life goes on;

they don't tell you that death goes on too." She flipped the omelette onto a plate and halved it.

"Jack told me how your husband died," said William. "How did you cope after something like that?"

"Cope?" Maggie put their plates on the table and took a sip of her wine. "I never thought about coping. I just kept on going, kept working at the café."

"Do you miss him?"

"That's the hardest question anyone could ask—and the hardest to answer. You have to get over it or you can't get on with your life, but you can't let go at the same time. I still haven't figured it out." She thought for a moment. "I miss his hairy chest! But I guess what I miss most is what I wanted him to be. I wish that he was more affectionate. I mean, he was a good man, but he had a kind of—I don't know what it was—like if he showed any tenderness it meant he was weak or a sissy or something." She fed more wood into the firebox. "There, we can build this up now the cooking's done; it's still a little chilly in here." Wiping her hands on a cloth, she sat down at the table. "You can't teach ghosts how to love." She picked at her omelette. "Lord knows I've tried."

William sat silently. Somewhere from behind his thoughts he heard Barbara's voice, *You watch yourself! There are women out there who would love to get their hooks into you!*

Maggie sighed and, as she took a bite of her omelette, noticed William's stocking feet. "Oh! I'm sorry! I forgot about your feet, they must be freezing on this floor!"

"No, I'm fine really—" William insisted, but Maggie was already up from the table and out of the room.

She returned with a pair of fleece-lined slippers. "Here, put these on. I'm afraid they're Rick's. Is that all right?"

"Yes, fine." William inserted his cold feet into the slippers. He felt humiliated, wearing another man's slippers while having dinner with his wife.

"How about you?" Maggie asked. "How have you managed since your wife passed away?"

"Barbara. Her name was Barbara," William responded, a little too forcefully. His omelette was growing cold on his plate. He didn't know what to say. Should he tell her that Barbara haunted his thoughts? Should he tell her about running until there was nowhere left to run to? About how inadequate he felt, about being reduced to blubbering jelly in the fog? Ghosts! He could tell her a thing or two about ghosts. "Uh, the same as you, I guess, carrying on from day to day." The lie was in his voice, but Maggie seemed not to hear, or perhaps she heard and understood, letting the lie tell the real truth.

"When Jeff came along, I think I had a relationship with him mostly to prove I was over Rick. I didn't really love him, infatuated maybe, but he was very charming and made me feel wonderful. He could be so romantic," Maggie sighed. "Too bad he was a crook, too! He said he was going to be my business partner, then cleaned out my bank accounts and took off!" She shook her head. "What a weird life."

"Is Tyler Westman charming?" William asked.

Maggie laughed. "Oh! That's just silliness! I don't know why famous people turn our heads. I guess it makes us feel special for a moment."

"He was charming enough to convince you to lend him your car." William regretted the remark as soon as he said it.

Maggie flushed slightly and concentrated on her omelette.

They finished eating in silence. William noticed a

shelf above the table holding a number of small, clay busts. "Those are interesting."

"Oh, they're only studies, practice pieces."

"You made them?"

"Yes, come on, I'll show you." They left the table, relieved to be released from the silence. Off the kitchen, a sun porch had been converted into a sculpture studio. "I actually went to art school, you know, two years in Chicago."

The place was a jumble of shelves lined with figures of birds, animals and people. "These are good." William tried to sound positive instead of surprised. "Do you sell them?"

"Sometimes at fairs and things; mostly they gather dust here."

"Did you ever want to do this for a living?"

Maggie laughed. "I'm one of those people with enough talent to make it look as if I could be an artist— and not enough talent to actually be an artist. Luckily, I realized it as soon as I finished art school. I think I knew I belonged here."

William examined a deer rendered in red clay. "Must be nice to know where you belong."

"I was brought up here and it felt like home. I was raised by my grandparents. They started the restaurant back in the nineteen-thirties when Jubilee was a copper boomtown. I was illegitimate, born out of wedlock, which was quite shocking in those days, still is today, I guess. Funny, people have been having illegitimate children since the Bible, and we still find it shocking. Anyway, my mother moved to Winnipeg and left me with my grandparents." She looked around at the clutter of her life. "So, I traded my artistic career for the glamour of being a restaurateur!"

"You're very talented," said William to Maggie's self-effacing laughter as they returned to the kitchen table.

William shared out the last of the wine; there was less than half a glass each. "Sorry, that's all I have," Maggie apologized. "I'm not used to having company." She put the dishes in the sink. "At least I won't get you drunk and try to seduce you!" she laughed.

William stood up nervously. "Let me help with the dishes."

"Oh no, leave them. You've been doing dishes all night."

William had come up close behind her at the sink. She turned around and looked up into his eyes. They saw each other's loneliness.

"I should go," said William.

Maggie gave him an inquisitive look. "Do you feel guilty?"

William backed away. "What?"

"About your wife's, I mean, about Barbara's death? Do you feel guilty?"

"Well, I—" William's thoughts thudded like doors banging in the wind.

Maggie crossed her arms and looked at the floor. "That's been the hardest thing for me, the guilt." She swallowed. "They said it was a hunting accident—that was the official verdict. Rick was alone in the woods and somehow managed to shoot himself through the forehead. A hunting accident!"

Anxiety gripped William's chest. He couldn't wait to get away. "I should go," he repeated.

Maggie's eyes came back from the distances they had gone to. "Oh, yes, I guess it is kind of late. Life goes on, you know!" she said over a self-conscious laugh.

With a, "Thanks for the food, it was delicious," and Maggie's, "Don't mention it, my pleasure," William plodded down the drab hallway, the wallpaper flowers like menacing eyes. Leaving at that moment felt like a mistake, turning his back on friendship, perhaps even affection, but William couldn't help himself. Slipping off the humiliating slippers by the door, he walked out onto the porch. With a final wave, Maggie shut the door leaving William alone with his choices on the dimly lit street.

As William drove home the fatigue from the long day crept over him. He was practically asleep on his feet when he reached the cabin, carrying his still-damp boots. He was surprised to find Denise ready to leave, her belongings piled beside the door. The bruise under her eye had faded to a soft shadow, as if she hadn't had enough sleep.

"What are you doing?" William asked, muddled.

"Going home," said Denise. "Danny's gone so I'm off to pick up the kids and head home."

"Gone where?"

"Don't know, just cleared out." She paused. "For now, anyway."

"Do you think he'll come back?"

"Probably. When he runs out of money or booze." She leaned forward and kissed William on the cheek. "Thanks for putting me up—or putting up with me!"

William smiled. He felt completely at ease with Denise. In fact, he had never felt so at ease with any woman, not even Barbara. "Jack says the spirits have been kind to me because I helped you."

Denise laughed. "The spirits sent me here to look after you. But, there's no reason for me to stay now that you've dumped me for Maggie."

"No, no!" William protested, disturbed that he

might have hurt her feelings. "I mean—" He blushed furiously.

Denise laughed again and punched him on the shoulder. "Just joking! Come on, help me with this stuff."

As she leaned down to pick up a bag from the floor, William noticed her amethyst pendant swinging on the thong around her neck. "Did Danny ever ask you about amethysts?"

"Huh? Yeah, he did. Why? Something going on?"

"I was curious." William picked up a bag. "Somebody said they overheard Danny talking about amethysts in a bar, that's all."

Denise snorted. "Danny talks about a lot of things—hardly ever says anything though. He has one of those wind-up mouths that keeps talking and talking, at least when he's drinking. I wouldn't put any store in anything Danny says when he's been drinking—which is most of the time." She cocked her head to one side thoughtfully. "You know, he did have a thing about amethysts. He got the idea that there was a deposit around here somewhere, even stole some of mine last year, the ones I use for my jewellery. He'd never admit it, but I know he took them. That's what we argued about the night he punched me. It was another of his get-rich-quick schemes—that usually turn out to be get-broke-quick schemes!"

They carried Denise's belongings out to her truck. She kissed him on the cheek again before she left. "Don't let that Jack push you around!" she warned. "And come see me when you want that dead spirit pulled out of your chest!"

William waved to the taillights as Denise roared off down the drive. The dust was too damp for her tires to raise a farewell cloud. As William walked back inside, he was thinking that Jack would probably move into the room Denise had vacated. He started to wonder where

Jack had been spending his nights. It hadn't even crossed his mind before. He puzzled about it after he went to bed until exhaustion blanked his mind and he dropped into the abyss of sleep.

CHAPTER SEVEN
SATURDAY

Little beams of sunlight seeped through the window and tickled William awake. He rolled heavily out of sleep and fumbled into the living room. The exhilaration of the night before had given way to a numb weakness. He felt as if someone had pulled a plug out of the bottom of his foot and let all his energy drain away.

"Nice pyjamas," Jack called from the kitchen. William stood there in underwear decorated in a delicate pattern of hearts and roses. They had come in the middle of a packet of three, hidden by the plain whites on the outside. With a growl he retreated to the bedroom and pulled on a pair of pants before making his morning pilgrimage to the outhouse. It was unseasonably warm, like a spring day. The lake was a dance of sunlight, the trees seemed to be stretching and yawning.

When he returned to the cabin, Jack had fresh coffee

made. William gulped it down greedily. "It's beautiful out. The weather sure is changeable. Every time we go outside it's different."

Jack agreed. "It's the time of year. Indians have a word for it: *nainauwahshee*."

"What does that mean?"

"The-time-of-changeable-weather," Jack deadpanned. He sipped from his cup and stared out through the kitchen window. "Thought we'd drive into town today."

William shook his head wearily. "Not today. I'm beat. I want to stay home, enjoy the sunshine." He drank more coffee.

"Maggie might need help at the café. Hate to think of her struggling away there all by herself."

William groaned, scratching the stubble on his chin. "Give me a few minutes to get ready."

Maggie wasn't there when they arrived at the restaurant. People William had never seen before were working the grill and serving tables. He and Jack were late enough to have missed most of the breakfast rush. A young blonde woman served them coffee at the counter and took their orders for breakfast.

William cleared his throat several times as if wanting to say something; whatever words were there kept jamming in his throat. After the waitress brought their food he was finally able to force out, "What do people around here do when they want to get together with someone?"

Jack shrugged. "Go and see them."

"I mean, there aren't any movies, or anything."

"Oh," said Jack, catching the drift, "you mean, like a date?"

"Um, not exactly, I was just thinking—"

"Thinking about Maggie, eh?"

"Uh, yes, I mean, I can't very well ask her out to dinner since she runs the only restaurant in town."

"Bowling," Jack intoned solemnly into his coffee cup.

"Bowling?"

"Yep. Take her bowling. There're lanes down at Fayette." Jack winked. "Be careful though. Around here, people consider bowling as foreplay."

"You can't be serious." Bowling was the least romantic thing William could imagine.

Jack shrugged again. "You'll find out. If you can't bowl you don't stand a chance. Come on, let's go." Finishing his breakfast, he slipped off his stool, leaving a confused William to pay.

William caught up with Jack outside the Jack o' Clubs Hotel. Across the street the warriors' huge white Lincoln looked like a cruise ship that had been ravaged by pirates. One of them sat on the hood. Jack went over and spoke to him. William stayed a good distance away. The two of them looked directly into each other's eyes as they talked. To William's relief, the warrior didn't even glance toward him. Jack crossed over and went into the hotel.

"What are we doing here?" William asked, following.

"Going to see those geologists." Jack took the stairs like a bird rising over a ridge.

William followed slowly, stopping to rest at the landing. "How do you know they're here?"

"The warriors have been keeping an eye on them for me." The worn carpet of the upper hallway was dimly lit by sconces of low-watt bulbs shaped like candle flames. Jack knocked on a door, raising a gruff, "Who is it?" from inside.

"Your fairy godmother," answered Jack. The door

opened a crack, barely wide enough for a single bloodshot eye to peer through. Jack pushed hard on the door, bringing a sharp cry the owner of the eye. Jack and William walked inside.

The Jack o' Clubs was an old hotel from the boom days; the room looked like it still had the original wallpaper. There were two beds, both messed up. A bottle of Canadian Club and some dirty glasses cluttered the nightstand. Beside the door, backpacks and aluminum cases, the kind used to carry delicate instruments, were piled in an untidy heap. Steve Mason stood behind the door with a hand to his nose. Frank Happer was at the foot of one of the beds looking nervous. They both seemed tired and dishevelled, and maybe a little hungover.

"Tell me about the gold," said Jack.

"What gold?" Mason feigned innocence. Happer darted him a nervous glance.

"George Ferris was found dead a few days ago," Jack said grimly.

"What do you mean? He's dead?" Mason's surprise appeared genuine. A little, high-pitched whine leaked out of Happer.

"He was killed out in the bush," said Jack. "Could be you had something to do with it."

That drew a reaction. "No, no," they both denied at once. "We haven't even seen George," said Mason. "Not since—when?—" he shot a glance at Happer for confirmation "—since last year when we hired him as a guide. We didn't even know he was missing until you told us, didn't know he was dead until now. Why would you think we had anything to do with George?"

Jack made an impatient frown. "We were up there yesterday, by your camp."

Steve Mason's eyes narrowed; Happer's eyes opened wide with terror.

"So?" Mason's voice was hard as granite.

"So," Jack explained, "we know George was up there too. He took something from your camp. He used an ATV to do it; it must have been too heavy for a man to carry alone. You followed his trail down to Eagle Lake."

Mason's face was blank. Happer sat on the bed, gnawing at a thumbnail.

Jack looked from one to the other "You radioed Billy Dawes to fly you out; then George turns up dead and his crazy friend suddenly finds the mother lode." Jack paused. "George Ferris was murdered. We found the body. Somebody split his head open with a rock. You tell me why we think you had something to do with it."

No one said a word. Mason looked defiant. Happer chewed his nails.

"Why did George raid your camp?" Jack's tone was firm.

"Shit!" exclaimed Happer. "We'd better tell him—"

"Shut up!" Mason shouted. "We didn't kill anybody. We have nothing to tell."

Jack remained calm. "You'd better talk if you want to get out of here." He nodded toward the window. "Have you seen those guys hanging around outside?"

"You mean the ones in that white car? They've been following us everywhere."

"They won't let you leave until I say so. And I won't say so until you tell me what George took from your camp."

Mason became agitated. "Who do you think you are? You can't keep us here!"

Jack maintained his composure. "So call a cop."

Mason's excitement increased. "There's a bus out of here tonight and we're supposed to be on it. We'd be gone now if that damn plane hadn't broken down." He tried to pace, but the room was too small. He ended up doing a frustrated pirouette. "We even tried chartering a plane from Thunder Bay, but they said this was Rainbow Airlines' route and they wouldn't fly it."

"Tell him, Steve," said Happer. "We have to be on that bus tonight. This is the only way."

"Shit!" Mason folded his hands in front of his chest as if in prayer. "You promise you'll let us leave if I tell you?" Jack nodded. "Okay. First, we didn't kill anybody. We didn't even see George; we didn't know it was him who took the—took the stuff. We thought it might have been him, but didn't know for sure." He sat down on the bed, trapped, defeated. "Last year we did a mineral survey of the ridge up there by Stillwater Lake." He licked his lips. "You've heard of Bre-x? It was a gold claim in the Philippines. They falsified the records and submitted phoney ore samples. It looked great on paper and investors bought shares like crazy. By the time people realized it was a scam, the con artists had made off with millions. Hundreds of millions."

"And you thought you could do the same thing?" asked Jack.

Mason sighed. "The geology was perfect. Everything I told you before about the rock formations was true. There should have been gold there. We surveyed the place pretty thoroughly last year, but couldn't find a trace of gold. Not a placer, not a vein, nothing. The geology is exactly the same as around the Holsum mine; it's the same greenstone belt. No one would be able to tell the difference between samples from Holsum and samples from Ghostwalker Ridge." His right hand formed into a fist. "We were so damn close!"

"You were going to salt the area with gold-bearing ore?" Jack asked.

Mason nodded. "That was the plan. We brought it in

with us, in a box marked GEIGER COUNTER. We planned this last year. It took us all last winter to gather the ore samples, filched most of them from Holsum and Red Lake. Our idea was to strike the claim in the late fall, but keep it quiet until the winter snow set in. That way, when we made the announcement and presented the ore samples, no one would be able to confirm the strike until next spring. By then we would be long gone with the money." He spread his hands in a gesture of modesty. "Not on the same scale as Bre-x, of course, just enough for us to retire on a tropical island somewhere, our own little piece of paradise, live the good life." His face reflected the pain of his loss. "The beauty of it, the thing that made it believable, was that there was already a legend of a lost gold mine up here, some old story of The Last Waltz Mine. We thought, with that provenance, people would invest even before the claim had been verified."

"So you could rip them off?" challenged William.

Mason shrugged.

"But George had ideas of his own? He took the gold samples from your camp?" Jack prompted.

"Yeah, I guess so," Mason agreed. "He must have figured out what we were up to, overheard us talking about it or something; I honestly don't know how he found out." He took a deep breath. "As soon as we discovered that the ore samples were missing, we knew our plans were blown. After that, all we wanted to do was get as far away from here as we could, before anyone connected us with the gold."

"Did you tell anyone after the ore was stolen?" asked William. "Did you call anybody on the radio?"

Mason shook his head. "No, we didn't tell anybody. We radioed for the plane to pick us up, that's all."

"You didn't call an accomplice, someone who could

have intercepted George and killed him?" William wasn't sure if Mason was telling the whole story.

Mason looked over at Happer.

"No," he said definitely. "We didn't have an accomplice. We acted alone." Mason's expression was defiant again.

Silence hung in the room like a piñata, with Jack holding the stick. "Well," he said at last, "you can be on your way. Come on, William, let's go."

"Wait a minute!" William put his hands up like a referee. "What about the amethysts?"

The other three looked at him. "What?"

"The amethysts," William repeated. "We thought you'd found an amethyst deposit and that George was somehow involved..."

Mason knitted his brows, perplexed. "No, there weren't any amethysts. We used that as a cover story, saying we were looking for amethysts. There never were any amethysts."

Jack jerked his head to motion William to follow and walked out the door, which closed quickly behind them.

"I'm confused," said William, following Jack down the stairs. "Danny and Andy and George were all looking for amethysts—and the geologists said they were too. How did you know about the gold?"

"Well," Jack chuckled, "I've never heard of anyone getting amethyst fever."

William felt more muddled than ever. "Let me get this straight. The geologists had gold ore with them up on Ghostwalker Ridge and George stole it. But what did he do with it? There wasn't any gold with him in the cave." He mulled it over. "Crazy Crazy! He has the gold! It was the ore George stole that he showed Doug Trimble. He must have killed George for it."

"Could be," said Jack. "As far as I know, he hasn't told anyone where the gold came from. The warrior I talked to told me nobody's seen him since he came into town that day; he seems to have disappeared."

"Should we call the police?" William asked.

"What for?"

"To tell them about Crazy Crazy."

Jack shook his head dismissively. "We don't know that he killed George. It's only one possibility among many."

"It all fits, don't you see?" William grew excited as his ideas came together. "The ore was too heavy for George to carry himself, so he had Crazy Crazy help him take it from the boat landing, maybe they put it in George's truck and drove it somewhere, then—"

Jack shook his head again. "You're getting ahead of yourself. If George had Crazy Crazy to help him, why did he go to all the trouble of taking his ATV over the ice to Eagle Lake? And if he was using his truck to move the gold, how did it end up back at his cabin where Lance and Caroline found it? No, there are too many unanswered questions to point the finger at Crazy Crazy."

William gave a dissatisfied grunt. "Well, what about the geologists? They were planning a major stock fraud. Shouldn't we tell the police about them?"

"They didn't hurt anybody." Jack shrugged.

"But conspiracy to commit a crime is still a crime," William reminded him. "And they could have been lying about the accomplice." He grabbed Jack's sleeve to stop him. "Wait a minute! Billy Dawes! The geologists radioed to Billy to pick them up, he could have gone after George, or called someone else—"

Jack cut him off with a laugh. "Lake Superior is more likely to dry up than for Billy Dawes to be mixed up in something like that."

As they left the hotel, Jack paused to talk to the warrior again. The warrior nodded and Jack headed back toward the Bronco with William in tow.

"You acted pretty tough in there," said William. "Especially when you pushed your way into the room."

Jack laughed. "Yeah, I've seen some of Tyler Westman's movies. Think his agent will call me?" Jack climbed into the truck and tilted his head back onto the headrest.

"What do we do now?" William asked.

"Let's go see Caroline and Lance," Jack said. "We'll find out if they knew what George was up to."

The sunshine lifted William's spirits. He hummed to himself in time with the bumps from the potholes as they drove out to see Caroline and Lance. George's truck wasn't there when they arrived. It was Caroline who answered their knock. "Yes?" she asked guardedly. In the glare of the sunlight, with no makeup, hair lank and dull, William was struck by how ordinary she looked. He wondered where her beauty had gone.

"Hi," said Jack. "You remember us, don't you? Jack and William? Can we talk to you for a minute?"

"What about?"

"About George; about your father."

"What about him?"

"We found out about something he was mixed up in, maybe it had something to do with how he died."

Caroline blinked hesitantly. "Okay, come in."

Inside, the cabin was a single room; half of it covered by a loft built under the rafters, accessed by a rickety wooden ladder. A few small, threadbare scatter rugs lay on the rough plank floor. In one corner, beside a potbellied stove, sat an old school desk and a beat-up chest of drawers. Everything in the place looked cracked, broken, or patched. Wooden chairs were held together by wire and nails. An unmade sofa bed took up most of the downstairs floor space.

Caroline rubbed her hands nervously on her jeans. "Can you help me fold this up?" she indicated the sofa bed. "I can't do it myself and Lance isn't here..." Her voice faded into an embarrassed silence. The three of them struggled to heave the stiff metal frame, lumpy mattress and rumpled sheets back into the sofa. Caroline replaced the worn cushions. "Please, sit down. Can I get you some coffee or something?"

"I'd love some coffee," said William, hoping that resorting to social conventions would help her feel more at ease. He sat down gingerly on a rickety chair.

"Tell me about Daddy." Beside the sink stood a Coleman two-burner camp stove; Caroline lit it and put a kettle on.

"There were a couple of geologists working up north of here," Jack explained, "at a place called Stillwater Lake. A couple of con artists. They planned a scam to stake a phoney gold claim, then run off with the investors' money. Looks like George was mixed up in it somehow."

"Gold! So that's what he was up to. The silly old fool! Just like Daddy, to get involved in some wild scheme and end up the loser." She leaned on the sink and shook her head.

"You didn't know anything about this?" Jack watched her reaction carefully.

"No. I suspected something, but I had no idea what." She looked out of the small, grimy window above the sink. "It's just like Daddy. He was always mixed up in something that ended up hurting him. And now this." She began to cry quietly.

William fidgeted, unsure if he should try to comfort her.

"I'm sorry," she said, "I'm okay, really." She pulled out a tissue, wiped her eyes and demurely blew her nose. "Before he came here, Daddy used to be a guide out in Alberta, he'd take rich Americans into the Rocky Mountains after bighorns and grizzlies. Some of them would pay him extra, a lot extra, to take them into the provincial parks where the hunting was better, but also illegal. Of course he got caught. The men who hired him said they had no idea they were inside the park boundaries, that Daddy had taken them there on his own. He lost his licence and his territory. When he settled up here I was so glad. There didn't seem to be any trouble for him to get into. Trust Daddy to find some." She began crying again. "God, I need a smoke." Taking a cigarette from a pack on the counter, she lit it with shaking hands.

"Where's Lance?" Jack asked.

Caroline gave a little choking laugh through her tears, as if she were trying to express several emotions at once. "Who knows where Lance is? Lance leads his own life. Comes and goes as he pleases. He is Lance Rockwell, after all, the actor." Bitterness was the emotion that won out.

William threw Jack a concerned look. Caroline's feelings were a minefield he didn't want to venture into.

Jack was unfazed. "Did Lance know anything about this? You said George called and asked you to come up."

Caroline poured hot water over instant coffee in chipped enamel mugs. She handed them to William and Jack, offering sugar and artificial creamer. William wondered what kinds of stories those mugs had to tell. Jack had told him of George and Crazy Crazy's drunken binges. He envisioned empty bottles, lights left burning over passed-out bodies on the floor. These mugs are like all of us, he thought. Chipped emotions, damaged people. He thought about what would have happened if he had turned to drinking after Barbara died. Where would he be now?

Caroline's voice brought him back into the room. "—don't know what happened," she was saying, inhaling smoke. "Lance wouldn't tell me anyway. I knew something was going on, because, well, we had some debts, some bad debts—we owed some not very nice people. Lance told me we would be able to pay them off soon, but didn't say how." She sat on the sofa, holding her coffee cup in both hands, staring into it. "Lance probably thought he was protecting me, the big goof." She seemed mesmerized by the coffee, never lifting her eyes from the cup. Smoke drifted idly from the cigarette in her right hand. "You've no idea what it's been like, what kind of life we've lived. When we first went to California it was great, we met some people and got invited to parties; even though we were broke we lived the high life. Everything was free. The drugs and liquor at the parties, all free. Someone let us stay in their place for free. Our new friends gave us expensive clothes because you can't be taken seriously in Hollywood unless you dress the part. Then someone set Lance up with an agent, he landed a small role in a daytime soap and everything looked fantastic, our dreams finally coming true." She lifted the cigarette to her lips without raising her eyes.

William sipped his coffee. It tasted bitter.

Caroline continued talking into the liquid darkness in her cup, smoke curling out of the corners of her mouth around her words. "The next thing we knew, people started asking us for money. We owed back rent on the place we were staying in. The clothes weren't free, we had to pay for those. And the cocaine, too. Not that we were big users or anything, at least I wasn't; Lance used it way more than me. And so suddenly we were in debt up to our yin-yangs. Our dreams came crashing down around our ears. Lance tried for another agent, but as soon as anyone found out who we'd been involved with they wouldn't touch us. Everyone knew the score except us, we were just too naïve. We actually thought Lance got parts because he was a talented actor." She leaned her head back and looked up into the rafters. "God, what fools we were. Lance had a few small parts, mostly in made-for-TV movies, but never earned enough to pay off the debt, which kept growing bigger and bigger. We had to do whatever these people said. We were slaves. Then Lance became secretive. He'd disappear for days at a time, wouldn't tell me where he'd been or what he'd been doing. Me, they mostly used as a courier. I'd deliver packages, I don't know what was in them. *Scripts* they called them. Delivering scripts. Yeah, right." She took another drag on the cigarette.

"Sometimes I was a driver. I'd chauffeur three or four starlets to parties, bachelor parties, stag parties, that sort of thing." Her untouched coffee captured her gaze again. "I could see what was coming. I was being introduced to the scene, groomed as a party girl. It wouldn't be long before I'd be in the back seat of the limo in a twenty-five-hundred-dollar dress and no panties on my way to a bachelor party." Sadness seemed to crush her down to a small and vulnerable child.

"Did George know what was going on? Did he know about your debt?" Jack's voice was soft as a down comforter.

Caroline shook her head. "I don't know, I don't think so. I didn't tell him and I don't think Lance did." She sighed. "Daddy and I weren't close. My parents separated when I was a baby; I grew up with my mother in Calgary. I didn't see much of Daddy growing up; he lived by himself in the mountains. I only really started to get to know him after Mommy died. He was the only family I had left." Tears puddled at the corners of her eyes, but didn't fall. "And I worried about him. I knew he was a big drinker, and Mommy died of liver cirrhosis." She stood up, pouring her cold coffee down the sink, looking through the window. "You know, I think Lance thought that if he did whatever they wanted he could keep me out of it. That's why he doesn't tell me anything: he's trying to keep me safe. The big goof."

Jack's voice was so quiet it was almost part of the silence. "Do you know Tyler Westman?"

Caroline added rage to her emotional brew. "Ty Westman! That piece-of-shit bastard! He's the one—" Anger swallowed her words like a dragon devouring virgins.

"Did Lance know a man called Crazy Crazy?" Jack asked.

Caroline couldn't speak through her fury. She shook her head in answer.

"How about Andy Polsky? Or Danny Burke?"

She stared through the window. "Here's Lance now. Ask him yourself." She crushed out her cigarette.

A truck door slammed and Lance Rockwell entered the cabin.

"What the hell are you doing here?" was his way of saying hello.

"They came to talk to me about Daddy!" Caroline practically screamed at him.

Lance matched her anger glare for glare. "What about him?"

"He was mixed up in some kind of gold-mine scam."

Lance's blue eyes danced like gas flames. "Get the

fuck out of here!" He made for Jack as if to grab him and physically throw him out the door.

"Lance!" Caroline screeched. "They're trying to help us!"

"Help us what?" Lance bellowed. "Get nailed for a murder rap?"

Caroline froze. "What?"

Lance wavered, then smiled; his acting training coming to the fore. "It's nothin', honey," he said in a cool drawl. "Nothin' at all. Why don't you boys leave?" He jerked his head toward the door. Jack and William stood up.

"No!" Caroline screamed. "I want to know! I want to know what's going on!"

Lance put his hands on her shoulders, lowering his head to look into her eyes. "It's nothin', hon, nothin' at all. I'll take care of it, okay? Trust me."

Caroline batted his hands away. "You had something to do with it, didn't you? You had something to do with Daddy's death. Did you kill him? Was it you? Did you do it?"

"Darlin', calm down—"

"No! I won't calm down! Lance, I want to know. I want to know *now*!" Her whole body was trembling, totally past any self-control. "If you don't tell me I'll call the fucking police myself! Do you hear me! I'll call them myself!"

Lance tried to take her in his arms, she pushed away from him. He flared at Jack. "See what you've done? Shit, I could have taken care of this!" He paced the small floor. "Look, it's not what you think. I didn't kill George. He called—" Lance groped for an explanation. He took a cigarette from the package on the counter and lit it. "Last fall I called him up, I wanted to see if we could make some money. We were broke and I saw this article in a magazine about how bear parts were being sold on the black market for thousands of dollars; I figured there must be bears up here and if George could hunt the bears, I could sell the parts and pay off our debt." Lance ran a hand through his hair. "He called me back and said he knew of something better than bear parts, something that would make us all rich; we'd never have to worry about money again. Said he'd found a lost gold mine, but I had to keep quiet about it." He looked at Caroline. "I told Ty."

"You told Ty! Are you crazy?" Caroline's words raked him like fingernails.

"I had to tell him something! He had us in his pocket and I wanted out. I told him we'd be able to pay him off, but Ty wanted part of the action—that was his price for letting us off the hook, he wanted his percentage. So last winter we came up here, Ty and me. He took me to his cabin, we had to land the plane on the fucking ice. George came up, too. He came on a snowmobile over the frozen lake." Lance stuck the cigarette in his mouth like he was trying to hurt himself.

"When was this? When were you up here?" Caroline demanded.

"Last winter. After the shoot for that slasher movie, remember that? We were on location in Chicago. As soon as my scenes were done, Ty flew me up." Lance paced again. "George laid out his plan for Ty. He said he had found this lost gold mine, The Last Waltz Mine; a very small seam of pure gold. But it was such a small seam, and had already been partly mined, that we wouldn't get much out of it. George had another idea; we could take the ore from the mine and spread it over a wider area and then sell the claims and make millions. He already had a place picked out. I'm not sure where it was; he said he was prospecting for amethysts and found this cave that would be the perfect place to store the gold, somewhere near a tree stump or something—"

"Hellbent Stump," William provided.

"Yeah, something like that. There was a lot of technical stuff about filing the claims and everything. George said he already had someone lined up to take care of that end of it. Ty wanted to send his own people up, but George said he wouldn't work with anyone except me, said he'd call when he was ready for me to come up. And then we left."

"He called again last week?" Jack prompted.

"Yeah, he called; Caroline and I came up. He told me where and when to meet him, over at the boat landing on the next lake. His truck was here at the cabin and I drove over there and he came in by boat with a box marked GEIGER COUNTER. We threw his tent and stuff into the back of the truck, then George and I carried the box through the woods; bitch of a thing to carry. On the way he told me how he'd broken into Ty's cabin, the one we'd met in, and spent the night there. He laughed about it, thought it was a great joke. We carried the box to the top of a hill and he showed me a hole and said it was the opening to the cave. He rigged a rope up on the box to lower it into the cave and," Lance glanced at Caroline, "as we were moving the box into position, he slipped, he just slipped—it was an accident—"

Caroline erupted. "It was you! It was you! You bastard!"

Lance lunged forward to hold her. "No! He was still alive. He—"

Caroline evaded his grasp and ran for the door.

"Caroline!" Lance called. He tossed his cigarette into the sink and ran after her. Jack and William followed. Caroline was nowhere to be seen outside. Lance yelled her name, swore and jumped into George's truck, spinning the tires in a dusty turn as he drove off, his head out the window, calling, "Caroline! Caroline!"

Jack and William remained on the porch watching the dust settle. They waited for nearly half an hour, neither one speaking. No one came back. "What should we do now?" William asked.

"I think we should return that camping stuff we borrowed," said Jack.

William was troubled by Lance's story. "Shouldn't we call the police?"

Jack shook his head. "You are one for calling the cops, aren't you?"

"Well," William began, but Jack wasn't listening, he was already walking toward the Bronco.

They spent the next couple of hours driving around returning the camping gear. As before, William stayed in the truck while Jack approached the dogs. William had forgotten to wash the porridge pot and asked Jack to apologize profusely to the owner. All through the trip, Lance's story festered in William's mind. He tried to piece it together with the geologists' story; with Crazy Crazy finding gold; with Andy Polsky and Danny and the amethysts. When they had returned the last of the equipment, William asked, "Should we go and see if Caroline's all right?"

"Good idea," Jack agreed.

George's cabin was deserted when they arrived. They waited around for a few minutes before heading home. As they drew near to William's place, they could see George's truck parked outside. William and Jack looked at each other as they pulled up behind it. They rounded the corner of the cabin and stopped. William's breath became short, his heart raced, he felt faint. Face down on the ground beside the front door lay the body of a man. He was lying in a pool of blood.

Jack bent down and searched for a pulse. "He's dead," he pronounced. It was Lance Rockwell.

The cabin door was wide open. Lying across the threshold, as if hastily dropped, was a rifle. Jack stepped around the body, over the rifle, and into the cabin. William walked, rubber legged, back to the Bronco and leaned on the fender.

After a short time, when William's breathing was nearly back to normal, Jack came over and put a hand on his shoulder. "No one in there," he said. "Now you can call the police."

William started to say that they would have to go into town; then remembered his own phone. He had been waiting for his service to be connected and hadn't tried it for days. At the front door he took a deep breath and, closing his eyes, edged past the body into the cabin. Tiptoeing across to the telephone, he used the sleeve of his jacket to pick up the receiver the way he had seen the police do it in the movies. A dial tone buzzed in his ear. Punching 9-1-1, his voice trembled as he said to the person who answered, "I'd like to report a murder."

William and Jack sat in the Bronco waiting for the police. The cab was warm in the afternoon sun. It was a long wait.

"What shall we say?" William asked. He felt a little spacey.

"Say anything you want," Jack replied.

"I remember," William chose his words carefully, "when you talked to them about finding George you didn't say anything about him being murdered. Or about Crazy Crazy shooting at us. Maybe we should get our stories straight."

"In my experience," began Jack, "it's better to say as

little as possible where the police are concerned. Answer their questions and tell the truth; don't offer any information they don't ask for."

"You've been in trouble with the police before?"

A complex look passed over Jack's face. "When I was young I did some stupid stuff. Mostly out of anger—maybe hatred, maybe frustration. I was so hurt by what had been done to my people that I wanted to hurt back." His mouth set hard, then softened slightly. "Eventually I realized that I was getting hurt more than I was hurting; I decided I had to try another way. I went back to school, earned my master's degree and landed a teaching position at Northern University. I was going to change the world." His face collapsed into sadness, perhaps defeat. "But the world changed me instead." He looked into the distance. "Yeah, I've been in trouble with the police before."

William didn't feel very confident about his ability to stand up under questioning. "I don't think I'm ready for this."

"You'll do fine," said Jack. "The spirit from that cave will help you. It will be fine."

The whole situation felt unreal to William, sitting there in his truck, sunshine falling on the windshield, a dead body lying on the ground. "Who did this?"

The muscles in Jack's face worked, as if he should have an answer but didn't. He shrugged. "I don't know."

"Tyler Westman." The name popped out of William's mouth.

"How do you figure that?"

"Well, he comes into town one day and the next day Lance ends up dead. Lance owed him money. Maybe they argued and Westman killed him, or had Dink do it."

"Could have been Caroline."

"Caroline?" That would never have occurred to William.

"Sure. She ran away, she came over here, Lance caught up with her and she shot him."

William couldn't believe it was Caroline. His mind ran over other possibilities. Crazy Crazy? The geologists? Was Lance killed by the same person who murdered George? What if the geologists had radioed down to Tyler Westman to tell him that the gold had been stolen and Westman had followed George and Lance to Hellbent Stump, killing first George and later Lance to cover his tracks? Tyler Westman, the gunfighter—how big a step was it from acting with guns to using them? William remembered the prowler the warriors had scared off. "Didn't you have the warriors watching this place?"

"Only when we were here," explained Jack.

William thought things over. "We missed lunch," he said.

Jack laughed out loud.

They waited.

Eventually the police arrived. First, a white Explorer with an O.P.P. crest on the door pulled up, light-rack flashing, the squawk of the radio echoing off the trees. It took a long time before one of the officers approached the Bronco.

"Hey, there," he gave Jack and William a nod. It was Ray Selkirk. "You reported a body?"

"Yes. It's around the front." William pointed to the cabin.

"Please remain in your vehicle," Selkirk said politely. He signalled to his partner, Constable Shaw, and they went around to the front together, returning to the Explorer a few moments later. Selkirk spoke into the radio.

They waited.

Soon, more cars showed up, some marked, some unmarked; there were people everywhere. There must have been a pattern or purpose to the activity; to William it looked like random movement. Uniformed and plainclothed police walked back and forth around the front of the cabin, some casually, some hurriedly. They hovered around George's old, blue pickup truck.

William's bladder was beginning to send urgent messages. A man and a woman in white shirts with dark blue epaulettes went by with a wheeled stretcher covered with a grey blanket. William reached his threshold of discomfort. Leaving the Bronco, he walked to the outhouse. He made it back to the Bronco without anyone taking any notice.

After what seemed like hours the stretcher-bearers retraced their steps, only this time a shape huddled under the grey blanket. They struggled with the heavy stretcher on the rough ground. A young man in a black topcoat came over and formally asked Jack and William their names. He wrote them down in a notebook. "You reported the body?" he asked. They confirmed that they had. "Would you come with me, please?" His tone was polite, but he wasn't giving them a choice. William felt his stomach jump. This was it.

The cabin was full of people. Some were making notes, some talked on cell phones, most appeared to be milling around aimlessly. William and Jack were escorted over to the kitchen table where a man in a blue suit and brown topcoat sat.

"You are—" he read their names out of his notebook. "Okay," he continued, "we need statements from the two of you—"

"Who are you?" interrupted Jack.

The man raised his eyebrows as if it were an unusual

question. "I'm Detective Inspector Bremner of the O.P.P. Criminal Investigation Branch."

Ray Selkirk came over and said something quietly into Detective Inspector Bremner's ear. Bremner regarded William and Jack suspiciously. "You're the guys who reported finding a body a few days ago?" They acknowledged that they were indeed the guys. Bremner thought for a minute, then signalled the young man in the black topcoat to come over. "This is Detective Sergeant Adams," said Bremner. He gave William a no-nonsense look, "You go with Adams." He pointed to Jack, "You come with me."

Adams directed William into William's own bedroom. Jack and Bremner went into the other. As William perched on the edge of his unmade bed, he was suddenly filled with panic at the notion that they might think he did it.

"Tell me what happened," invited Adams, moving a pile of books off a chair and sitting down. He had a neat, Mel Gibson haircut. Nervousness tightened William's throat. He stutteringly told about arriving home and finding the body. Adams wrote it all down in his notebook. "Did you know the deceased?"

"Slightly. He was the son-in-law of the other man we found, George Ferris."

Adams wrote. "Ah yes, we received the report; we planned to question you again about that; we were waiting for instructions from headquarters. Tell me about it."

Anxious monkeys with ice-cold fingers jumped up and down William's spine. His words twisted and came out backwards. As he struggled for coherence, William was aware of Adams' doubting frown.

"Seems odd that you should find two bodies in just

a couple of days, and one of them in your own home. What do you have to say about that?"

William didn't have an explanation.

Adams nodded thoughtfully, his pen poised over his notebook. "When you discovered the body, the front door was open, is that correct?"

"Yes."

"There was no sign of forced entry. How do you suppose the perpetrator gained access to your cabin?"

"I don't know. I must have forgotten to lock the door."

"Are you normally so forgetful?"

William couldn't answer.

Adams spent a few minutes flipping back through the pages of his notebook. "You seem nervous, Mr. Longstaffe. Do you have anything to be nervous about?"

"Uh, no. I'm not used to this, finding bodies, being questioned by the police, um—" Without prompting, William launched into a garbled account of the connection between Lance Rockwell, George Ferris, Tyler Westman, and the gold scam.

Adams tapped his pencil against his book. "That's all for now," he said, as if he knew there was something he should have asked, but couldn't think of what it was. "Thank you for your co-operation. If you will wait here for a moment." He left the room.

After Adams left, William realized he was clasping his hands so tightly they hurt. He stood up and shook them out. Taking a deep breath, he looked out of the window at the gathering dusk. Would they believe him? Would they arrest him? Barbara's voice came out of the shadows, *You get yourself into these situations and rely on me to rescue you; well, I'm sick of it!* William closed his eyes, and sighed.

A few minutes later Adams opened the bedroom

door. "Detective Inspector Bremner would like to talk to you."

In the front room, Jack was waiting by the front door. Bremner stood at the table with another man in a white shirt and narrow black tie. "We need to take your fingerprints," he said flatly. Noticing William's look of panic, he added in a more conciliatory tone, "to differentiate your fingerprints from the perpetrator's. This is, of course, completely voluntary on your part and can only be done with your consent, but your co-operation—or lack of it—will be noted."

The man in the white shirt pressed William's fingertips one by one onto an inked pad and then onto cards on which William's name was already filled out. Another pile of cards sat on the table marked with Jack's name. When he was finished, the fingerprint man handed William a plastic squirt bottle. "You can wipe your hands. This will take the ink off." His hands were still a dull grey after scrubbing with a paper towel soaked in the cleaning solution.

"You can leave now," said Bremner. William choked with relief. He wasn't going to be arrested. "Don't go far, we'll have more questions for you later," Bremner added. "Is there somewhere you can stay the night?"

William tensed again. It hadn't occurred to him that he wouldn't be able to stay in the cabin. Jack came to the rescue. "We'll stay at Denise's place. My sister's."

"Where's that?" Bremner asked, taking out his notebook. Jack gave directions. Bremner wrote them down and looked confused. "Well, somebody'll know where it is," he said, flipping the notebook shut. He told a young constable to take them to their vehicle.

By the time they stepped outside, it was full dark. A corridor of yellow POLICE LINE tape led to the road; it looked like a police auction parking lot, completely blocked by vehicles. William's Bronco was boxed in. Video cameras and microphones appeared out of the darkness as they were besieged by reporters. William shielded his eyes against the glare of the lights.

"What can you tell us?" they shouted one over the other. "Is it true that the dead man is Lance Rockwell?"

Jack smiled and waved at the cameras. William was flustered. "I don't have anything to say," he mumbled.

The constable took them back inside and talked to Bremner, who sighed and shook his head. "Leave the keys to your vehicle and I'll have someone deliver it to you as soon as the road is clear." William handed over his keys. "Okay," Bremner said to the constable, "drive them where they want to go."

Outside, the reporters surrounded them again, peppering questions, pushing microphones. Jack kept smiling and waving. William wanted to pull his coat over his head.

"You people keep back!" the constable yelled, with no noticeable effect. Jack and William followed him down the drive until they reached the last police car in the line. Behind it were three or four vans belonging to the news people. "Move your vehicles!" the constable shouted again.

One of the reporters shoved a microphone up to his face. "Are these men under arrest?"

"Move your vehicles now!" the constable ordered, opening the back door of a police car for Jack and William. A steel grill separated them from the driver. There were no handles on the insides of the doors.

Engines started as the reporters squeezed their vehicles hard over into the brush on the side of the narrow road. There was barely enough room for the police car to squeeze by.

"Take us to the Kozy Korner Kafé," Jack called out

in a friendly tone. The constable didn't answer. The radio squawked intermittently on the way into town. Pulling up outside the café, he opened the back door for William and Jack. "Thank you!" said Jack cheerily. "Don't forget to tell Detective Inspector Bremner where to bring our truck!" The constable made a screeching U-turn, then raced away to the north. "Maybe we should have given him a tip," said Jack.

A van pulled up and reporters piled out. They pounced again.

"I'm sorry," William said, irritated. "We don't have any information for you. You will have to talk to the police."

"But sir—" An aggressive woman pushed a microphone forward.

William was losing his patience. "I can't tell you anything. Please, leave us alone."

Jack smiled and waved again as they went into the café. The reporters, mercifully, didn't follow.

As William and Jack entered, everyone in the restaurant looked up, their attention drawn by the commotion raised by the reporters. Jack smiled and William hung his head. Except for a few persistent rubber-neckers, the crowd quickly lost interest when they realized the excitement was over.

The café seemed quieter than the night before. The young blonde woman they had seen earlier was serving and a young man with long black hair tied back in a ponytail worked the grill beside Denise. Maggie had disappeared into the back on William and Jack's arrival. She reappeared a few moments later and hurried over to where they sat at a recently vacated table. "Hello, you two," she said brightly. She had put on a clean apron, brushed her hair, added a glisten of fresh lipstick and a whiff of perfume.

"Need any extra help tonight?" asked Jack playfully.

Maggie laughed. "Not tonight! I managed to call in some extra people to help out; it was only last night that the rush took us by surprise. But I have your number taped to my phone in case of emergency!" She touched William on the shoulder and smiled with sparkling eyes as she left them with menus.

"How did the questioning go?" William asked Jack.

Jack chuckled. "I don't think he believed a word I said. How about you?"

"I think I confused him," William said. In a safe place, relieved at being released, William allowed himself a quiet laugh. "It was pretty funny now that I think about it. I was really nervous and everything I said was mixed-up; I think he even forgot what we were supposed to be talking about." He laughed, then quickly sobered. He felt bad about laughing while Lance lay dead.

"Don't worry," Jack said. "Those spirits of the dead, they like laughter. It helps them on their journey. Gravity is only for the living."

Maggie came to take their order.

"Did you hear about Lance Rockwell?" Jack asked her.

Maggie drew in a breath and put a hand over her open mouth. "Oh my word, I'd forgotten, and everyone's been talking about it! I've been so busy. You're the ones who found him, aren't you? You poor dears! Are you all right? What a shock it must have been!" She made a funny little shuffling motion as if torn between talking to William and looking after the other customers.

"We'll tell you about it later," said William. He ordered toast and camomile tea for his jumpy nerves. Jack wanted a hot beef sandwich. Maggie lightly touched William's shoulder again as she bustled away. William's eyes followed her the same way they had followed the naked Fiona up the stairs.

"Maggie sure looks nice tonight," Jack observed.

William blushed and changed the subject. "Have you thought more about who killed Lance?" he asked. Jack's face was inscrutable. William guessed what he was thinking. "You're going into the spirit world to ask your helping spirits, aren't you?"

Jack smiled. "You're learning. We'll find out what the spirit helpers say first. Everything else is idle speculation."

It was hard for William to believe that the man he was talking to about the spirit world had once been a university philosophy lecturer. "How do you reconcile the spirit world with your philosophy background?"

Jack was mildly surprised by the question, but there was a sadness about him as well. "It's all the same," he said. "Different philosophies give different world views, different approaches to life. The spirit world is another way of approaching reality. Western philosophy is based on the intellect, on reason. The spirit world is based on experience. In this world," he knocked on the table, "what is important is what you think and what you believe. In the spirit world, none of that is important. All that matters is your experience."

"And truth," William added.

Jack smiled, melancholy colouring the edges of him. "Yes, and truth."

"What made you leave philosophy behind and seek out the spirit world in the first place?"

Maggie appeared with their food. Beside William's toast she placed a chicken salad sandwich. "In case you needed a little more," she said before being called away to another table.

"I wanted," Jack began and hesitated, "I needed—"

A light steam rose from his meal, miraging his features. "I made a mistake," he said. "I went too fast. There is a path to follow for those entering the spirit world. But I couldn't wait. In my intellectual conceit I thought I knew everything, I thought I could take a shortcut. Anton, my teacher, warned me, but I wouldn't listen. Instead of avoiding the destructive spirits, I went to them. That's how I met Wendigo. Now I can't escape him." A lost look clouded his eyes. "I didn't—" He sighed. "It's no accident that these deaths occurred here. It's because of Wendigo. Wendigo will always bring death to my door."

"You mean, Lance was killed because of Wendigo? And George?"

"No, Wendigo didn't cause the deaths, but the fact they happened around me, that's Wendigo's doing."

William munched. As Jack talked, he had eaten all the toast and half the chicken salad sandwich. "You should eat," he told Jack. "Your food's getting cold." Jack nodded and started on his meal. William finished his sandwich and sipped his tea. His mind churned over Lance's murder and the links to George Ferris, unable to sort it out. He felt like someone lost in a strange city, wandering in circles through unfamiliar streets.

When Jack finished eating he said, "Come on, we'd better tell Denise she has house guests."

Jack spoke to Denise over the counter while William told Maggie where they were staying. Maggie said she would try and come over after she closed up.

They had to wait for William's Bronco to arrive. Since Maggie was too busy to sit and talk, William went for a walk around the town. The reporters were gone. The walk didn't take long. Jubilee was not a big town. He passed the General Store, the tiny one-teller bank, the hunting and fishing outfitters, the community hall, Drake's Garage, a snowmobile and outboard motor repair shop, a church. The tavern at the Jack o' Clubs Hotel was loud and full to overflowing; people, beer glasses in hand, spilled onto the sidewalk outside. William walked out to the school at the south end of town. Tents and trailers were pressed up hard against each other, the tents glowing softly in the darkness from their internal lights. Muffled guitars and singing came from some of the trailers. William kept going until he was beyond any human sound. He craned his head back and looked at the sky. The moon had not yet risen and the stars twinkled above him like so many missed moments of happiness. When he and Barbara were young, their love was as strong as the gravity that held the planets in their orbits. But Barbara was gone, and any chance of love. The futility of life ran its cool fingers through his hair. "Barbara!" he called into the night, "let me go!" No answer came from the shadows of the trees, nor from the wind, nor the unrisen moon. William stood in the chill darkness, waiting, but could hear no answer to his plea.

Eventually, feeling empty and alone, William turned back toward the wilderness of people. By the time he reached the café, his vehicle was parked out front. The last customer had left. Maggie and Denise and their helpers were cleaning up. Jack was waiting by the door. He tossed William his keys. "Ready to roll?"

William looked for Maggie. She was at the counter, gathering the cash out of the register. He gazed across at her. It seemed too impersonal to wave good-bye from the doorway, but walking over seemed so obvious. His body twisted in indecision, feet pointed to the door, shoulders turned toward the counter. He untangled his feet and marched across the room, painfully aware that everyone was watching him. "We're leaving for Denise's," he announced when he reached the counter, standing next to Maggie, sensing her perfume, watching the light play in her auburn hair.

"Okay," she said expectantly, leaving the way open for him to say more.

"Well, see you later." William practically ran for the door.

"Smooth move," said Jack as they climbed into the Bronco. William growled.

They drove north out of town, past the Rainbow Lake road, past the Trout Lake Road, past any sign of habitation. Jack pointed to the left. William slowed and turned onto a dirt road. The headlights swept a sign identifying Iron Lake Reserve. They passed rows of small square houses with lighted windows. Jack gave directions to a little bungalow at the end of a road. It didn't have a foundation; the house sat on stacked concrete blocks. The side of the house where they parked was painted pink; the front was sky blue.

Jack knocked and the door was opened by a young girl in Raggedy Ann pyjamas. "Uncle Jack!" she squealed, throwing her arms around him in a joyous hug. A boy, a few years older, appeared behind her, equally delighted to see Jack. A Border collie nosed into the excitement, tail wagging frantically.

They entered directly into a small living room with a beat-up couch and armchair, a scarred coffee table and a TV. A decorated Christmas tree sparkled in one corner and Christmas lights winked around the window. Jack saw William's look of surprise.

"You like the decorations?" he asked with a playful smile.

"Isn't it a bit early for Christmas?"

"Momma likes them!" piped up the girl. She sat on the floor and hugged the collie. "Has them up all year 'round. Says it makes the place look cheery."

"Ah," William responded. "And what's your name?"

"Jessie!" she said with a giggle and a grin. She had Denise's long raven-black hair.

"I'm Toby," said the boy.

"This is Muffin!" Jessie waved the dog's paw to say hello.

"My name's William," he introduced himself.

"Are you going to be our new daddy?" Jessie asked.

William was flabbergasted. Jack threw his head back in a full-throated laugh.

"Momma said Danny was gone," continued Jessie seriously. "We need a new daddy."

Jack picked her up and gave her a hug. "William's not your new daddy. He's just going to stay here tonight."

"You too?" Jesse was excited. "Like, a sleepover?"

"Yes," agreed Jack, "like a sleepover. Shouldn't you be in bed by now? It's awful late."

"Momma said we could stay up till she came home," Toby informed them authoritatively.

"Nice house," said William politely, settling on the creaky couch.

"Momma says one day the wind's going to blow it over," Jessie informed him with delight, as if she couldn't wait for the adventure.

"Why is it up on blocks?" William asked, concerned for his safety.

"It was Danny!" shrieked Jessie.

"Yeah! Danny did it!" Toby agreed.

Jack laughed. "That's Danny's doing all right. Danny moved in with Denise, but Danny can't live on the reserve because he's white. He was working on a road crew over on the highway and one day he brought the whole crew over with all their equipment and they moved the house down the road off reserve land. They stacked it up on those concrete blocks, hooked up plumbing and wiring, then left it. Danny always said he was going to put a proper foundation under it; I guess he hasn't had the time yet." He went into the kitchen.

Jessie shrugged in a hopeless gesture. "And now Danny's gone, so it'll *never* be fixed!" She jumped on the couch and cuddled next to William. The dog scrambled up beside her. "Read me a story?" she whispered timidly.

"Okay," said William.

With a shriek of delight, Jessie slid off the couch and gathered up a pile of books from under the Christmas tree. They spilled behind her as she hurried across the room and dumped them on the couch beside William. "Read this!" She held up an illustrated copy of *Anne of Green Gables*.

The sound of a car came from outside. William looked out the window to see Denise's truck pull up. A minute later, Denise and Maggie came into the house.

"You two!" were Denise's first words. "Bed! Now!"

With a few groans of, "Aw, Momma," and final hugs for Jack, Jessie, and Toby scurried off to bed, Muffin the dog trotting behind.

Denise went to tuck in the kids. Maggie moved Jessie's books, sat on the couch beside William and placed her hand in his. He stared down at their nestled palms. He didn't know what to do. Should he just let her hand lie in his, or should he hold it tightly, give it a squeeze? Jack rescued him from his indecision by returning from the kitchen with steaming cups of pale, clear tea. "*Maskikik*," he said. "Medicine. Help you sleep."

William extricated himself from Maggie's grasp to

accept his cup in both hands. Denise came in and collapsed into the easy chair. "Boy, that was a long day. I'm beat!"

Maggie wanted to know everything that had happened. William patiently recounted the events of the last few days, the trip to Eagle Lake, the meeting with the geologists, culminating in the discovery of Lance's body. Maggie shook her head. "Who could have done such a thing? And why on earth did they do it at your house? It's unbelievable; it doesn't seem real."

No one had an answer. Maggie sighed. "So the whole gold rush is a fake! What a disappointment! All those people coming from all over. I had someone in the restaurant today from Arizona. Can you believe it? Arizona." She thought for a moment. "You know, we should just have a big party and send everyone home."

Denise brightened. "Yeah! We could rent the community hall like we did for the Jubilee Day Dance last summer! Hire a band—"

The two of them quickly sketched a plan for a Gold Rush Ball.

"When?"

"Dunno. Couple of days to arrange the bookings; how about next Saturday?"

"Okay, let's do it!" Maggie concluded.

The couch creaked as William shifted uncomfortably. He sipped his tea. It tasted like grass.

"I'd better be off," said Maggie. "Another long day tomorrow. Denise, will you drive me home?"

"I'll take you," offered William.

"Oh! That would be nice." Maggie took leave of Denise and Jack and joined William in the Bronco. The highway lay before them like an awkward silence. When the tension finally overflowed, they both spoke at once. "You know—", "That was—", Maggie had the grace to laugh, but William lapsed into a foolish silence. He realized he didn't know how to act around Maggie. After years of having Barbara direct his every move, he felt at a loss on his own. Words echoed around inside him, too faintly for any sound to make it out of his mouth.

"I didn't have a chance to ask you how you felt after … you know, after finding Lance." Maggie's voice was gentle as an old love song.

"Oh, um, okay, I guess. I mean, it was a shock, uh, made me feel kind of queasy."

"Well, I think you're very brave."

"Brave?" That was a term no one had ever applied to William.

"Yes. I mean, you left everything behind and moved up here, then find yourself mixed up in these deaths. I'm not sure how I would cope with all that; certainly not as well as you seem to be doing."

"I don't know how well I'm doing; I haven't managed things very well. Even moving up here wasn't a well-planned decision; I didn't prepare properly like I should have. I can't focus on my book; I just wander around, following Jack without any direction of my own. I feel like I've run out of places to run to, like I've gone beyond some kind of limit, like on old maps where they'd fill in the blank spaces with *here be monsters*."

"Do you plan to stay here? Or will you go back to Toronto?"

William sighed at the petty complications of his life. "I don't have anywhere to go back to. I sold my house to my son. He and his wife needed a place, so I put the house in his name. He pays me a little every month, I thought it would provide me with some income to supplement my pension and help him out…" He knew he was rambling and blew away the unsaid words with a sigh. "I don't know what I'm going to do right now.

Wait and see what happens, I suppose." His own words irritated him like spiny beetles crawling in his ear. Was he really such a victim of circumstance? Had he ever been anything else?

"I know how hard it is to go out into the world," Maggie commiserated. "You'd think I'd be used to it, all those years in a restaurant, but every day it's a struggle." William's self-pity had touched her own. "Every day I see myself in the mirror and wonder, Who wants to look at me?"

William was astounded at this admission. "What do you mean?"

"Well, look at me." She gave self-deprecating laugh. "I'm hardly Gwyneth Paltrow. With my body all you need is a net and some sand and you could have a game of beach volleyball."

They reached Jubilee and William drove to Maggie's house.

"There's nothing wrong with the way you look." He searched for a compliment. Unused to caring for anyone else's feelings, he could only utter a lame, "I think you're beautiful."

Maggie laughed. She leaned over and kissed him on the cheek. "And I think you're amazing!" She jumped out of the truck, her Good-night! lost in the slam of the door. William left his headlights on the front of the house until, with a final wave, she went inside.

Amazing, William repeated to himself on the way back to Iron Lake. Maybe, he hoped, there's a chance for a new life after all.

Denise and Jack were talking quietly in the living room when William returned. The Christmas lights reflected in Denise's hair, filling it with colour. "Where's the Big Chief going to sleep?" she asked Jack.

"William can have the couch," decided Jack. "I'll take the floor."

Denise fetched a couple of tattered sleeping bags, then left Jack and William to look after themselves. The couch creaked and groaned as William lay down.

Sleep was next to impossible. Every time William moved, the couch let out a squeal. Even when he did manage to doze off, the complaining couch woke him whenever he rolled over. His mind teemed with images of Maggie, Lance, Barbara, Tyler Westman, Toronto, the naked Fiona. Finally, he decided to give up on sleep; at that moment he drifted off.

CHAPTER EIGHT
SUNDAY

William opened his eyes to the faint grey of early dawn. Light came from the kitchen, accompanied by the murmur of soft voices. The dog stood beside the couch watching him, tail wagging.

William went into the kitchen, Muffin padding at his heels. Jack sat at a rickety old chrome-legged kitchen table with a flecked yellow Formica top. At the stove, Denise stirred porridge in an enamel pot. She wore her blue housecoat and big fluffy slippers. She glanced at William and said something in her native tongue. Jack smiled.

"You want some porridge?" he asked.

William nodded yes and sat down. Denise set three bowls on the table, one plastic and the other two mismatched stoneware. She ladled porridge into the bowls and generously sprinkled brown sugar on top. Jack took a handful of spoons out of a drawer. They were all different sizes and patterns. William's had a bent handle. He tried to straighten it, but couldn't untwist the obstinate metal.

"No one's ever been able to straighten that spoon!" Jack chuckled. "We always give it to the guest. Legend has it that the man who can straighten that spoon is the man Denise will marry!"

William flushed. "What about, uh, Danny; isn't he—"

Denise spoke in her own language again. "Denise says," Jack interpreted, "that Danny could only straighten one thing, and it wasn't that spoon!" He laughed out loud.

A sleepy Jessie shuffled into the kitchen, trailing a blanket behind her. She climbed onto Jack's lap and buried her head in his chest. He cradled her tenderly. Muffin nosed her toes.

Their heads turned simultaneously to the sound of vehicles outside. At a knock on the front door, Jack and Denise exchanged a perplexed glance. Muffin ran ahead as Denise went to answer it. A man's voice tersely asked for William and Jack. Jack slid out from under Jessie, leaving her curled on the chair. In the living room they found Bremner and Adams at the door with two uniformed constables.

"William Longstaffe," Bremner said, his voice flat, expressionless, "you are under arrest for the murder of Lance Rockwell." He turned to Jack. "Jack Crowfoot, you are under arrest as an accessory to the murder of Lance Rockwell. Please come quietly." The dog woofed playfully, wagging her tail.

During the ride to Fayette, William's initial shock gave way to depression. Bremner's declaration had so overwhelmed him that he was hardly aware of being handcuffed and bundled into the back of a police car. It felt like a dream, his mind wouldn't admit that he had been arrested.

Jack and William were taken down in separate cars. The Fayette O.P.P. station was a low, nondescript brick building. They were escorted through the back, into a short hallway of white painted concrete blocks with two doors marked Washrooms on the left and three steel doors on the right. They were not what William expected to find in a jail: ordinary fireproof doors with narrow windows of wire-reinforced glass; exactly, William noted ironically, like the classroom doors at the university. A constable opened one door and prodded Jack through it, before opening another door and standing aside to let William walk into his cell. The constable removed the handcuffs, then asked William for his belt and shoelaces. The door closed and William heard the lock click. There was no handle on the inside. A smell of strong disinfectant overlaid lingering odours of vomit and urine. William's stomach dropped like a runaway elevator.

The cell was small, the walls unpainted concrete block. Rough greyness oppressed him from all sides. Fastened to one wall was a bunk with a foam mattress covered in a stained, striped material. A window of wire-reinforced glass high up in the back wall admitted a dim haze, as if the daylight were afraid to enter. A recessed light bulb protected by a metal guard shone from the centre of the ceiling. William sat down on the bunk and waited.

Every once in a while a face appeared briefly at the window in the door, studied him, then disappeared.

After a time that wasn't quite long enough for William to catch up to his plunging stomach, the door opened. He was handcuffed and led to the front office, where a corporal completed the arrest forms. William answered the questions dully. Out of his numb mind a thought struggled up. "Shouldn't I have a lawyer?" he asked. The corporal informed him that Detective Inspector Bremner was in charge of the case and William could ask him when he came in. William wasn't sure if he was within his rights to insist. He decided to shut up and wait.

On the way back to his cell he was allowed to use the washroom across the hall. Going to the bathroom wearing handcuffs while a police officer watched was the most humiliating experience of his life.

Once more in the cell with his handcuffs removed, William stood behind the locked door, head bowed, his body drooping as if the gravity in that little room was several times stronger than anywhere else on earth. He had no idea how long he had been standing there when the door opened and a young constable stuck his head in. "We're getting sandwiches for lunch. What do you want?"

William was stunned. He hadn't even thought about food. In prison movies, the closest William had ever been to incarceration, the inmates were given a metal plate with a dollop of mush on it. "Um, uh, tuna fish on whole wheat."

The constable wrote it down. "And to drink?"

He needed something tranquillizing. "Uh, herb tea; maybe camomile."

"One camomile herb tea. Won't be long." He turned to leave.

"Wait!" William called. He looked down, embarrassed. "What if I have to use the washroom?"

"Bang on the door; someone will take you across the

hall. These are just holding cells while we wait for transport to Thunder Bay, so they don't have their own facilities. Government cutbacks." The door closed, the lock turning with a decisive click.

A little later lunch arrived. It came in a paper bag with PHIL'S SANDWICH SHACK printed on the side. Underneath it said, Home of Phil's World Famous I-Wish-I-Had-One Double Decker Sub! William sat on the bunk and started to eat Phil's lunch. His stomach was in such a knot that he could only manage a few bites. He sipped the tea. It didn't help.

William felt grubby and smelly. There had been no chance to wash up that morning or to change his clothes. He was sweaty from the tension.

The door opened. Handcuffed once more, he was led to an interview room. Detective Inspector Bremner sat at a small table. William took the chair across from him.

"Now, Mr. Longstaffe, there are some very serious charges against you. You have been arrested for the murder of Mr. Lance Rockwell."

"Shouldn't I have a lawyer?" William made a timid attempt to assert his rights.

"You'll get your chance to speak to a lawyer. Right now you have some questions to answer. The way I figure it, you were in with George Ferris on this gold scam. Then, for some reason, you decided you couldn't trust or didn't need George anymore, so you killed him out in the woods where you thought the body would never be found."

"But we told you about finding George's body."

Bremner ignored the interruption. "George had already called in Lance Rockwell, his son-in-law. That's probably why you killed George, you were afraid he would tell too many people about the scheme and blow it before you had a chance to cash in. Perhaps Lance

Rockwell knew you had killed George and was blackmailing you, so you killed him."

"That's preposterous!" William shouted. He was bewildered. Bremner's story made a kind of evil sense. William didn't know where to start to correct him.

"Is it?" Bremner asked sternly. "Where were you yesterday, Mr. Longstaffe?"

"I was with Jack, we went to return the camping gear he borrowed." The words stuck to his tongue like half-licked postage stamps.

"And can you identify any of the locations you visited?"

"No. I followed Jack's directions, I don't know the area well, I went where he told me."

"So you can't account for your whereabouts at the time of the murder?"

"I can, I told you!"

"Can anyone besides Mr. Crowfoot confirm your presence at any of the locations?" Bremner asked.

William swallowed. "No. I stayed in the truck because of the dogs."

Bremner looked at him skeptically. "The door to your cabin was open, but there was no forced entry. How—?"

"I explained that! I must have forgotten to lock it!"

"Come on, Mr. Longstaffe, a school kid could come up with a better story!"

William ground his teeth.

Bremner leaned forward. "We have other evidence, Mr. Longstaffe. Very damning evidence indeed." He paused dramatically. "We found your fingerprints on the rifle, the gun that was recovered at the scene and is believed to be the murder weapon."

William felt an ice-cold hand grip his heart. "That's

impossible! I never touched the gun! You're making this up!"

"I wish I were, Mr. Longstaffe," said Bremner gravely.

William launched into an incoherent self-defence, panic leaping around inside him. Rambling, repeating himself until, all talked out, he lapsed into a defeated silence. He didn't think they had believed him before, and he didn't think anyone would believe him now.

Bremner listened unblinking before signalling the guard to take William to his cell. This time the handcuffs were left on. William paced back and forth beside the bunk while his mind went over everything—what had happened, what had been said, what left out. His panic, once on the loose, could not be contained. It prowled the cell with him like an angry tiger.

William thought over what Bremner had said. Were his fingerprints really on the rifle? He didn't remember touching it, but had he? He went over the scene at the cabin. No, he had gone inside to use the phone, but he hadn't touched the gun. He had never handled a firearm in his life, so how could his fingerprints be on the gun that killed Lance Rockwell? Bremner must be lying. But why? What could he possibly gain by inventing evidence? Unless, for some ulterior motive, Bremner wanted him in jail and invented the fingerprints as an excuse. Maybe Bremner was in on the gold scam and wanted him and Jack out of the way!

William shook his head and dismissed the thought as imagination fuelled by desperation. Yet there had to be a way out. Could he turn invisible? Could he call on the spirit from the cave to help him? But Jack had been arrested too, so the spirit world didn't seem to be helping him much. William paced.

He banged on the door to call a guard to take him to

the bathroom. No one came. He banged again and yelled. It took a while, but a constable finally came and took him across the hall. It was just as humiliating as before.

Returning to the cell, William sat on the bunk and tried to calm down. What could he tell Bremner to convince him of his innocence? What did he actually know? He ran through the sequence of events in his mind.

The year before, Lance had talked to George about ways of making money. George somehow knew about the geologists' gold fraud scheme. He planned to steal their samples of gold-bearing ore and took his ATV up to Eagle Lake in the winter in preparation for their return. He discussed his plans with Lance and Tyler Westman at the Eagle Lake cabin, without mentioning the geologists. After George raided the geologists' camp, he and Lance carried the gold ore to Hellbent Stump. There George fell and broke his leg, then someone killed him. Who? Lance? Andy Polsky? Crazy Crazy?

And what happened to the gold? Crazy Crazy found it, but where?

Lance was the key to everything. If Lance hadn't killed George, he must have known who did. Lance was murdered to keep him silent. Who else knew that Lance was involved in the gold fraud with George Ferris? William returned to the thoughts he had before, thoughts about Tyler Westman. Lance had said that Westman wanted part of the action; maybe he wanted all of it. Everything William could think of pointed to only one person: the gunslinger actor, Tyler Westman.

A nerve-wracking hour later, a corporal came and took William back to the interview room. He sat across from Bremner, his cuffed hands clasped tightly on the table. He twitched with tension.

"I know who did it," William blurted out. "And why."

Bremner stared at him, not saying anything.

William was sweating. He hunched forward tensely. "Tyler Westman," he revealed.

Bremner continued to stare at him without a word.

"You see..." William explained his reasoning. In conclusion, he added, "He probably killed George as well."

Bremner stared at him in silence for a few moments longer, then cleared his throat. "After the interview with Detective Sergeant Adams at your cabin, we checked up on Tyler Westman." Bremner tapped the file in front of him. "He didn't arrive here until after you reported the discovery of George Ferris's body; we have the flight records from Thunder Bay. Therefore, he couldn't have killed George Ferris."

William looked down at his clasped hands.

"As for any connection with Lance Rockwell, he will be interviewed." Bremner put his head back and stared at the ceiling. "I'll be straight with you, Mr. Longstaffe." His forehead furrowed as if he had not yet completely made up his mind. "We could keep you overnight. But—" he leaned forward and looked straight into William's eyes, holding his gaze for a long moment before speaking "—we're letting you go. Charges dropped."

"What!" William froze warily.

Bremner leaned back again, looking pleased with himself. "The evidence we had to link you to the murder was the fingerprints. Partials of your fingerprints were found on the weapon; that's why we issued the arrest warrant. However, further analysis has shown that the prints may not have resulted from your handling of the weapon; they may have been transferred to it by person or persons unknown."

"I—I—" Each of William's teeth seemed to be moving

independently. His mouth couldn't form the words. "I don't understand. How could anyone do that?"

"It's quite simple really. There are special materials for it; however, you can do it with ordinary sticky tape. All you need is a source. Were there any unwashed cups or glasses left around your place yesterday morning?"

"I don't remember. There could have been."

"Our theory is that after using the weapon, the perpetrator entered the premises and found a used glass or coffee mug. He, or she, then used some tape to pick up the prints from the source. By putting the tape on the weapon, your prints were transferred onto it."

"Oh my God!" William exclaimed. A feeling of relief began to creep through him.

"The rifle wasn't registered. We're checking on it, but don't expect to find anything. The prints were suspect from the beginning, actually," continued Bremner. "The placement was all wrong. There were prints where there shouldn't have been any and none where they should have been. But it wasn't until the tests came back today showing traces of the tape gum that we knew for sure. We have someone at your house right now trying to identify where the prints were lifted from, in case the perpetrator left any prints of his or her own."

"You knew the prints were suspect, yet you arrested me anyway?" William's mood was a tangle of relief, excitement, fear, and anger.

"Your involvement in this matter was, and still is, very suspicious. I'll admit it's all circumstantial at the moment; there are, however, a lot of other charges we could hold you on if we wished. You knew of the geologists' conspiracy to defraud, but didn't tell anyone. That could be aiding and abetting. There's also interfering with a police investigation, among other things. Yes, we have enough to put you away."

"But you're not going to?" The words held equal parts of hope and suspicion.

Bremner nodded thoughtfully. "We'll see. Depends on how co-operative you are. You help us with the investigation and we'll see how it goes from there. Now, let's review your story again."

William gave a suspicious look. "You knew the fingerprints were false before you brought me in here. Why did you accuse me of murdering Lance?"

"We couldn't be sure until the proper tests on the fingerprints were carried out. And, as I said, you remain under suspicion. For all we know, you were the one who transferred your own prints to the weapon to make it look as if someone else were trying to implicate you. I was just shaking the tree to see what fell out."

"And what did fall out?"

"Not much." He paused and gave William a piercing look before adding, "Yet."

William dropped his eyes. "That's why you didn't want me to have a lawyer. You never intended to press the charges."

"It's Sunday, Mr. Longstaffe," Bremner said. "Lawyers don't work on Sunday." He consulted his notes. "Now, we have to go over this once more."

William held up his hands. "Do we need the handcuffs?"

Bremner scraped his chair back, opened the door and yelled something down the hall. A constable came in and removed the handcuffs. "Okay," Bremner sat down, "let's start at the beginning." William went over the whole thing again. In detail. Over and over.

For the cell door to finally open, to be allowed to walk out without handcuffs, was to William like being raised up out of a wheelchair by a faith healer, a miracle of incomprehensible dimension. Grinning stupidly, he went to the front desk to recover his shoelaces and belt.

There he encountered one more surprise: Caroline Rockwell. She turned lost eyes on William, seeming not to recognize him. She looked as forlorn as a stray dog. William greeted her cautiously, not sure what kind of reception he would receive.

"Oh, hi," she said, with a failed attempt at a smile.

"What are you doing here?"

"They picked me up this morning and brought me here. I've been answering questions." Her eyes moved randomly, as if searching for something to hold her attention.

"Are they letting you go?"

"Yes, I think, I—" Her sentence crumbled into an inaudible mumble.

"Come, on," said William, after collecting his things, "let's get out of here." He took Caroline's elbow and walked her to the door. With every step the tension in his neck and shoulders hardened into an armour of muscle. With every step he expected a voice to call from behind him, "Mr. Longstaffe, one more thing—", starting a sequence of intrigues that would lead back to the cell, back to locked doors and dim windows. William grasped the handle of the front door and pulled it open. He wanted to run, to make a final dash, but he let Caroline go first before walking through himself and hearing the door swish closed behind him. William stood on the step and breathed deeply.

Car doors opened in the parking lot and reporters sprang out with tape recorders and cameras. William realized he had no idea how he was going to get home. His grip on Caroline's elbow tightened as he prepared to stand his ground against the onslaught of reporters when he noticed someone waving off to the right. There was a big white car with two figures beside it, Denise and Maggie. "Come on!" he barked to Caroline and hustled her across the lot.

They reached the car seconds ahead of the reporters. The mufflerless engine was already rumbling as Caroline and William jumped into the back seat. Denise dropped her heavy foot on the gas pedal and spun the wheel at the same time, sending the land yacht into a slewing turn out of the parking lot, north onto the highway.

Maggie was in the front with Denise. Jack was already in the rear seat. William sighed and leaned back into the torn upholstery.

Maggie asked, "Are you all right?"

"Yes, I guess—no—I don't know..." The acceleration of the car flattened William against the seat.

"Well, we'll have you home soon. How are you, Caroline?"

"I'm okay," she said in a lost voice to match her lost eyes.

"We've been waiting all day," said Denise. "We came down here this morning and waited for you. They told us they were holding you here until they could arrange to transfer you down to Thunder Bay, but I talked to my Grandmother Flora and she told me they would let you out today, so we waited."

"Weren't we lucky to get this car?" Maggie's eyes shone with excitement. "Tyler Westman still has my car and we couldn't all fit in Denise's truck, so she borrowed this for us."

"On loan from the warriors," Denise smiled into the rear view mirror. "They warned me not to scratch it!"

"And you've been on TV!" Maggie announced. "The reporters were in town to cover the gold rush and having a local murder was like a gold mine to them!" She caught herself. "Oh! I'm sorry, Caroline! How thoughtless of me!"

"It's okay," Caroline whispered.

Maggie chattered to cover her embarrassment. "It's because Lance Rockwell was once in a daytime soap opera that this has really made the news. It was that one, *Heart of the City*, right, Caroline? It takes place in City Hall, all the goings on in the mayor's office. I don't think I ever saw it, I never have time to watch daytime TV, although I have been thinking of putting a TV in the restaurant, you know, over the counter."

William turned to Jack. "When did they let you out?"

"A few minutes before you."

They didn't need to say more. The deadness in their voices summed up the whole experience. William put on his belt and began to re-thread his laces.

"Caroline, dear," Maggie looked over the back of the seat, "what happened? How did you end up here?"

Tears bloomed at the corners of Caroline's eyes. She swallowed them back with a trembling breath. "When I ran away yesterday, I ran into the woods. I could hear Lance calling, but I just ran." She dropped her eyes. "I got lost, I guess. I finally came to the lake and followed the shore back to the cabin. There was no one there. I grabbed my purse and walked into town along the highway. I saw a bus outside the hotel and bought a ticket; it took me down to Thunder Bay, but that used up all my cash and my credit cards were maxed out. I didn't know where to go; I wandered around, ended up at a marina down by the water." Her voice grew softer. "I felt somehow that being near water would help me. The marina gate was locked, but the fence was torn down on one side. I climbed over and walked around listening to the sound of my footsteps on the wooden dock, to the sounds of the boats rocking, of water lapping on the pilings. I found a boat with a motor on the back and it felt like, if I could be out on the water everything would be all right; so I untied the boat, started the motor and went out on the lake. It was dark. Looking back, I could see the lights on the shore and it seemed that if I could run farther away all the bad things would be left behind. So I kept on going until the city was nothing but a little glow on the horizon. I shut off the motor and sat there in the dark." Her words faded to a whisper. "I thought that if I could slip into the water, everything would be okay; it would solve everything. I put my hand over the side of the boat; the water was cold, so cold, but it felt soothing. I stood up to step over the side and lost my balance. I fell back into the boat and banged my elbow; it hurt. I lay there holding my elbow, looking up at the stars; they were so beautiful. It seemed as though they had a message for me, as if their twinkle sent some sort of code that I could understand if I watched long enough. So I watched; watched the stars; watched the moon come up; everything looked beautiful. It was a cold night, but I didn't feel cold, I felt protected, safe. I stayed there all night. When the sun came up I started back toward the shore, but ran out of gas." Tension crept into her voice again. "I didn't know what to do. I thought of trying to swim to shore, but I'm not a good swimmer. Then the Harbour Patrol boat came and picked me up. The police brought me up here, asked me questions about Daddy and Lance." Her voice rose with up-welling emotion. "They told me Lance was dead. They took me to identify his body." Tears strayed down her cheeks, feeling their way tentatively, like blind people in a strange room.

William took her hand; she cried silently, unaware of his touch. The Town Car rumbled north.

Denise drove to George's cabin to drop off Caroline. "Do you need someone to stay with you?" Maggie asked as Caroline slid her hand out of William's. "Or, would you like to come and stay with me for a while?"

"No, I'll be okay, really." Caroline imitated a brave smile.

"I don't think you should be alone," William interjected.

"I need to be alone, that's best right now." Caroline climbed out of the car. "Thanks for the ride." She shut the door and went into the cabin.

"Poor dear," said Maggie. "I hope she'll be all right."

Poor dear, thought William. It seemed cold comfort, after all she had been through, to be called a poor dear.

"Your truck's still at my place," Denise said to William over the back of the seat. "Do you want to get your truck now, or do you want to go home first? You can't stay at your place, the cops have it sealed off as a crime scene, but maybe you can pick up some stuff, a change of clothes or something."

"Take me to the truck." His voice had a bite that surprised even himself.

Denise cranked the wheel and drove toward Iron Lake.

As they turned off the highway at the Iron Lake Reserve, Jack asked William, "You want to hike out into the woods tomorrow?"

"No, I don't," William snarled. "I'm not going anywhere." William's emotions, worn thin by his anxious morning at the police station and by Caroline's story, were at the breaking point.

"The cave where we found George's body needs to be purified. We have to cleanse the death out of it." Jack paused as if waiting for William to say something. "The harmony is disturbed," Jack added "The spirit in that cave is not very happy, that's why you were arrested, that's why—"

William's brittle emotions snapped. "Jack, I'm not going anywhere with you, now or ever, understand? I don't want anything more to do with you. Since you came along I've been shot at, found two dead bodies, and been arrested for murder. That's enough. I can't take anymore. So leave me alone, okay?"

As Denise pulled up to the house, the car was not even at a full stop before William had his door open. He ran to his own vehicle.

"William?" Maggie called after him, "where are you going?"

"I'm going home!" he yelled back, louder than necessary.

"I don't think you can. The police—"

"Well, too fucking bad!" he screamed, wrenching open the driver's door and climbing in. The Bronco roared to life, tires spinning in the gravel as William pulled away. If he had looked in the rear-view mirror, he would have seen three startled figures staring after him through the obscuring dust. He kept his eyes straight ahead as he hurtled out of their lives.

When William arrived home, the first thing he did was to rip down all the yellow POLICE LINE tape and stuff it into a garbage can. Inside, the place was a disaster. Dirty footprints covered the floors. Glasses and mugs, dull silver with fingerprint dust, cluttered the table and the kitchen counter. He attacked the mess in a frenzy of cleaning: tearing sheets off beds, washing dishes, scrubbing floors. His mind worked like a munitions factory in wartime. What was he going to do? He couldn't stay there. Return to Toronto? Maybe move somewhere far away, Halifax or Vancouver—maybe Tuktoyaktuk. What did it matter where he went? Who would care?

The ring of the telephone in the midst of his fretting made him jump. He had forgotten about his service being connected. It rang on and on, insistently. He wasn't going to answer, but finally picked up the handset like a wrecker swinging a sledgehammer.

"Daddy! Thank God! Are you all right?" It was his daughter, Stephanie. "Peter! It's him!" she called away from the receiver.

"Yes, yes, I'm fine, everything is okay," he lied.

"Why didn't you call me? I've been frantic. Peter and I have been on the phone all day trying to find you. We tried the police; finally the phone company gave us your number, it was a new listing—anyway, that's not important, listen, I'm coming up, my flight's all booked. I'm leaving tomorrow morning and I'll be in Thunder Bay by 11 o'clock. Then I'll fly up to the lake. Why didn't you call me?"

"I'm sorry, I should have called, but, uh, Stephanie, don't come up. It was a misunderstanding, that's all."

"Daddy! We saw you on TV! You were arrested! How can you say everything is all right?"

"Really, everything is fine, I'm fine."

"You don't sound fine, you sound weird."

"Stephanie, I'm all right, really. There's no need for you to come here; in fact, I'm thinking of coming back home."

"Oh! When?"

"I haven't decided yet, I'm just thinking about it. Give me some time; I'll call you."

"What happened? They said on the news there was a murder."

"Yes, there was; I'm too tired to explain it to you right now. I'll call you in a few days."

"Okay," she agreed doubtfully. "You promise me you'll call?"

"I promise."

"Daddy, I'm worried about you."

"There's no need to worry. Everything will be all right."

"Peter wants to talk to you—"

"Not now, I'll talk to him when I call back, I'll talk to both of you." They said their good-byes and hung up. William stood with his hand on the receiver, dissatisfied. He knew he had added another brick to the wall between Stephanie and himself. He had painstakingly built it over many years.

William looked at the wall. "I can't even talk to my own children," he told it. As expected, it responded with wooden silence.

He heard Barbara say, *You never think of anyone but yourself. If I walked out of here tomorrow, you probably wouldn't even notice I was gone.*

Having lost all track of time, William was surprised to see it was dark outside. He busied himself with the airtight woodstove.

What's the matter with you? the voice persisted, *Can't you say anything? Are you going to give me the cold silent treatment like you always do? What kind of man are you?*

That was the question. What kind of man was he? A man who ran away from the past with no future to run to? Opening a bottle of red wine, he poured himself a glass. He had run away from his children; he had run away from Jack and Maggie and Denise. Sprawling on the couch, he drank glass after glass of wine; the perfect complement to his banquet of self-pity. Tipping the bottle once more, he was befuddled to find it empty. He had drunk the whole thing.

Leaving the empty to roll on the floor, William stumbled to bed, seeking the relief of a stupefied slumber.

CHAPTER NINE
MONDAY

The following day bloomed warm with sunshine again, a miniature summer in the middle of fall. William swallowed coffee as an antidote to his hangover, then went for a walk along the lakeshore, hoping to find some answers. He felt like someone looking for lost car keys in their sock drawer, not because they could be there, but because it was the only place they hadn't looked. He found only rocks, trees, sky, and sparkling water—answers to some questions perhaps, but not the ones he was asking.

On returning to the cabin, he saw a dark blue car parked beside his Bronco. As he approached, the car doors opened. Out stepped Tyler Westman, Dink, and Fiona. William stopped, his muscles zinging with adrenaline as his body prepared to run. Tyler Westman moved toward the front door as Dink circled around to William's back.

"Thought we'd have a little talk," Westman said. "Mind if we step inside?" Without waiting for a reply, Westman opened the door and went in. William followed with Dink at a threatening distance behind him.

"You look like a man who could use a drink—could use a few, actually," Westman laughed. William hunched in defiant silence. "Well, maybe it is a little early. Fiona!" Fiona entered wearing a black, low-cut, ankle-length evening gown with a denim jacket and sneakers. Her breasts lunged against the fabric as she walked. "Fi, why don't you make us some coffee?" Tyler Westman had on his cowboy outfit; Dink wore his suit, purple shirt unbuttoned to show off his gold chains. "Let's all have a seat." Westman took command of the sofa, Dink sat at the kitchen table. William stood where he was.

"We're flying out of here today," Westman informed him. "Our private plane is waiting for us over by the resort. We'll pick up the Zodiac at the other lake, then we're gone." He tossed Maggie's keys onto the coffee table. "Thought you could drive us up to the float plane dock and then take the car back to your lady friend. Sure do appreciate her lending it to us, made our stay here a whole lot more enjoyable, didn't it, Dink? Oh, and by the way, I left a couple of autographed pictures there on the dash as a little thank you; figured she could put them up in her restaurant, sort of a Tyler Westman Ate Here kind of thing, you know? Come on now, sit down. Nothing to be afraid of, we're just bringing the lady's car back is all."

William sat in the armchair.

"News that this gold rush is fake is all over town. Haven't seen so many disappointed faces since I announced I was retiring from movies!" Westman leaned forward with his elbows on his knees, "Now the thing is, we were staying over there at the hotel in town," he paused and looked directly at William, "and we had us a little visit from the police." He sat back.

Fiona brought mugs of coffee. As she leaned over to put one on the table in front of William, he could see down her dress to the curving line of her breasts. He looked away quickly. She oozed over to the sofa and curled up beside Ty.

"What we want to know is," continued Westman, "exactly what you told them."

William sat, his fingers clenching the arms of the chair. He saw Westman's eyes move over to Dink. "I told them what I knew," William answered.

"And what—*exactly*—was that?"

William recounted what he had told the police about stopping at Tyler Westman's cabin on the way back from finding George's ATV.

"Well, that sounds pretty harmless, a couple of curious locals dropping in on the big movie star." He paused and sipped his coffee. "But they seemed to think they knew a whole lot more about me than that." He looked hard at William. "They had the impression that I knew Lance Rockwell, that we had some kind of dealings together; some kind of gold mining fraud that I was mixed up in. Hell, they were almost ready to say *I* killed Lance Rockwell, ain't that right, Dink? Luckily, I had an alibi tighter than a bull rider's cinch—so did Dink and Fiona. Now, who do you suppose gave them the idea that I knew that piece-of-shit Rockwell?"

William shrugged. He heard the scrape of a chair as Dink stood up from the table.

Westman held up a hand. "It's okay, Dink. Mr. Longwilly here is taking the Fifth Amendment. Do they have the Fifth up here in Canada? Must have something like it, I guess." He leaned forward again, frowning at his clasped hands, searching for the right words. "What we want to impress upon you, Willy, is that it's not such a good idea for you to go talking about things you know nothing about. This is just some friendly advice, you understand, but I've heard of cases where some fools said the wrong things about someone else, untrue things, you understand, and the consequences that followed made those fools wish they had shut the fuck up in the first place."

William, his mouth set, stood up and walked over to the woodstove. He picked up the box of matches from the kindling box and took out a match. "You want to threaten me?" he asked. All the adrenaline in his body flowed to his vocal chords giving his voice a violent energy. "You have a career, a reputation, a standing in Hollywood." He struck the match against the box, it flared into flame. "This is just one match," said William, "but this one match could start a fire that could burn down a whole a city. You want to threaten me? I'll start a fire under you that will burn your life to ashes. I'll call the tabloids and tell them about your drug dealing and how you enslave and use people. I'll blow the lid off your career. I'll burn you to the ground!"

Silence hovered as the match burned down to William's fingers; he had to break his dramatic pose to blow it out. Tyler Westman began to clap slowly in mock appreciation of William's performance. He walked over to William and, snatching the matchbox from him, grasped a fistful of matches and struck them all together on the box. They hissed into flame. Westman held them in front of William's face. William could feel the heat on his nose and cheek. "For every match you've got, I have a hundred. How would you like to spend the rest of your life in fear, never knowing when someone is going to jump out and beat the crap out of you, when your house is going to burn down? How would you like the police to find a kilo of cocaine on you and spend the next ten years in jail? How would you like that to happen to your daughter, or your son, or your grandchildren?" He dropped the still burning matches on the wood floor, poking William in the chest, hard. "Don't play with fire, Willy boy, you might get burned."

He turned to the door, jerking his head at Dink and Fiona for them to follow.

"Wait!" William called. "I want something." Sulphur smoke rose around him as the matches on the floor burned out, leaving black scorch marks on the polished wood.

Westman snorted. "*You* want something?"

"Yes," said William. "I'll leave you out of the picture, and I'll get Jack to do the same, if you let Caroline go."

"Caroline?" Westman smiled as he understood what William was asking. "Well now, she owes us quite a chunk of change." He looked toward the ceiling while he considered. "Fiona, what do you think? She's your meat." Fiona shrugged. Westman nodded. "Okay, but understand, we aren't making a deal here, because there's nothing for us to deal; there's nothing to link us to Lance or his criminal activities or his death. But seeing as how poor pretty little Caroline has lost her husband, I guess we can cut a little slack for the grieving widow." He pointed a warning finger at William. "You tell her she better not set foot in California again. Ever. Hell, she better not go west of Kansas." He motioned to his confederates and opened the door.

Dink picked up the keys. "We'll leave the car at the float plane dock," he said as he walked out.

In the silence following the departure of Tyler Westman and company, William began to shake. The anger, the fear, the excitement all churned within him. With uncertain steps, he crossed the room to the front door. He remembered a dream in which he found himself on a high-wire platform far above the ground with an expectant crowd watching below; he had never walked a high-wire before and there was no net. That was exactly how he felt.

He slowly negotiated the path to the lake. He had lost control of his legs, they went in awkward directions, leaving him wobbling off balance. Reaching the flat rock beside the water, he sat down with a relieved sigh. The rock was warm from the sun and the heat helped him relax. Looking out over the shining lake, seeing the dark pines, the birch and aspen in their fall colours, the blue sky flecked with small white clouds, William felt a calmness descend over him. Perhaps he could find answers there after all. Maybe he had been asking the wrong questions.

The sputtering start of a plane engine echoed over the lake, followed by the full-throttle roar as the plane lifted off the water, seeking altitude over the treetops. With a wide rising curve, the yellow wings turned away, leaving only the sound of the engine behind, until that too was swallowed by distance.

When he felt up to it, William made his way along the lakeshore toward the float plane dock. Maggie's blue Plymouth was beside the Rainbow Airlines office, the keys in it, Tyler Westman's signed pictures on the dash. William tore them into little pieces and threw them into the wind.

He drove into town and parked as near as he could to the Kozy Korner Kafé. Maggie wasn't there. The blonde waitress told him she would be in for the supper rush if he wanted to come back later. William thanked her and drove to Maggie's house. Repeated knocking at the front door failed to draw any response. He went around the back. Through the windows of the sun porch he could see her standing before a clay bust. She wore an apron heavily stained with reddish-brown clay. Her hands and arms were smeared with it up to the elbows. As he watched she reached out a hand and smoothed a feature on the bust with her thumb, then stood back thoughtfully.

William mounted the three wooden steps and knocked. Maggie gave a startled jump. Flinging open the door she threw her clay-wet arms around him.

"Oh, William! Thank God you've come. I was so worried. I almost went to see you a thousand times, but I didn't know what to say. You were so angry and—oh! I'm so glad you're here."

Stepping back, Maggie drew William into the house. He walked the tightrope over the threshold without a net.

"Come in, come in," Maggie urged, gesturing him into the kitchen. "Oh darn! Look at the mess I've made of you!" She brushed at the clay impressions her arms had left on his shirt. "Would you like some coffee? Here, sit down, let me clean you off a bit." She grabbed a wet dishcloth from beside the sink.

"No, no, it's okay, really, don't worry." William waved off the cloth.

Maggie washed her hands at the sink; William sat at the table, an awkward chasm of kitchen between them. William attempted to start a bridge. "Tyler Westman came to see me today."

"Ty Westman? Went to see you?"

"He brought your car back." William proceeded to describe his confrontation with Westman and how he had bargained for the salvation of Caroline. Maggie sat at the table beside him, coffee forgotten.

"That's what he called her? Meat? That's disgusting!" She reached out and put both her hands over his. "You were very brave standing up to him like that."

William glowed under her praise. "I have no idea where it came from, that whole business with the match. I've never done anything like that before."

"Are you sure Tyler Westman wasn't involved in Lance's death?" Maggie wondered. "What if he was? That was a big promise to make!"

"He said he had an alibi for Lance's murder. I didn't ask what it was; I guessed that any alibi he came up with would be a good one. And if it turns out that he was involved, it's one promise I won't mind breaking."

"Does Caroline know?"

"No, I came to look for you, to bring your car back."

"To hell with the car! We have to tell Caroline, she must be worried sick!"

Hurrying out of the house, Maggie took the passenger seat of the Plymouth, leaving William to drive.

"Westman told me that the news about the gold rush being phoney had broken in town," William said.

"Yes, after you told us on Saturday night, I started telling people in the restaurant as soon as I opened up this morning. It didn't seem right for everyone to be set on striking it rich when there wasn't really any gold. The whole town is in turmoil."

As they drew up to George's cabin, they could see Caroline sitting on the jetty, looking out over Reese Lake. She turned at the sound of the car, but didn't leave the dock.

"Hello," she said as William and Maggie approached, glancing up at them from the corner of her eye. Maggie gasped. Caroline looked like she had been in a train wreck; her face bruised, her lips swollen.

"What happened?" William's stomach churned.

"Ty Westman paid me a little visit this morning. He reminded me not to say anything about him to the police."

"He's gone," said William. "He flew out a little while ago."

"At last!" sighed Caroline. "I can't believe that fucking bastard is finally out of my life. He said he was going, but you never know what to believe with Ty."

"He beat you up?" Maggie's brows knitted with concern.

"Yeah, shows, huh?" Caroline put a hand up to her cheek. "Him and Dink both took a shot. I guess I'm lucky I'm alive, or lucky they didn't take me with them." She looked out over the lake. "He let me go, you know. Said I was free as long as I didn't say anything about him to the cops. Told me never to go back to California, or even to cross the border again." Taking a pack of cigarettes out of a shirt pocket, she put one to her lips and flinched with pain. "Shit! I can't even smoke." She threw the cigarette into the lake; they watched it bob on the water. "Lance used to say that smoking was our way of ridding the world of tobacco. The big goof!"

"Westman told you that this morning?" Little pieces of William's mind clustered around the thought like iron filings drawn to a magnet.

"It wasn't much of a surprise, really." Caroline spoke to the water. "It was Lance who was worth the money to them, he's the one they had by the balls, they could control him because he was trying to protect me. Without Lance they didn't really have anything, just another actress wannabe with a flashy smile and a swimsuit-model body, and they've got a thousand of those, prettier and more co-operative than me, so they dumped me. Not that they really lost anything. The debt they laid on us was all made up; there wasn't really any debt, just the consequences of not paying them what they wanted. And they wanted everything."

"Do you think Westman really did kill Lance?" The question was out of William's mouth before he thought about it.

Caroline shook her head. "No. Ty was here on Saturday, before you and Jack came over. He warned us off and Lance was all agreeable, but you could see how scared he was. Ty liked that. After Ty left, Lance took off in the truck, but he came back when you and Jack were here, when I ran away."

"Westman could have met up with Lance after you left." William tried to see things from a new angle. "Maybe Westman went over to my place and Lance happened to come over at the same time and Westman killed him."

Caroline shook her head once more. "No. When I told you before that I walked into town, I was lying. I was with Ty. When I came back here after running away, he was waiting for me, him and Dink. They'd come for Lance and me, to take us back to LA. When Lance didn't show up, they took me to the hotel in town; they were going to come back for Lance later. I told them I needed some smokes and, when I went downstairs to the lobby, I saw the bus stopped outside and walked right out the front door and got on it. You know the rest." She sighed. "I was with Ty and Dink when Lance was killed. I'm Ty's alibi." Her sombre eyes smouldered over the lake.

William was out of things to say. As they left, Maggie said, "If there's anything you need, just call me."

William was moody on the drive back to Maggie's house. "If Westman visited Caroline before he came to see me, then he had already told her she was free. That's why he agreed so readily to let her go, it was already a done deal. The whole scene at my cabin was Tyler Westman acting. He was playing me along."

"I still think you were very brave. It took courage for you to try to help her. You did a good thing. You're a good man." Maggie put a hand on William's arm and left it there until they reached her house.

Inside, Maggie offered coffee again and William absently accepted. "Are you okay?" she asked at William's distracted air.

"I thought," the glacier of William's feelings began to melt into words, "I thought I was helping someone and it turned out to be another failure, like everything else in my life."

"What do you mean, another failure? What you did was wonderful."

William shook his head. "Everything I've tried, I've failed at. As a professor, a husband, a father." He sat at the table and stared at the floor. "All the years I was at the university, I never made it to department head, was never good enough at the politics. Even as a teacher I didn't amount to much, no one was sad to see me go when I left, most people probably didn't even notice." William's self-pity welled up. "When I was a graduate student, I really believed I had something to bring to literary criticism, but my ideas never caught on—the opinion of other scholars was that my approach was too diffuse, my conclusions unfocused. One colleague called my work erratic."

"I'm sure you were a good teacher," Maggie offered, trying to cure a tumour with an Aspirin.

William didn't hear her. "Barbara was always disappointed in me. I could never do anything right. We fell apart and could never glue the pieces back together. We were in love when we got married, I know we were, but we lost it somehow." He wavered on the verge of tears. "I wanted that back, the love we had when we first met. But she died! She died and we never had the chance! All those years of trying so hard and failing; of not being the husband and father I was supposed to be; not being the man I was supposed to be—all those years of my life were lost, do you understand?" He grabbed Maggie's arm, pleading, tears running down his face. "All those wasted years, I never had the chance to make them up to her. She died and my life was lost too!"

Maggie squeezed his hand. Pulling a tissue from a box on the table, she gently dried his tears. Her own eyes were brimming.

William took her hand and, closing his eyes, pressed it, still formed in a clumsy fist around the tissue, against his cheek. They sat there until William could open his eyes without fear of unleashing a flood. "I, I'm sorry," William stammered, releasing Maggie's hand and rubbing his face with his sleeve, "I kind of lost it there for a minute. I shouldn't be talking to you about this; I guess all the tension…"

Maggie held his face in both her hands, speaking directly into his eyes. "You are not a failure. If you tried your best all your life, you haven't lost anything. You did a very brave thing today—no one who was a failure could have done something like that. If Barbara didn't appreciate you for who you are—not who she wanted you to be, but who you are—then she lost a wonderful man."

William put his hands over Maggie's and dropped his head. "Thank you for being kind. I'd better be going."

"I'm not being kind." Maggie held his face, forcing his eyes up to meet her own. "I think you're very brave and I admire you enormously."

William, embarrassed at his emotional outburst, retreated into his familiar coldness. He removed her hands from his face. "I'd better go," he said, rising from the table.

"Are you sure you're all right?" Maggie asked doubtfully.

"I'm fine, I'll be fine." William's dead voice put an end to the conversation.

"Maybe you should get a dog," suggested Maggie.

"A dog?"

"Yes. There aren't any psychiatrists in Jubilee, so when people need help working through their feelings they get a dog."

William wondered how everything in his life could turn out wrong. Earlier, she had given him a warm embrace, now she was telling him he needed a dog. He couldn't leave fast enough. On his way down the narrow hallway to the front door, he remembered that they had come in Maggie's car. His own vehicle was back at his cabin.

"Take my car," said Maggie. "I can walk to work." She shushed William's objections. "It's not far. It's a nice day. I do it all the time. You can bring the car back later. Bye." She shut the door, leaving William alone on the step with his carefully packed emotional baggage. He had wondered what kind of man he was. Maybe now he knew.

William spent most of the night prowling around his cabin, unable to sleep. Random emotions darted through him, erratic as escaped zoo animals. For the brief periods when he did doze off, he woke up in a sweat about all the things he had revealed to Maggie. He had never opened up like that with anyone before and the unknown consequences of his confessions brewed in his imagination. What if she told everyone in the restaurant? What if he went into town and everyone laughed at him, knowing that he'd been crying in Maggie's kitchen? And what did Maggie think of him?

Underneath his fussing was the fear that he was no longer in control of himself. He had broken down in front of someone who was practically a stranger, yet he had never talked about any of his troubles to Barbara. His inner conflicts, kept tightly bound for so many years, were beginning to unravel. Perhaps, if he had talked to Barbara about his feelings, their relationship would have been different, his whole life would have been different. Why hadn't he trusted her? Why hadn't he trusted himself?

CHAPTER TEN
TUESDAY

At four in the morning, William gave up on sleep. He turned on all the lights, washed, shaved, dressed, made coffee, ate and sat down at his desk to work on the notes for his book in an attempt to bring some order and direction to his life.

He had barely started work when he was interrupted by the sound of cars outside. William sat frozen in his chair. Had they come to arrest him again? The knock at the door was sharp and commanding, only serving to deepen William's dread. The banging progressed to a pounding. William descended the steep stairs from the loft and opened the door.

"Glad to find you up," said Detective Inspector Bremner. With him were Sergeant Ray Selkirk and Constable Shaw. Shaw was dressed in a camouflage suit complete with hat. Jack stood behind them. "May we come in?"

As they crowded through the door, William asked, "What's this about?"

"Mr. Longstaffe, we would like to request your help in our investigation," said Bremner as if reciting a memorized text. "In view of the connection between Lance Rockwell and George Ferris, and in view of the murder of Lance Rockwell, we have decided it is urgent that we act on your report of the death of George Ferris and make every effort to recover the alleged body."

William stared at him blankly.

"You see," Bremner dropped into a more conversational tone, "we need to establish the facts of Lance Rockwell's death. The evidence of Caroline Rockwell suggests that George Ferris called his son-in-law and asked him to come here from California, presumably to help with the gold fraud. If they were conspiring, then George Ferris is a suspect in Lance Rockwell's murder."

William did a double take. "But, George was already dead. He couldn't have killed Lance."

Bremner was unfazed. "It has not yet been established whether George Ferris is alive or dead. So far, all we have is your testimony. We need to find the body, if there is one, and formally identify it. Then we can rule him out as a suspect."

"What does this have to do with me?" William asked.

"We would like your help in recovering the body."

William laughed. "I wouldn't know where to look. Ask Jack. It was his spirit helpers that led him to the body."

Bremner appeared slightly embarrassed. "That's just it, Mr. Longstaffe. Mr. Crowfoot has agreed to assist us; however, spirit helpers don't really fit very well into police reports and are not readily accepted by the courts, so we were hoping for corroboration of a less mystical nature from a more reliable witness. You were there when the body was found and we would like you to confirm the site."

"No," said William emphatically. "I'm not going back there."

Bremner continued as if he had not heard. "There is a helicopter standing by. Our plan is to fly in a recovery team. According to Mr. Crowfoot, there is nowhere to land at the site; we will drop the team by winch and remove the body. Mr. Crowfoot has declined the use of the helicopter and says he will walk in. You can either hike in with Mr. Crowfoot, or be dropped with the recovery team."

"Do I have to be dropped? Couldn't I identify the site from the air?"

"The body was allegedly found in a cave which cannot be seen from the air."

"It doesn't matter," William shook his head dismissively, "I'm not going."

Bremner considered. "We could bring charges of obstructing an investigation against you, Mr. Longstaffe. In addition, you returned to your domicile without permission, crossed a Police Line and possibly destroyed valuable evidence. Failure to participate in this investigation could be construed as an attempt to prevent the further disclosure of evidence. There might be evidence at the alleged site of George Ferris's death that you wish to keep concealed—"

"God damn it," William shouted, his tattered feelings quickly finding a focus in anger. "You make me so goddamn mad!"

"Calm down, Mr. Longstaffe. We are politely requesting your assistance in our investigation and reminding you of the possible consequences should you refuse to assist. We can't force you to participate."

"You—" William's words tangled behind his teeth. "If you're not forcing me, what the hell *are* you doing?"

Bremner paused and looked reflective. "We are trying to determine the extent of your involvement in the deaths of George Ferris and Lance Rockwell."

William stared back and didn't say a word.

"Now, if you prefer to walk in with Mr. Crowfoot, Constable Shaw here will accompany you. He will be equipped with a radio to call in the helicopter when you locate the site."

William sighed and reached for his hiking boots beside the door.

William drove the Bronco over to George Ferris's camp with Ray Selkirk's Explorer in front, Bremner's unmarked car behind. It made him feel like a criminal all over again. By the time they reached the cabin, dawn was breaking and William was in a foul mood. The uncurtained windows glowed with light, a sign that Caroline probably wasn't sleeping too well either. As William, Jack, and Shaw put on their backpacks, Bremner went up to the porch. He noticed Caroline's battered face when she came to the door. "What happened to you?" he asked.

"I fell," she replied.

Bremner regarded her skeptically as he explained about the mission to retrieve her father's body. Caroline simply nodded and shut the door.

Bremner and Selkirk drove off, leaving William and Shaw to follow Jack in search of the corpse. It was a gorgeous day for a hike, one of those bright, crisp fall days full of joy and energy even as everything around was dying. It was only a week since William had made the trip before, but he found it noticeably cooler—there was a definite chill of the oncoming winter in the air.

They skirted the sparkling lake and headed into the trees. Jack glided through the bush like a swimmer through water. William dogpaddled in his wake; Shaw brought up the rear, avoiding drowning only marginally better than William.

No one spoke. William was still too angry to talk to Jack, although he couldn't say specifically what he was angry about. Vague, unfocused feelings dogged his footsteps. Everything irritated him: the forest, the police, the murders, Maggie, life. He was out of his element, although he had to smile when he thought about what his colleagues in the English department would say if they saw him now. The more he imagined it, the funnier it became and a little chuckle escaped from his grim mouth. Jack threw a glance over his shoulder.

"Can we rest for a minute?" William asked.

"Shit, that's rough going," grumbled Constable Shaw.

Jack's eyes, when he looked at William, seemed apologetic. "You feeling better?"

"Yes, I am," William responded, a little surprised. It was amazing how his mood had changed in the past few minutes.

"The spirit from the cave is helping you," commented Jack. "Helping you feel better, cheering you up."

Shaw's policeman's eyes shot from one to the other with a perplexed look.

"I was afraid that spirit would magnify your anger," Jack went on, "but that spirit wants you back, so it's making things better for you."

"What are you talking about?" William wasn't ready for any more mumbo jumbo about the spirit world.

"I told you once before," continued Jack, "be careful what you say. The spirits, they act on our words. Once you say something, you can't take it back; those feelings are in the air. Spirits can magnify or diminish them. You said you didn't want to have anything more to do with me. The spirits could have taken those words and amplified them and we might never have met again. Instead, the spirits turned your anger. The spirit from the cave likes you and wants to keep you from harm. The spirit made things work so you would return to the cave."

"You mean, I'm here, not because of any murders or police investigations or anything else, but because a spirit wants me?"

"Yes," said Jack matter-of-factly. "You must be strong. That spirit can either help you or overwhelm you. You have to make that spirit your friend, or it will suck the life right out of you."

"And how, exactly, do I do that?" William's voice was as dismissive as a bio-tech executive talking about the environmental dangers of genetically modified crops.

"Could be tricky," said Jack, very seriously. "You haven't been trained in working with spirits. It takes years to master. Many who try don't succeed and end up dead or crazy. It's a dangerous path."

"Can you give me a crash course?" William scoffed.

Jack pursed his lips. "All that matters is how strong your own spirit is. If you are strong enough, you will be able to withstand the spirit in the cave; if not, it will overwhelm you. I will do what I can to keep the spirit calm, but in the end it all comes down to you."

"Are you trying to scare me?"

"No, just warn you. I think you have the strength."

Shaw was growing restless. "How much further is it?"

"Oh, a ways yet," said Jack. "We're maybe halfway there, maybe a little less. Ground's rougher further on, slower going."

"Shit," cursed Shaw, "if it's any rougher than this I'm asking for extra pay. Bet those bastards in their cushy seats in the chopper are laughing their asses off at me having to slash through this shit."

William eyed the holstered gun on Shaw's hip. "What if we run into Crazy Crazy again?" he asked Jack quietly.

"He's gone," Jack replied.

"Gone where?"

"Billy was going to fly him down to Thunder Bay this morning. I went over to Billy's place last night and Crazy Crazy was there. He wanted Billy to take him to have the ore samples assayed right away, but it was too late to fly down. Billy kept him at his place overnight; he was afraid to let him go into town in case he started a riot."

"Did he say any more about where he found the gold?"

Jack shook his head. "No. Billy and I tried to tell him about the scam, but he wouldn't listen, insisted that Billy take him to Thunder Bay."

"What were you doing at Billy's?"

Jack smiled. "I went with the warriors to keep an eye on your camp; I stopped in to see Billy on the way over."

"Let's move out," Shaw growled.

As Jack predicted, the trail became rougher. Shaw kept up a steady stream of curses, swearing every time his foot slipped on a rock or a branch slapped his face.

William's mood, on the other hand, continued to lighten. He found it strange that, except for the deer and a few chipmunks, they hadn't seen any animals on their trips into the bush. At the next rest stop he asked Jack about it. Jack laughed.

"There have been a lot more than you've seen," Jack informed him. "You have to learn how to look. Then there's the noise. You and Shaw make more hullabaloo than a bear in a bramble patch. Animals hear that noise, they take off. Another thing is the smell. You don't smell like you belong here. Soap, aftershave; bugs love it, but other animals run a mile. And on top of that, almost everything that ever lived out here has been shot. The price of progress." He gave a wry smile; it showed more sadness than irony. "Too bad nobody asked the animals if it was a price they wanted to pay."

They eventually reached Hellbent Stump and passed through the narrow alley between the Stump and the Chunk, emerging into the clearing of the scree. "About fucking time," said Shaw. He took a hand-held radio from a pouch on his belt and started to call for the helicopter.

"Not yet." Jack stopped him. "We have to climb up to the top." He pointed to the ridge towering above them. "We'll have lunch here, then climb up."

"Let's go up now," insisted Shaw. "I'll call for the chopper and we can eat while we're waiting for it."

"Better if we find the body first," said Jack, "before we call in."

Shaw glared at him, surprised and angry. "I thought you knew where it was!"

"I knew where it *was*," Jack replied calmly. "I don't know where it is."

"What are you talking about?" Shaw easily made the quantum leap from irritation to rage. "You mean I've been busting my ass through the bush and now you're telling me you don't even know where the damn body is?"

"I'll take a look." Jack went toward the cliff face. William rose to follow; Jack stopped him. "No. You wait here. Now is not the time for you to meet the spirit." He walked over the scree and disappeared through the bushes. Even though the bushes were mostly bare of leaves, the dense tangle of branches still obscured any evidence of the cave.

"Shit!" exclaimed Shaw, walking around impatiently. "Where'd he go?"

"There's a cave in there," William told him. "That's where we found the body."

Shaw didn't acknowledge the answer; he resumed his pacing. William felt quite calm. When they had reached the cliff, he had a feeling of coming home, as if this was where he belonged. A desire to follow Jack into the cave flamed within him. Jack reappeared and walked back to where the others waited. "Body's gone," he said.

Shaw swore.

"Let's eat," said Jack.

Jack opened the backpacks and distributed paper bags from Phil's Sandwich Shack. There was tuna fish for William (someone had remembered), chicken-on-a-bun for Jack, and, for Shaw, one of Phil's World Famous I-Wish-I-Had-One Double-Decker Meatball Subs. Shaw ate voraciously, finishing long before Jack or William, even though the sub was three times as big as their sandwiches. There were also two apples, a pear, and a container of salad that Jack and William split after Shaw declined to partake.

William lay down on a bed of tumbled rocks and munched on a pear. After the muscle-wrenching struggle of the trail, even rocks felt comfortable. The sunlight lay warm on his face, the breeze blew slightly cool. A picture-book sky overhead dotted with a few fair-weather cumulus clouds completed William's feeling of perfect peace and contentment like the ribbon on a present. He would probably have dozed off if Jack hadn't said it was time to go. "Dangerous for you to fall asleep here," he said. "You need all your wits about you."

William sat up. "Why did we come in the hard way from George's cabin instead of on the easy trail from Trout Lake?"

"What!" Shaw barked. "There's an easy trail!?"

Jack ignored him and Shaw stomped off to wait in sullen silence at the base of the bluff.

Jack explained to William, "I wanted to see if anyone had been using that trail since George's death."

"And had they?"

"Doesn't look like it."

"Have you figured out who made the trail and why?"

Jack began to pack up. "I guess George made it. He wanted a secret way in to Hellbent Stump; for two reasons. First, he needed a route to the boat landing at Trout Lake. He was last seen on Tuesday of last week when he filled up some gas cans. He probably took his boat over to the Trout Lake landing that day in his truck, then drove back to his own camp. The next morning, Wednesday, he left his truck at his camp, walked to the Stump on his secret trail, then followed the old logging road to Trout Lake. From there he took his boat up to Eagle Lake. Caroline and Lance arrived on the Wednesday, but George was already gone."

"He told Lance to meet him at the boat landing to help carry the gold ore to the Stump," William added.

"Yeah," Jack agreed. "He went up to Eagle Lake on the Wednesday, and we know he camped overnight, so he must have raided the geologists' camp on the Thursday morning and headed back. That was the day of the really heavy rain."

"He broke into Tyler Westman's cabin and stayed the night there." William was starting to get the facts straight. "That means he must have met Lance at the boat landing on Friday."

Jack nodded. "They carried the gold ore to the Stump and that's when George fell."

"When Caroline reported George missing, Lance already knew he was dead."

"Come on," Jack said, "let's go. Shaw looks like he's about to piss himself."

"Wait, what's the other reason? You said there were two reasons George made the trail."

"He intended to hide the gold ore at Hellbent Stump; he didn't want anyone to know what he was up to, so he made a secret trail."

After packing up, they climbed to the top of the Stump. The view was more awe-inspiring than before. William shaded his eyes against the sun and looked out over the vast evergreen forest. Jack cleared away the detritus covering a fissure and cautioned Shaw the way he had warned William on their first trip. "Walk on the bare rock. Don't step on a debris pile, even if it looks solid."

Jack led the way over the rock, through the erratic patterns of dead branches and drifts of brown needles, to a large open fissure. William could tell by the scuffmarks around the edge that it was the opening to the cave where they had found George's body. It looked slightly different. William speculated that the wind or the rain could have rearranged things. On examining the lip of the hole more closely, it appeared to be a lot more marked up than it had before.

Jack signalled them to wait and began to study the ground around the fissure. He wandered farther and farther away from the edge of the cliff, until he disappeared from sight in the trees.

William sat down to wait and immediately became sleepy again. Shaw remained standing. They didn't speak. They had nothing in common except for the fact that they were both standing on the edge of the same cliff. William watched Shaw and was amazed how two people could be so far apart. He felt a familiar sense of estrangement, an inability to relate to others. "Takes all kinds to make a world," he mumbled to himself, but wondered what kind of world they had made.

Jolted from his reverie by a curt, "Let's go," from Shaw, William saw Jack waving some way off. As they moved toward him, William became aware of the smell. He knew instantly that it was the smell of death. Shaw swore. The hairs on the back of William's neck prickled. A wave of memories of Barbara overwhelmed him, scattering his consciousness like shards of a shattered mirror. He felt the cold cloak of death wrap around him. The world spun and went black.

When he regained consciousness, Jack was bending over him. "Go back and wait by the edge," Jack said, helping William to his feet.

"No," said William, "I'll be okay." There was something here he had to face, something primal and visceral he needed to come to terms with.

Jack led them to another wide, deep fissure partly covered with dead branches. The smell was very strong. "The body's down there," Jack indicated.

William leaned over the edge and peered into the darkness. "Is there another cave down there?" he asked, surprised that his voice didn't tremble.

Jack shook his head. "Not here; that's a blind fissure." He nodded to Shaw. "You can call for the helicopter now."

Shaw spoke into the radio. A garbled reply burst from the speaker. Shaw listened intently, then said, "They'll be here in about twenty minutes." Holstering the radio, Shaw snorted and held his nose. "Let's get way from this smell. We'll wait by the cliff edge, it's the most open area, easiest place for the chopper to drop its payload." Back at the edge, Shaw removed an orange plastic cylinder from his backpack. Extending a short aerial and flipping a switch, he set it on a rock.

"What's that?" William had never seen anything like it.

"GPS beacon," explained Shaw. "Global Positioning System. It'll tell the chopper exactly where we are."

The minutes dragged by as they waited for the helicopter. No one spoke. William breathed deeply. He couldn't clear the smell from his nostrils; it clung to his nose hairs and was drawn in with every breath, filling him with a feeling of sickness and decay. The puffy white clouds had turned grey and ragged, as if chunks of broken concrete had been flung into the sky.

Occasionally the radio squawked and Shaw spoke into it. Any feelings of well-being William might have had were long gone. His tuna fish sandwich seemed to have come alive in his stomach and was trying its best to get out. Finally the *whup-whup-whup* of the approaching helicopter troubled the silence. Shaw took an orange signal cloth out of his backpack. William and Jack helped him to spread it out on the ground, weighting the corners with rocks.

The Search and Rescue helicopter arrived and hovered overhead. A side door slid open and a winch arm swung out. A man in a military-style jumpsuit descended in a sling. The sling was retracted and another man lowered. Next came an aluminum stretcher with a large black bag, resembling a sports equipment bag, strapped to it. As soon as the stretcher was down and uncoupled, the helicopter banked and left with a hurricane blast of wind.

The new arrivals were all business. They didn't waste any time on introductions. One of them had a corporal's chevron on his shoulder and a flash that said SPENCER; the second man's flash said SCOTT. Carrying the stretcher and the black bag between them, they followed Jack to the fissure where the body was hidden. Quickly sizing up the situation, the rescue team cleared the debris from around the opening. From the black bag, Spencer took out a climbing harness, rope and surgical masks. He handed out masks to everyone, although they didn't do much to block the smell. Scott snapped on the harness and the corporal belayed him down into the fissure. Shaw offered to help, but received a quick shake of a head in reply.

When Scott reached bottom, his teammate let the rope go slack. Some shouted instructions echoed up from the depths. Spencer took a second rope and a sling from the black bag and lowered them into the hole; then unfolded a flat, rectangular bag with a zipper down the middle, a bag big enough to hold a body. After a few minutes a call of "Okay!" came from the chasm.

The corporal asked for Shaw's help. They each took a grip and began to haul on the lines. As William wasn't needed, he walked back to wait by the cliff edge. This was more than he could face. He pulled off his mask and let the fresh breeze clear his head.

After a while the others came toiling toward him. Jack, Shaw, and the two rescuers each carried a corner of the stretcher. On it was the black body bag secured with three blue straps.

When they reached the clearing, all of the men removed their masks and breathed deeply. Shaw had already radioed in for the helicopter; it could be heard approaching in the distance. Soon it was thundering overhead and the stainless steel winch cable was lowered. Scott attached the cable to the stretcher, shoulders hunched against the downdraft, then stood back and signalled for it to be taken up.

Without warning the helicopter, not waiting to winch up the stretcher, banked, gained altitude, and flew away, the dangling stretcher whipping through the treetops. The sudden blast of wind from the rotors nearly knocked William off his feet. As the sound of the beating blades diminished, William heard a gunshot. Turning, he saw Crazy Crazy on the edge of the clearing with a rifle to his shoulder. His body bucked against the recoil as he fired into the air at the retreating helicopter.

Shaw was shouting, "Drop your weapon!" He drew his gun and held it in a two-handed grip pointed straight at Crazy Crazy, feet apart in an aggressive stance, voice an angry command. "This is the police! Drop your weapon!"

In an almost leisurely movement, Crazy Crazy swung the rifle around, drawing a bead on Shaw. William saw Crazy Crazy's body jump as Shaw fired. Two more shots from Shaw were followed by Maurice Crécy falling backwards, almost in slow motion, a look of disbelief on his face.

Shaw kept his gun trained on the body. He advanced cautiously until he was standing over the limp form on the ground, hands white around the pistol grip. "You!" he barked at Scott. "Secure the weapon!"

Scott crept over in a half-crouch, ready to hit the ground at any movement from the downed man. He grasped Crazy Crazy's rifle by the barrel and stepped away quickly.

"Check for life signs!" Shaw ordered.

Again, Scott approached in his half-crouch. Reaching out tentative fingers, he felt Crazy Crazy's neck. After a moment he looked up at Shaw. "He's dead," he pronounced.

Shaw continued to stand tensely pointing his gun at the body. Scott stood up and moved around beside Shaw. He put one hand softly on Shaw's shoulder. "It's okay," he said gently. "He's dead. You can relax."

That was easier said than for Shaw to do. He was so pumped with adrenaline that he couldn't turn his attention away from the source of danger, even though the danger was past and Maurice Crécy was no longer a threat.

William looked at Jack, surprised to see him simply standing there, watching. To William, Jack was a man in command of every situation, someone who could have stepped in and stopped all this. His eyes seemed unfocused, as if he were watching from a long way off. On his face was a look of profound sadness.

While Scott stayed with Shaw, Corporal Spencer spoke into the radio and called the helicopter back. He looked at Shaw and his partner. "They're going to unload the body and clear the stretcher, then come back for us."

There was nothing to do but wait. Scott eventually persuaded Shaw to move away and sit down, still holding his gun. William noticed Jack examining the pile of rocks and branches beside the cave opening. Spencer answered intermittent squawks from the radio. Crazy Crazy lay lifeless on the rocks.

William was relieved to finally hear the helicopter approach. It hovered overhead and the stretcher was lowered. Spencer and Scott put Crazy Crazy's body into another black body bag and secured it to the stretcher. After attaching the stretcher to the winch cable, it was hauled up and a sling was lowered. The two rescuers helped Shaw into it and he was winched up into the air. Corporal Spencer turned to William. "You coming with us?" he asked, his voiced raised against the whirr of the helicopter.

William looked over at Jack, standing silently apart, and shook his head. "No. We'll walk out."

"You sure?" the corporal asked. William nodded. "Well, be careful." He passed the hand-held radio to William. "Here, take this radio. If you need anything, call in." He shot an uncertain glance at Jack. "You sure you're okay?" William nodded again.

The sling was lowered for Scott and Spencer in turn. The helicopter rose and flew off for the last time. The corporal waved from the open door. William waved back and waited on the brink of the precipice until the machine had diminished to a speck in the sky and the sound of the spinning rotors was overshadowed with silence.

William had no idea what to do. He picked up the backpacks. Jack stood looking down at the rock splashed with blood. William felt helpless; he could find no appropriate thing to say. "Ready to go?" he asked.

Jack didn't look up. "I could have prevented this," he said under his breath. "It didn't need to happen. Raven didn't show me this."

"How could you have known?"

"I was going to ask the warriors to watch Crazy Crazy, but I didn't. I thought Billy was flying him down to Thunder Bay."

"It's not your fault." William searched for something comforting to say. "You said yourself nobody knew what Crazy Crazy would do next. He was a wild card, beyond your or anyone else's control."

The words didn't seem to have any effect on Jack. He stood, shoulders hunched, staring at the ground. William put a hand on his shoulder. After a minute, Jack nodded as if concluding some inner conversation. "Let's go," he said. "We still have to cleanse the death out of that cave." He reached for his pack. "First there's something I want to show you."

William took a last look at the bloodstained rock. It could have been the earth itself that was bleeding, red gore oozing out of the stone, death welling up, seeking him. He shuddered. "Do we need to cleanse this place too?" he asked.

Jack considered. "No. The soul is gone. He knew the way to the Lodge of the Dead. The rain will wash away the blood and that will be cleansing enough. Caves are different. Death can get trapped in a cave and great harm can come." He pondered for a moment more before moving silently off.

William followed Jack back to the fissure where the body had been hidden. The smell was still strong even though the corpse had been removed. On the bare rock near the opening sat a green metal box, about the size of a microwave oven. The words GEIGER COUNTER were stencilled in white on the side.

"It was down there with the body," Jack explained.

"Is there anything inside?" William was almost afraid to look.

Jack flipped the lid open with his foot.

William stared uncomprehendingly at the contents. "Its rope."

Jack tipped the box over, the lines spilling out in a tangled heap. He knelt down and separated them into two piles. One was a thick yellow polyethylene rope with evenly spaced knots along its length; the other consisted of a number of thinner, shorter grey pieces tied together. Jack pointed to the second pile. "Know what this is?" William shook his head dumbly. "It's the painters from the boats at the Trout Lake landing all tied together."

William couldn't grasp the significance.

Jack shoved the ropes back into the box and flipped the lid shut. "Come on, let's get away from this smell." He led the way back to where Crazy Crazy had fallen. As they approached, the slash of blood on the ground gave William the impression of a sinister smile.

Jack walked over to a large boulder about the size of a moving van. He patted it affectionately. "This is a glacial erratic, left here when the glaciers melted 11,000 years ago. It was brought here from up north, probably from around the Bone River area. See this dark veining?" The rock was streaked with alternating layers of light and dark stone. "It's typical of that area, don't find it around here though." The rock was an irregular shape, one side forming a large overhang. Jack crouched down and peered into the recess before reaching under to brush aside an accumulation of brown pine needles. He moved aside. "Take a look."

William squatted. "Ow!" he grimaced as stabs of pain shot through his knees. He leaned stiffly forward, peeking into the shadows where Jack had cleared the debris. He saw a pile of small, jaggedly shaped, light-coloured rocks. He picked one up; it glinted with a crystal sheen. A dull yellow vein ran through the centre surrounded by a network of fine capillaries.

"It's quartz," explained Jack. "The yellow stuff—" he pointed to the thick vein "—is gold."

"Gold?" William examined it in wonder. He had never seen the metal in its raw state.

"Yep," said Jack. "That's what all the excitement is about, right there in your hand. It's why George died and why Lance died and why all those people from all over the country have suddenly decided to drop in and visit the charming metropolis of Jubilee."

"How did you know it was here?" William asked.

"I thought it might be; I looked for it while we waited for the helicopter."

Jack sat down, leaning against a tree. William stretched out his legs, exciting more stabs of pain from his knees.

"Are these the stolen ore samples the geologists brought up in the Geiger counter box?" asked William. "And is this where Crazy Crazy's ore samples came from?"

"Uh-huh," Jack confirmed.

William turned the chunk of ore over in his hands. "Was it here all the time?"

Jack looked slightly abashed. "Yeah, I missed it. Remember when we first came up here, all the branches from around the opening to the cave were piled off to one side? Well, the box of gold was hidden under there. I didn't check because I assumed it was just the cleared debris from the hole. I didn't realize that something was concealed underneath it. And I wasn't looking for gold at that point. It was buried under this boulder later, when George's body was moved." He shook his head. "If I had found it earlier, things might have turned out differently."

"What about the ropes?" William asked

"The two ropes, the yellow poly rope and the boat painters, were most likely used to move the body from the cave to the fissure where we found it. That means there were two people. Hauling a dead weight out of that cave would have been hard work, too much for one person." Jack seemed to have recovered his equilibrium; he talked without any hint of the shock of Crazy Crazy's death.

"Why didn't they take the body out through the other entrance, the way we went in?"

"They probably didn't know about it. It's not visible

from the outside, and, as you found out, not easy to find even from the inside. George came across the cave while he was out here prospecting for amethysts and decided it would be a good place to store the gold until they could distribute it to the phoney claims—"

William interrupted. "I thought the amethysts didn't exist. I thought they were merely a cover story for the geologists."

"They were a cover for the geologists; they were real for George. He really was out here prospecting for amethysts. Remember the amethyst jewellery Denise makes? There are a number of local craftspeople who use amethysts in their work. George was convinced there was an amethyst mine around here."

"Denise said her supplies came from some kind of co-operative," William commented.

"Yeah, a co-operative called Mother Nature." Jack smiled. "Lance told us that he and George were lowering the box of ore samples into the cave when George slipped and fell. What did they need to lower the box? A rope. That would be the yellow poly rope. It was knotted like that to make it easier to climb in and out of the cave."

Jack paused and thought for a moment. "This isn't complete because we don't know all the facts, but this is what I have figured out so far: George fell and broke his leg while he and Lance were hiding the gold in the cave. We found George's body and told Lance about it. He went to tell someone else; remember how we saw Lance driving away right after we told him? Lance and person or persons unknown decided to move the body. They needed more rope so they took the painters from the boats at the landing. They hid the body in what they thought was a deep and inaccessible hole, dumped the ore samples under the boulder, put the ropes in the box and dropped it down the fissure with the body."

William considered all this, his mind juggling ideas. "Then who killed George? Was it Lance after all?"

"He said he didn't, but he could have." Jack mused on the point. "If he didn't, he must have gone for help after George fell; whoever he met killed George."

"The same person who later helped him move the body? Could it have been Crazy Crazy?"

Jack sighed. "Could be; we don't know at this point."

"Could your spirit helpers show you?" William asked, partly as a joke.

Jack sagged with sadness. "I have asked. Raven kept bringing me back here. I thought he was trying to show me the gold, Raven likes bright things." He rubbed his face with his hands. "But the death was still here haunting that cave, and that attracted Wendigo. Wendigo confused everything. I made a mistake. I thought the death here was George's death, stuck in the cave, but I think Raven was trying to show me Crazy Crazy's death. Wendigo clouded everything so I couldn't interfere, couldn't stop Crazy Crazy from dying so that Wendigo could have his feast."

William felt uncomfortable. "Wendigo was here?"

Jack nodded. "Oh yes, Wendigo was here." He turned his eyes to the sky. The clouds had gathered into towering cumulous banks. "Wendigo and I are inseparable. Denise told you about my wife, Sarah. She's—I guess you'd call her mentally ill. Sarah lives in her own world, out of touch with reality. When she started to lose her mind, I thought I could reach her, bring her back. I found someone to train me in how to enter the spirit world. But she was slipping away faster than I could follow; so I tried to take a shortcut. Instead of following the training, I sought out a spirit to be my helper." He looked down at his hands. "I didn't find a helpful spirit like you did. I found Wendigo. I was strong enough that Wendigo didn't consume me completely, but wasn't strong enough to escape his grasp. Now Wendigo and I are bound together. Any time there is an unnatural death, Wendigo draws me into it. George, Lance, Crazy Crazy—Wendigo brought me into all their deaths." He fell silent.

"What about Sarah?"

Jack's body sagged further, as if his bones were crumbling inside. "I couldn't help her. Wendigo pulled me away from her. Anton, my teacher, he tried to reach her too; even he couldn't find a path into the world she had gone to. She was too far away, too far."

William waited in respectful silence.

Jack stood up. "Come on, we still have to cleanse that cave."

The trail back down the bluff was hard on William's knees. By the time they neared the cave entrance, he was hobbling. When they reached the scree, Jack held up a hand to stop.

"What—?" William began.

Jack silenced him with a sharp hand gesture.

William bent over and rubbed his knees. It wasn't until he raised his head that he saw the man standing on the scree, his head tilted back, looking up at the top of the cliff. Beside him a large dog sniffed the ground. The man was holding a rifle.

"Wait here," whispered Jack and moved off silently through the trees. William sat down as quietly as he could. The figure with the gun was too far away for William to distinguish any features. The man began to make his way toward the base of the cliff when Jack appeared out of the bush and walked up behind him. The dog ran at Jack, barking savagely. It stopped a few feet away, holding him at bay.

Startled, the man tripped as he turned, falling hard on the rough stones, dropping the rifle. "Spur!" he shouted. The dog backed off, growling, as the man lumbered to his feet.

William left the cover of the trees and stumbled noisily over the loose rocks of the scree, his knees flaring with every step. The man's suspicious eyes watched him. It was Andy Polsky in a hunter's cap and multi-pocketed vest. The dog charged at William, but a sharp, "Spur!" from Polsky checked it.

Andy Polsky flicked his eyes back to Jack. "What are you doing here?"

"What are you doing here?" Jack countered.

"I'll go wherever I damn well—"

Jack cut him off. "Did you hear the shots?"

Polsky's eyes narrowed to slivers. "Yeah."

"Crazy Crazy is dead."

"Crazy Crazy? Dead?" A frown creased Andy's forehead, but his eyes didn't change. "Who shot him?"

"I didn't say he was shot." Jack's face was poker blank. "I only said he was dead."

Polsky's face grew mean. "What are you trying to do, trick me?"

"I want to know what you're doing out here."

Polsky became meaner. "I come out here, like I told you before, I come out here to make a hiking trail up to the top of the Stump."

Jack nodded toward the gun on the ground. "You make trail with a rifle?"

The big shoulders shrugged. "Thought I might run into a deer, get some meat."

"Little early for deer. Hunting season doesn't open for a couple of weeks yet."

The shoulders shrugged again. "When you need meat, you need meat. Nobody around here pays attention to hunting seasons when they want to eat."

"It's a long way to pack meat, all the way back to the road."

Polsky made an even deeper shrug. "Maybe I'll carry out a haunch, come back for the rest later."

"Did you see Crazy Crazy out here?"

"I didn't see anybody. I was coming in from the west, from the highway; heard the helicopter; heard shots. I just got here, trying to figure out what was going on. Thought maybe they were flying in prospectors or something—something to do with Crazy Crazy's gold."

"What do you know about the gold?"

Polsky's shoulders hunched forward threateningly. "What do I know? What business is it of yours what I know?"

"Andy, listen to me," Jack said in a placating tone, "George was murdered here. The helicopter came in to take out his body. Then Crazy Crazy came out of the bush and started shooting. He was shot by a cop. George's son-in-law was shot dead the other day too. That's three people dead, and it all revolves somehow around this gold. It would be a good idea if you told me what you know."

Andy's eyes remained narrow. He reached down and picked up his rifle, examining it for damage. "Let's sit down," he said. They walked back to the edge of the trees and sat. William made a futile effort to find a comfortable seat. Polsky held the rifle across his lap, one hand on the barrel grip, one on the stock, ready to use it. The dog stood a few paces off, a low growl coming from its throat.

"Last year," Andy began, "George told me about an amethyst deposit around here, showed me a handful of crystals, good quality, strong colour, even planes. Wouldn't tell me where they came from. Wanted my help, said he was broke and needed a partner to invest some capital to develop the site when he found it. So we came out here looking, me and George, and he brought that Crazy Crazy along too; they were pretty thick together, always drinking.

"A few weeks ago, George tells me he was wrong about the amethysts, that there are none, but I know he's lying; I think he's found something and he's trying to cut me out of the deal. Then I hear from Billy that those geologists are back up by Stillwater Lake, the same ones who were here last year, and guess what they say they are up there looking for?"

"Amethysts," interjected William.

Polsky nodded. "I think maybe George is working with the geologists, he was their guide last year. They're up by Stillwater Lake, but I figure George knows something about the Stump, so I keep looking around here. Then one night about a week ago, I'm at the hotel bar and there's George and Danny, and George is asking Danny about earth-moving equipment, because Danny works on the road crews in the summer, you know? Well, I laid into George about shafting me and he says there aren't any amethysts, that the ones he showed me he got from Danny who'd stolen them from Denise. Denise wouldn't say where they came from, Danny even socked her one he was so mad when she wouldn't tell him. I still thought George was lying, but he was drunk and argued like a drunk, so I left. That's the last time I saw him."

"But you kept trying to find the amethyst deposit?" Jack prodded.

"Yeah. I knew there was something going on even if I didn't know what it was. Then one day I met Crazy

Crazy at the Stump here, and he was pointing a gun at me and yelling about gold. I couldn't figure out what he was saying, but he was—" Polsky searched for the word, "—agitated, he was very agitated. Kept on telling me to keep away. Some people in town say gold is what made him crazy in the first place. Anyway, we hear some noise and it distracts him and he wanders off. I follow him and I see you two. Crazy Crazy hides in the woods, but I go up on top of the Stump. There's an opening to a cave that George and I found, you knew about that, right?"

Jack nodded.

"Well," Polsky continued, "I can see that someone has been there. I look down into the cave and there's George, dead as a moose head on the wall. So I hightail it out of there. Don't want anything to do with that. Then I hear shots and I figure Crazy Crazy must have shot at you. I hiked back to the road where I left my truck and went home."

"You didn't know anything about the gold?" William asked.

Andy Polsky shook his bushy head. "Nope. First I heard about any gold was when Crazy Crazy was pointing a gun at me. I thought the little bastard was going to shoot me for sure."

"So this time you brought your own gun?" Jack gestured toward Andy's rifle.

Andy patted the stock. "Yeah, well, a man must protect himself somehow. Never know what you're going to run into."

"And you didn't tell anyone about seeing George's body or hearing the shots?"

Polsky kept his eyes on his gun. "Not a soul. I've got a business to think of. Stories like that are bad for business. Hard to attract customers if they think they might end up dead in the woods."

"Why did you come back?"

"When I came out here with George looking for the amethysts, I saw the great view from the top of the Stump and I had the idea of running trails out here. That's what I was doing, cruising trails. Like I said, I heard the helicopter, then the shots; it was all over by the time I got here."

Jack stood up. The dog growled louder. "Andy, you can't run trails out here. This is sacred land, there are burials around here. You start cutting out here and the warriors will be on you before you can blink."

Polsky looked sullen. He didn't contradict Jack, but gave a sneaky look out of the corner of his eye.

"Well," said Jack, "we'd better head out. Which way are you going?"

Andy pointed into the trees. "Same way I came." He stood up shouting, "Spur! Go!" The dog bounded into the bush, Andy Polsky faded after him.

Jack and William started back over the scree. "Do you think he'll come back?" William asked.

"Depends on whether he thinks it's good for business."

"Do you think he was telling the truth?"

Jack shrugged. "Probably as close to the truth as Andy Polsky ever gets."

"On the day that Crazy Crazy shot at us, you said someone else had been up on the top of the Stump, that was Andy Polsky?"

"Yeah, but I didn't know who or why until today."

William looked up at the sky. The tops of the towering cumulus clouds had become flat. The bottoms had turned greenish-black. "Do you think it's going to rain?"

Jack considered the clouds. "Could be. Don't usually get thunderstorms this time of year. It's been sunny and warm for the last couple of days, high pressure; if there's a cold air mass moving in from the north, it could give us some thunder."

"A thunderstorm!"

"That's usually what it means," Jack pointed to the anvil-shaped clouds, "when they go flat on top like that."

William panicked. "What will happen to us if we're caught out here in a thunderstorm?"

"We'll get wet, I suppose. Let's go, there's work to do."

William surveyed the treetops. "What about lightning? Won't we be hit by lightning?"

"We'll ask the spirit of the cave to keep you safe. Come on. We need some wood." He picked up a stick, broke it over his knee and held up one of the broken pieces. "About this size."

William stumbled around the edge of the scree gathering fallen branches.

"That's lots," said Jack. He opened William's backpack, removed two flashlights and refilled it with the sticks. He gave William a serious look. "Now is your time to be strong. You have to keep your wits about you, don't let yourself become confused, don't let the spirit in the cave take control of you. If you feel yourself losing control, I want you to sing." Jack chanted a few syllables that sounded to William like, *nay-haw-nay-nay-haw*. Jack made him repeat them over and over. "We don't have time for you to find your own spirit song, so I am lending you one of mine. This is a powerful song, not to be misused." He looked intently into William's eyes. "Be strong."

"Jack, you're scaring me," William's eyes darted back and forth over Jack's, seeking reassurance.

"This is no time for fear; you have a task. You knew

it when we found the body, but you couldn't face it then, you had to turn away. Up there, you were alone. Now you have the spirit of the cave to help you."

"What do I have to face?"

"Only you can know that. It's between you and whatever is trying to destroy you. Let's go." Picking up his pack and a flashlight, Jack disappeared behind the bushes.

William followed Jack through the dull-leafed branches and into the cave entrance. Pushing the backpack full of wood ahead of him, he was surprised at how easily it slid along the rocks. His fatigue disappeared. A sense of peace began to creep over him, replacing his apprehension; he felt almost euphoric.

When he could stand up straight, William immediately shone the flashlight on the wall, studying the opening, making sure that he could distinguish the cleft from the other shadows in the rocks. Turning back toward the centre of the cave, he saw Jack kneeling in the half-light taking something out of his backpack. He unrolled a deerskin shirt covered with intricate beadwork. Silver and black wings unfolded over the shoulders; a wolf's head intertwined with a bear and a raven on the front. William thought it was one of the most beautiful things he had ever seen. Jack pulled on the shirt and, taking the deerskin bag from the backpack, unpacked his drum. William glanced at the wall again to make sure the opening was still visible. It was so obvious that he wondered how he ever could have had trouble finding it.

"I need the wood," said Jack, softly. William carried his backpack over and emptied it on the floor.

Jack used the sticks to build a small fire. "Sit there,"

he instructed, pointing off to the side of the cave. "Sit with your back against the rock and don't move."

William sat down as directed, trying to arrange his legs in a way that put the least stress on his knees. "How long will we be here?"

"As long as it takes." said Jack. He took a small deerskin pouch out of his backpack and held it up. "Tobacco. Offerings for the spirits."

"What are you going to do?" William asked. "You said we had to cleanse the death out of the cave, is that right?"

Jack sat back on his haunches with the tobacco pouch cupped in his hands. "Everything in the world works in concert with everything else, everything works in harmony. But sometimes the harmony is disturbed, things shift out of balance. It is our task to restore the balance. That is why we are here on earth. None of the other beings in the world, animals, plants, fish, birds, insects, can change their environment, only humans can do that. We were given that special ability by Gitchi Manitou, the Great Spirit, so that we can restore harmony where it is lost. Gitchi Manitou put us here to maintain the balance of the world."

"Human beings have brought more discord into the world than harmony." William observed.

"We can choose whether to use our abilities to destroy or create." Jack lapsed into silence and tended the fire. William watched the smoke as it rose straight up in a thin, blue-grey column through the opening overhead. After a few minutes Jack stood up, faced the east, and scattered a little of the tobacco. He gave a short chant before making a quarter turn and repeating the scattering and chanting. After paying his respects to the four directions, he sprinkled some of the tobacco into the fire. The sweet aroma of the tobacco tinged the crisp tang of the woodsmoke. William breathed it in. Jack began to chant to the soft beat of the drum. William closed his eyes as the smoke enfolded him like a warm, comforting blanket. He drifted away on the drumbeat.

The smoke began to change. It grew darker and seemed to wrap around William in constricting bands. The fragrance turned acrid; William felt the disturbing tingle of the smell of death in his nostrils. He struggled to open his eyes, but found them pasted shut by the smoke. He heard Barbara's voice from far away, Don't leave me, William; don't leave me—

His arms and shoulders strained; he was unable to move, trapped in a black cocoon.

Barbara's voice became stronger, You cheated me out of the love I could have had!

William's breath came in short gasps. The bonds around his chest were too tight for him to breathe. Barbara's voice grew louder until it filled his head, forcing out all his thoughts, booming into the hidden corners of his mind: William, it's not too late! I am here with you now. William, give me your love. Love me, now.

William's breathing had almost stopped, his eyes clenched so tightly shut it felt like his eyeballs were being forced against the back of his skull.

A single raw nerve-ending within him began to sing. *Nay-haw-nay-nay-haw*. With what little breath he had left he squeezed the song through his vocal chords. He forced it louder. Barbara's voice was still calling to him, but he stopped listening, compelling all his concentration onto the song. It gained in volume, pushing the voice back, lifting the suffocating weight of the dark smoke. The shadows around him melted away like morning mist burning off a lake. He opened his eyes.

A thin wisp of blue smoke rose languidly from the remains of the fire. Jack was gone. William sat, his back against the wall, breathing heavily. His heart was pounding slowly. He tried to stand up; pain exploded in his head, forcing him down again. He watched the smoke until it was no more than a whisper.

William hauled himself to his feet, grimacing against the stiffness in his knees. His head ached dully. Heartbeat and breathing were returning to normal. His backpack and flashlight were gone. He looked around, searching for the cave opening, but was unable to orient himself. Panic tightened his throat.

With an effort William calmed himself down. He had to figure it out. Looking up at the ceiling opening, he turned so that it was directly behind him. Walking straight ahead brought him to the wall, the few steps feeling as long as an endless journey. He stared at the rock. Very little of the light from the opening reached back that far; all he could see was dark stone and darker shadows. Closing his eyes, he pictured the entrance in his mind. Holding the image, he opened his eyes and examined the wall. At first he saw only a jumble of shadows, but they abruptly resolved into a shape and the opening appeared before him.

With a sigh of relief, William crawled into the darkness. He crawled through the passage easily and stepped out into daylight.

Jack sat on a nearby rock, no longer wearing the deerskin shirt, the backpacks at his feet. "Hi," he said as casually as if meeting a friend in the park.

William blinked at the light. "What happened?"

"You tell me," said Jack.

They sat down on the scree and William recounted his experiences in detail.

"You faced what you had to come to terms with, whatever had power over your life," Jack said.

"Why didn't you stay with me? Why did you leave me in there alone?"

"Let's say," Jack replied after a thoughtful pause, "that when you wrestle with spirits you have to do it all by yourself." He examined William through narrowed eyes. "Looks like you did okay. Still have all your arms and legs and stuff. At least, as much as I can see. Yep, you did good." He patted William's shoulder. "Of course, if I was you I'd check inside my pants, but maybe that's being over cautious."

William was rattled. "What? What do you mean, inside my pants? What's wrong?"

Jack laughed. "It was a joke, a bad joke. Pay no attention. Come on, I want to show you something."

"Wait a minute," William stopped him. "What do you mean, I did good? What would have happened if I hadn't?"

Jack lifted his backpack. "The spirit in that cave wanted to keep you. You had to show you were strong enough to get out of the cave on your own. Now that spirit will be your friend, your helper." He thought for a moment, trying to decide on how best to explain it. "Spirits either help you, or possess you, or they are indifferent to you. That's the way spirits are, there aren't any other alternatives for them. You were too strong to be possessed, so the spirit has become your helper."

"What if the spirit had possessed me?" William asked, concerned at what sounded like a close call.

"Well," said Jack mischievously, "we wouldn't be out here talking about it. Come on." He walked along the base of the cliff until he reached the cleft between the Stump and the Chunk. A shadowy crack ran along the bottom of the Chunk, parallel to the ground. Jack, slipping off his pack and taking out a flashlight, lay down flat and wriggled into the tight space.

"Jack!" William called; there was no answer. With a sigh he lay down and crabbed sideways into the opening. Wider in the waist than Jack, he forced himself through, scraping his back along the rock. The passage was short, hardly more than a body width. William found himself in a small chamber, barely big enough for the two of them to crouch together. Jack shone his flashlight on a crevice in the wall. It glowed dull purple.

"What is it?" William reached over and put his hand in the cranny. It felt smooth and angular.

"It's amethyst," said Jack. "Natural, raw amethyst."

"Amethyst!" William repeated in wonder. Jack ran the light over other crannies in the walls and ceiling, all bearing gardens of crystals. "It's so beautiful!" William exclaimed.

The wall behind them was heavily chipped away, some of the seams completely mined out. At the far end of the cave, Jack shone the light into an opening about as wide as a man's shoulders. It tapered away into the distance, bristling with purple crystals as far as William could see.

William gazed around in awe. "So there were amethysts after all. This is what George and Andy Polsky were looking for. Lucky they didn't find it."

Jack shook his head. "The spirit of this cave keeps it well hidden. No one would ever find it by accident. I could only show it to you now because you have a spirit helper of your own." Jack switched off the light, plunging them into darkness. The crystals held the light briefly, leaving an afterimage of violet lightning on William's retinas.

"Very few people know of this cave," Jack kept his voice low. "There's a reason I showed it to you. We may need the help of the warriors before this is through. Up until now, they protected you because I asked them to;

now they will protect you to preserve the knowledge of the cave. They will respect you for the knowledge you hold." William felt Jack grasp his arm. "You must understand the seriousness of this. The warriors will die for you if you ask them."

The air in the small space felt thick.

"Or kill," Jack whispered. "You must be respectful, be careful what you say and speak only absolute truth around the warriors." Jack flicked on the light again and shone it on a nest of crystals. Picking up a loose stone from the floor, he tapped the base of one violet spear until it cracked. He broke off the piece, and handed it to William. "This is for you. Keep it with you always; it will help you stay strong."

William took the crystal, about the size of his little finger. It lay like a sliver of solid light in his hand.

"We can go now," said Jack.

William eased out of the cave, clutching the crystal tightly. Once outside, they gathered their packs and prepared to leave. The thunderheads on the horizon had begun to move in, a slowly advancing threat. "Do you think we can be home before the storm breaks?" William stooped a little to make himself less like a lightning rod.

Jack regarded the sky. "Hard to say. Air masses this time of year are confused. Those clouds could stall where they are, or catch a shear wind and be here in a matter of minutes. The sooner we start, the better." He picked up his knapsack. "Raven must be making more amethyst."

"What do you mean?"

"That's what amethyst is, frozen lightning. Raven steals it from the sky and hides it in the earth. Once, long ago, when the earth was dark, it was Raven who brought the light. Now Raven stores light as crystals in case the darkness comes back. Summer lightning makes white quartz crystals, but autumn lightning makes the purple amethyst."

They began the trek back along George's secret trail. They hadn't gone far when William had to stop. Fiery pain screamed in his knees. "Jack, I don't think I can make it. I can't walk any further. My knees are shot."

Jack observed the sky through the trees. "It's getting late, we don't have much time. It will be dark soon, and that storm is moving in."

"I can't help it. I'm sorry, Jack, I can't go on." William sat down and tried to rub the burning away. "Anyway, there's something I should tell you." He described his encounter with Tyler Westman and his conversation with the battered Caroline.

Jack regarded him with respect. "You actually did that with the matches? And didn't back down when he threatened you? That was very brave of you."

"That's what Maggie said. I'm not sure if it was brave or foolhardy."

"It was brave," confirmed Jack. "It took strength and courage. No wonder you could withstand the force of that spirit." He glanced at the sky again. "We'd better keep moving."

William stood up, took a tentative step, winced, looked despairingly at Jack.

"Okay," said Jack, "let's try another mode of travel."

"I still have the radio, I could call for the helicopter to come back and pick us up." William shrugged off his pack and rummaged for the radio.

"Let's try something else first. Let's try turning invisible."

William groaned. "Jack, this is no time for medicine man stuff, I'm in serious pain here. I think we should call for the helicopter." Spirits and stories about Raven were all very well in their place, but William was dealing with physical suffering, which, he thought, put things in a different perspective.

"Let's try this first. Remember what we did last time?" Jack repeated the instructions for moving while invisible. "Grab hold of that tree beside you and make yourself indistinguishable from it. Then, find something else a short distance away. There, see that tree with the bent trunk? Reach out and grasp that tree and blend with it. That way you will move from one place to the next. Ready to try?"

William sighed and placed his hand on the tree trunk. He closed his eyes and tried to let himself become the tree. He opened his eyes again and looked at Jack. "How do I reach the other tree? It's way over there."

"You have to kind of project yourself, just make yourself *be* there."

William rolled his eyes before closing them again. The faster he got this over with, the sooner he could call for the helicopter. He pictured the tree with the bent trunk in his mind and tried, concentrating as hard as he could, to project himself. Opening his eyes, he found himself in exactly the same place as before. "This isn't working. Let's call for help."

"You're trying too hard. Relax. Make yourself more diffuse. That's the hard part. In the cave, it was your ability to focus your energy that helped you ward off the powers trying to overwhelm you. But for this, you have to go to the opposite end of yourself, let yourself be all fuzzy and indistinct."

William's mouth twitched in a wry smile. He remembered the comments other scholars had made about how vague his writings were. I guess I know how to be unclear, he thought.

"Don't close your eyes completely, close them halfway to make everything look blurry, that will help."

William stifled a sigh and touched the tree again. Relaxing as deeply as he could, he blurred his vision and singled out the tree with the bent trunk. He tried to remain unfocused and extend himself forward. After a few minutes, he gave up. "I can't do it," he said, opening his eyes fully. Everything looked different. He realized he was standing with his hand on the tree with the bent trunk.

Jack smiled. "Sure you can."

William looked around again, trying to comprehend what had happened.

Jack helped him slip on his backpack. "Don't get all focused again, stay diffuse. Now, try for that outcrop of rock over there."

William let himself blend with the tree, then reached out for the rock. It took a couple of tries and reminders from Jack to relax, but he soon felt the cold stone beneath his hand. His mouth opened in awe. "I really did it?"

"Yes, you really did," encouraged Jack. "The spirit from the cave is helping you. Keep going."

Wobbly and uncertain as a kid learning to ride a bike, William continued to move through the forest. He lost all sense of time, all sense of place; when he eventually stopped moving, he couldn't understand where he was. He gazed around in a daze. His hand was on something metallic. He examined it closely, trying to figure out what it was. It was silver and shiny and seemed to be attached to something, something big and dark.

"William. It's me, Jack. You can come back now. We're here."

Everything was a blur. He looked at the shiny metal again. It was a handle! A shape took form around it. It was the Bronco! He was standing with his hand on the door handle of the Bronco. Jack stood beside him, holding his arm. William looked around, still too muddled to talk. It was almost full dark. The square frames of the windows of George Ferris's cabin were golden with light.

"We're here," said Jack.

The front door of the cabin opened, spilling light into the dusk. Caroline Rockwell stepped out onto the porch, her arms folded tightly across her chest. "Who's there?" she called; a tremor in her voice.

"It's Jack and William," Jack called back.

"Oh, thank God," Caroline breathed. "There's been a break-in! Someone broke into my cabin!"

Jack looked at William. "You okay?"

William nodded dumbly. Jack took his arm and led him toward the cabin. Caroline shuffled nervously, her arms still tightly folded. Her blonde hair shimmered around her swollen angel face, the bruises hidden by make-up. "What happened?" Jack asked.

"I went into town today," Caroline explained, "and when I came back the door was broken in. I'm scared. With Lance gone I—" she gulped air. "I don't have a phone so I couldn't call anyone and I don't have any way of getting back into town, the police still have Daddy's truck and—"

"Is anything missing? Did they take anything?" Jack's voice was calm and steady.

"I don't know, I mean I can't tell." Caroline sounded confused. "This is all Daddy's stuff and I don't know what's missing and there isn't anything here worth stealing anyhow, I mean, Daddy didn't have anything valuable—"

"Let's take a look inside," Jack interrupted. They

went in. Caroline had been tidying up; the sofa bed was folded away; the precarious chairs were lined up in a row against one wall.

Jack crossed to the desk. "Was there anything in here?" He opened the top drawer.

"I don't know," Caroline replied. "I never looked in it."

Jack opened another drawer full of papers: old receipts, cheque stubs, outdated hunting and fishing licenses. He closed the drawer and shrugged. "I can't tell if anything's missing." He took a last look around and pointed to the gun-rack on the wall. "George's shotgun is there," he said, "but his rifle is gone."

Caroline looked puzzled. "You mean, someone broke in to steal Daddy's rifle?"

"Could be, but why would they leave the shotgun? If they were stealing guns, why not take them both?" Jack thought for a moment. "Was the rifle here when you went into town, or was it gone before that?"

Caroline shook her head, "I don't know, I never noticed."

"Okay," Jack said, "we can go to William's place and call the police. Or we could take you into town."

"Yes! Please!" Caroline said breathlessly. "I want to go back to town. I couldn't stay here alone tonight."

Jack's brows knitted. "You said you were in town earlier. How did you get there and back?"

"Oh," Caroline explained, "a man came by, he lives on the next lake, Trout Lake, and said he had heard about Daddy and Lance and wondered if there was anything he could do to help and offered to drive me into town and I've been stuck out here all alone and so of course I said yes. He took me into town and I went shopping, bought some food and stuff, and afterwards he drove me back. After he dropped me off, I found out that the door had been broken open and I ran after him down the drive, but he was gone and I've been here going crazy ever since."

"Who was this guy?" asked Jack.

"Oh, his name's Harry, Harry Perkins," said Caroline. "He was very nice."

"Did you stay with him while you were in town?"

"Oh yes, we were together the whole time. We went to the General Store and he bought groceries too—well, except for when I was having my hair done, I haven't been able to properly wash my hair since I got here."

"He left you alone while you had your hair done. How long was that?"

"Well, I had to wait a while because I didn't have an appointment, I dunno, about an hour I guess; I'm not really sure, I'm not very good with time."

Jack asked William for his keys and went outside. William helped Caroline put out the lights. It was only then he noticed that the place was lit solely by kerosene lamps: the cabin had no electricity. On the way out, he pulled the door to, closing it as best he could against the broken lock. Jack already had the engine running as William and Caroline climbed into the Bronco.

The town of Jubilee was still alive with the remains of the gold rush; echoes of drunken dreams rolled out of the hotel bar. Jack parked in the first open spot he could find and the ragged trio walked to the Kozy Korner Kafé, William hobbling on his spent knees. The café was full and noisy. An arm waved to them over the crowd. Detective Inspector Bremner sat at a table with Sergeant Ray Selkirk.

"We've been waiting for you," said Bremner. "Here, sit down. We were afraid you were lost, about ready to send out a search party." He looked at Caroline. "Hello, Mrs. Rockwell. I didn't expect to see you here."

"Caroline's place was broken into today," William said.

Bremner looked surprised. "When did this happen?" he asked. Caroline told her story again. "Oh boy," Bremner gave a weary sigh, "this is going to be a long night." He turned to Selkirk. "You'd better go over to the Ferris place to investigate the break-in. I'll stay here and take a statement from Mrs. Rockwell." Bremner looked at Jack and William. "You two stick around. I need your statements about what happened out there in the bush today."

Jack looked at Bremner. "Why don't you call Harry Perkins and ask him to come in and corroborate Caroline's story? He was out at George's camp, maybe he saw something, or someone; he might be able to help with your investigation."

Bremner gave a wry smile. "I might do that. It will save some time and we already have a lot to deal with tonight. Sergeant Selkirk can arrange it." Selkirk left and Bremner flipped to a fresh page in his notebook. "Now, Mrs. Rockwell—"

Jack shooed William toward the door.

"Hey!" barked Bremner, sharply enough that heads turned at nearby tables. "Don't go anywhere! As soon as I'm done here I want to talk to you!"

"We won't go far," said Jack vaguely, mumbling under his breath, "At least, no further than we have to," as William followed him over to the cash register where Maggie was ringing up a bill. William stood stone-faced, his nerves knotted as the embarrassment over crying in her kitchen returned.

"Oh," said Maggie, "I heard about poor Crazy Crazy, isn't it terrible? Are you feeling any better, William?"

"I'm fine," he answered blankly. "Your car is still over at my place."

"Don't worry," Maggie smiled playfully, "I know you won't steal it!"

William looked away.

"Can we talk to you in the back for a minute?" asked Jack.

"Oh! Sure." Maggie's eyebrows arched in surprise as she led the way through the swinging doors. Jack crossed the kitchen to a door at the back and opened it.

"Thanks, Maggie," he said. "See you later."

"Where are you going?" she asked. The same question was on William's lips.

"Not far." Jack stepped through the door. With an awkward good-bye to Maggie, William turned to follow. Maggie grabbed his sleeve, stood on her tiptoes, and gave him a peck on the cheek. William felt the knots tighten within him. He tried a smile, but his jaw was so tense he could only manage a crooked grimace. He hurried after Jack down the alley behind the café as quickly as his knees would allow.

Why is everything so difficult? he wondered. Why can't things be simple between people?

He had seen the look in Maggie's eyes as he turned away from her, a look of hurt and confusion. William had seen that look a million times in Barbara's eyes. The shock stopped him dead. He had never noticed the pain in Barbara's eyes before; he had seen only the anger. Finally, he understood. It was like stepping back from an impressionist painting and seeing the vague blotches of colour resolve into a field of flowers or a pond of water lilies. Whenever he had retreated into a cold distance, Barbara funnelled the rejection into anger. All her screaming: she was trying to reach him, but it served only to drive him farther away. That is where their love had gone, lost in a distance that was nowhere at all.

Where did he learn to react like that? How could he not see for all those years? Why was he so afraid?

William looked up and saw Jack's silhouette in the entrance to the alley. "You go ahead," he called. "I'll wait here."

Jack came back toward him. "What's happening?"

"Uh, my knees hurt," William heard himself say, knowing he was avoiding his emotions. He took a breath. "I was thinking about Barbara, our relationship." Even as he grasped for the words they fled like wild horses over distant hills.

"You had a shock today in that cave," said Jack gently. "You encountered something big. When you are shaken up like that, things don't settle down the same way they were before. It will take a while before you feel solid again." He took William by the arm and walked him down the alley.

Out on the street they saw the warriors' car parked near the hotel. Jack dragged William over to it. One of the warriors stood eye to eye with Jack. Jack spoke to him in their own language, indicating William with a jerk of his chin. The warrior turned a pair of burning eyes on William and nodded.

Jack led the way back to the Bronco. With William in the passenger seat, he drove north out of town. In the side mirror, William saw a car with a single headlight on high beam come up fast behind them. The light caught the mirror and reflected into his eyes, blinding him. "What was that all about?"

"Just arranging some help in case we need it," replied Jack.

"Why did that warrior look at me and nod? Did you say something about me?"

"I told him about the spirit of the cave and that I

had shown you the amethysts. He acknowledged you to show that he respects your knowledge."

"Am I not supposed to tell anyone about the amethysts? Is it a secret?"

"What you do with the knowledge you have is up to you. Act however the spirits guide you."

The side-mirror had gone dark. "They aren't following us anymore," William commented.

"Aren't they?" asked Jack.

When they reached the Trout Lake Road, a pair of headlights flew past them in the direction of town. William looked back and saw the distinctive taillights of Harry Perkins's Jaguar.

"I take it we're going to Harry Perkins's place," William stated. "You only wanted Bremner to call him into town to get him away from his cabin."

"Uh-huh," Jack nodded.

"What for? What do you hope to find there?"

"Dunno," said Jack. "Just have a look around."

Jack inched the Bronco along the dark road to avoid the jarring potholes and pulled into the parking area at the boat landing. He reached into the back seat and fished flashlights out of his pack, handing one to William. Jack slipped out, closing his door quietly, and set off down the road toward the last cabin. William followed.

All the cabin windows were dark. Lightning flickered on the horizon from the hovering storm, thunder grumbled distantly. Jack went up to the door, stood back and kicked. The door flew open. Jack walked inside with William so close behind that his chest touched Jack's back. The door led into a kitchen, which opened directly onto a living area with a small couch, an easy chair, and a coffee table. Off to the side was a door leading to the one bedroom. They went in.

It was a small room with barely enough space for a bed and a nightstand. A doorless closet revealed a row of neatly hung clothes. Jack rummaged around in the closet while William checked the nightstand. In the bottom drawer was a locked metal box. William held it up. "Is this what we're looking for?"

Jack took it, giving it a gentle shake. "Could be," he said. "Let's see what's in it."

He carried the box back to the kitchen and put it on the table. "See if you can find something to open it with."

William pulled out a cutlery drawer and picked up a dinner knife. "How's this?"

Jack took the knife and began to work on the lock. William opened another drawer and found a screwdriver, a hammer and a pair of pliers. "There are some tools here."

Jack put down the knife; it had bent without any effect on the lock. He took the screwdriver, positioned it over the hasp and gave it a whack with the hammer. The lid popped open. Jack dumped the contents on the table. William's flashlight illuminated a pile of papers. The top piece was a certificate of incorporation for the Lucky Foot Mining Company Inc., signed by the president and CEO, H. Perkins.

Jack pulled another document from the pile. "Look at this." It was headed, Articles of the Crazy Luck Mining Company, proprietor, G. Ferris. The rest were similar legal documents, all to do with mining companies, some in George's name, some in Harry Perkins's name, and some in both.

"What do you make of it?" asked William.

"Looks to me like Harry and George set up a network of companies, probably to market the phoney gold shares."

"Does this mean Harry Perkins was George's partner?"

"Looks like it. Perkins is a stockbroker; he must have planned the financial end of it, George did the grunt work."

William shuffled through the papers. "How did you know all this would be here?"

Jack's face was in shadow, leaving William unable to read his expression. "Raven brought me here in a vision, told me the key to the secrets was here; told me to wait for a sign, to wait until the dead man's locks were broken. Raven loves a riddle. When George's cabin was broken into, I came here. The dead man's locks were broken."

"I still don't understand."

"Some of these papers must have been at George's cabin. Perkins had to get them back because they were proof of his connection to George. When it came out that the gold rush was a bust, Perkins had to start covering his tracks."

"He made sure Caroline was out of the way by taking her into town," William said, "and while she was having her hair done, he went back to George's cabin and broke in and took them—"

"—to remove the evidence of any link between him and George," concluded Jack. "Okay, let's put this back."

"Shouldn't we take it to the police?"

"Better if they find it here, I think," said Jack. He stuffed the papers into the box and closed the lid.

"What if Harry notices the lock is broken?"

"Hopefully he won't have time. We'll go back into town and tell Bremner."

William hesitantly agreed. "Our fingerprints must be

all over the place. What if the police find our fingerprints on the box?"

"Then you'd better get a good lawyer," grinned Jack. He returned to the bedroom and deposited the box in the nightstand drawer.

William was still puzzled. "If Crazy Crazy found the gold, how did they file all these claims?"

"These aren't claims, that's different. These are mining companies. They would file the claims when they produced the ore samples and the companies would own the claims. I would guess that they set up a lot of little companies so each one could own a claim or two, then it wouldn't look like only one company owned the whole gold field."

"How does Crazy Crazy fit in?"

"I don't know. He was pretty strung out with gold fever. I don't think he was part of George's plan; even George knew Crazy Crazy was too unreliable to trust with a secret. But George might have let something slip, maybe on one of their binges, something about gold out at Hellbent Stump. But the gold was hidden after George's death, so George couldn't have told him where it was. I think Crazy Crazy must have found it on his own, poking around out there, just like I did. Maybe he was still looking for the amethysts and stumbled onto the ore. He's too dead to tell us now. Come on, let's go before our friend Harry comes back."

Lightning danced around the sky as they made their way back to the Bronco. Thunder rumbled through the darkness. The cool night air had released the storm, ominous low clouds rolling in quickly.

Jack took the driver's seat and started the engine.

William gratefully stretched his knees in the passenger side footwell.

"We haven't learned very much," William observed. "We still don't know how George was killed, or who killed Lance, for that matter."

"Seekers after gold dig up much earth and find little," Jack quoted a saying.

"I remember that," said William, memories tinkling in the back of his mind. "A Greek philosopher, um—"

"Heraclitus," provided Jack. "Fifth century BC." He snapped on the headlights. "One of my favourite philosophers; remembered for twenty-five hundred years for stating the obvious. Things like, You can't step into the same river twice." He shifted into reverse. "Harry Perkins is the key to all this. You stick him into any of the gaps in our logic and everything makes sense." Lightning flashed, thunder close behind.

William began to put the pieces together. "When George fell, Lance went for help. Who would he go to except George's partner, Harry Perkins?"

"Only instead of helping to rescue George, Harry drops a rock on his head." Jack backed out of the parking space.

"And after we found George's body, we saw Lance driving away to the north. Where would he be going except to tell Harry? And earlier that morning, when we saw George's truck being driven wildly on the highway, it was Lance returning from Perkins's cabin."

Jack shifted into gear and began to bump down the road. "Then George's body was moved using a rope made from the painters of the boats at the landing down the road from Harry Perkins's cabin."

A sudden flare of intense light blinded them. Jack jammed on the brakes and skidded to a stop. Two headlights on high-beam blazed before them. A vehicle blocked the road. Through the glare, it was impossible to make out what kind it was. A figure emerged from the driver's door and moved to the back. The trunk lid opened and closed, the figure walked back to the front. As it stepped past the headlights toward the Bronco, William saw the silhouette of a rifle. Jack saw it too. Slamming the gearshift into reverse, he floored it, spinning the Bronco back into the boat landing parking space.

The window beside William exploded in a crash of shattering glass. He heard the gunshot as the splintered glass sliced his face and fell down his collar.

Harry Perkins approached the Bronco, the rifle trained on William. Jack sat poised for action, one hand on the wheel, one on the gearshift; one foot on the clutch, the other feathering the accelerator.

"Get out!" Perkins commanded; his voice deadly as a lethal injection. Lightning skittered through the night, thunder boomed. Perkins's eyes were flat as a prison guard's.

Jack doused the headlights and shut off the engine. William opened his door and fell out of the Bronco, landing hard on his knees. He felt someone helping him up. It was Jack. Perkins covered them with the rifle. Lightning stabbed out of the clouds, shimmering on the gun barrel, thunder sharp as a bullet.

Jack whispered in William's ear. "Hold your crystal." William fumbled in his pocket, closing the amethyst in his fist.

"You, with the flashlight," said Perkins, "turn it on." William didn't move, in shock from the exploding window. He realized he still held his flashlight in his hand. He turned it on. "Get going, up that trail," Perkins ordered.

Jack steered William toward the trail, the same old logging road they had used to return from Hellbent

Stump the night Harry Perkins had generously provided a ride back to George's cabin. The lightning flashes were closer together, the thunder climaxing in a carnal crack.

William plunged into the eye-poking trees, over the shin-biting rocks. Jack was behind him, steadying him with a hand on his back. Then came the rifle, full of gunpowder and jacketed lead, Harry Perkins's finger on the trigger.

William's knees screamed with every step. He fell, dropping his flashlight. "Get up!" yelled Perkins over the thunder.

"I can't," William shouted into the ground. "I can't walk. My knees! I can't walk!"

"Carry him," Perkins commanded. Jack helped William pick up his flashlight and climb onto his back. William shone the light down the trail before them as Jack trudged on.

Jack began to make a low noise in his throat, like a hum or a chant.

"*Shut up!*" snarled Perkins.

"Got to keep Wendigo away," said Jack calmly in his backwoods dialect. "You're out in the bush at night, Wendigo going to come for you for sure. Have to sing the sacred songs to keep him away, or he eat you up!" Jack resumed his low hum.

"Shut up, I said!" Perkins's tone grew harsher. "Keep moving!"

The trees shook in a violent gust of wind. "Hear that?" asked Jack. "That's Wendigo, coming closer."

"It's the storm, you idiot. Shut up and keep moving!"

"That Wendigo, he's a bad spirit," Jack went on. "He grabs hold of you, tears off your arms and eats them in front of your eyes. The more you scream, the more he likes it. He breaks your legs so you can't run away, then rips open your belly and eats your guts while you're still alive."

Multiple flashes of lightning flared around their heads. The air was so full of static it made their hair stand on end, their skins tingle. "Shut up!" yelled Perkins, his voice drowned by thunder.

Jack droned on, "He tears your head off and scoops out your brains and fills your skull with evil spirits, then puts your head back on and you become a Wendigo, roaming the forest forever looking for living men to eat!"

Jack slowed down; then stopped walking altogether as he delivered his monologue. Perkins jabbed William in the back with the rifle barrel. A sharp snap of twigs came from off to the left. Perkins jumped. A grinding noise, like rocks being crushed together, came from the right. Perkins swung the rifle toward the sound.

They had reached the Gulp. William grasped that Perkins intended to drop them down the bottomless hole, never to be found. William was terrified; a pure seam of fear ran through his being. Every muscle was bone-snapping tense; throat twisted shut, eyes spasmed open. William trembled, insides turned to water. He knew he was about to die. His hand clenched tight over the crystal, gripping it like a last hope. "Listen to him!" William shouted over the thunder, his voice high pitched and brittle. He slipped off Jack's back. Lightning scrambled the shadows into monster shapes. Thunder galloped overhead, echoing into the hollows of the Gulp.

"Listen to him!" William pleaded. "We know all about the gold fraud. The police know too. They're looking for you right now. You won't get away with it. Let us go! Turn yourself in; it's your only hope!"

"Shut up!" Perkins yelled, his eyes darting erratically.

Jack leaned close to William's ear and whispered, "When I give the word, shut off your light and become invisible."

"Get over there!" Perkins motioned toward the edge of the Gulp with the rifle. From close behind came a low moaning sound that faded into the death-knell toll of thunder. The grinding noise came again, seemingly all around them.

"That's Wendigo," said Jack ominously, "he's close now." The trees shook violently. "I think he's here!"

"Shut up!" shrieked Perkins, levelling the rifle to shoot.

A branch snapped, as if under a heavy footfall, right beside Perkins. He turned quickly, almost losing his balance, firing wildly in the direction of the sound. A death-cry scream came from the trees.

"Now!" whispered Jack. William flicked off the light and stepped sideways into the shadows of the trees, letting himself blend into the patterns of needles and bark, into branches and the biting scent of sap. He embraced the darkness like a father finding a lost child. William went so deep even the penetrating lightning could not reach him, nor the searching claws of the thunder.

Another death-cry ripped the darkness. Perkins was intermittently outlined by the storm-light. Another low moan groaned close beside him. He swung around and fired blindly. Trees shook and more branches snapped. Perkins fired again, first to the right, then to the left. "Who's there?" he yelled, spinning in a disoriented circle, firing again and again.

Death-cries erupted in a frenzy, first here, now there, then everywhere at once. Trees shook with inhuman force. Perkins backed away, swinging the gun to cover his retreat. He fell over backwards. More branches snapped around him and the moaning grew louder, closer. Perkins jerked to his feet, dropped his gun and ran headlong into the bush, arms flailing. Between two peals of thunder, an ear-splitting scream rent the night. Whether it came from Perkins or not, William could not tell.

"William!" Jack's voice came from a long way off, like someone calling in a dream. "William!"

William became aware of being shaken. There was a light coming from somewhere. He wanted to sleep; to slip down into a deep lake of oblivion and be watched over by mermaids with flowing hair and soft, shapely tails waving sensuously in the depths.

"William!" The shaking continued. The light grew brighter. William blinked. Jack was shining a flashlight directly into his eyes. He squinted and waved the light away. Jack shook him again. William was vaguely aware of occasional crackles of thunder.

"Come on, we have to get you out of here. Can you stand up?" Jack's hands were under William's arms, half helping, half dragging him to his feet. "You really were invisible that time. Even I couldn't see you. That spirit must have helped you, known you were in danger and helped wrap you in darkness. But when you go too deep into invisibility, sometimes it's hard to find your way out. Some of the old medicine men, they would go so deep they could never come back and were invisible all the time. Ghostwalkers they were called, but they weren't ghosts, just men who were invisible. Still some around, they say. They're so invisible even death can't find them; they wander around invisible all the time, like spirits. You should be careful; you have a natural talent for becoming invisible and we don't want to lose you. You need to learn some control."

William could hear the voice, but Jack could have been speaking in a foreign language for all he understood. He looked around. It was so dark the whole world was one featureless shadow, except where the cone from the flashlight splashed on rocks and branches. Lightning continued to spark in the sky, but it had moved off, no longer directly overhead.

"Can you walk at all?" At Jack's voice, William looked down at his feet; they seemed like strange, distant objects he had never seen before. "Come on." Jack grasped his sleeve and pulled him forward. William took a step, stumbled and fell in a boneless heap.

Then the rain came. The leading edge of the thunderstorm had passed, pulling the rain clouds behind it. It was a hard, cold-front rain, naked and furious. William knew he was wet, he thought of the mermaids again. He felt something tugging at him, urging him up, but he didn't want to go, he wanted to stay there with the mermaids in the comforting water. He felt himself lifted onto Jack's back, rain-thrashed darkness spinning around him.

Jack's steady steps rocked William in his daze. The rain hammered his back. Thunder rumbled softly in the distance.

William's awareness returned all at once, like someone slapped out of sleep. And with the awareness came the terror. He saw himself on the edge of the yawning hole in the earth; the gun aimed at his heart; the deranged look in Harry Perkins's eyes in the lightning flares; the hair-raising, skin-crawling static; the thunder; the moans and the inexorable footsteps of the approaching Wendigo. He saw death. William screamed.

Jack put him down. William was breathing in short, quick gasps, his eyes wild, muscles trembling. "It's okay," soothed Jack. "It's okay."

William looked around. They were on a dirt road. To the left, dim light crept through the night. Harry Perkins's Jaguar, headlights still on, fading as the battery died. Before him, the Bronco. They were back at the boat landing. The downpour had softened to a steady rain, a reassuring patter of normalcy. William remembered wet Sunday afternoons, reading a book by the fire, Barbara in the kitchen, the smell of roast beef filling the house, the kids upstairs, their quiet play flaming into momentary arguments, subsiding into murmurs again.

"William!" Jack took his arm and led him to the Bronco, helping him into the passenger seat. William felt detached, as if he were floating. He watched from a weightless distance as Jack went over to move the Jaguar. With a low *rurr-rurr* from the weak battery, the engine purred to life. Jack parked the Jaguar at the landing and took the driver's seat of the Bronco.

After a slow, splashing journey through the potholes, they turned onto the highway. The wipers swished rhythmically, the headlights feeling their way through the rain. William had the sensation they were sitting perfectly still, that the road was moving beneath them. He thought that if he sat in one place long enough, the earth would rotate under him and he would end up somewhere else.

Jack steered onto another dirt road. It twisted in the darkness like loose rope. They stopped at a house and the headlights picked out a blue wall. Or was it pink? William was amazed that the house was off the ground, suspended in mid-air. He looked at it wonderingly as Jack helped him out of the Bronco.

There was a door; there were people. He saw Denise's face pass in front of him, then Maggie's. He found himself lying on the floor. Denise was kneeling beside him with a smudge of smoking grasses in her hand. She was chanting. The smoke smelled sweet. William breathed it in and felt himself drift on the fragrance. He saw feathers. Denise was waving a fan of feathers over his chest. Her hand began to shake uncontrollably.

William was in a cave. A small fire burned in the centre. To the left was a dark tunnel William knew he must not enter. He turned to his right. A deer stood beside him, a buck with a full set of antlers. William stretched forth a curious hand to touch them. "If you follow me," the deer said, "I will heal your wounds."

A bird flew up in front of him, flapping its wings around his head, but it wasn't a bird, it was Denise with wings coming out of both sides of her head. Talons the size of butcher knives, sharp and curved, plunged into his chest. His vision was filled with blood. He screamed.

William ran, ran as hard as he could toward a dark tunnel. Something was chasing him, he didn't know what, something terrifying, something dark and deadly. He had nearly reached the tunnel when a flickering blue flame pulled him back.

CHAPTER ELEVEN
THURSDAY

William awoke in a bed. Daylight brightened the curtained windows. They were curtains he had never seen before, white with a rose-coloured ruffled border. He was in a double bed with an iron bedstead, covered by a white sheet and a flowered duvet. A dresser with an oval mirror stood next to a pine wardrobe. Flower-pattern wallpaper covered the walls. A couple of pictures filled in the spaces, a pastoral landscape and one of a cougar crouching on a rock. He lay for a moment looking at the ceiling. A square light fixture hung from the centre.

Something was on his face. He reached up and touched it, then sat up and looked in the dresser mirror. A large gauze pad was adhesive-taped to the right side of his face. His right eyelid had a blood-encrusted scratch. The other side of his face was bristly with grey whiskers. He felt hungover, as if he had been on a giant bender.

Throwing back the covers, William dragged himself out of bed. He was in his underwear; shirt and pants draped over a chair beside the dresser. The shirt had been washed; a brown stain of blood still discoloured the collar. His glasses were on the dresser.

After dressing, he went out into the hall and started down the stairs. His knees protested mildly. The staircase descended into another hallway; William recognized Maggie's front hall. He made his way through the house to the sun porch at the back. Maggie was staring at a lump of clay. She looked up as William entered.

"Hello, sleepyhead," she said, turning back to the clay. "I thought I'd try something abstract, try working with pure form. What do you think?"

"I'm not a very good person," said William. It jumped out. Whatever was brewing inside him had to come out, he had no control over it.

Maggie laughed at the non sequitur. "That's a funny thing to say! What on earth do you mean?"

"With Barbara—I never knew—"

"Wait," said Maggie, taking off her clay-stained apron, "come into the kitchen." Placing a hand on his shoulder, she directed him to a chair and sat him down. "Now, tell me what you mean."

"With Barbara, I was always so distant. I ran away from her anger, but she was angry because she couldn't reach me; we ended up hurting each other. And I didn't know; I couldn't see what I was doing. Peter and Stephanie, what have I done to them? I didn't mean to hurt anyone, especially not them, not my family, but I was afraid, afraid of her anger, I was so afraid." The sadness was too deep for tears.

Maggie took both his hands in hers. "You haven't

done anything wrong. You were just being human. It happens to everyone. If I were to tell you some of the mix-ups Rick and I got into, oh boy! We all go through this. You're not a bad person."

William stared emptily at the floor. "But she's gone and I can't make it right."

"It is right," said Maggie. "That's the way you were and whatever happened was right for the two of you. You can't judge your life from outside, you have to live it from inside. If she was a screaming bitch and you were a cold fish and you couldn't figure it out between you, then the two of you deserved to be unhappy."

William looked at her in surprise.

"It's true," Maggie stated. "There's no blueprint for a perfect relationship, there's only us poor dumb humans blundering around in some emotional swamp, and we make of it the best we can, and if we hurt other people along the way, or they hurt us, out of stupidity or lack of insight or plain bull-headed stubbornness, then all we can do is go on from where we left off and try our best not to let it happen again. Want some coffee?" She went to fill the coffee maker on the counter. "Anyway," Maggie added, "now you are changed."

"What?"

"Denise took that dead spirit out of your chest. She said it would take a while, maybe a few days, before you recovered. You feel upset, but it will pass. You'll have these moments of deep despair and giddy happiness until you find your natural balance again."

"What are you talking about?"

Maggie tilted her head. "Don't you remember?"

"Remember what?"

"Jack brought you over to Denise's place the night before last. You were in some kind of daze. Jack said you had met Wendigo. One side of your face was all cut and bleeding, you were soaking wet, you were a mess. Denise said Wendigo had shaken loose the dead spirit in your chest, so she took it out."

"You were there?" William felt the whisper of a memory.

"Yes. I don't think I helped much, but Denise's Grandmother Flora told her it was important for me to be there. Denise has been teaching me a few things, some things about healing and restoring balance, things I guess I need in my life. She belongs to a healing lodge, did you know that? Anyway, after work yesterday, she asked me over to her place. She said her Grandmother Flora told her she had some important spirit work to do and she needed my help. So, I went over and then Jack brought you."

Confused images juggled in William's mind. "I sort of remember seeing you and Denise. And there was a deer, and a bird with huge talons. I remember being in a cave." More images hovered on the edge of consciousness, out of reach.

"Jack said you were afraid and your fear made you run in the wrong direction. He had to grab you and pull you back."

William felt bewildered by it all. "How did I get here?"

"Jack drove us. We decided this would be the best place for you until you came around. You slept right through yesterday and all last night. It's Thursday today. You lost a day; you must have been completely exhausted."

"And Denise took the dead spirit out of my chest?"

"So she says." Maggie poured coffee and brought it over to the table. "Oh, you must be starving, too. I'll make you something"

"No, wait, I'm not hungry, I want—I guess—I don't know what I want."

"It's all right." Maggie put on a kitchen apron. "You'll feel better after you have something to eat."

William stood up. "I think I should go."

Without looking up from her food preparations, Maggie said, "I think you should sit down and eat."

"Well," William hesitated.

She turned to him. "Why do you think you're here? Why didn't you stay at Denise's or go back to your own house? You're here because Grandmother Flora said that I am the one who will help you find your balance again. A relationship knocked you out of balance and a relationship will restore it for you." Maggie went back to preparing the food. "I have no idea what I am supposed to do, but if you want my help, I'll try my best and that's all I can do." Her knife snicked through a tomato.

William sat down quietly and sipped his coffee. "What's Grandmother Flora like?" he asked.

"I don't know," said Maggie. "I've never met her. Denise says she's been dead for fifteen years." She sliced some cheese. "Anyway," she added, "you can't go home. My car is still over at your place and Jack has your truck."

Maggie put a plate of cheese and tomato sandwiches in front of William. "How's your face?" she asked. "Does it hurt?"

Except for the tape pulling when he talked, William hadn't even been aware of it.

"We cleaned it up as best we could; washed it with antiseptic and put a sterile dressing on it. There were bits of glass all over, we got most of it out; you should go to the hospital in Fayette as soon as you can to have it checked. I'll change the dressing after lunch. I changed it a couple of times while you slept. You stopped oozing blood, but talking and eating might open it up again. You're lucky it missed your eye. There's one small cut there on the lid; a scratch really." She fingered his collar. "Sorry about the bloodstain. I washed the shirt; the stain wouldn't come out. Lucky it doesn't show too much."

William had hardly taken his first bite when a knock sounded at the front door. He ate while Maggie went to answer it. His cheek complained at the chewing. He put the sandwich down on his plate as Maggie showed Jack into the kitchen.

"Ready to go?" Jack asked.

"Um," William mumbled around his half-chewed mouthful.

"If you feel well enough, I'll take you home. There's some policemen lurking around who've been looking for us. For some reason, they don't like to be kept waiting."

"Go on," said Maggie, "we can talk later. I'll get your jacket. When you come back, I'll change that dressing for you."

William sat in the passenger seat of the Bronco while Jack drove.

Jack gave William a playful grin. "How're things going with Maggie?"

"Maybe I should get a dog," William replied.

"Good idea," said Jack.

William looked out the glassless passenger window. "What happened the other night?"

Jack kept his eyes on the road. "What do you remember?"

William recounted his disjointed experience with the bird and the deer.

Jack remained silent for a few minutes. "We'll talk about it later. Now is not the time for explanations.

Explanations are intellectual. You need to stay with your emotions. For now, don't worry about what happened, just enjoy feeling unglued."

As they rolled down the highway, William asked, "One thing I'm not clear on is the relationship between Perkins and Tyler Westman. George appeared to be working with both of them, but were Perkins and Westman in this together?"

"I was confused about that too," Jack confessed. "Nothing that Raven or Wolf showed me connected Westman and Perkins. I think George was acting on his own."

William went over what they had learned. "We know George was involved with Perkins because they set up the mining companies together; and we know George made a deal with Tyler Westman when they met at the Eagle Lake cabin last winter. But it was the geologists who were planning the gold fraud; where do they fit in?"

Jack shrugged. "Either George knew about their plan and approached Perkins, or Perkins knew about it and recruited George to steal their ore samples."

"Was Perkins working with the geologists?"

Jack shrugged again. "I don't know. Mason and Happer didn't know anything about Perkins's arrangement with George, that's for sure. And Perkins wasn't in on George's plan to relocate the gold ore to Hellbent Stump either, because George called in Lance to help him with that. I think George was keeping everyone in the dark."

William rubbed his temples. "George told Lance and Westman that he had discovered the lost gold mine; he didn't tell them about the geologists or Perkins, but when George fell and broke his leg, Lance went to Perkins for help."

Jack agreed. "Looks that way. George must have sent him there. I guess he didn't have anywhere else to turn."

"George also told Westman that he had someone to look after the technical details. He must have meant Perkins. Did George still expect Perkins to handle the business end of things, even though he was working with Westman?"

"Some of the incorporation documents we found in Perkins's cabin had George as the sole proprietor. George might have thought that, with mining companies set up in his name, he could pull off the gold scam on his own and help Caroline." Jack sighed. "I have a feeling that George hadn't worked out all the details. He had the gold, he would deal with Perkins and Westman when the time came."

William shook his head sadly. "All this happened because George was trying to help his daughter."

"Yeah, he just wasn't a very good thief."

They drove in silence until William commented, "Those warriors did a good job."

"Good job of what?" asked Jack.

"Of making it seem as if Wendigo was out there in the woods with us."

"Oh," said Jack.

"They sure scared Perkins. Me too. I guess they saved our lives."

The highway took them north out of town; the cold wind through the missing window made William's face ache. They passed a car parked crookedly on the soft shoulder, the hood and trunk lid wide open.

"Stop!" William shouted. Jack slowed and pulled off the road.

William opened his door and strode back to the parked car, ignoring the protests from his knees. A long, wide slick of oil trailed away behind it: the sign of a major engine problem.

Jack came up beside William.

"That's the warriors' car," William stated, staring at the stranded pile of scrap.

"Looks like it," said Jack.

"How long has it been here?"

"Quite a while. It was here when I drove you from Denise's down to Maggie's place. We passed it on the way."

"If their car broke down here, how could they have been in the woods making Wendigo noises with us?"

"That's a puzzle," said Jack.

"You're not going to tell me it was really Wendigo out there in the woods, are you?"

"Could have been," said Jack. "Or maybe it was the wind and some really big chipmunks." He walked back to the Bronco, William following moodily behind.

On the road to Rainbow Lake, instead of taking the turn to William's cabin, Jack followed the north fork toward Rainbow Lake Resort.

"Where are we going?" William asked.

"Thought we'd talk to Billy, see what's happening," said Jack, pulling up beside the Rainbow Airlines office. They could see Billy down on the float, leaning over the engine of his plane.

"Hey, Billy," Jack greeted as they neared the dock.

"Hey, Jack," Billy responded cheerfully. "How's it goin'?" He saw William's bandaged face. "Whoa! What happened to you?"

William shrugged. "Ran into a window."

"Looks bad. You gonna be okay?"

"Small cuts, big bandage, that's all," William explained.

Jack interrupted, "You hear about Crazy Crazy?"

"Yeah," Billy nodded. "Poor guy. He was one strange little dude, but he shouldn't have ended up like that. It's real sad."

"You were supposed to take him down to Thunder Bay, to the assay office."

"Yeah, I know," acknowledged Billy. "After you left the other night he stayed here overnight. I don't know what would have happened if he'd gone into town; the person who started a phoney gold rush? Man, he would have been ripped to pieces. He wouldn't believe it was all fake; he had his ore samples and that was enough for him. Anyways, old Crazy was going to tag along on my run. I've been making extra flights down to Thunder Bay to keep the stores in town supplied, especially the café. You wouldn't believe how much food Maggie has been going through.

"Anyways, he wakes me up at first light the next morning and we're all ready to leave when I start losing hydraulic pressure. I take a look and find a leak and when I tighten it up, wouldn't you know it, the fitting's cracked. I tell Crazy Crazy to wait while I change the fitting and bleed the system, but by the time I'm done he's gone. Couldn't have taken more than half an hour to fix it; I guess he wandered off, maybe forgot why he was here, you know what he was like. Then I hear he got shot up there on the Stump. Made me feel real bad. I mean, if it hadn't been for that leak, I would have flown him down to Thunder Bay and he would probably still be alive today."

"Yeah, well, that's the way she goes sometimes," said Jack. "Thanks for filling us in."

"Hey, no problem, man," said Billy, "anything I can do to help. One good thing's going to come out of all this anyways, I've made enough money for a down payment on a new plane. Get rid of this sorry heap. This old girl won't be passing too many more flight inspections."

"Well, good luck, Billy," said Jack.

"See ya around." Billy returned to his engine.

Jack took the south fork and drove to William's cabin. After parking the Bronco, they walked around to the front. William stopped and gasped at what they saw. There, on the ground beside the door, wild-eyed and trembling, huddled Harry Perkins. He was barely recognizable. His clothes, caked with mud and dirt, were in tatters, bloody cuts visible through the tears; a gash ran down his mud-splattered face beside his right eye; his grey hair was stained red with blood.

"Oh my God!" William exclaimed. He opened the door while Jack helped Perkins to his feet. They took him inside and sat him at the kitchen table.

"Get some bandages," said Jack.

While Jack heated a pan of water on the stove, William hurriedly went for the first aid kit. They helped Perkins out of his grimy, torn clothes; Jack cleaned his wounds with warm water. Perkins's breathing was ragged; he continued shaking uncontrollably. Jack bandaged the cuts, William fetched clean clothes. "Make some medicine tea," Jack said as he helped Perkins dress. "And William," he added, "call the police."

Jack went to the bedroom for a blanket; William placed a call to the police, then found the mustard tin of *maskikik* tea. Perkins huddled in his chair trembling, his unfocused eyes darting randomly. Jack wrapped the blanket around Perkins's shoulders and sat with him, murmuring reassurances in comforting tones.

When the tea was ready, William placed a mug of it on the table.

"Tell me what happened," Jack encouraged him quietly.

Perkins turned toward him, his eyes were hollow pits. "Wendigo," he whispered, shivering.

"Yes, Wendigo came," Jack nodded, "but he's gone now. You're safe here. Try some of this." He guided the mug to Perkins's lips and helped him drink. "Tell me about Lance."

"Lance." Perkins was still trembling. "I killed Lance. I had to. He wanted to go to the police."

"And George?" Jack asked softly.

"Yes, and George. He was in the cave. He was hurt. There was no other way."

"Okay, take it easy," said Jack soothingly. "Drink your tea and tell us what happened."

The mug rattled against Perkins's teeth as he took a drink. It took several minutes of Jack calming him down before his shaking abated enough to talk.

William watched Perkins with morbid fascination. He had never seen a murderer before, let alone been in the same room with one. Perkins looked like he had aged twenty years. Gone was the confident and commanding manner; he hunched over his tea a broken man, head bandaged, cheeks sunken, hair matted with blood. But it was the eyes William found most disturbing. They looked as if the life had been scooped right out of them.

"Start at the beginning," Jack suggested. "Tell us about the geologists and the gold fraud."

Perkins took a deep breath. "I'd made some disastrous investments," he began hesitantly, "with other people's money, investments I was sure would pay off—but they didn't and if anyone found out about what I had done, it would mean jail. I was on the brink of losing everything." Once he started, the story spilled out of him. "Last spring I met with two geologists, Mason and Happer, we discussed the possibility of finding gold in the greenstone belt—particularly in the exposed drift called Ghostwalker Ridge north of Jubilee. They told me that the geology was promising and there was a legend of a lost gold mine, but the whole area had already been surveyed with metal-detecting aircraft without finding anything. I thought that the geology and the story of the lost mine made a gold strike in the vicinity believable. I decided that if we couldn't find it there, we could put it there.

"I was desperate; my life was going down the tubes. I worked out a plan to salt the area with gold-bearing ore and convinced the geologists to come in with me. They were going to rediscover the lost gold mine and pull a Bre-x. You know about Bre-x?"

Jack nodded.

"But it all went wrong. Mason and Happer got scared and wanted to pull out. I decided to go on without them, and everything went out of control."

Jack spoke in a gentle voice, "They were in pretty deep, they got as far as bringing the gold ore up here. What scared them off?"

Perkins seemed to shrink in his seat. "My greed. Why have a little when you can have it all?" He put both hands around the tea mug and held onto it tightly. "The plan was to announce the strike and pre-sell shares before the claims were verified; the share price would be based on the geologists' reports, the physical samples and the legend of the lost mine. I bought that cabin up here in order to manage things first hand." Jack helped Perkins drink more *maskikik*.

"The original deal I made with the geologists," he went on, "was that we would sell shares up to twenty million dollars, then make a run for it. That would be ten million for me and five million each for the geologists. But I knew we could make more, at least three or four times more. It would be riskier, a lot riskier. I tried to convince Mason and Happer, but they wouldn't go for it. They were nervous; they didn't want to take any more chances than necessary. They seemed on the point of backing out, so I reassured them that we would stick to the original plan and increased their share to seven million each."

"Where does George Ferris fit in?" Jack asked.

"I began to think that the geologists were the weakest link in the scheme. Once I had their report, I didn't really need them; so I decided to cut them out. They wouldn't be able to say that the reports were falsified or they would be admitting to fraud. But I still needed a front-man, someone to find the gold and announce the discovery." Perkins fixed his dead eyes on the tea mug, his voice becoming a monotone drone.

"One day, shortly after I had bought the cabin, I noticed a truck parked at the boat landing. There were two men in it, both very drunk. They told me they were going out into the bush prospecting for amethysts. One of them, a man named Crazy Crazy, started talking about gold and the other one, George Ferris, repeated the story about the lost gold mine.

"I invited them back to my cabin, fed them more drinks. The crazy man passed out and I eased Ferris around to the subject of gold, that maybe there was gold around there and that maybe I knew where it was and how would he like to make some big money, in the neighbourhood of a hundred thousand dollars?" The blanket slipped off one of Perkins's shoulders; Jack reached over to pull it up again.

"Well, Ferris jumped at the chance, so we made a deal. I didn't trust his crazy friend; I made him promise to keep it to himself. We planned to let the geologists plant the ore samples, then Ferris would find it and announce the strike." Perkins drank more tea. "I returned to Toronto and created a web of companies in order to sell off a lot of small claims instead of one big parcel in order to spread the risk. I laid everything out ready, then came back up this fall when the geologists were planting the ore. They didn't know about my arrangement with Ferris. We were so close when everything began to fall apart."

"Did you have anything to do with George stealing the ore from the geologists' camp? Or was he acting on his own?" William asked.

Perkins shook his head. "I didn't know anything about that. The next thing I knew, a wild man was pounding on my door saying that Ferris had sent him, that Ferris had been hurt and needed help. The man said he was Lance Rockwell, Ferris's son-in-law. He led me to Hellbent Stump where Ferris lay at the bottom of a cave with a broken leg and a box of gold ore.

"I climbed down a knotted rope into the cave and asked Ferris what was going on. Ferris said he had decided to hide the gold somewhere for safekeeping. I didn't believe him for a minute. I guessed that George had formed a partnership with Rockwell and was trying to double-cross me. Ferris was in a lot of pain from his broken leg, he begged me to help him. I knew we would need to call in a Search and Rescue team to get Ferris out of the cave and to a hospital; that would put the whole venture at risk. Weighing Ferris's worthless life against sixty to eighty million dollars wasn't a hard choice to make, so I—" Perkins hesitated "—I picked up a rock and bashed his head in." He shuddered and held his face in his hands.

"What happened next?" Jack prompted.

Perkins took a breath. "I climbed back up the rope and told Rockwell it was too late to save Ferris, that he had died of his injuries. Rockwell was in a panic. I told him to go home and that I would look after everything. I hid the box of gold and the rope under some rocks, covering them with branches and pine needles. Then, on the Monday, Rockwell came to my cabin and told me Ferris's body had been found."

"Jack and I found him," said William, refilling Perkins's mug with tea. "We told Lance about it on the way home, then we saw him driving off to the north. I guess he was on his way to tell you that George had been found."

Perkins nodded. "The next day, we went back to Hellbent Stump and moved the body. We hauled it out of the cave and dropped it down the deepest fissure we could find. Rockwell got upset when he saw Ferris's smashed head. I told him that an animal must have done it, but I don't think he believed me; I think he suspected that I had killed Ferris.

"I still thought everything could work out, I didn't want to let it go. I told Rockwell that if he would give me the mining company certificates from George's cabin, I would transfer them into his name. I was starting to have my doubts about him; he was becoming erratic. He would turn up at my place at odd hours all stressed out. Something was bothering him, something more than the death of Ferris, but he wouldn't tell me what it was. Rockwell was scared; wanted me to promise that the gold scheme was a sure thing."

"Do you know Tyler Westman?" William asked.

Perkins looked up and blinked his soulless eyes. "Westman?" He shook his head. "No, never heard of him."

Jack put a hand on his arm. "Go on."

Perkins took another deep breath. "One day Rockwell arrived at my cabin in a panic. He said that you two had been to see him and that his wife had disappeared. He was acting insane; he thought you knew too much. I suggested that we talk to you, try to make a deal. Rockwell had a rifle with him that he had taken from Ferris's cabin, so I took my own rifle as well. We drove to your house in Ferris's truck, but you weren't home. Rockwell wanted to go to the police and tell them about Ferris. He was sure they would find out anyway and the sooner we turned ourselves in the better it would be.

"I told him that we couldn't go to the police because I had killed Ferris and that he would be charged as an accessory to murder. Rockwell went berserk. He was waving Ferris's rifle around, and I was afraid he was going to kill me. So I shot him and left him on your doorstep. I took his gun and left my own rifle, along with Ferris's truck, at your cabin and walked back to my own place on Trout Lake." Perkins stared unseeing at the wet rings on the table.

The sound of a car outside broke the tension. Jack went to open the door for Sergeant Selkirk and Constable Shaw. As he spoke to them quietly, William stuffed Perkins's bloody clothes into a plastic bag.

Selkirk walked over to the table. "Harry Perkins?"

Perkins showed no reaction.

"Would you come with us, please?" Selkirk took hold of Perkins's arm and brought him to his feet. Perkins didn't resist. Selkirk escorted him to the door where Shaw took him outside. Selkirk turned to Jack and William. "We'd like you to come down to the station as well. We need you to make a statement."

"We'll drive ourselves down and meet you there," said Jack.

Selkirk nodded and left.

"I'd really like to wash up and change my clothes," said William.

"Don't worry," Jack assured him, "Justice is blind. And hopefully doesn't have a sense of smell either."

The drive to Fayette was an uneventful drone. William folded his arms across his chest and stared glumly out of his glassless window at the wearying repetition of rocks and trees. William hated it. He hated the colour of it, the sameness of it—he hated everything. The further they travelled from Jubilee, the worse his mood became.

"Relieved that it's all over?" Jack asked. William didn't change the set of his face. "You may feel weird for a while, but it will pass. These mood swings must be killing you!"

William's frown deepened. His feelings prowled from anger to self-pity and back again, like a cougar pacing in a cage. "You know—" he rubbed his forehead "—I can't get over the feeling that Tyler Westman is involved in all this. Caroline said that Westman was waiting for her at George's cabin after she ran away. But Lance must have gone back at some point for the rifle. Do you think Lance and Westman met there?"

"I don't know," said Jack, "but Caroline knows more than she's saying. I have a feeling she knew Lance was dead the night she got on that bus. She was Westman's alibi for the time of Lance's murder. That must have been her bargaining chip: she would provide the alibi if he would let her go free."

William watched the relentless passage of the trees as the wind blew back his hair through the shattered passenger side window.

Bremner was waiting for them at the Fayette police station. By way of greeting he demanded, "Where the hell have you been?"

Jack was led away by Sergeant Selkirk. William was

coerced into the little interview room. Bremner and Adams pushed in behind him, Adams forcing William down into a chair. Bremner put his knuckles on the table and leaned across to put his face close up to William's. "Where the hell have you been? I told you not to leave the restaurant, but you sneak out, disappear for a day, then turn up with a man who confesses to two murders. Now, where have you been?" Bremner's voice had built into a shout, little flecks of spittle flew into William's face. Their eyes locked.

"I was asleep." William's voice was a grenade of controlled anger. "I had a dead spirit taken out of my chest."

Bremner's voice dropped to a soft threat. "Look, Mr. Longstaffe, you're an intelligent man, you're an educated man, do you understand what kind of trouble you are in? Do you realize that you are throwing away your whole future if you don't co-operate with us?"

Their eyes wrestled, neither budging. William leaned forward until he was nose to nose with Bremner. "Either charge me or fuck off."

Bremner's expression changed into that of a man who had just lost control of his bowels. He broke away and walked to the door. "You deal with him," he said to Adams as he strode out without looking back.

Adams shuffled through the papers in his file, his face down to hide his expression while he brought his laughter under control. "Okay," he began seriously, "let's start with the incident at Hellbent Stump. We know you left from George Ferris's cabin Tuesday morning accompanied by Mr. Crowfoot and Constable Shaw."

Together they went through the events surrounding the death of Crazy Crazy. As they talked, William's anger gave way to sadness over the troubled man's senseless death. He was careful to call him Maurice Crécy, not Crazy Crazy. It made him feel better to use his name, as if they were talking about a person and not a caricature.

"Okay," said Adams, moving on, "let's talk about what happened after you left the Kozy Korner Kafé." William began to describe the confrontation with Harry Perkins, drifting into a monologue, not so much of the sequence of events, but of his internal state, of the claustrophobic trees, of the cold claws of death at his throat as he stood on the edge of a bottomless grave with a bullet waiting in the barrel of a gun a heartbeat away.

"You escaped by making yourself invisible, is that correct?" Adams managed to keep the skepticism out of his voice. He pursed his lips at William's affirmative reply. "And how did Harry Perkins come to be at your cabin today?"

William recounted the finding of Perkins at his front door.

"If you will wait here for a few minutes, Mr. Longstaffe." Adams gathered up his files and left.

William leaned on the table and sighed. He stared straight ahead, his mind as blank and exhausted as the prison walls.

He became aware of someone calling his name. "Mr. Longstaffe?" Adams was standing across the table from him. "Are you all right?" William nodded dumbly. Adams gave him a concerned look. "We are going to keep you here overnight. You are not under arrest, but we will hold you as a material witness. Do you understand?" William nodded again. "We are keeping you here due to your previous failure to remain voluntarily. Do you understand?" Another nod. "Please follow me."

William followed Adams back to the same cell he had occupied before. It seemed the only difference between being a witness and a criminal was that witnesses weren't handcuffed. William lay down on the bunk, feeling the weight of his fatigue. He felt as if he were falling backwards into the Gulp; he could see Harry Perkins's bullet flying toward him in slow motion. Out of the darkness came the deer's head. "If you follow me, I will heal your wounds," it said. William reached out. "How do I follow you?" More a plea than a question. "I don't know how. I'm not strong enough."

William dozed off, to be awakened when a young constable, with STEELE on a patch over his pocket, popped his head in. "Chinese okay for supper? We're ordering in. Anything special you want?"

William said no, and stared at the ceiling. He felt as deflated as a flat tire.

About forty minutes later Constable Steele returned. "Food's here. Come on, we can eat in the staff room." William followed him to a windowless, concrete block room. Prison architecture seemed to be the same whichever side of the bars you were on. A row of vending machines glowed along one wall. Two brown paper bags smelling of hot and sour sauce waited on a table. Jack was already sitting with another young constable. As the policemen distributed paper plates, William took a chair across from Jack. "Dig in, guys," prompted Steele enthusiastically. "This is better than the stuff you'd usually get." He pointed to the vending machines. "Cruel and unusual punishment, having to eat that stuff." Both officers laughed. They dropped into conversation about the Maple Leafs and a stolen car they were looking for. William ate, not really tasting anything.

"You okay?" Jack asked.

William lifted mournful eyes from his plate. "How do I follow the deer? I don't know what I'm supposed to do."

Jack put down his fork. "It's not really following; it's

more like freeing yourself from the cocoon of restrictions you have been wrapped in so you can find your true path." He reached over and tapped William on the chest. "You have a big hole there to fill. We can't put a bandage on it like we can your face. Everything may feel impossibly hard for a while. Trust the deer; it will guide you to your path."

William noticed the officers staring at them. "Giving some medical advice," said Jack cheerily. The officers shrugged and returned to comparing the strengths of the Leafs to the Oilers.

After the meal, William and Jack were shown the staff lounge. There were couches and a TV. A coffee table was piled with magazines. "Your cells won't be locked," Steele informed them. "You can watch TV in here if you want, we've got satellite. Just don't leave the building."

"I'd like to make some calls," said William.

"Sure, pay phone's right there in the hall."

William felt his pockets for change. "I, um—"

"Well, seeing as how you're a witness and everything, I guess the department could spring for a phone call or two. Come with me." Steele led him to an empty office. "You can call from here; dial 9 for an outside line."

William sat at the desk and called directory assistance for the numbers of Maggie's house and the Kozy Korner Kafé. He tried the café first, but Maggie wasn't there. He tried her home number. She answered on the first ring.

"Hello, Maggie, it's William."

"Oh, William, where are you?"

"Everything's fine." He explained about being held as a witness. "I'm not locked up, can even watch TV if I want." There was a pause. The thin copper wire stretching from Fayette to Jubilee did not make a connection between them. "Um, Maggie, I—"

"Yes?"

Break the cocoon, let the past go. "I, uh, I don't want you to save me."

"What?"

"You know, Denise or her Grandmother Flora said that you were the one to help me find my balance. Well, if we are going to have a relationship, I don't want it to be because you are saving me. I want it to be because, you know, because of us, because of you and me."

"William, I—"

"And I wanted to say that I appreciate all your help and care."

"William, I—"

"I've got to go; I just wanted to tell you those things. Hope your sculpture works out, you know, the pure form one. It looked interesting. Bye now." He hung up before she had a chance to say anything his old condescending self might consider trite or sentimental—any touch, however gentle, that would hurt his still tender wounds.

William was trembling. One more call.

"Hello, Stephanie?"

"Daddy! Where are you! I've been going frantic! I—"

"Stephanie, listen to me. Everything is all right. I'm fine."

"Daddy, I'm coming up there."

"Steph, please don't do that, not yet."

"But Daddy!"

"Stephanie, I called to say that things will be different from now on, something's happened that's changed me."

"Daddy, you're scaring me."

"Don't be scared, everything is okay, in fact, it's more than okay, everything is good, very good. I called to say I love you very much and that I—"

"Daddy—"

"No, let me finish, I have to do this, I may say it badly, but I want—" William grappled with a storm of unformed thoughts. "When you were growing up, I made a mistake and I want you to know that I have realized it and that I will be a better father to you and Peter and a better grandfather to Colin and Stephen."

"Daddy, what are you talking about? You weren't a bad father, you're a good father."

"That's not what I mean, it's not about being good or bad, it's—I made a mistake, that's all."

"Daddy, I'm worried about you. What's going on? What's this all about?"

"Look, Steph, I have to go."

"When are you coming home?"

William took a deep breath. "I might have changed my mind about that."

"Daddy! I think I should come up."

"No, Stephanie, I'll call you later and we'll talk about it."

"Well, okay," she agreed reluctantly. "You promise you'll call?"

"Yes, I promise." He said good-bye and hung up. He sighed. *Changing myself is the easy part,* he thought. *The hard part is other people.*

William left the office and found Steele at the front desk. "I'd like to go back to my cell." William had almost said room. It sounded strange to ask to be put in a cell, and ironic at a time when Jack was telling him to free himself of his bonds.

"No problem," said the young constable and led the way.

Back on his bunk, William went over his conversations. Was he making a worse mess than he was in before? Could he free himself from the trap he had made for himself? It sounded like a good idea, but how exactly was he supposed to do it? And what consequences would follow? William's exhaustion overcame him and he faded into sleep.

CHAPTER TWELVE
FRIDAY

William was roughly awakened the next morning by Constable Shaw. "Hey, get up, Bremner wants to talk to you." He threw a plastic bag on the bunk. "You've got half an hour." He stopped at the door. "Oh, and here," he tossed another package on the bunk. "Bremner sent that for you."

In the plastic bag were a disposable toothbrush, a squeeze packet of toothpaste, a disposable washcloth, a small bar of soap, a disposable razor and a large paper towel. Everything the disposable person needs, thought William. The other package said STERILE DRESSING in green letters.

William went across the hall to the bathroom and cleaned himself up as best he could. As the damaged side of his face was too raw to shave, he decided not to shave the other side either. Guess I'm growing a beard, he thought as he replaced the dressing. He hadn't had a beard since graduate school.

Shaw was waiting in the hall when he came out and led the way to Bremner's office. Jack was already there when William entered. "Sit," said Bremner, jabbing a finger at them. "You are co-operating with us as witnesses. I thought we'd meet in here instead of the interview room, make it a little less formal." He gave William a stern look. "Perhaps a little less threatening." Bremner poured coffee for them into paper cups. "Mr. Harry Perkins has given us a full confession as to his involvement in the phoney gold scheme, and the murders of George Ferris and Lance Rockwell." He paused and leaned back in his chair. "For some reason, judges don't like confessions. They throw them out every chance they get. So if Perkins's lawyer claims the confession was made under duress, or that improper procedure was followed because somebody looked at him cross-eyed, and the judge dismisses it, then we're back to square one." He leaned forward over the file again. "Therefore, we need corroborative evidence to show a judge that even if the confession doesn't stand up, we still have enough to go to trial. We need your help in substantiating Perkins's confession." He opened a file on the desk. "I'm going to tell you what Perkins said, then I want you to tell me what you know about it, got it?" Jack and William nodded. "You may be repeating things you have said in previous interviews, but we're trying to form a complete picture here."

William asked, "Where is Perkins?"

"He was transferred down to Thunder Bay last night after we recorded his statement." Bremner proceeded to read out Perkins's confession about the murders of George Ferris and Lance Rockwell, repeatedly questioning Jack and William about their versions of the events.

"Do you have anything else to add?" he asked when he came to the end.

William sat up. "What about the rifle and the fingerprints?"

"Perkins says he bought the rifle second hand from an ad tacked on a supermarket bulletin board in Toronto. He left it at the scene knowing that it could not be traced back to him. The fingerprint transfer was something he had seen on a TV crime show. He used some tape from your desk to lift the prints from a mug in the kitchen. It was clumsily done, strictly amateur hour." Bremner shook his head. "People watch too much TV," he declared. "We did find some gum residue on one of the mugs in your kitchen, but no other prints." Bremner fixed his eyes on William. "You should be more careful about locking your door in future. Anything else?"

Both Jack and William shook their heads.

Bremner referred to the file again. "That brings us up to the events of last Tuesday night. You left the Kozy Korner Kafé, against instructions, I might add, and went to Mr. Perkins's cabin."

"But first we found out that Caroline's place had been broken into," William filled in. "It was Perkins who drove her into town. He had the opportunity to return to the cabin and steal the papers that connected him to George Ferris while Caroline was at the hairdresser's."

Bremner frowned. "Yes. We called Perkins into town to confirm Mrs. Rockwell's story; on returning home he found a vehicle parked at the boat landing. Fearing intruders, he waited until he saw two people coming from the direction of his cabin. He recognized you immediately. Until that moment he still believed he could get away with the gold scam. There was nothing to link him to either the Ferris or Rockwell murders. He was sure that Ferris's body wouldn't be found, and even if it was, no coroner would be able to tell if Ferris's fatal head injury was deliberate or accidental. Perkins had recovered the documents linking him to Ferris; and with everyone out of the way, even Ferris's unreliable friend Maurice Crécy conveniently dead, he was in the clear.

"When he saw you at his cabin, he decided he had to get rid of you two as well. He didn't know how much Rockwell had told you, or exactly what you knew about Ferris's death. He retrieved Ferris's rifle from his trunk and took a shot at you, shattering the passenger side window of your vehicle. Then he directed you into the bush with the intention of shooting you both and dropping your bodies into a large pit he had seen on the way to Hellbent Stump."

"The Gulp," William provided.

"What?"

"The Gulp, that's what it's called."

"Ah." Bremner made a note on his pad. "What happened next is unclear. Perkins was unable to account for his whereabouts from the time you last saw him in the woods Tuesday night until he was discovered at your front door yesterday. All he would say was, *Wendigo*." Bremner gave them an inquisitorial stare. "Perkins suffered a number of cuts, abrasions, and contusions. Are you sure that he was not with you during the time he was missing? Maybe you roughed him up a bit, took a little revenge? Can't say I would blame you if you did."

William was outraged at the suggestion. He stood up, ready to tell Bremner what he thought of the idea, but Bremner held up a hand to stop him.

"We aren't going to have a repetition of yesterday, Mr. Longstaffe." Bremner frowned severely. "I suggest you sit down and control yourself."

William sat, fuming.

Bremner busied himself with the file, shuffling papers,

reviewing reports. After a few minutes he said, without looking up, "Well, we have your statements about what happened that night. You have a lot to explain, especially about disappearing for a day, but I suppose that isn't pertinent to this case at the moment. I think we have enough to convict with or without the confession. Thank you, gentlemen, you are free to go."

"Wait a minute," said William, swallowing the remains of his anger. "What happened to the geologists?"

Bremner rubbed his eyes. "Steven Mason and Franklin Happer. We're still looking for them. They took a bus out of Jubilee on the day Lance Rockwell was murdered. The same bus, coincidentally, Caroline Rockwell was on. We traced them to Thunder Bay where they disappeared. We'll catch up with them eventually." He smiled. "We always do."

"Thank you," William said as they left the office, although he had no idea why he said it. He had nothing to thank Bremner for. As they crossed the parking lot to the Bronco, William asked Jack, "How did Perkins get to my front door? Did the warriors leave him there? Were they the ones who beat him up?"

"That was Wendigo's doing," said Jack. "Wendigo is attracted by death, he took Perkins to a place where a death had occurred, where Lance died. Lucky we cleansed the death out of that cave or Wendigo might have left him there. Then we would have had to go out into the bush to bring him back."

William made a dissatisfied frown. "If Wendigo is supposed to eat people, why didn't he eat Perkins?"

"I'm a spirit talker, remember? I talk to Wendigo. I asked him not to."

"Wendigo does what you say?"

"He did that night," Jack shrugged. "Lucky for us, or we might have been eaten too!"

William felt a chill run up his spine. "Come on, Jack, be straight with me. Was it really Wendigo out there, or was it the warriors?"

"Next time you see those warriors," said Jack mysteriously, "you ask them!"

"Hungry?" asked Jack as he drove the Bronco back to Jubilee.

William gave a noncommittal grunt. He hadn't thought about food. He laid his head back on the headrest, letting himself be mesmerized by the passing scenery.

"We can get something to eat at the Kozy Korner," Jack suggested.

William didn't respond. He watched the landscape fly by, the occasional cut through multicoloured rock, revealing the strata that had taken millions of years to lay down. He felt as if he were looking deep into the core of the earth, as if he were being shown something hidden, some secret lesson about how things went together and why.

"I still don't understand," he said to Jack, "about this dead spirit Denise took out of my chest."

"Think of it like a scab on a cut," explained Jack. "A protective covering over all your inner hurts. After Wendigo loosened it up, Denise pulled it off."

"So now my inner hurts are exposed?"

"Well, sort of more freed than exposed. Your feelings were always controlled before, repressed. Now you have the opportunity to respond to the world, and other people, in a feeling way."

"The deer said that if I followed it, it would heal my wounds. What does that mean?"

"You'll have to find that out for yourself. Each

person's path is unique." Jack paused, searching for words. "Healing isn't something that happens and then you're healed and it's over. Healing is a process that we work through all our lives; it's our path, it's our life's work. The world is continually damaging us and we are always seeking to restore the balance."

"It's a cruel world," quoted William facetiously.

"Not cruel," said Jack, "just a world that is constantly seeking harmony."

"Does anyone ever find harmony and balance in their lives? Have you?"

Jack shrugged. "The irony of it is that the very search for balance is what pushes things out of balance. Harmony for the wind is whistling through the sky, but that stirs up the water and the water gets all roughed up and loses the level it is always seeking. So the balance is that sometimes the wind blows and sometimes it is still, sometimes the water is rough and sometimes it is calm. It's the same with the forces in our lives. Our lives can't be calm all the time; our path is to find the harmony between the rough and the smooth. That's where the Deer spirit will lead you, into an understanding of your own life."

William remained silent for the rest of the trip, losing track of distance and time; he was surprised when Jack pulled up across the street from the Kozy Korner Kafé. He followed Jack through the door and looked around for Maggie. She wasn't there.

"You know," he said, "I'm not really hungry." He chewed his lower lip. "I still have to return Maggie's car, why don't you drive me home and then I'll take her car back?"

"Sure," said Jack with a shrug.

William drove the blue Plymouth to Maggie's house and knocked on the door. Getting no response, he walked around the back. He could see Maggie working on a sculpture in her studio, could hear Neil Young's "Heart of Gold" playing very loudly. He watched her completely absorbed in her work, arms moving like a ballerina's as she searched for a shape in the clay. William thought of creeping quietly away, leaving the keys in her mailbox, slipping out of her life.

Instead he climbed the steps and knocked on the door. She didn't hear him. He knocked again, louder. Maggie looked up, startled. Seeing him she ran to the door, flung it open, threw her clay-stained arms around him and pressed her face against his chest. William thought she softly said his name, but couldn't hear clearly over the music.

He let one hand slide over her shoulders like a sheltering wing. The other he ran through her hair, feeling the softness of it. They stood there holding each other for a long time.

Eventually Maggie broke away and went to turn the volume down. "Come in, come in," she urged. "I was so worried about you."

William didn't want to talk; he just wanted to hold her. He had made up little conversation openers like, I brought your car back, and, The police are finished with Jack and me, but all such thoughts went out of his head. He took her in his arms again and pulled her close to his body, letting the past go, letting everything go except the sensation of holding another person—a person who wanted to be held and embraced him back.

"Welcome home," she mumbled into his shirt.

CHAPTER THIRTEEN
SATURDAY

The news that the gold strike was fake had people leaving the town of Jubilee almost as fast as they had come. Saturday night brought the Gold Rush Ball. Maggie and Denise had organized it. They booked the community hall, bought a temporary liquor license and hired a country band from Sault Ste. Marie called King Cab and the Eighteen Wheelers.

The evening was a great success. Even though a lot of the gold seekers had packed up their dreams and left town, the hall was still so crowded that exuberant partiers, trying to drink away their disappointment, overflowed into the parking lot and down the street. The men outnumbered the women about fifty to one; it was like a gigantic boys-night-out with all the men trying to impress the women by out-toughing, out-shouting, and out-drinking everyone else. It made for some very interesting dancing.

Jack, William, Denise, and Maggie shared a table near the stage. William had loaned Jack one of his more subdued checked shirts and they looked masculine in clean flannel and blue jeans. Denise's black hair, picking up highlights from the stage lighting, ran over the shoulders of a mauve blouse. Amethyst earrings sparkled when she turned her head. The bruising around her eye had completely faded. Maggie had her auburn hair tied back in a loose ponytail, brushing the back of a forest green dress. She wore a single amethyst crystal on a gold chain around her neck.

William felt in his pocket for his own crystal. He would ask Denise to string it for him later. His face had healed enough that he didn't need the bandage any more, his cheek a calamity of scabbed-over cuts, partly hidden by an advancing beard. The band was so loud William and Maggie couldn't hear each other talk. They tried to discuss the events of the previous few days, but spent most of the conversation shouting, "What?"

When the band took a break, two men came up to the table. It was Danny and another man, about as big as Danny, only more serious looking. Danny gave Denise a sloppy grin. "Hey, babe," he said. Denise didn't respond. "I've come back," he said, increasing the grin.

"Well, you can just go away again," said Denise without looking at him.

"Hi, Danny," said Jack. "Hey, Anton." Anton nodded back.

"Denise," Danny announced, spreading his arms wide, "I'm a new man!"

Denise glanced at him from the corner of her eye. "Looks too much like the old one to me," she said, averting her eyes again.

Danny sighed. He reached into a pocket and pulled out a wad of bills. Ostentatiously peeling some off, he placed them on the table in front of Denise. "There," he said, "that's for you to get your house fixed up. Now, would the old Danny have done that?"

"You taken up bank robbing?" asked Denise.

"Denise, I worked for that money. You ask Anton here." He asked for her. "Anton, how did I come by that money?"

"Work," said Anton.

"There, you see?" beamed Danny. "I worked for the money and now I'm paying off my debts. And one other thing: since the night I left I have not had one drink. Not one itty-bitty little drink, not even a whiff of a beer cap. Nothing. Nada. Niet. Not a thing. Not a drop. Absolutely nothing. Right, Anton?"

"Nothing," agreed Anton.

"Look," said Danny, "can we sit down here so I can explain? I'll tell you the whole story."

William touched Maggie's arm. "Maybe we should go outside for some air."

"No, no, no," interjected Danny. "I want you guys to hear this too, I want everyone to know. Now, can I sit down?"

Denise nodded.

Anton produced two chairs, seemingly out of nowhere as there didn't appear to be any empty seats in the place. Danny put his elbows on the table and leaned toward Denise. "That night I popped you one, gave you a black eye, right? You know I only get like that when I've been drinking. Well, one night I went over to William's camp to hit him up for some cash, you know, to get my truck fixed—I knew you'd been staying there and I thought I could work the sympathy angle. As I'm walking over there, I hear these screams coming from the woods, scared the crap out of me.

"Then Jack and Anton here jump out in front of me, only they don't look like Jack and Anton, they look, I don't know, really scary, like ghosts or demons or something. They grab me and tell me I have to go with Anton, he has this job to guide some people on a wilderness trek. Hikers, at this time of year, can you believe it? Jack tells me not to come back if I'm going to be popping his sister."

Jack sat very still, eyes closed, listening attentively.

"So Anton and I go with these campers who turn out to be some guys who are going off into the wilderness to find spiritual renewal in the trees or something like that. We hike into the backcountry for a few days and every night they sit around the fire and take turns talking about themselves and then all the other guys show support for the speaker and say something nice about him. Well, they invited Anton and me to join in these little gab sessions and I'm like, I don't think so, but a couple of nights later I start talking and telling stuff about myself I had never told anyone before, some really dumb stuff I had done, fighting, stealing cars, getting busted, hitting Denise. And these guys, instead of telling me what a loser I am and how I had messed up my life, they all said good things about me and, you know, I started to feel pretty good about myself."

Denise stared off into space, feigning indifference.

"One night they're talking about how being out in nature had given them a renewed sense of themselves and they asked me how I felt and I started crying, I couldn't believe it, I'm crying in front of all these guys and instead of heckling me telling me what a wimp and a crybaby I was, they said I was great and told me how brave and wonderful I was, and you know, I felt wonderful, like I had a renewed sense of myself. Then they asked Anton, who hadn't said a word the whole time—and Anton has spent so much time in the bush he probably can't get any more renewed than he is, right, Anton?"

Anton grinned.

"And Anton stands up and looks around the group and says, 'My friends, you have given this man his life back. I thank you.' And all these guys have tears running down their cheeks and they start hugging me and hugging each other and I'm okay with it and I even hug Anton and like he doesn't knife me or anything. And in all that time I didn't have one drink and I don't care if I never have another drink. And on top of that," Danny added in his excitement, "they paid us for guiding them." He took a deep breath. "So what I'm asking you, Denise, is, will you give me another chance? I really love you. And I don't want to go through the rest of my life with no one to hug but Anton."

Denise played with her coaster for a minute, holding everyone in suspense. Finally she looked up at Danny and, with a challenge in her eyes, said, "Okay. I'll give you another chance."

Danny jumped up and shouted "Yee-haw!" which didn't draw any attention in the general commotion.

"But," said Denise dramatically, "there are conditions."

"Sure, Denise, anything you want," said Danny, beaming.

"First, you never hit me again."

"Never, never again," said Danny solemnly with his hand over his heart.

"Second, you fix my house."

"I will fix your house, Denise," assured Danny. "I will fix it better than—"

"Now don't go making promises you can't keep; that's another condition. Just fix it."

"I will fix it."

"Okay," Denise nodded. "Three—I don't know what three is yet, but it'll come to me."

"Anything you want, Denise," said Danny.

"Well, don't you lie to me."

"I've never lied to you, baby."

"What about those amethyst crystals you stole from me? You lied about that."

"It was only once," said Danny with a look of shocked innocence. "I'll never do it again,"

Jack leaned forward. "What did you do with those crystals, Danny?"

Danny looked down. "I gave 'em to George Ferris. He knew the country around here pretty good and I thought he might be able to find where they came from." Danny shrugged. "Nothing came of it, no harm was done." He looked pleadingly at Denise. "Come on, baby, what do you say?"

Denise held up a warning finger. "And you've got to be good to my kids! Or else!"

"I'll be great to your kids!" Danny pushed back his chair, gathered the money from the table, and gave Denise a long, slow kiss. Cheers came from the surrounding tables. "Let's get out of here, babe," said Danny. "I've got a spoon to straighten!" Denise flashed a big smile around the room as she and Danny left together.

William thought for a moment. "So it was Danny who started George looking for the amethysts."

Jack nodded. "Yeah."

"And it was Danny outside my cabin the night when the warriors did their death-cries?"

"Yeah."

"Why didn't you tell me? I was so scared and you wouldn't tell me what was going on."

Jack smiled at him. "You needed the fear. The fear was helping you find your path, shaking you out of your rut. If I had told you it was Danny out there, you would have relaxed and lost all the benefit of your terror." He gestured toward Anton. "William, this is Anton, my teacher." Anton gave a slow nod.

William stared at Anton, who smiled impassively. Before William could say anything, the band started up with a bouncy number that blew away the possibility of further conversation. William was watching the gyrations on the dance floor when he suddenly remembered something. "Oh no!" he cried, putting a hand to his forehead. "I forgot! I was supposed to call my daughter! She'll be insane with worry!"

"It's not too late," Maggie shouted over the music. "Do you want to do it now?"

William nodded. Signalling goodnight to Jack and Anton, he and Maggie pushed their way outside. There was as much noise and commotion outside as within.

As they cleared the edge of the crowd, they met Caroline Rockwell on her way to the party. She was wearing tight jeans and a white satin cowboy shirt embroidered with red roses under a denim jacket. Her makeup and the dim light hid any bruising that remained from her encounter with Tyler Westman. Her swollen lips had subsided to a fashionable puffiness. With her golden curls, she looked like a million and a half bucks.

"Hello, Caroline," Maggie greeted her. "How are you?"

"I'm fine," said Caroline. "Or, at least better than I was. I'm not crying every five minutes."

"Going to enjoy yourself at the party?" William asked.

"I hope so," said Caroline. "I need some fun."

"Well, be careful," said Maggie. "You've experienced a terrific loss, both your father and your husband; you're probably still pretty fragile."

Caroline put a hand on Maggie's arm. "Thanks, I really am okay. I've been thinking things through about Daddy and Lance, about my life." Her eyes glistened. She bravely blinked back tears, "I need to grow up a little and get on with my life. And I'm going to hang around here, at least for a while, and see what happens. I can't go back to California even if I wanted to, but I'm never going back to that kind of life. If I have a chance to start over, it may as well be here as anywhere else. I have Daddy's cabin to stay in, and the truck. I guess I'll look for a job and see how things work out."

"It just so happens," said Maggie, "that I'll be hiring some extra help for the restaurant soon. When you feel a little more settled, come see me at the café."

"Really? Oh, that's great!" gushed Caroline. "If there's one thing I'm experienced at it's waitressing. That's what I did when Lance and I were trying to get established, until all that other shit happened. The glamorous world of show biz!"

"Have a good time!" Maggie waved.

"I think I saw Brad Pitt in there," William added.

Caroline laughed and walked off, shoulders set toward a new life.

"She certainly is a beautiful woman," Maggie observed as they continued down the street to the Bronco.

William took her hand. "Yes," he agreed. "Having someone who looks like that working for you certainly won't be bad for business!"

"Now that's a sexist remark!" teased Maggie. "What if it works the other way and all the wives make their husbands stay home to keep them away from her?"

"That's a sexist remark as well," William noted. They both laughed. "Why are you hiring new staff for the restaurant? Denise isn't leaving or anything, is she?"

"No, nothing like that," said Maggie, the clouds of their breath mingling in the chill night air. "This gold rush thing has been good to me. I made enough money to pay down my debt, so I'm going to be able to do better. I can hire some extra people and give Denise more work and a raise. She was only working part-time and it's hard to raise two kids on what a part-time waitress makes; it broke my heart that she tried so hard and yet she was so poor. Maybe now with Danny—but I don't know. Anyway, I'll have more free time for myself, I can spend a little more time on my sculpture. For the last few years I've done nothing but work and sleep. It's been hell; hopefully things will be better from now on."

"That's great," William said, "glad to hear it."

"How about you?" she asked, "how are things going with your book and everything?"

"Well, I haven't really worked very much on the book," he admitted. "I've been a little preoccupied with getting arrested and almost being murdered and things like that. Maybe I'll be able to work on it over the winter." William released her hand and put his arm around her shoulder. "You know, um, maybe we could go down to Fayette some evening and do something."

"Like what?" Maggie frowned, her tone doubtful.

"Well, um, go for Chinese food or something."

"Oh!" Maggie breathed a sigh of relief, "for a moment I thought you were going to ask me to go bowling!"

"Well, if you'd rather go bowling—"

"No, no, Chinese food would be fine. A change from the Kozy Korner anyway." She leaned close to him. "You know," she began hesitantly, "almost every time we've been together we've ended up talking about you and Barbara and I want you to know that I'm not going out with both you *and* Barbara; if we go out it has to be just us."

William stopped, took her by the shoulders, and gazed into her eyes. The uncertain light from the sparse streetlights diffused their features into soft shadows. "I will probably never be free of Barbara, she was a big part of my life, but I want to leave that behind. It's you I want to go out with. I'm not looking for a Barbara replacement, far from it, I, um—"

"I understand." Maggie embraced him, closing her eyes, pressing her cheek against him. "I'm still trying to let go of Rick as well." She laughed lightly. "Maybe Barbara and Rick will run off together!" Her arms tightened around William, the mist of her breath holding so many words unspoken. She quickly broke away and looked up at him, concerned. "What's the matter? You're trembling."

William was tingling all over, he felt like his bones had turned to rubber. "I don't know," he laughed, "maybe it's gold fever."

Or, he thought, perhaps it's love.

It felt like a good way to start a new life. William took hold of Maggie's hand and walked down the street as if he were following a deer along a woodland trail.

Author's Note

This is a work of fiction. Although the shamanism described in the book is based on research, experience, and interviews, no attempt was made, out of respect for the sacredness of Native North American religions, to accurately portray the beliefs and practices of Canada's Native Peoples.

John C. Goodman lived in British Columbia and Ontario before moving to St John's, Newfoundland and Labrador, where he lives and writes.